JOURNEYS FROM HOME

Also by Julia Lisle

The Changing Years
A Perfect Match

JOURNEYS FROM HOME

Julia Lisle

HEADLINE

First published in 1997
by HEADLINE BOOK PUBLISHING

10 9 8 7 6 5 4 3 2 1

British Library Cataloguing in Publication Data

Lisle, Julia
    Journeys from home
    1.Domestic fiction
    I.Title
    823.9'14[F]

    ISBN 0 7472 1847 1

Typeset by
Letterpart Limited, Reigate, Surrey

Printed and bound in Great Britain by
Mackays of Chatham PLC, Chatham, Kent

HEADLINE BOOK PUBLISHING
A division of Hodder Headline PLC
338 Euston Road
London NW1 3BH

To Philippa
in admiration of her courage

ACKNOWLEDGEMENTS

I would like to thank Ian Hay Davison and Judy Thomas for being so generous with background information. Also Michael and Gisela, my brother and sister-in-law, for lending us their house in Florida. We thoroughly enjoyed the research undertaken there.

As always, many thanks to my husband, Keith, for all his support during the writing of this book, and to my editor, Clare Foss, for her patience and advice.

Chapter One

Afterwards, Louise Henderson couldn't understand what made her tell such a whopping lie.

She wasn't by nature a liar. 'Lies are used by inadequate people who can't face up to things,' she'd told the twins as they were growing up.

Mark, their father, thought that was too harsh. 'Small lies, little white lies, can save people's feelings. They do no harm.'

'There's always another way of putting something that avoids untruths,' Louise had argued. (It wasn't often she contradicted her husband.) 'Otherwise who will believe you when you give real praise?' So she hadn't told the children that their performance in the school play was marvellous – RADA hopefuls they were not. Instead she'd praised the verve Emma had put into her characterisation and complimented James on his lovely speaking voice.

Louise reckoned her approach had worked because when she'd taken them off to Heathrow Airport that morning, they'd been full of confidence. Emma and James were to travel round the world for their gap year, starting in India.

The parting had gone well. She'd been afraid both she and they would be in tears. After all, it was the first time the twins had gone abroad on their own and this was such an adventure. There were so many unknowns that they must, surely, feel a little nervous. But she should have known that they would be far too excited to suffer from either nerves or tears. On the way to the airport Emma pretended to have lost her passport, then when they arrived James remembered he actually had left his toilet bag in the bathroom, so they had to buy him replacements in the airport chemist's. That had nicely used up any available time that could have lapsed into sentimentality. Finally Louise checked they had their telephone credit cards and suggested the odd call, say once a week, so she and Mark wouldn't forget they had children.

Emma grinned at the impossibility of that, hugged Louise and said, 'This is your chance, Mum. To do something, I mean, something you always wanted to and couldn't because you had to run round after us and Dad.'

Louise hugged Emma back, feeling the warmth of the lithe body that was so much taller than hers, letting the energy that

1

spilled out of that athletic frame flow into her. Then she hugged the equally tall and spare James. He overcame his dislike of emotional displays, put down his guitar case and actually kissed her. 'Ems is right, Mum. Now that we've gone, you can do something for yourself.' Then, just for a moment, it seemed nerves were going to get the better of him after all because his voice cracked and he blinked hard.

'Darlings,' she said, laughing through the tears that threatened but didn't spill, 'I never wanted to do anything but bring you two up – and look after your father. But don't worry, your dad's still here and I'm enrolling for a degree in nuclear physics tomorrow!' Which sent them off laughing. Louise had never been known for her intellectual capacity. Wicked tennis player, wonderful mother and wife but no great shakes in the brain department, that was the general verdict.

She stood in the middle of the busy check-in area and watched her two eighteen-year-old children walk into the departure hall and out of her life.

It was like watching half of you – no, seventy-five percent – vanish like water down a plug hole.

Nothing would ever be the same again.

Of course Emma and James would return but they'd be different people. Experiences Louise hadn't shared would have shaped their characters. They would be older, wiser, changed in ways she would have to struggle to understand. It was the start of life on their own. College would follow and then jobs. Never again would she share their lives in the same way. She'd had the nurturing bit, it was time for letting go.

Standing on the busy concourse with people hurrying this way and that, Louise felt quite light-headed. She picked out her car keys from her handbag and looked at them. Thirty minutes away was an empty house with two devastated bedrooms. The last thing she wanted was to go back and start sorting out dirty clothes.

It was a beautiful summer's day; she could ring round and see if anyone wanted a game of tennis. Or she could go swimming in someone's pool then lie in the sun gossiping. There had to be someone else with nothing much to do.

She wandered over to the parking-fee machines to get her ticket franked. Took money out of her purse to insert into a metal mouth. Then suddenly replaced everything in her bag and walked smartly out of the terminal in search of the underground.

It wasn't until she got to her husband's offices near Chancery Lane that she realised a sleeveless check shirt, shocking pink tailored shorts and strappy sandals were not the most suitable of outfits for a visit to one of the partners in a top accountancy firm.

The huge, streamlined building seemed almost as busy as the air terminal. The Commercial Division was on the fifth floor and

2

Louise took the lift, amused at the looks her long bare legs were given by the soberly dressed men and power-suited women who shared it with her.

The front-desk receptionist eyed her with interest and summoned Mark's secretary.

'Mrs Henderson,' said June Barker with genuine warmth, 'how nice to see you. It's ages since you've been in.'

June had been with Mark for over ten years. Heading for forty and with a big build, she dressed in dark, self-effacing, well-tailored clothes and was enormously efficient. Pressure never bothered her; late nights getting together reports and accounts she took in her stride. Only discourtesy ever disturbed her equilibrium. Mark always said he wouldn't know what to do if she decided to leave. Louise liked her and appreciated the way she smoothed so much in his extremely busy life.

'Is my husband around?' she asked. 'I thought if he was free I'd get him to take me to lunch.'

And how she wanted him to be free! She'd missed him so badly at the airport. Now she wanted to tell him all about the twins' departure, have him suggest something pleasant to take away the awful pain of their absence.

'Ah.' June looked concerned. 'He's been in a meeting all morning. It's due to finish just about now but I'm not sure . . .' She broke off as the double doors of the big room they used for major meetings opened and Mark came out, surrounded by what seemed to Louise to be dozens of people.

He saw her at once and his long face creased into worry lines. 'Darling! How did it go? No trouble, I hope?' He slipped an arm around her shoulders and gave her a quick kiss.

The light-headed feeling was still there and her body seemed to belong to someone else. Nothing really connected. She saw the crowd of men, who were in fact only six, studiously talking amongst themselves and not looking at her. Then noticed that one of them was, in fact, a woman. Her charcoal suit, discreet white blouse and short fair hair had blended in so well with the other grey suits, she had seemed one with them. But there was nothing masculine about her face. The short hair merely emphasised its femininity. Large eyes an interesting shade somewhere between grey and green, nicely emphasised with make up, a controlled but full mouth painted soft coral, strong cheekbones and small chin, all said this was an attractive woman.

'Everything went fine,' Louise said cheerfully to her husband. 'Absolutely fine. I thought you might take me out to lunch so I can tell you all about it.'

She knew Mark had wanted to come with her to see off Emma and James, but there had been this meeting. All through the twins' lives, it seemed, he had either been away or in a meeting. She'd

3

been the one to attend parent/teacher evenings, speech days, sports days and carol services.

Mark's dark blue eyes flickered, taking in her, his secretary standing poised a little way back from the two of them and the chattering group of five men and one woman. His expression was at once irritated and concerned. 'I'm sorry, darling, but I can't. We're lunching upstairs and carrying on with our discussions.' He looked at her and it was as though he took in her appearance for the first time. 'What have you done with the car?'

How typically male – always worried about parking!

Louise flashed him a brilliant smile. 'I left it at Heathrow, took the tube.' She shivered slightly; the air conditioning in these offices was fierce.

Concern overcame irritation. 'But that means you'll have to go back there before this evening.'

Louise had forgotten, she really *had* forgotten, about the dinner for the Americans over to discuss the details of a merger Mark's firm was handling. He was currently second in command of the Commercial Division, hoping to take over when the Managing Partner retired in a couple of years. She had helped him entertain on similar occasions many times. Usually she drove home afterwards but tonight they'd planned on her staying with Mark in the Chelsea flat he'd recently bought.

'Getting too old to drive back eighteen miles?' she'd joked when he'd announced his purchase.

'Not quite! No, I'm really looking ahead. The twins will be needing somewhere in London to live after university and this was such a snip. Property is on the up again, it's going to be a good investment.' Which was no doubt true but Louise had still thought it an oddly impulsive gesture on the part of her normally cautious husband.

However, she had enjoyed decorating and furnishing it in a simple style, bearing in mind that its ultimate purpose was as a base for the young, and Mark got into the habit of staying there when he wanted to be able to drink more than one glass of wine in an evening.

'Ah, well,' Louise said even more brightly. 'The car can stay at the airport till tomorrow.' The thought of going back there and either driving home and taking the train or coming straight back into London again was unnerving. All those people, all that traffic, all that time alone with just her thoughts.

Mark opened his mouth and she waited for him to say how foolish that would be, given the charges in the short-term car park, then he shut it again. 'Tell you what, give me the keys and the ticket, and I'll get someone to bring it in. June,' he turned to his secretary, 'can we spare George?'

'I'll get on to him now,' she said, and went to pick up a phone on the reception desk.

4

The sole female detached herself from the group of men and came up to Mark. 'Would you like me to take everyone upstairs, so you can follow in a little while?' The voice was low and self-possessed, the glance towards Louise nicely non-committal.

Mark visibly brightened. 'Thanks, Robin. Oh, I don't think you've met my wife yet. Louise, this is Robin Howard. She joined us recently from our New York office. Louise has been to the airport, Robin,' he added, as though that explained her eccentric clothes.

As if it mattered she wasn't in a grey suit or some chic little number! Louise smiled brilliantly and held out her hand. 'Robin, how nice to meet, Mark's told me so much about you.' Well, he had mentioned the name, had said great things were expected of this new colleague. What he had failed to mention was the new colleague's sex.

'Louise, I'm really pleased to meet you, hope we can spend some time together soon. You'll forgive me if . . .' Robin waved a hand towards the group of men, now watching them with unconcealed curiosity.

'Please, I know how important this is,' Louise said graciously. 'Mark will be along in a moment.' The light-headedness was now lifting her into the stratosphere.

She heard Mark asking, 'Are you sure you're all right, darling?' as she watched Robin Howard skilfully shepherd the men along the hall and into the lift.

'Perfectly,' she said as the lift door closed on the group. 'If you could organise the car, that would be wonderful. I'll see you at the flat later, shall I?'

'Well,' his voice was doubtful, 'I think you'd better meet us at the restaurant. We're probably coming straight on from here. Is that all right?'

'Perfect!' She heard her own bright voice as from a long way off. 'I'll go and get my hair done and find something to wear. Now, run along, you don't want to leave all the looking after to Robin.'

He said, 'No, indeed,' in rather an odd voice, and gave her a quick kiss. 'Till tonight, then.' He walked off towards the lifts with that swift, slightly jerky stride that seemed to come with the long legs the twins had inherited.

'Everything's organised with the car, Mrs Henderson,' June announced. 'George will park it as near to the flat as he can. If you're not there, he'll bring the keys back here and give them to Mr Henderson.' She looked closely at Louise. 'Are you sure you're all right?'

'Absolutely,' Louise said with great determination. 'Thank you so much, June. Must go. Hair to get done, you know?' She wheeled about and walked firmly out of the office.

Somehow she got herself to the hairdresser's. She didn't have an

5

appointment and her regular stylist wasn't available. She told them anyone would do and they gave her over to a young man with a long ponytail, very tight trousers and very loose top. He admired the thickness of her dark hair, chopped it much shorter than normal and kept up a flow of amusing chat about the latest scandal as though he realised she couldn't be relied upon to do much in the conversation line herself. 'There,' he said at the end. 'Those gorgeous peepers of yours look twice as large now.' For a brief moment Louise came down from the stratosphere. Yes, her grey eyes had somehow been emphasised by the new, bouncy dark curls. And she thought she definitely looked younger than the thirty-nine years her passport proclaimed.

Louise overtipped the young man and took herself off to Knightsbridge, floating along the pavements seemingly without effort.

Mark never minded her buying a new dress as long as it was stylish. Louise knew he wanted her to look good. It was her slopping around in jeans and sweat shirts that irritated him.

She found an ultra-short dress and jacket in bright yellow linen that was outrageously attractive and equally expensive. She bought new shoes, too, then went to Harrods beauty department and flexed her credit card some more on toiletries and make up before catching a taxi to the flat for a long, sybaritic bath. By that time she felt she needed alcohol and poured herself a whisky from the bottle Mark kept there.

She hoped that somehow he would manage to end the discussions in good time so he could come back for a shower and change before dinner. But it grew later and he didn't appear.

Normally Louise paid little attention to her make up; a quick flick with the mascara brush and some lipstick was her usual routine. Tonight, though, she spent a long time in making sure she looked her best, applying foundation and powder plus the merest hint of blusher before subtly blending both grey and silver eyeshadow in a new way and finishing with two coats of navy blue mascara instead of her usual rapid brush with black.

The new dress flattered her cleavage and made the most of her excellent legs, helped by the high heels of the shoes she'd chosen. Louise stared at the chic woman in the mirror and thought, Who are you? No one I've met before, that's certain.

The waiter at the restaurant recognised her, though, and his smile was warm as he announced that Mr Henderson and party had just arrived and would she follow him, please? He led the way towards the back of the restaurant and Louise was conscious of admiring glances following her. They combined with the whisky to give her an unusual feeling of confidence.

The others had obviously just got settled. She noticed immediately that Robin had found time to change her grey suit for a rose pink silk dress that subtly outlined her good figure. Serene and composed, she looked someone content with her self-image.

Mark rose the moment Louise approached, his eyes alight. He told her she looked wonderful and introduced her to the five Americans. At a quick glance, they all looked the same. They were all medium-sized, short-haired and dressed in well-cut suits. They all had a confident, upfront manner. They shook hands and gave her almost identical admiring glances. Then they all sat down and picked up their previous conversation. Louise took the place that had been left for her. There were two Americans between her and Mark, two more between her and Robin, which meant she could expect no help from either of them.

The one really good thing about these evenings was the food. Mark always made sure they ate somewhere really good. This evening it was Scott's in Mount Street.

'Are you interested in food?' Louise asked the man on her right. His name was Roy Horowitz, from Chicago. They were all from Chicago.

'Hey, food's important!' Roy beamed at her. 'I mean, you are what you eat, right?'

'And what do you like to eat most in Chicago?' Louise asked, head held slightly to one side, eyes firmly fixed on his protuberant blue ones. She had perfected a way of listening that suggested whatever she was hearing was completely fascinating.

They ordered and after the subject of food seemed to be exhausted, Louise switched the conversation to Roy's family. That was usually safe for at least the first course, after which she would turn her attention to Brewster Williams on her right.

Roy told her in minute detail the saga of his two elder children by his first wife, his two younger children by his second and all about his latest wife, who preferred to have no children at all. Louise kept her expression rapt. Soon he would ask her about her own family, then there would be a chat about the twins. He might even manage to summon up some interest in her, ask if she had a job. But when she then explained that her family was her job, his interest would vanish. The moment she declared herself a wife and mother was the moment she ceased to exist as a person in her own right. It had happened so many times, Louise told herself she should be used to it by now. And after all, she herself believed that being a wife and mother was the most important job there was. Out of the corner of her eye she could see Robin holding forth on the position of the British government on the European single currency. The American on her left was listening with deep attention.

'Mary-Lou has this very stressful career in real estate. She says that and me is enough for any woman, so no children,' Roy announced. 'Say, this Chablis is definitely potable!' He raised his

7

glass to Mark across the table. 'I find I can trust a man who knows his wines!'

'Glad to hear it, Roy,' Mark said, briefly breaking off his conversation and raising a glass back.

'Now, little lady, just what do you do with your life?'

Louise ate the last of her scallops and considered the question. 'What do I do with my life?' she repeated, holding his gaze with hers. 'Well, I suppose my life could be described as stressful as well. Probably not as stressful as Mary-Lou's but, yes, stressful.' She drew the word out. Once again, she had this sense of being detached from what was actually happening.

'Stressful, you say? Now that sounds interesting. Just what is it that makes your life stressful?' Roy also dragged the word out, not in a mocking way but almost as though he didn't believe she could be involved in anything more taxing than choosing new curtains.

And then it came. The big, whopping, thumping lie. 'I edit a women's magazine,' Louise said. A marvellously effervescent feeling rose in her as she heard her voice utter the words and saw the change in Roy's expression. 'A brand new one. We hit the news stands next month. Aimed at thirty-somethings with taste, talent and ambition.'

'Say, that sounds really interesting.' There was respect in his voice. 'Mary-Lou is always saying she needs a magazine that has a mind of its own. So what were you doing at the airport this morning? Taking some time off from your duties?'

'Heavens, no!' Louise laughed and gave her head a little toss. 'I was saying goodbye to a young pop star who has just given us a sensational story. Making sure the rest of the press didn't get on to him, you know? Can't tell you his name but it's all hot stuff! Tomorrow I'm going to be working on his mother's side of the story. Where she went wrong, what she did right, all that. My readers will find themselves caught between the two.'

'My!' said Roy. He appeared at a loss for a moment then addressed himself towards the other end of the table again. 'Mark, you never told me what an intelligent and go-ahead girl your wife was!'

'She certainly is,' Mark said positively, but his expression was ever so slightly puzzled. It fuelled Louise's extraordinary sense of floating in some rarified stratosphere, safe amongst soaring and wheeling predatory birds.

'We're privileged she found the time to come out this evening,' Roy persisted, shooting another admiring glance at Louise. This was heady stuff.

'Well, the twins have certainly kept her occupied.' Mark gave his wife a warm smile but she could sense impatience held sternly in check.

'Twins!' Roy chuckled. 'Say, hasn't your hubby got a real sharp sense of humour? But Mary-Lou tells me some men can feel threatened by achieving wives, like to deny that side of their existence. Not that she has any trouble in that direction, I'm really proud of her accomplishments.'

'Oh, Mark's proud of me,' Louise murmured, beginning to wonder where her lie was taking her. 'It's just I like to keep my two lives separate.'

Roy looked again towards the other end of the table. 'Hey, Mark, you don't get involved in Louise's publication then? You keep out of it, right? Well, let me tell you – wrong! You need to share in marriage, you know? I'm sure she would find you a real fascinating subject to plan a feature around. Top accountant makes ideal husband . . .'

'Oh, Mark is always fascinating,' Louise put in, beyond caring where this was going but vaguely aware she needed to bring Roy's attention back to her end of the table.

It was too late.

'Publication?' Mark's voice sharpened. 'What publication?'

'Why, the one she's editor of,' Roy said in surprise before Louise could intervene.

Mark just looked at his wife. 'Louise?'

She drank more of the wine, letting it buoy her up even further amongst the creatures that flew so far above the mundane earth. 'Roy's such fun.' She flashed him a scintillating smile. 'I've been indulging myself, spinning one of my fantasy scenarios.'

The American looked startled then a certain reluctant admiration crept into his face. 'Say, you can spin a good line,' he said. 'Mary-Lou has fantasies too. In her dreams she's the first woman President of the United States. She's even talking of running for the Senate . . .' The conversation switched to politics and Louise realised that his interest in her had evaporated.

9

Chapter Two

'I just don't understand why you said it!' Mark tugged off his tie and undid the top buttons of his shirt then sat on the bed to unlace his shoes.

Louise felt drained. Her head was aching and she no longer felt lighter than air. She lay back on the bed, fully dressed, and said nothing.

'You put me in an impossible position. I could only think it was a joke! But what was the point?'

'A moment of madness,' she murmured, wishing he would stop.

'I mean, it's not as though you've ever said you wanted to edit a magazine,' Mark continued as his shoes dropped heavily to the floor.

Louise put a hand over her eyes and wondered if it would matter if she went to sleep in her clothes.

'If it had been something you really thought you could do, I might have understood it.' Mark removed his shirt and trousers and went into the bathroom. 'I tell you,' he called out, 'I could see Robin thought it was very odd.'

Louise sighed, levered herself off the bed and took off her jacket. 'Undo me, will you?' She presented her back to Mark.

Clamping his toothbrush between his teeth, he skilfully lowered the zip then undid the little hook at the top.

There were no more questions as Mark launched into the ritual two minutes of brushing up and down. Louise slid out of the dress and hung it up with the jacket. She took off her underclothes, slipped on the nightgown she kept at the flat then sat down at the dressing table and applied cleansing milk to her face.

The first wipe of the tissue made her face look like a melting clown's. She pulled a second tissue out of the box and cleared her eyes. Then another tissue to reveal her mouth. As she worked, tears started to well up, coursing out of her eyes as though a spring had been unblocked. Louise used both hands to pull more tissues and wiped urgently, pulling and pushing at the soft skin, heedlessly dropping the soiled pieces of paper on the dressing table before tugging more from the box. And all the while the tears fell.

Then her shoulders started to shake. From somewhere deep inside her a terrible sob tore its way upwards. She gasped, tried to

11

control it and found another forcing its way through her throat. She brought her tissue-laden hands to her mouth and attempted to stifle the sobbing, staring at herself in the mirror with wild eyes.

'Darling, darling!' Mark was behind her, he looked frightened. 'Whatever's the matter?'

'They've gone,' Louise got out through the shuddering sobs. 'My babies have left me.'

'Oh, darling!' He pulled her to him, burying her face in his chest, stroking her hair. 'I didn't realise. No wonder you were so odd this evening. Hush, it'll be all right, I promise you.'

Even though Louise could feel his arms around her, she still felt dreadfully alone. Grief overcame her.

She had a dim awareness of him taking her to bed, holding her until her sobbing gradually eased and at some point she cried herself to sleep.

The next thing she was conscious of was Mark shaking her awake.

'Darling, I have to go. I've brought you a cup of tea, will you be all right?' He sounded worried.

Louise wondered where she was for a moment then forced her swollen eyes open. Mark was standing beside the bed, a cup in his hands, eyes anxious. Gradually everything came back to her. She struggled into a sitting position. 'That's kind,' she said, taking the cup and drinking some of the tea. It tasted marvellous, deeply aromatic. 'Lapsang, my favourite.'

Mark looked pleased. 'I know. I got some only the other day. Look, will you be all right if I leave now? Only I've got to carry on with the discussions, you see.'

Louise did. She looked at her watch. Eight o'clock. 'I'll be fine, darling. I'm sorry about yesterday,' she said in rush. 'I don't know what happened.'

He sat on the bed. 'It was the children leaving like that. Of course you were going to be upset. I blame myself for not realising how much it would affect you. I should never have asked you to join us last night.'

'It would have been nice if we could just have been together.' Her voice was quiet, uncertain.

'I know, darling. I know. But you do see that it just wasn't possible? However, I should have told you to stay quietly at home. Will you be all right to drive? The keys to the car are in the living room with a note of where it's parked.'

Louise gave a quick sigh, put the empty cup on the bedside table and said, 'Of course I will! You go off to work, I'll be all right, promise!' She gave him a bright smile.

Mark went to the door, then hovered there for a moment. 'Look, I'm probably tied up until late this evening but tomorrow I should be able to get home at a reasonable hour. Why don't you ask some

12

people round? It's ages since we did any entertaining. Isn't it our turn to have Colin and Nicky?'

Louise nodded, but wondered. Normally Mark never wanted to entertain. He said he worked so hard most of the week, was away so often, that when he finally managed to get home he just wanted to relax. She always had to bully him into letting her ask people round, remind him how he enjoyed being with their friends on the rare occasions they got together. Now he was obviously trying to please her. Should she say she'd much prefer to be alone with him?

But after all, what would they do, just the two of them? No Emma to come bounding in, all cheek and fun, teasing Mark into a good humour, wheedling something she wanted out of him. No James to be quizzed on his school work, to get all touchy and slope off to his room from where sounds would drift down of either heavy metal or classical music. No discussions between her and Mark on the children, what they needed, what should be done about them, what they had been doing. There had always been so much to talk about when the twins were around.

'Lovely idea, darling,' Louise said. 'I'll give them a ring and see if they're free.'

'Right, then.' Still Mark lingered. 'Might have a bit of an idea for a little treat. Something to put the sunshine back into your life.'

Louise looked expectant.

'Need to fix one or two things first, though.'

He gave her a big grin, blew a kiss across the room and left.

Louise thought about staying in bed for a little as an unusual luxury but there didn't seem much point, so she threw back the duvet and took herself off to the bathroom.

Which was just as well as in the middle of her shower she remembered the call from her mother that had come just after she'd got to the flat the previous afternoon.

'So that's where you are!' had been her mother's greeting. 'I rang you at home and got no answer so I thought it worth a try. I expect Mark is taking you out to cheer you up.' Louise didn't say anything. 'You must be so miserable now the children have gone,' her mother continued. 'I remember how I felt when you got married. Of course, you only moved a few miles away but it was as though you'd gone to the ends of the earth.'

'I saw you nearly every day!'

'I know, but it wasn't the same as having you at home. So I know just how you feel.'

'I'm fine, Mother.'

'So, how did it go?'

'Well, I took Emma and James to the airport this morning . . .'

'Did you cry?'

'No, Mother, I didn't. None of us cried. It all went very well. How are you?'

13

'The arthritis isn't too good today but I'm managing. Now, dear, I thought it would do you good to have a little diversion. There's a coffee morning tomorrow and I've said you'll come with me. Then I'll take you to lunch at that little place that's just opened round the corner from me. Such a nice woman is running it, we've become quite friends.'

'That's very kind of you, Mother.' Louise heard the lack of warmth in her own voice and managed to find a more lively tone as she said she was looking forward to seeing her mother the next day and rang off. Then immediately forgot all about the call.

Until now.

But there was no need to panic, she had plenty of time.

It was, in fact, only just after nine-thirty when Louise drove up to their house. The weather was once again beautiful. She put the car away and went to change into something her mother would think suitable for a coffee party. Heading for her bedroom, she hesitated outside Emma's room. She put a hand on the door knob and stood still, feeling its cool porcelain roundness, while she gathered her courage to enter the empty room.

Abandoned clothes were everywhere. So were make up, tennis racquets, trainers, a hockey stick, sweat bands, several dozen CDs and a flock of fluffy animals.

Louise started to pick up dirty clothes from the floor and put them in the wicker basket that stood behind the door. Then her eye fell on Barbar, the balding teddy bear that had accompanied Emma everywhere since her baby days. The day before the twins left, Barbar had actually been packed into one of the enormous rucksacks that were the only pieces of luggage they were taking. 'I can't go without him,' Emma had declared, stashing T shirts, pants and socks on top of his limp body.

'What a softie!' James had scorned, coming to ask Louise what had happened to his other pair of jeans. The ones he wasn't wearing.

She'd fetched them from the airing cupboard. 'Heavens, Mum, you haven't ironed them!' Emma was equally scornful. 'Leave us a bit of street cred!'

'They'll be all right by the time they've been rolled around in the rucksack for several weeks,' James said quietly.

'If you intend taking the pair you've got on,' Louise said to him, 'get them off. They're filthy!'

'Mum!'

'They'll practically stand up on their own!' She grabbed the back of the jeans and hung on.

'OK, OK,' he said with resignation, went to his room and changed into a pair of old shorts then came back with the dirty trousers.

By the time she'd returned from putting the discarded jeans into

14

the washing machine, Barbar had been removed from the rucksack and was sitting on Emma's pillow. 'She's decided a sundress and two extra T shirts win over her infancy fixation,' James said, lying on Emma's bed, his feet next to Barbar, head hanging over the end, arms dangling. That way up his face looked narrower than ever but the navy blue eyes under the heavy dark eyebrows were more arresting. Upright, James never seemed fully to open his eyes on life; hooded by heavy lids, they remained unfathomable. 'By the time we complete our circumnavigation of the world, she might be ready to enter adulthood.'

Emma tossed a pair of rolled up socks at him. 'Just because you think you've done all your packing, there's no need to try and come the big brother on me.' The twenty minutes between their births had always been highly significant to both of them. She hefted the rucksack. 'Ugh, it still weighs a ton!'

'Take everything out,' ordered Louise, clearing a space on the floor. 'You don't need all that make up nor all those sweaters.' She removed two heavy cable knits from the pile, leaving a soft lambs-wool one, then started going through the bottles and tubes of cosmetics, paring down the collection to the basics. 'And where's that Immodium I got you?'

James squirmed round on the bed so he could watch her. 'How are you ever going to manage without us, Mum? I mean, what'll you do with your days?'

'Oh, you!' Emma plumped herself down beside him and bent over, her head swinging as she searched beneath the bed. 'Life doesn't revolve around you, you know! Without us, Mum can start living again.'

'I'm living very nicely now, thank you,' said Louise, opening one of the drawers in Emma's dressing table and trying to find a space for the make up she'd taken out of the toilet bag.

'But you know what I mean.' Emma looked up from her search for a moment. The twins were as different in looks as they were in personality. Emma had Mark's fair, curly hair, cropped almost as short as his, but Louise's wide face, large grey eyes and generous mouth. She even had the dimple beside the left corner that deepened whenever she smiled. James looked much more like Mark but in character Louise felt he was closer to her. Both twins, though, had their father's long, lean figure; Emma just under six foot, James just over. They towered over Louise's five foot five.

Emma was back to searching beneath the bed. She dragged out a multi-coloured T shirt. 'Oh, no! It's dirty! Mum, I really wanted to take this with me!'

'Have you heard about washing?' James asked her. 'I mean, like, while travelling? Because I'm not going to do yours.' Though prone to fits of forgetfulness, he was the more organised twin.

15

Unprompted, he had equipped himself with a tube of concentrated washing liquid for his rucksack, and a medical kit.

Louise took the dirty T shirt, ran down and dropped it into the washing machine with the jeans. When she returned upstairs, Emma had ruthlessly removed yet more items from her make up. 'All I really need is a lipstick and some blusher. Oh, and an eyeshadow. And I suppose mascara would be a good idea . . .' Back went each discarded item. She looked up at Louise. 'Thing is, Mum, if Dad has to go abroad on business, you could go with him now, couldn't you? And take up golf.'

'Darling, of course I can! I'll be so busy, I won't even realise you've gone.'

Now, sitting on Emma's unmade bed, hugging Barbar to her chest, Louise remembered their parting and tears pricked again at her eyes. She hadn't expected Emma to worry about her. James, yes, he was the thoughtful one, but not Emma, who blithely assaulted life as though it was a game that had to be mastered in the shortest time possible.

She couldn't stay in this room any longer. Dumping Barbar, Louise fled downstairs and into the garden.

Chapter Three

The Hendersons lived in what had once been a small Surrey village. Over the years its proximity to London had increased its desirability to commuters; large gardens had been converted into small housing estates and fields had been incorporated into the curtilage of what was now too large to be called a village. Smart dress shops, motor showrooms and delicatessens had taken over from the local provisions shops, now superseded by a large supermarket. Lost in the thickets of neo-Georgian detached, semi-detached and terraced houses, were a few scattered survivors of the original large Victorian and Edwardian family properties, most with gardens truncated by the lucrative sale of plots to hungry developers.

Eighteen months after Louise and Mark had married, Mark's mother had died. Then Victor, his father, had announced that he was moving into a retirement home. 'Got to get settled before I go gaga. Don't want anyone to have the problem of persuading me into surrendering my independence – much better if I bite the bullet now,' he'd said. His two daughters, both married and with children, had heaved sighs of relief and agreed that this would really be for the best.

They had not been so relieved when Victor had then declared he was handing over the family home to Mark and Louise. 'You girls are nicely set up, married to chaps able to provide for you, don't need my help. Though there'll be something for you when I finally fall off my perch, don't you worry about that. Mark is still making it up the ladder, only right he and Louise should have the house.'

Of course in those days, in the late-seventies, the house hadn't been worth a tenth of what it was now. Even so, large and solidly Victorian, with six bedrooms, two bathrooms and an acre of garden, it was enough to cause a rift in the family that had never been satisfactorily healed.

'Why did you do it, Father?' Louise had asked once after her two sisters-in-law had left with husbands and children after yet another sticky family get-together. 'You could have put the house on the market, divided the proceeds between Mark, Fiona and Patricia, and we would still have had enough to get a reasonable house.' (Mark and Louise had been living in a flat in Battersea when his mother had died; it was far too small after the twins had arrived and

17

they'd been in the process of looking for something more suitable with a mortgage they could afford for three months by then.)

Victor had sighed and stretched out on one of the old steamer loungers under the shade of the tulip tree, looking elegant in well-pressed cotton trousers, the neck of his shirt decorated with a cravat. 'Sarah and I bought this house when she was expecting Fiona. We saw it as a family home. I didn't want it to go to developers or be split into flats. The girls have lovely houses already.' Fiona was married to a highly successful Harley Street gynaecologist and Patricia to a high-flying barrister. They had large houses one in Esher and one in Cobham, each with swimming pool, tennis court, designer kitchen and Jacuzzi. 'I knew you would give it the care it needed.' And Victor reached over and patted Louise's hand.

She had always got on well with him. Sarah she'd found rather intimidating, a trifle *grande dame*. When Mark and Louise became engaged, Louise had wished her father were still alive. A family physician of the old school, he'd known how to charm women like Sarah Henderson. Victor, with his twinkling eyes and straight-forward manner, Louise had found much easier. He'd skilfully built up a family timber firm into a successful player in the burgeoning DIY business of the sixties and seventies. So successful, in fact, the company had been bought out by one of the high street names, leaving Victor and Sarah very nicely situated – until it had been discovered Sarah had cancer and their life together had fallen apart.

Louise had loved the house from the very first time she'd seen it. Behind the slightly austere, gabled frontage were large, beautifully proportioned rooms, a graceful oak staircase and generous hall and landing. The kitchen was huge, and when the twins were growing up it had been the family room.

Sarah's decorative taste had run to embossed wallpapers and heavy velvet curtains. Over the years, Louise had very gradually redecorated, doing all the work herself. She had given due credit to her sisters-in-law for introducing her to Osborne & Little and Designer's Guild. Glazed chintz had replaced the velvet curtains and dralon upholstery, the embossed wallpapers had been stripped and Louise had taken a course in marbling and rag rolling.

The day was heating up into another scorcher. Already there was little trace of morning freshness left as she wandered through the garden, pulling off the dead heads from the shrub roses as she went. She'd made as many changes here as in the house. Sarah had liked formality: straight herbaceous borders, hybrid tea roses, savagely pruned shrubs, and a summer house as square as the lawn. Now beds blowsy with drifts of perennials and laxly growing shrubs wound their way through an irregularly shaped area of grass down to an orchard. The apple trees were bearing well this year. The June drop had left a heavy burden. Loiuse could never bring herself to remove immature fruit to improve the yield of what was left. To her

18

it was like aborting unsatisfactory foetuses. An extreme thought, quickly dispelled from her mind as she checked the plum tree, thick with golden-green fruits, not the ubiquitous Victoria.

The sun's fire was filtered through the leaves of the trees. How hot would it be in India? Emma and James would have landed in Delhi by now and be on their way by local transport up into the hills. Like the sahibs in the days of Empire leaving the heat of the city for the refreshing air of the higher regions. Louise tried not to think about terrorist situations, revolting Sikhs, ethnic disturbances.

She looked at the bees buzzing round the deep purple of *Buddleia davidii* – 'Black Knight' – and thought, Nothing was watered last night. She would have to remember to switch on the irrigation system as soon as the sun dipped. One turn of a tap and thousands of small sprays would leap into life, imitating rain on the flower beds and lawns. Louise had rather liked the involvement of first standing and holding a hose pipe and then, later, moving the automatic spray from place to place in the garden, seeing the plants welcome the life-giving water. But Mark had said it was all a waste of her time. Modern technology should be installed.

Waste of time! What was she to do with all the time that now stretched before her?

With a ring of her bicycle bell Mrs Parks rounded the corner of the house on her mountain model, well-developed arm and leg muscles gorgeously displayed in a smart, co-ordinated shirt and skirt outfit that was undoubtedly a cast off from one of her other 'regulars'. Louise had been part of her little group of clients for four years now and didn't know what she would do without her. Quite apart from the ruthless efficiency with which she kept the housework under control, Louise thoroughly enjoyed her company.

'It'll be the twins' rooms today, no doubt,' her daily said as Louise came up the garden path towards her. She leaned the bicycle against the kitchen wall and took off her baseball cap. (It kept her hair in place while she rode, she'd once explained.)

'A cup of coffee?' asked Louise, leading the way into the kitchen.

'Later, when I'm into my routine.' The question was always asked and always answered in the same way. Emma had once suggested Louise give up but she felt it showed consideration and that maybe one day Mrs Parks would welcome a coffee on arrival.

Not today, however. She took yesterday's breakfast plates off the kitchen table without comment and loaded them into the dishwasher.

'There are the twins' rooms, the beds need stripping and I should sort out Emma's dirty clothes but my mother's invited me to a coffee morning . . .'

'*And you'd rather finish them yourself,*' Mrs Parks completed Louise's sentence for her. 'Quite understand, duck. Felt just the same when my Kev left home. Why don't we do what we can before

19

your mum arrives, then I'll give the lounge a bit of a turnout.'

'How's he doing now?' Louise felt guilty at not having inquired before this. It must be all of six months since Mrs Parks's last had flown the nest.

While she collected her tool box of cleaning materials, the hoover (so powerful it tended to swallow bedclothes if given half a chance) and the long-handled fluff collector, Mrs Parks gave Louise a non-stop commentary on her offspring. 'Oh, he loves it. Says me and Trev must come out. Says even if there had been the jobs over here, he'd rather be there. Life's so easy.' The cleaning materials were checked. 'Going to need a new polish soon, I'll leave it out after I finish to remind you. And we should see the birds! he says. Well, Kev's always been one for the girls. Mind you, here they never knew what he was on about. Said him being a palaeontologist put them right off. Can't think why. Once you know how to pronounce it, there's nothing to it. I know he's a lot to do with dead bones but they've been such a long time dead, it can't matter, can it?'

'Fossils, aren't they?' murmured Louise, following her up the stairs then being allowed to bundle up Emma's sheets as Mrs Parks whipped them off the bed. She avoided looking at Barbar.

'That's right.' Mrs Parks used the encouraging tone of a nursery school teacher. 'Still got the lot he collected when he was a lad. Keep them in his room, I do. Somehow that makes me think he'll be back one of these days.'

'I'm sure he will,' Louise said heartily, fishing out more clothes from under the bed.

''Mazing, in't it? You give them something to put the dirty ones in and it's as if it's never there.' Mrs Parks removed the handful of T shirts, shorts and pants from Louise and put them with the bed linen.

'Got time for James's room the same, 'ave we? Afore Mrs Russell comes? Then I can get on with the hoovering an' all that while you goes out for your coffee.'

'We can make a start anyway.'

'Keeping well, is she, your mum?' asked Mrs Parks as they moved next door. She got on extremely well with Louise's mother.

'She's just fine,' Louise said briskly, trawling underneath James's bed heedless of her smart Escada shift dress. The only thing she found for her pains were a number of dust balls.

''E's always been the tidy one,' observed Mrs Parks, emptying the contents of the second clothes basket on to the outspread duvet cover. 'I'll add Emma's to this lot, shall I? 'Ow's she going to keep track of all her bits and pieces going across all them places, that's what I wonder.' She switched on the vacuum cleaner and pushed the long nozzle under the bed, dust balls vanishing into the interior with the speed of vandals before the police.

The door bell rang. 'That'll be Mother.' Louise escaped downstairs with relief. The twins' bedrooms had the look of the *Marie Celeste*; everything as normal except for the absence of their owners. Which was a ridiculous thought because normally they wouldn't be there anyway. Even in the holidays they would have been up by now and out doing something. At least, Emma would have been. James would probably have been practising either the piano or his guitar. No matter how persuasive Emma was in suggesting he come and play tennis or go swimming or up to London – and Emma could be very persuasive – he usually insisted on spending the mornings on his music.

'Very nice, darling,' approved Betty Russell, giving her daughter's appearance a keen glance as Louise opened the door to her.

Mrs Russell was wearing a sprigged cotton dress and jacket. She was a small woman with a neat figure, carefully peroxided hair and an air of helplessness. Beneath the fluttering, however, she was in total control. Betty Russell had always believed it was up to the woman to keep her husband's interest, which she had done by allowing him to think she depended totally on him while making sure his life ran as smoothly as any busy doctor's could. During Louise's teenage years, she had produced a steady stream of advice on how to get and keep your man. When her husband had succumbed to a heart attack at the early age of fifty-two, Betty had taken it as a personal insult.

Now she stepped into the hall. 'I'll just have a few words with Mrs Parks, before we go.'

Betty believed in maintaining good relations with any home help. She was also genuinely interested in Mrs Parks's family.

She spent ten minutes going through the details of each of the Parks children's current activities. Then she and Louise set off in her little Metro, the car leaping forward in the way it had, Betty never having mastered the business of letting in a clutch but refusing to switch to an automatic on the grounds that she didn't trust such things. 'How that woman managed to bring up four such successful children, I'll never work out,' she said. 'It's not as if that husband of hers could have been much help.'

Trevor Parks was a self-employed plumber who suffered chronic back problems, a distinct disadvantage in his profession, and spent more time explaining his inability to deal with leaking pipes and stopped drains than actually working.

'Perhaps that's where they get their scientific bent from,' suggested Louise, hanging on tight as her mother took a roundabout with reckless enthusiasm.

'But *two* doctors, a dentist and a palaeontologist? Well!'

Louise wasn't sure if the last exclamation concerned the Parks children's achievements or was directed towards the BMW that had taken his revenge for being cut up at the roundabout by overtaking with only an inch to spare, swinging ahead just in time to avoid a bumper-to-bumper confrontation with an articulated lorry.

Louise had discussed her mother's driving with Mark. 'Honestly, she's going to kill either herself or someone else one of these days. She shouldn't be allowed on the road.'

'She's no worse than fifty per cent of other drivers.'

'But they aren't my mother!'

'Don't worry, darling. You know Betty. She always manages to come up smelling of roses. Anyway, there isn't a thing you can do about it.' Mark had grinned at her. 'I'd back her against the rest of the road hogs any day.'

'How's Mark?' asked her mother now, changing down with a grating of gears as she pulled sharply into a minor road without a signal, leaving a furiously hooting car behind her. 'Missing Emma, I'll be bound. He has such a good relationship with her.'

She always managed to underline Mark's failure in achieving the same sort of relationship with his son without directly mentioning the fact. Or was it that Louise was ultra-sensitive on this point?

'He suggested we ask Nicky and Colin round tomorrow night.' Louise had rung Nicky before leaving London and issued the invitation, apologising for the shortness of the notice. Nicky had said not to be silly, they knew what Mark's schedule was like and they'd love to come.

'Oh, how sensible, darling. I remember when you left home, I cried every night for a week. If only someone had organised me into some entertaining!'

Louise felt a familiar sense of impatience take hold of her. Why hadn't her mother organised *herself* into going somewhere or having friends round? She had no lack of them. Betty Russell's days were well filled with coffee mornings, bridge afternoons and the occasional evening with the local Conservatives. Yet somehow she managed to make Louise feel constantly guilty that she didn't do more for her mother. Then, as always, she was filled with remorse at her own lack of understanding. 'You must have been exhausted after all the wedding preparations! What a pity one of your friends didn't make sure you had something nice to do.'

This elicited a small, slightly shame-faced, laugh. 'Well, actually a couple of them did take me out for the day. But it was the evenings when I felt most lonely.'

Louise had exhausted many years ago the number of ways it was possible to respond to this. 'Where are we going?' she asked instead.

This morning's coffee party turned out to be in aid of the Tory Party.

Held in a large house that looked as though it had been built in the seventies or early-eighties – pillared portico, neo-Georgian symmetry to its windows and garage – it had been erected in a verdant setting that maximised the plot's mature trees. Expensive landscaping had produced a rich profusion of shrubs. Tidily pruned specimens each occupied their allotted space in the bark-blanketed beds edged with bright begonias. The beds themselves had been allowed a certain freedom and meandered through lawns whose grass had been clipped to within a millimetre of its roots. A Grecian temple looked as though it might provide changing facilities for the large, kidney-shaped pool, surrounded by generous expanses of terracing. On the flagstones were a number of tables with garden umbrellas and comfortably cushioned chairs. A side table offered an urn and rows of coffee cups and saucers. Smartly dressed ladies dispensed refreshment to an assortment of equally smartly dressed guests who ranged in age from thirty something to well over eighty.

'There's Nonie Rose – it's her house we're using this morning.' Betty Russell sounded excited. 'It's the first time she's agreed to have a function, they haven't been here long.' Tucking her arm through her daughter's, she marched her firmly up to a deeply tanned woman in her forties. Brilliantly gold hair was flicked into a helmet of chrysanthemum petal ends, a well-used face was brought alive by protuberant eyes of electric blue and a slash of geranium red for a mouth. Her figure was as controlled as her plants, splendidly arrayed in tailored white trousers topped with a short-sleeved lime green jacket that appeared to have nothing underneath but a deep cleavage. 'Nonie, do let me introduce my daughter, Louise Henderson. I know you'll have so much in common. Mark, her husband, is in the City, too. Your Derek probably knows him.'

Before Louise, averting her eyes from the cleavage, had time to ask just what Derek Rose did, they were interrupted by a commanding woman in her fifties, wearing a cotton dress and jacket which looked as though they could have been bought in the same shop as Mrs Russell's.

'It's Louise, isn't it? Your mother said she was bringing you and we're just so pleased to see you at one of our little gatherings. I've been asking her if we can't prevail upon you to let us hold a function at your lovely home, now that you are no longer so involved with your family. They have left home, haven't they?' she added, as though Louise's unresponsiveness had introduced a moment of doubt. It didn't last long. 'Of course they have! Your mother tells me they're going round the world! Such lives the young lead these days. What wouldn't I have given to do that sort of thing when I was their age! Instead, it was straight into secretarial college and then marriage. No time for oneself at all!'

'This is Mary Holland, our Ladies' chairman,' Louise's mother said with pride. 'I told her I was sure you'd have lots of time now to help with fund raising and . . . well, things,' she finished lamely, as if suddenly aware that this suggestion was not finding favour with her daughter.

'You are kind, Mrs Holland,' said Louise, a feeling of desperation taking hold. The last thing she wanted was to get drawn into a round of social events such as this. On the other hand, Mark had mentioned it would be no bad thing if she could get involved with the local Conservative Association: 'I wouldn't mind getting on terms with our MP, I'd like to be able to nobble him every now and then.'

What could she say? One thing she was quite sure of, she wasn't going to utter even a little white lie. Not after last night.

'I don't think I can consider it at the moment,' she said carefully. 'I'm afraid the house is due for an overhaul. We've done nothing to it for the last twelve years and the redecorating is going to take all my time.' She watched Mrs Holland's face fall and wondered what Mark would say. But the house did need attention and this was something she would enjoy doing.

'Oh, dear, I know what a job that is going to be! Still,' Mary Holland rallied, 'you will of course want to hold a big party when you've finished and perhaps we can help there.' Her voice held the confidence that their future cooperation was a *fait accompli*.

'Lulu! How wonderful to see you!' Louise was grabbed and given an enthusiastic kiss on the cheek. 'I never dreamed you'd be here!'

'Polly, where on earth have you sprung from? I didn't know you were back!' Louise smiled warmly and allowed herself to be pulled away from the older women with a hurried apology and taken to a table a little apart from the main area.

'Now don't move from there, I'll get us both some coffee,' Polly Fawkes said, and was off.

Louise glanced back at her mother but Betty seemed to be happily talking with a number of other women her own age. So she watched Polly insinuate her way to the front of the coffee queue, her blade-of-grass figure chic in pink linen, the platinum blonde hair, so pale it was almost white, cut short like a boy's to show off her well-shaped head, make up discreetly making the most of her astonishing green eyes. Polly looked, in fact, like a millionaire urchin who hadn't forgotten her roots.

They'd become friends through the tennis club. For three years they'd played regularly once a week until Polly and her businessman husband had left England eighteen months ago when he'd been moved to Paris. Louise had missed her more than she'd imagined. Polly's ironic outlook on life was very stimulating.

She arrived back with two cups of coffee, two chocolate Hobnobs and a clutch of raffle tickets. She carefully placed the cups on the table, looked at the biscuits with distaste then put them to one side with the tickets. She sat down with a sigh of relief. 'Thank heavens for someone I can talk to. I was just about to leave when I saw you.'

'When did you get back? Why haven't you rung me?'

'Ten days ago and I've hardly had a moment. You're top of my list, promise, darling! But it was all such a rush! Willoughby has been put on the main board and in charge of some company or other they've just acquired. He's supposed to turn it around in a ridiculously short time so we've had to give up Paris and come back here.' She glanced around with a look that said precisely where she would rather be. 'Thank heavens we never let the house! Pooh swore she'd never forgive me if she couldn't spend her holidays here.' Pooh was Polly's fourteen-year-old daughter. 'Now, of course, she's mad as anything that we're leaving Paris. That's the young for you!' She gave a light laugh and twisted the huge sapphire ring on her wedding finger. 'As to what I'm doing here, ask Willoughby. He told me he wants to get closer to the party and I wasn't to lose any time in offering my services.'

'Sounds just like Mark,' Louise commented with a touch of gloom.

'How is my favourite man? Oh, I've missed you both! You're so lucky to have such a charming husband. Willoughby doesn't improve with age.'

Willoughby Fawkes was a dry, self-contained man who was reputed to have an amazing business brain. According to Mark, he was little short of a genius.

'So how are the children, those darling twins?'

'Gone off round the world yesterday morning.' Louise tried to sound cheerful but felt misery fill her chest like water pouring into a balloon, stretching the thin rubber until it threatened to burst.

'Oh, you poor thing!' Polly leaned across the table and grasped Louise's hand with her thin one. 'Never mind, think of all the fun you can have now!'

'That's more or less what Emma said. Except I think she fears I don't know how.'

'Perceptive little soul, your Ems. Wish my Pooh showed half her sensibility.'

'Where is she at the moment?'

'Staying with friends in the Loire Valley, expected home at the end of next week in time to get ready for school. We've hardly seen anything of her these holidays.' Polly sounded as though that wasn't altogether a bad thing.

Louise leaned forward. 'Look, are you doing anything tomorrow night? We've got Nicky and Colin Webber coming round for a meal. Why don't you and Willoughby join us? It would be such fun, just like the old days!'

'Oh, darling, I'd love it. But we're supposed to be going to some dreary drinks party.'

'Is it local, can you come on afterwards? Mark says he's going to be home early, which usually means by eight-thirty, so we won't be eating much before half-past nine.'

Polly's face lit up. 'That sounds great. I'll drag Willoughby away and we'll be with you just about the same time as Mark.' Her eyes gained a wicked glint as she raised her coffee cup. 'Here's to us, and here's to you and your freedom. I'll make sure you know how to enjoy it!'

Chapter Four

Mark backed his Mercedes out of its parking space on Friday night with less than his usual care. He couldn't wait to get home.

The long discussions with the Americans had been tedious in the extreme. In the end, they'd got the desired result but it had been an exhausting business.

It had not helped, either, that he had felt Robin Howard assessing every word he spoke.

Her own contributions to the negotiations had been low-key but eminently sensible, her manner relaxed and confident throughout.

Which was more than Mark could say of himself.

Robin's appearance on the scene had taken him by surprise. A couple of months ago, Douglas Pargeter, the firm's Senior Partner and also Managing Partner in charge of the Audit Division, had suggested lunch. Mark had been instantly alert; Douglas only ever suggested lunch when he had something of importance to impart. Usually he preferred sandwiches in the office or, at the most, a quick beer at a local pub. The fact that he took Mark off to The Greenhouse was even more significant. Douglas's parsimony was legendary. If he was willing to push the boat out at a fashionable restaurant, there was either something extremely pleasant in the offing or a major difficulty.

There was a whiff of the sinister about Douglas, Mark decided, not for the first time, as they took their seats. Beneath all the well-bred manners and cultivated charm, honed by Eton and Cambridge, writhed a devilish wisp that warned he should not be taken at face value. Particularly when he was putting himself out to be pleasant.

It had been Douglas's charm, City connections and infinite capacity for taking pains that had guided the small firm he'd joined in his thirties into the mainstream and, via a series of ever more important mergers, ultimately to become one of the top account-ancy firms in the country. Now heading for sixty, with a pleasant Gloucestershire home and a wife who preferred country living, he'd made no secret of his decision to retire in eighteen months' time. There would then be a general reshuffle and Mark had hopes he would be put in charge of the Audit Division.

As they sat in the taxi going towards Mayfair and Douglas gave a lively account of his weekend spent visiting some friends in Yorkshire, watching their highly priced horseflesh dominate the York races, Mark grew increasingly confident that the purpose of this lunch was to confirm his present position as acting head of the Acquisitions Department, thereby clearing the way for the major step up when Douglas retired.

Mark had been given the responsibility of running Acquisitions when the actual head had had to take sick leave some six months earlier. The time must now have come for the firm to acknowledge that he wasn't coming back. It had been obvious to Mark as soon as poor Howard, yellow-faced, gaunt and racked with pain, had given up the daily struggle to get into the office, that he wasn't going to get better. Mark supposed courtesy demanded that the fact he'd been more or less running the department for several months before Howard collapsed be only half recognised by the 'acting' tag. Now it seemed as if his position would be ratified.

Douglas, his poker face bland and pleasant, spent the first two courses indulging in a general discussion of business and the way the company was going.

When the bread and butter pudding arrived, he ate the first few mouthfuls in reverential silence then looked across the table at his junior and dropped his bombshell. 'Robin Howard is returning from the New York office. Acquisitions needs another high-flying partner so you're going to have someone to work alongside.' He dug his spoon into the pudding again.

Mark pushed his away from him and stared at the Senior Partner. At first he couldn't believe it. This wasn't about ratifying his position. Indeed, it sounded dangerously like undermining it. 'What exactly does that mean?' he demanded.

Douglas blew out disdainfully through pursed lips, a habit he had when anyone questioned a statement of his. 'I said, you'll work alongside each other.'

Mark couldn't leave it there, however dangerous pressing him might be. 'You mean, we are going to be joint acting heads of department,' he said flatly. 'Is that really necessary?'

Douglas pounced on the last word. 'Necessary? Well, let's see, dear boy. Acquisitions has grown rapidly over the last few years. It provides a healthy segment of our profits.'

Mark cursed himself as he noted the faint look of distaste on the Senior Partner's face. So far Mark's progress through the firm, from university onwards, had been trouble-free. Now an element of doubt had been introduced. He was going to have to fight for his position. And if he wasn't confirmed as Head of Acquisitions, he could say goodbye to running the Audit Division when Douglas retired.

Mark had met Robin Howard. They'd both been involved on a project a couple of years earlier. Sharp mind, excellent manner. Top women accountants still weren't as common as top women lawyers but if anyone could break through the glass ceiling it would be her, of that he had no doubt. It had never occurred to him, though, that her advancement could be at the expense of his own.

Questions raced through Mark's mind. Had he failed in some way he hadn't realised? One or two things hadn't gone quite as well as they might but for reasons that had had nothing to do with him. He could see that but had Douglas decided differently? Then there was the fact that his ability to pull in major new clients seemed to have declined recently.

'Could be a good decision, Douglas,' he said, speaking positively. 'Could free me up to do a little more prospecting.'

'Quite, dear boy. I thought you would see it my way.' Douglas laid down his spoon on an empty plate with a little sigh of contentment. 'Coffee, don't you think?' He waved at the waiter. 'And brandy?'

The question hung in the air.

Mark didn't hesitate. 'Not for me, thanks, Douglas. I leave spirits for the evening.'

He nodded with approval and ordered coffee.

'Yes, this could be a most valuable development. The only thing is,' Mark leaned forward slightly, his gaze holding the other man's, 'I'm disappointed you didn't discuss it with me earlier. Presenting it as a *fait accompli* suggests I don't have your complete confidence.'

He held his breath.

Douglas gave one of his snake-like smiles. 'It was a Senior Partner decision. When you're there, you'll understand.'

Oh, devious Douglas! The merest hint that Mark was still headed for the top. Given a moment after informing him that he now had serious competition in the Acquisitions Department.

Mark had returned to the office with his mind in a ferment. Not only was he going to have to cope with a threat to his standing in the firm, that thread involved a woman.

Mark was the first to agree that women deserved equal opportunities with men. Fine minds, some of them, and no reason why they shouldn't perform just as well as their male counterparts. Particularly in areas such as advertising, sales and the service industries. However, he didn't feel comfortable working alongside them. You just didn't invite girls into the men's locker room for golf or rugger, and that went for business, too. All right, it was an old-fashioned point of view but he felt there was something fundamental about it.

As usual in the evenings, the traffic along the Cromwell Road was static. Mark sat with the engine idling first outside the Gothic glories of the Victoria and Albert museum and then the Natural History Museum, his mind a jumble of uncomfortable thoughts. The fact that Robin Howard had provided such excellent support in the discussions with the Americans was both a relief and a cause for concern.

Then there was the little matter of why he had found it so difficult to tell Louise that the new partner in the department was a woman.

He should, of course, have told her at the start. But he wasn't in the habit of discussing the office with his wife. She was reasonably intelligent, of course, but there was no way she could understand the sort of things he was involved in: major audits, mergers, takeovers and all that. Which was fine with Mark. He hadn't married Louise for her business acumen. Still, that lunch with Douglas and the news of Robin Howard's advent had rattled him and he'd have liked a little sympathy and understanding. But it was the day the children had broken up and they'd all gone to a musical to celebrate. Louise had been full of the twins' plans for their gap year and how much money they'd managed to save. The moment had passed and had never really resurfaced.

And it was hardly surprising Louise had got caught up in all the excitement and planning. He'd never have believed the twins could be so single-minded about a project. They'd really gone at it hammer and tongs. Which had pleased him. Especially seeing that James could give his attention to something other than music.

The traffic gradually crawled over the flyover towards Hammersmith and then the Hogarth roundabout and on towards Richmond. Mark breathed another sigh of relief. Unless there were any more holdups, he should be home within twenty minutes. Home with his loving wife at a reasonable hour for a quiet evening spent working in front of the television. It made him feel quite odd to think of home without the background of noise and activity that was inseparable from his children. No wonder Louise had reacted so strongly the other night.

Darling Louise. Mark couldn't remember the last time she'd given him cause for concern. It had been joy all the way ever since he'd seen her for the first time at a tennis tournament. Louise had reached the semi-finals of the singles. He'd been admiring the punch of her service, the shortness of her skirt and shape of her legs, not to mention the curves so invitingly displayed as she scampered around the court, when she'd dashed forward to return a short ball, stumbled and skidded straight into the net, ending up on her back as her opponent played a gentle lob just over her head. It had been the way she'd laughed, got up and dusted herself down that had decided Mark this was the girl for him. Fresh from his triumph in his finals and ready to take on the world, he'd made sure of an introduction to her as soon as she came off the court.

Louise had gone on to win that tournament and they'd started a swift courtship that ended in marriage before the next. Held just after their honeymoon, Mark had won the men's singles, Louise

30

had successfully defended her title and together they'd won the doubles. He always reckoned that day had set the pattern for their marriage.

Mark hailed the advent of the twins as another triumph, two for the price of one, so to speak. While he'd carved out his career, he had always felt secure in the knowledge that Louise was looking after home and family.

Held once again in a queue at traffic lights, his attention was caught by the girl driving the car next to him. She had a look of the young Louise: short dark curls and a small, retroussé nose. She turned slightly to address a remark over her shoulder to a young child of perhaps five years old, probably a girl though it was difficult to be sure with its T shirt and short hair. The child saw Mark and pulled a rude face, then looked extremely pleased with itself. The sort of thing Emma would have done.

The driver looked over her shoulder and caught the expression. Instead of chiding the child, she laughed and looked at Mark with a cheeky smile and a shrug of her shoulders. Had he been a different sort of man, he realised, he would have wound down his window and started a conversation.

Instead he looked straight ahead and thought of Emma with nostalgia. Then felt renewed sympathy for his wife. He'd spoken to Louise on the telephone yesterday afternoon – briefly because he'd been interrupted by June with a transatlantic call and hadn't had a chance to get back.

Never mind, this evening they'd be able to have a proper chat. He'd forget work for once. After all, it was Friday evening. He'd find a nice bottle of wine and they'd have a cosy meal, just the two of them. And he had his treat for her all lined up. He smiled to himself as he turned off the main road and on to the final stretch. Louise should be thrilled with what he'd arranged.

Mark parked his car in the garage and went straight into the kitchen. A pungent, unidentifiable but definitely unpleasant smell hit his nostrils.

'Oh, no!' Louise cried as she slammed the microwave door shut.

Mark went and kissed the back of her neck. 'What disaster has hit now?' It was unlike Louise, who was normally efficient in the kitchen. He hoped she wasn't going to throw another wobbly.

'That's the second lot of caramel I've burned,' she wailed. 'I didn't have time to clean the glass jug from the last lot so I used a plastic one and now it's melted and there's brown gunge all over the oven. How could I be so stupid!'

Mark dumped his heavy briefcase on the nearest work surface, tugged his tie undone and shrugged himself out of his jacket. 'We both need a drink, I've had a hell of a day. How about a martini, or would you like something stronger?' It was one of their standard jokes, dating back to the time Louise had rejected his offer of a

31

martini on the basis it would be just red vermouth while she wanted a real pick-me-up. This time the remark brought no smile of recognition.

'Darling, do you want to start drinking before everyone comes?' she asked.

Too late Mark saw the round table in the corner laid for six. Memory flooded back. 'Isn't it just Nicky and Colin?'

'The Fawkeses are back from Paris. I ran into Polly yesterday and asked her and Willoughby too. Since we were already having Nicky and Colin, it seemed like a good idea.'

Unconsciously Mark straightened his shoulders. 'But you've still laid it in the kitchen!'

'I told Polly it was casual. I didn't think you'd want all the fuss of the dining room.'

He said nothing but abandoned the fridge and ice to open the back door and fan the air.

'I'll light a scented candle,' said Louise. 'By the time they arrive, it should be fine.' She poured sugar into a pan and went across to the gas stove. 'I've made *Oeufs à la neige* for pudding. All it needs is the caramel topping.'

Mark brightened. It was one of his favourites. He leaned against the work island and watched her heat the sugar. 'You know, I'd forgotten you were going to ask Nicky and Colin.'

'It was your suggestion,' she said with a brittle note in her voice.

'Right, right,' he agreed hastily. 'And it'll be great to see them, it's ages since we were last together.' He went and took the pan off the stove then wrapped his arms around her. She turned towards him, rested her head in the curve between his shoulder and his chin and gave a tiny sniff as her body melted into his. 'Hey, none of that,' he said gently, running his hand down one of her tight little buttocks and on to a naked thigh. 'The kids'll be back before you have time to realise they're gone.'

Louise held up her face for his kiss. 'I know, I'm just being silly. I'll be all right, I promise. You can't be maudlin with Nicky around.'

A shower and change of clothes made Mark feel better. Dressed in jeans and short-sleeved polo shirt, an extra dry martini inside him, he rubbed his fair hair with a towel and combed it into place, the short curls damp-darkened. He threaded a Gucci belt through the waist loops of his jeans and gave his stomach a pat. More than a hint of flab there, the perils of sandwich lunches. (Louise had mentioned she thought it was the alcohol he consumed but Mark didn't really think that could have anything to do with weight. Beer maybe but not spirits.) Perhaps he'd ask Colin for a game of squash tomorrow . . .

He ran down, taking the stairs two at a time. 'Where's the ice

32

bucket?' he shouted, looking at the empty space in the cupboard where it was normally kept.

'I've taken everything on to the terrace. It's such a lovely evening, I thought we could have our drinks out there.' Louise stood in the kitchen doorway.

Mark feasted his eyes on her. 'You look good enough to eat!' She'd changed into peppermint green cotton pants with a top in the same green striped with sherbet pink. 'A neapolitan ice cream, let me have a lick!' He reached for her, grasping both buttocks this time and pulling her tight against him.

Louise wriggled out of his hands as the door bell rang but there was a nice little bounce to her walk as she went to greet their guests.

Chapter Five

'Now don't let Mark bully you,' Nicky said to her husband as they waited outside the Hendersons' front door. She had wanted to go straight in but Colin had said, no, they must wait, Louise and Mark mightn't be ready for them.

'I never do,' he said now shortly. He thrust his hands into the pockets of his chinos and jiggled some change.

Oh dear, Nicky thought, said the wrong thing again! Why couldn't she be like Louise, who seemed to understand just how everyone should be handled? But she wasn't going to allow anything to upset her this evening. This evening Nicky felt absolutely marvellous and being asked to supper with Louise and Mark had made everything perfect.

Colin and Mark went way back. The fact that Colin was a partner in a small firm of local solicitors instead of a high-flying legal eagle in the City didn't matter to Mark. Anymore than it mattered to Louise that Nicky patronised the local nearly new instead of being able to buy the sort of clothes she could. Or that when they came to a meal, the Webbers' whole house could have fitted into the kitchen, or almost. Nicky told herself not to exaggerate. She and Colin lived in a very nice house built in the thirties with a more than decent-sized garden – luckily bought before property prices had shot up so much. It had been a real struggle to keep up the mortgage at first; now they couldn't believe how fortunate they'd been.

The door opened and there was Louise, looking marvellous and greeting them as though they were the only people she wanted to see. She always gave Nicky such a warm feeling.

And out on the terrace was Mark. Heavens, every time Nicky saw him she realised he was more attractive than she'd remembered. He and Colin were both tall but Mark was somehow better put together. Not that Colin wasn't good-looking but he was beginning to lose his hair, which was as fair as Mark's but finer. His high forehead was now higher than ever and his kind eyes were sort of lost behind his spectacles whereas Mark's blazed in that dark, dark blue, so dark you sometimes thought they were black. And his nose was strong and straight, patrician, not splayed out like Colin's. He'd kept his figure, too. Colin's broad shoulders, which had been so powerful in the rugby scrum, were now matched by a thickened waist and broad beam.

'How's my favourite man?' Nicky sparkled up at Mark.

'Nicky! Looking as great as ever.' He gave her a smacking kiss on each cheek that lit the little glow he'd always fired in her, ever since that first time Colin had brought her to meet his great friend all those years ago.

Nicky ran a hand self-consciously through her bright red curls. She'd never been a great beauty but she knew how to make the best of herself. The 'carrot top' of the school playground had given way to 'flame-haired wonder' when she left, and Colin was always telling her she hadn't changed a bit. She'd seen in Mark's eyes that first time they met surprise at Colin's choice. At first she'd thought it was because she came from the Midlands and didn't have the same sort of accent, so she'd been defensive. Not prickly so much as a bit more jokey than usual. Because she knew that Mark had been at Oxford with Colin. He had told her so much about his best friend. How they'd both been cricket and rugger blues, had chased girls and crawled pubs together. 'He got a two-one while I just scraped a second,' Colin had said. 'Mark could have got a first, if only he'd put in a bit of work. But he said it was more important to make the most of the experience. I thought he'd become an entrepreneur, do something really exciting. Instead he got articled to the firm of accountants he's still with. He said accountancy was the key to a brilliant business future and suggested I do the same. But I always wanted to practise law.' It had all seemed incredibly glamorous to Nicky.

Later she'd realised that she was different from Colin's usual girlfriends not because of her background but because she was so much more attractive and sparky. She discovered that he was normally rather shy with the female sex and realised that it had been she who had made the running with him. She'd been attracted by his solidity, his presence, the sense of security he gave her. All right, maybe he didn't have Mark's charm and good looks but he suited her. And she suited him.

'Life's rosier for seeing you!' She made a business out of fluttering her eyelashes at Mark, who was never averse to a bit of flirtation. Not that it meant anything, Nicky knew that, he was far too happy with the lovely Louise. Still, it didn't do any harm if you showed someone you thought they were attractive. She'd never do anything more, of course.

Louise brought out a small dish of spicy sausage slices to have with the drinks.

'How are you enjoying your freedom?' Nicky asked her.

'She doesn't see it as that,' Mark said quickly, slapping Colin on the back.

'Oh, you have to be positive.' Nicky slanted a quick grin up at him. 'Think freedom, Louise!'

36

'Pay no attention to Nicky,' Colin said easily, taking the dish from Louise and handing it around. 'She's terrified of the day when our two leave home.'

'How are Riff and Raff?' asked Louise.

Nicky couldn't remember how Robert and Richard, now twelve and eleven, had earned their nicknames but they'd instantly stuck. 'Smarting under the worst reports they've ever had, and that's saying something!' She collapsed into one the garden chairs on the generous-sized terrace. 'Oh, this is wonderful. What an evening!' She looked out at the charming tangle of greens and golds that strayed into the distance. 'What's that marvellous smell?' She twisted round in the chair to look at the rose growing up the house. That pink would look great on their back wall. She was just about to aşk the name when Louise said, 'Nicotiana,' and gave a wave of her hand towards tall, willowy plants with white trumpet flowers growing between silver-leaved shrubs. 'Tobacco plants.'

Nicky tried not to feel hurt that Louise had felt the need to translate the Latin.

'White wine for you, Nicky?' Mark asked.

She nodded. 'I've some news,' she announced proudly as he handed glasses to her and Louise. 'I've got a job.'

'You're never letting her loose, are you?' Mark demanded of Colin. 'She isn't safe!'

For the briefest of moments Nicky felt resentment. Just because she'd always played the unruly girl who was the life and soul of the party, there was no need to think that she couldn't handle herself in an office! Then her customary good humour took over. After all, it was a compliment, really, wasn't it?

'You have my permission to kick him,' Louise said sweetly. 'Tell us all about it? It sounds very exciting.'

But before Nicky could say anything there was the distant chime of the door bell.

'Ah, Polly and Willoughby.' Louise got up and went back into the house.

'I thought they were still in Paris,' Colin said. 'Is it permanent or are they back for a visit?'

'I think it's for good but I haven't spoken to Willoughby yet. Louise ran into Polly at some coffee morning yesterday. Ah, here they are.'

Polly came through the french windows from the drawing room, talking animatedly to Louise. 'It was the most *boring* party, darling, no trouble dragging Willoughby away at all. The moment he knew we were to come here, he lost any interest in staying, thank heavens.'

Nicky had forgotten the way Polly always made her feel dowdy. And Paris seemed to have given her an additional chic. That little navy shift dress must be French, there was nothing to it really and yet it looked so special. Of course, if you had a figure like hers, anything would look good. Nicky's legs were excellent but her figure was the original British pear shape. She compensated by wearing really short skirts but now, beside Polly, she felt her outfit looked vulgar.

'Nicky, you're always a sight for sore eyes.' Willoughby appeared behind his wife and advanced towards her. Nicky braced herself for a couple of wet kisses. Paris didn't seem to have improved him at all. He was still the same slack, loose-limbed figure he'd always been. You'd have thought Polly would have got that flab off him, made sure his suits looked tailored. His clothes must surely be expensive, everything else in their lives was, but you would have thought they'd been handed down by someone even larger than Willoughby because they never seemed to fit properly. And the combination of his thick lips and the way hair grew all over the backs of his hands always made her feel odd.

Whenever they met, Willoughby gave Nicky the unsettling feeling that he wouldn't mind making a serious pass at her, should the right opportunity present itself. Not that he said anything, it was just the way he looked. She wondered what Polly saw in him. Of course, his being such a successful businessman meant his wife was well supplied with everything that made life comfortable, but even so! I mean, thought Nicky, a girl like Polly could have had anyone.

There followed several minutes of general merry-go-round: exclamations of delight at seeing each other again, Willoughby saying how good it was to be back in England, Polly admitting it was wonderful to be with old friends again but Paris had been such a delight – and Mark getting more drinks. Nicky noticed how the women were all served white wine while the chaps were pressed to have martinis out of a pre-mixed jug. Not that it worried her you understand? But it was interesting.

'Nicky's just told us she's got a job,' Louise said as the party settled with their drinks.

'No! Really? Tell all,' Polly demanded, her beautifully shaped head with its short white-blonde hair held invitingly to one side, an expression of eager interest on her urchin face.

Nicky's elation faded. 'Oh, it's nothing sensational. I'm going to be secretary to the head of the college down the road.'

'That the place we once thought about for James?' Mark asked. Louise nodded.

Nicky knew they'd rejected it as not academically successful enough. James had gone to Mark's public school for a year, despite Louise's warning it was all wrong for him. It had been a disaster. James had had something approaching a nervous breakdown and had had to be taken away. In the end he'd joined Emma at the local grant-aided school, where Riff and Raff were currently juniors.

'It's perfect for me. Means I'll be free in the school holidays, most of the time anyway. There was a lot of competition,' she added with a touch of smugness. 'I thought I didn't stand a chance but the head said personality counted for more than recent experience and he was looking for someone cheerful who could get on with people, be tactful and discreet.' She gave a small, self-deprecating laugh. 'I thought if anything got me the job it would be my French.' How she'd worked at that, at school and afterwards! She'd had real flair and it had been so interesting. 'Instead I got it because I'm not a gossip!' Nicky felt she'd done enough talking about herself. 'I'd love to talk to you about Paris sometime,' she added to Polly.

'But why get a job?' Mark asked idly. 'Fed up with life at home?'

'The boys aren't doing at all well at school,' Colin said, his voice level. 'We've decided they've got to go somewhere else and that means a bit of a drain on the old finances.'

'That's terrible, Colin,' said Louise. 'Emma and James have done very well there.'

'Have they, darling, actually?' queried Mark, getting up to refill glasses. 'Oh, I know their A level results were reasonably good, thank heavens, but education is about more than academic achievement.'

'Right, Mark. Manners, savoir-faire, connections.' Willoughby ticked them off on his fat fingers. 'The old-boy network still counts.'

'Less and less these days,' Colin stated quietly. 'In fact, sometimes I think it can be a positive drawback. Still, the boys need much more individual attention than they are getting at the moment.'

'Going private seems the only choice we've got,' Nicky put in. 'But the fees are just astronomical so the only thing is for me to go back to work. Otherwise . . .' She shrugged expressively. 'Getting this job is fantastic, I never thought I'd find anything so quickly.'

'Lucky head, say I.' Mark poured more wine into her glass. 'Just hope you don't distract him too much from his duties.' He gave her a twinkling glance and passed on to Polly.

'We'll eat in a few minutes, Mark.' Louise's voice sounded a warning note as she got up.

Nicky followed her into the kitchen. 'Need a hand?'

'Oh, you are an angel! Would you like to shake that dressing then add it to the starters? I hope you don't mind eating in the kitchen?'

'Yours is so nice, I wouldn't mind never seeing the dining room.' Nicky carefully spooned vinaigrette over little dishes of melon with prawns and grilled red peppers.

'How are you going to manage a job and a family?' Louise brought a beautifully dressed salmon from the fridge and placed it on the island.

Nicky fished a tissue out of her shoulder bag and wiped up a bit of dressing that had spilt on the polished pine table. 'It shouldn't be too bad. The boys will be at boarding school, after all, so it'll just be

39

Colin and me. He never seems to mind what he eats anyway.' She gave a little giggle. 'I expect I'll be shopping at Marks and Sparks for ready-to-eat meals.'

'Have you settled where the boys are going?'

'It's all organised. Nowhere very grand but the school has a good reputation for getting the most out of its pupils.' Nicky mentioned a minor public school not too far from them. 'At the moment they don't seem to be learning anything. No discipline! Riff and Raff just spend the whole time either skiving or disrupting the rest of the class. I don't think any of their teachers will be sorry to see the back of them. There, that's all done. What's next?'

Louise stood back and surveyed the table and her preparations. 'How do you feel about the job?' she asked abruptly. 'I mean, actually going back to work?'

Nicky brightened. It was the first time anyone had asked her this. She sat on the edge of the banquette and smoothed down her skirt. 'I'm looking forward to it. You miss using your mind, you know? And all those skills? And being with other people. Life's pretty social round here but it's not quite the same, is it?' She'd really missed office life when Robert had come along and she'd given up her job.

Louise drew out a chair and sat down beside her. 'I thought you had to have word processing and all that to get a job these days? You didn't use a word processor before when you worked, did you?'

'Uh-huh.' Nicky shook her head. 'But I could see I'd want to get back to work at some stage so I took a course at the local adult education.'

'You never told me that!'

'No?' Nicky looked down at her hands. 'Well, I wanted to make sure I could do it first.' That wasn't really it, though, more a case of there not being any opportunity. She didn't see all that much of Louise nowadays. It wasn't as though their children were near enough in age to do things together. When Nicky and Colin had first got married, the Webbers and the Hendersons seemed to have lots of evenings together. But over the years those occasions had grown fewer and fewer. She and Louise would bump into each other in the supermarket sometimes, have a quick conversation then end by saying they'd ring and make a proper date. And sometimes they did.

'Was it very hard?' asked Louise.

Nicky shrugged. 'Not once I got into it. All a matter of getting your mind in gear really. I used to pop into Colin's office at lunchtime and practise on his secretary's machine. She's been ever so nice, really helped me. I'd do some of her work while she was shopping so it helped her too.'

'I envy you,' Louise said slowly.

'Me!' squeaked Nicky, looking first at her hostess then glancing round the huge kitchen with all its gadgets, its island work unit and

40

the comfortable dining area so beautifully set for the meal they were going to eat. Not a 'designer kitchen' as such, but what a contrast to hers: small and badly planned. They'd been going to rip it out and start again but what with the children coming so quickly, and then the recession, there'd never been enough money.

'Now the twins have gone, the house seems so empty. I really don't know what I'm going to do with my time.'

'But you've got Mark!' The words were out before Nicky realised what she'd said or the way she'd said it.

Louise's big grey eyes met hers and Nicky stared back, knowing she should say something else and unable to find the words.

'So I have,' Louise said slowly. 'And you've got Colin.'

'That's right! We're both so lucky,' Nicky added enthusiastically. 'Shall I call the others in?'

Louise got up briskly, went over to the island and started cutting up a baguette. 'That'd be great, thanks.'

Nicky went back to the terrace and found the conversation had moved on to how Willoughby was going to turn round some company or other. Colin looked a little out of things. She went up to his chair and ran a hand along his shoulders, feeling the warmth of his solid flesh. 'Louise says it's all ready,' she said merrily, cutting straight across Willoughby in full flow.

'Great.' Polly got up with alacrity. 'I could do with some food.'

She set off for the house, followed by Mark, carrying the wine.

'I'll bring the martini jug,' said Willoughby.

Nicky turned to the table and picked up the ice bucket. She believed in making yourself useful.

It was a shock to find Willoughby's hand round her waist and his thick lips nuzzling her neck. 'Too long since I've had the pleasure of admiring those gorgeous legs,' he said into her ear. His hand slipped up to clasp one breast in an eager gesture. 'How about lunch sometime?' The suggestive way he said it made Nicky's toes curl, and her whole body revolted against his touch.

'Missing the Parisian *putains*, Willoughby?' she enquired silkily, and trod on his toe.

There was a sharp intake of breath and the hand was removed. 'Only being friendly,' he said sulkily. 'No need to be like that!'

Nicky clasped the ice bucket to her. 'After you, Willoughby,' she said – she had no intention of offering her rear for any further friendly gestures. 'Or do you need cooling off?' With a neat gesture, she dropped an ice cube down his collar.

Over the meal Nicky made a point of being ultra-enthusiastic about everything. In fact, the evening that she had been so looking forward to, that she'd felt so good about, had turned sour. Colin was very quiet. Even Louise failed to bring him out. Polly was – well, Polly; sophisticated, brittle and in control. Nicky had always wondered about Polly. About how deep things went under that shiny surface or whether it was all as shallow as it appeared. Mark and Willoughby dominated the conversation.

It hadn't taken long for Willoughby to recover from having to shimmy the freezing bit of ice down his back and out through his trouser leg. He'd stomped up the garden path but by the time he'd reached the kitchen, it was as if nothing had happened.

Now he sat discussing business as though his mind had never wandered to other matters. Neither man really allowed the women to have a say, though Polly dropped in acerbic comments from time to time, which Willoughby ignored and Mark listened to in an indulgent manner, continuing afterwards as though she hadn't spoken. Louise made sure everyone had food and wine, quietly filling glasses when Mark was too involved in the discussion to notice they were empty, but didn't say much.

Nicky began to grow irritated.

'The thing with the single currency . . .' Mark said, leaning his elbows on the table and jabbing a finger towards Willoughby.

'The thing with the single currency,' Nicky said loudly, 'is that it's like the channel tunnel: anything that makes it easier to get to Paris has got to be a good thing. Isn't that so, Polly?'

Polly smiled, her asymmetrical face creasing engagingly. '*Tu as raison, ma chérie!*' There was no trace of the irony that so often coloured even the most commonplace of her remarks. 'I miss Paris every day. It's going to be a long time before I forgive Willoughby for bringing us back.'

'Not me, darling, the company.' He helped himself to more of the strawberry pavlova Louise had produced for pudding.

'Company, schmompany! You could have got another job!' She glared at him across the table. 'You uprooted me from here, dumped me in Paris without so much as suggesting I might have a choice, made me go to French classes, insisted I make a stylish home for you to entertain in. Then, just when I've got the whole thing beautifully organised and am starting to enjoy myself, what happens? Upsticks and back here, *that's* what happens.' She sat back and drained her glass of wine, pushing it towards Louise for a refill without apology.

Wow! Thought Nicky. Something has really got into her! She'd never seen the normally ultra-composed, sophisticated Polly turn on her husband like that before.

For once Willoughby appeared lost for words. 'But,' he tried, looked helplessly towards Mark then back to his wife, 'I thought you liked living here.'

'Did you ask me?' she demanded. 'Was there any discussion? Where's this famous equality we all talk so much about these days? I think Nicky's got the right idea.' She raised her glass to her. 'Get a job, have some independence.'

Nicky went quite pink with pleasure at being singled out in this way. 'Colin and me – Colin and I, that is – we discussed it all. About the children's school and me getting a job and everything.'

'Yes,' he put in, the first words he'd spoken for some time. 'I've always felt we're a proper team, Nicky and I.' A sudden warmth flooded through her at the look he gave her. Good old Colin, always supportive.

'Lucky you,' Polly said quietly.

'But this is a great chance,' Willoughby said loudly. 'After I turn this company round, I'll be ready to take on the chairmanship.'

'So that makes it all right, does it?' Polly's voice dripped a sweet acidity. 'Willoughby's career is careering along, hell for leather for the top, and Polly will smooth everything along the edges, is that it?' Nobody said anything. 'I should never have abandoned PR. Well done, Nicky, for getting on with your life again.'

'I've never noticed you resenting the material rewards my career has brought us,' Willoughby said stiffly.

'Money. That's what it all comes down to, doesn't it!' Polly stated in a high, slightly unsteady voice.

'No.' Willoughby's voice strengthened. 'It's about doing a job you think is worth doing. It's about teamwork, not only in your office but in your home.' The rest of them seemed to have been forgotten now as Polly glared at her husband across the table and he glared back.

Mark looked uneasy then poured some more wine into his glass and lifted it. 'I'm glad you mentioned Paris, Nicky – and you, Polly – because there's something I want to tell Louise and I think this is a good moment.'

Nicky watched him raise his glass and look straight at his wife. 'Darling, I've fixed it so you can come with me to Paris next week and we can stay on for the weekend. A little second honeymoon for us now that the children have gone. Once I've got my meetings out of the way, it'll be just you and me in gay Paree.'

Nicky grabbed her glass. 'That's wonderful, Mark! Oh, Louise, you'll have such fun.'

'Yes,' Polly said, looking depressed, 'I envy you.'

Louise seemed quite overcome. 'Paris? I didn't even know you were going, Mark!'

Chapter Six

'Whew,' said Mark as Louise started clearing the table, 'I've known easier evenings!'

Louise transferred what was left of the pavlova on to a small plate and covered it with clingfilm. 'Polly seems really upset at having to leave Paris,' she commented. Which was an understatement; she'd never seen Polly like that before.

'Doesn't she just! I don't envy Willoughby with her in that mood.'

Louise thought she didn't envy Polly in the car going home, not with the way Willoughby had been looking at her.

After the meal Mark had taken the men off for a game of snooker.

A few years ago, when Mark became an equity partner with a share of the profits, Louise had suggested they build a swimming pool or tennis court, or both. 'James and Emma could bring their friends home,' she said. 'It would be such fun.'

'But think of the upkeep! We have the tennis club just round the corner and no end of friends with pools. All we'll do is attract the worst element the kids mix with, and find ourselves buying Coca-cola and beer wholesale. Much better to build an extension for a billiard room. That could be in use the whole year round.'

Louise thought a billiard table would attract just the element Mark was against but she could see it wouldn't be any good telling him that. And it meant they could redesign their bedroom to give them each a bathroom and Mark a proper dressing room.

Once installed, the full-size table had been a definite asset. Both James and Emma loved playing, as did their friends, and Louise surprised herself by how good she became. And the table provided a fun way of spending time with their friends after a meal.

But tonight Polly had stated in a voice you didn't argue with that she'd rather not play, she wanted to give Louise ideas for her visit to Paris. Louise could see Nicky was disappointed but all she said was, 'Paris? Oh, that's much more exciting than a whole load of balls!'

And the three women had had an animated conversation. At one stage Polly and Nicky had switched to French, talking so rapidly that Louise was unable to follow.

Finally the men had returned and Mark had asked if he could get anyone a brandy. 'No thanks, sweetie,' Polly said, getting up and giving him a kiss on the cheek. 'I must take my man home, we've a lot to get through tomorrow.'

'We have?' Willoughby sounded grim. 'Tomorrow is Saturday and I intend to enjoy my weekend.'

'You are going to help me get the house straight. I don't want Pooh coming back to chaos.'

She received from Willoughby the sort of look that said, 'Wait until I get you on your own, but he managed a graceful goodbye to Louise.

Polly had given her an unexpectedly strong hug. 'Great evening, darling. Give you a ring next week with those addresses.'

Then Louise and Mark started clearing the kitchen.

'I think Polly can keep her end up,' Louise said now, investigating the remains of the main course.

'And wasn't Colin quiet?' Mark started stacking the dessert plates into the dishwasher. 'Even when we were playing snooker, he hardly said anything.'

'You and Willoughby didn't give him much of a chance over supper. I hope you involved him a bit more during your game.' Louise put the remains of the salmon into a plastic container and thought maybe it hadn't been a good idea to mix the Webbers with the Fawkeses. She'd forgotten just how dissimilar they were.

Mark reached for the fish plates. 'Colin needs to lighten up a bit more. I was always having to drag his nose out of a book when we were at Oxford. If it hadn't been for me, he'd have spent all his time studying. Nicky's been the best thing that could have happened to him but I sometimes think she could have done more to encourage his ambitions. He should have found a job amongst the big boys. He could be partner in a top firm by now if he'd really tried.' Mark finished the plates and began fitting in the glasses, cursing when he couldn't find room for them all. 'I gave him two or three introductions he could have followed up. Instead, here he is stuck in a tuppenny-ha'penny local firm, having to send his wife out to work.'

'He is a partner and I think he likes being where he is. Colin's very reliable and thoughtful but he hasn't quite got your drive, darling. I don't think he'd want to cope with the pressures of being in a City firm.'

Mark gave up on the glasses and stared at her. 'You really think so? I mean, about Colin's being happy to be buried in a backwater?'

For all his brains, Mark could be very obtuse about people sometimes. 'I'm sure you've talked to him about it. What does he say?'

'Oh, that he likes being in general practice. Trouble with him is, he's lazy.'

'He is not!' Louise said firmly. 'He works extremely hard. And I think Nicky's delighted to have a job.' She threw away the remains

46

of the beans and mange-tout. Mark always said that when the time came they had to eat recycled vegetables, he'd turn his toes up. 'I think she's looking forward to it.'

Later, as Mark slipped into bed beside her, she said, 'I've been thinking about the house.'

His hand, on its way to turn out his bedside light, stayed in mid-air. 'What about it?'

She put down her book and slipped a little way down the pillows. 'Don't you think it's time it was redone?'

'Redone?' His gaze travelled round their bedroom with its matching wallpaper and curtains. 'Looks all right to me.'

'Because you haven't really looked. The sun's bleached the paper by the window in here and in the drawing room; in the twins' rooms the paper's actually begun peeling off. There's scratched and chipped paint everywhere – and it's all looking hopelessly out of date.'

'It is?' asked Mark in an altered tone.

'While the children are away, I thought I'd redecorate.'

He turned to her, his eyes appalled. 'Don't you remember how long it took the first time?'

'Two years, I think, but that was because the twins were so small and I had to look after them as well.'

'Two years of paint pots everywhere and never being able to have people round without apologising for the mess. Two years of you always up a ladder and always exhausted. And do you remember how long this room and the billiard room took you after the builders had finished? I suggested they did the decorating but you said you wanted to do it.'

'Don't you remember how over budget they went?'

Mark was not to be put off. 'I'm not going through that again.'

'But the house really does need redoing.'

He flopped against the pillows. 'These days we can afford professionals.' He turned to her again, full of purpose, the way he was when there was a busy day at the office ahead of him and he couldn't wait to get there. 'You get on to some firms and get a few quotes. Stress the importance of their finishing quickly. I want everything ready by Christmas.'

'Christmas!'

'That's four months away, for heaven's sake.'

Louise thought of the size of their house, the unlikelihood of anyone being able to start immediately and the fact that she hadn't any idea of what she wanted done. In her imagination she had envisaged several weeks spent happily scanning magazines, visiting interior design shops, discussing ideas with Polly and some of her other friends. Then gradually going through the house room by room, perhaps gaining inspiration as she went. She levered herself up on one elbow so she could see Mark properly. 'This will be a major project,' she said repressively.

'It'll cost enough!' He pulled her down on top of him and started to reach for the hem of her short nightie. 'Look, darling, I can see this is something you'd like to get your teeth into and that it could be a nice occupation while the kids aren't here. Why not get a specialist to help you?'

'You mean an interior decorator?'

'Hamish at the office had his place done a few months ago and said his wife had found a marvellous girl. I'll get the details from him.'

Louise felt his hands slide up the backs of her thighs, taking the nightie with them. Saturday tomorrow and no need to get up early. 'That'll make it even more expensive,' she said languorously.

'Well, if we're spending all that money, we want to make sure the end result will justify it.'

'Mark! That sounds as though you don't trust my judgement!' Louise pulled away from him and tugged down the nightie.

'Darling.' He reached for her again. 'That's not what I meant at all!' His hands caressed her thighs underneath the flimsy material, his movements slow and unhurried. 'You've got wonderful taste! But why not use professional help to make the most of it? Eh?'

It sounded sensible but what had seemed an all-involving project was beginning to sound more like a matter of delegation.

Mark's hands gently drew her nightie up over head. 'Make some appointments for when we get back from Paris. What do you think of my little idea?' His voice was honeyed, slow and seductive.

Louise snuggled against him, ran a finger through the hairs on his chest, inching it towards where he was most sensitive, loving his sudden intake of breath. 'It sounds absolutely wonderful, darling. I can't wait to get there.'

When Mark had first started travelling abroad, he'd suggested she came too but Louise had never wanted to leave the children. She said she'd prefer to leave travelling until they'd grown up.

And now they had.

'It'll be like a second honeymoon,' she said, moving her hand further down his body.

'Mmm,' Mark murmured, his mouth closing on hers.

She forgot all about her redecoration plans.

On Monday Louise rang a couple of builders and made appointments for them to come round the following week.

Then Mark was on the phone with the details of the interior decorator his fellow partner had used. Louise sighed but rang her immediately and made another appointment for after the Paris trip. The girl sounded very obliging and friendly and Louise began to think that maybe working with someone else on the house might be fun after all.

After that there was nothing that called for her attention. Mark, as usual, was working late that evening so there was no meal to get and Mrs Parks would be coming tomorrow so no point in doing the dusting. Then the doorbell went. It was Polly.

'Darling I've brought my Paris address book.'

'How kind, come in for coffee. You look as though you're about to join the army!' Polly was looking as terrific as usual in Bermuda-length shorts in a very subtle shade of khaki and a matching sleeveless shirt with safari pockets. The multitude of brass buttons was matched by a pair of gold earrings.

'Poor them! I've no sense of discipline,' Polly giggled as she followed Louise into the kitchen and watched her put the kettle on. 'Though I think I could wake them up, add a touch of imagination to the drill.' She stood to attention and made a smart salute, then collapsed on to the banquette. 'And I could certainly do the logistics bit. When I think of how I've master-minded all our moves, no army wife could have done better.' Paris hadn't been Willoughby's first assignment. At various times Polly had had to create homes in Brazil, India and Korea. Always with stints in London in between.

'Do you think you're here permanently now?' Louise asked as she made the coffee.

Polly shrugged her shoulders. 'Who knows? Willoughby thinks he's in line for Managing Director when John retires next year, then he'll be sending everybody else round the world.'

Louise led the way out on to the terrace, then had to go back for pencil and paper as Polly brought out a fat Filofax. Names and addresses were thrown out like bird seed, Polly sketching in the background to each with speed and economy. 'Very good on medium-priced clothes that are that little bit different. You'll never see anything like them over here. Make Mark get you at least one outfit, you'll never regret it . . . Marvellous hairdresser, better than two hours at the psychiatrist. I think I shall have to keep going back at least once a month.' Then she glanced at Louise and said, 'Not that you haven't got an excellent cut now, darling. Perhaps leave Alex for next visit. Now, this is a great bistro in the Marais district, ideal for a little lunch, nothing remarkable but everything so very French . . .'

On she went until at last Louise interrupted with a laugh: 'We're only going for four days. You've giving me enough for four months!'

Polly looked up from her little book, a bemused expression on her face. 'So I am! Forgive me, darling, I just miss it all so much. I wish I was coming with you!'

'Why not?' Louise suggested light-heartedly. 'Mark will be in meetings all Thursday and Friday, you could show me Paris.'

'Oh, Lulu, would that I could! But with Pooh coming back at the weekend, there's just too much to do at Whiteways.' She closed the

49

Filofax with a snap and replaced it carefully in her handbag.

Louise was taken aback. She hadn't expected her suggestion to be taken seriously. 'Just what is it about Paris?' she asked curiously.

Polly shot her a hooded look. She picked up a biscuit. Sharp white teeth broke into the crisp confection and a shower of crumbs fell on to her shorts. They lay there unnoticed. 'Paris,' she said dreamily, 'is just such an experience.'

'Did you meet lots of people?'

Polly came out of her trance. 'Of course, darling. You know Willoughby. Half his success comes from making sure he knows all the right people. He has such a knack for getting on terms with them.'

Louise wondered how he did it – and when. Poor Colin hadn't been given a chance the other night.

'But did *you* make any friends?'

Polly brushed away the crumbs from her shorts. 'One or two,' she said casually. 'After all, one or two are really all you need, aren't they? If they're the right sort.' She paused as if struck by a thought. 'Look, here's Marie-Claire's number.' She grabbed Louise's piece of paper and added to the list. 'I'll ring her and say you'll be in touch; she was such a good friend to me and I know she'd love to meet you. She speaks very good English.'

'That's terribly kind but I'm not sure we'll have time to meet people.' Louise stared down at the detail-loaded piece of paper.

'You mean, you want to keep Mark all to yourself?' Polly gave her a wicked smile.

'We don't get many opportunities just to be on our own,' Louise confessed. 'And I'm really looking forward to this time in Paris.'

'Second honeymoon and all that? But now the children have gone, you'll be able to have lots of those.'

Louise laughed. 'I suppose we will. All right, I'll ring your friend . . . what's her name?' She squinted at Polly's scribble.

'Marie-Claire Desrivières. She's great fun, doesn't take anything too seriously.'

'Like you and me, you mean?' Louise grinned, remembering times she and Polly had spent together: playing tennis, having lunch, swapping recipes, taking the children around. Always there had been lots of laughter and Louise supposed she would say Polly was one of her best friends. But how well, she wondered now, did she in fact know her? Their relationship had always been so light-hearted. Whenever the conversation looked like taking a serious turn Polly always said, 'Heavens, that's far too deep for me.'

'Exactly, darling, like you and me.' Polly stood up. 'Now I must be on my way. Willoughby wants me in London this evening for some business do and I've booked myself a massage and hair appointment. Then I've got to check out a personal trainer.'

'Personal trainer?'

'Must keep the body beautiful and the working parts working. You don't expect me to join some sweaty exercise class, do you?' Polly shrieked with laughter. 'If you could see your face, Lulu! No, but seriously, you should come in with me. Do you a power of good. You feel so marvellous afterwards!'

'Oh, Polly, you're wonderful. Whatever did I do while you were in Paris?'

'Got far too serious, it seems to me. Lighten up, Lulu.'

That was what Mark had said Colin should do, thought Louise as she saw Polly off. Had she really lost her zest for life? Would she find in Paris what Polly obviously had?

Chapter Seven

Louise was enchanted with Eurostar. 'It's like the Orient Express brought up to date! Even to the little lamps at each table.' She flicked the smooth semi-circle of opalescent glass with her finger.

Mark grinned at her from the opposite first-class seat. 'You look like a child at the pantomime.'

'I feel a bit like one. I can't remember when you and I last had a holiday all on our own.'

He frowned briefly. 'It won't be a holiday until Saturday. I'm sorry I shan't be able to take you round during today and tomorrow, but you won't mind, will you?'

Louise smiled reassuringly at him. 'I'm going to have a ball. Polly has given me five thousand addresses.

'Ah, yes, Polly!'

'What do you mean, "Ah, yes, Polly!" in that tone?'

Mark flicked the pages of the Eurostar magazine that had been on the table between their seats in a gesture that gained time. Then he seemed to come to a decision. 'I had lunch with Willoughby yesterday.'

'And?' Louise prompted.

'He said they'd left Paris not a moment too soon, that Polly was involved with some Frenchman. You don't look surprised.'

'She hasn't said anything but I suppose, yes, I did have a suspicion something might be going on. She was so upset at having to leave and there's such an excited air about her whenever Paris is mentioned. Did Willoughby say if he knew who it was?'

Mark shook his head. His fingers flicked again at the magazine pages.

'So what makes him think it's true?'

'Oh, you know, little things. Like telephones being put down when he answers, and Polly being particularly nice to him when he comes back after a trip.'

'Perhaps she was just pleased to see him again!'

'Willoughby?' Mark laughed sardonically. 'What beats me is why she married him in the first place. I can quite understand why she stays with him but could she see right from the start that he was destined for the top, with all the trappings that go with it?'

'What a cynical remark!'

53

'Well, can you think of a better reason?'

'Polly always does everything Willoughby wants,' Louise said slowly. 'I think she really cares about him.'

'Polly only cares about herself.'

Louise opened her mouth to defend her friend then closed it again as she saw Robin Howard coming down the train towards them. The accountant looked extremely elegant in another grey suit and ivory silk blouse. Her face lit up as she spotted them. 'Ah,' she said, 'you're here already. I got caught by the traffic.'

'We didn't have to battle with it,' Mark said smugly, getting up and removing his briefcase from the adjacent seat. 'Our train brought us right into Waterloo.'

Why hadn't Louise realised Robin would probably be going with them to Paris? After all, Mark had said that the first couple of days were going to be concerned with business.

She still felt cheated.

Now, of course, Robin was going to share their table, leaving her an awkward third at their business discussions. For both of them were now taking papers out of their respective cases.

'Hi! The gang's all here!' An attractively ugly man of medium height with huge ears, large nose and lovely tawny eyes stood beside their table. He was accompanied by another man and a woman. 'I thought Val was going to make us so late we'd miss the train.'

'That's right, blame it all on your poor wife.' A woman who looked about Louise's age smiled without a hint of bitterness. A tad taller than her husband, she had a commanding presence, dark hair swept up in a French pleat and a classically strong face with straight nose, high cheekbones and a wide mouth. Not pretty but elegant. She took off her cream coat and revealed a matching dress.

Mark rose again. 'Hi, Neil, glad you made it. You know Robin, of course, and this is Louise, my wife. Lulu, meet Neil Lewin, he's the legal eagle working with us on this project, and this is his assistant, Don.' From behind Neil and his wife a younger man in his late-twenties pushed forward a serious face with heavy black glasses, and murmured hello.

Louise held out her hand. 'Delighted to meet you, Neil, I'm the passenger on this trip.'

He beamed at her. 'Not the only one. Meet my wife. She insisted on coming even though I said she'd be on her own most of the time. But we're going to stay on for the weekend.'

Louise grinned at Val. 'So are we. What's the betting the meetings go on over Saturday? Have we been sold a pup, do you think?'

'Probably, but who cares?' Val tossed her smart coat on to the rack above the seats, looked at the papers that now covered the table then indicated the one for two on the other side of the aisle. 'I think this one is ours. You and I are going to enjoy ourselves while they, poor things, are handcuffed to their wretched files.'

Louise moved across with alacrity. 'Mark didn't tell me another wife was going to be on the trip.'

'Probably didn't know. I swung it on Neil at the last minute. I should be at the office but I wondered what in heaven's name I was doing, slaving over hot papers when I could be in Paris.' Val settled herself down opposite Louise and opened her hazel eyes wide.

Louise laughed, suddenly liking her very much. 'You work?'

'I'm an accountant.' Val twisted her pleasant mouth into a derisive moue. 'For my sins.'

'You don't mean that!' Louise insisted. If ever a woman looked in command of herself it was Val.

Louise received a confident smile, 'No, you're right, of course. I love my work. But I love skiving off to Paris more!'

'Is your firm like Mark's?'

Val shook her head. 'I'm in industry, in the finance department of a construction company.'

'Be the financial director in a few more years,' Neil chipped in from across the aisle. 'That is if she manages to stop taking time off like this.' He grinned at them and Louise thought how relaxed he looked. Don, Robin and Mark were already frowning, pulling at an ear lobe or flicking a pencil, but he seemed remarkably laid back.

There was a slamming of doors, then the train pulled smoothly away from the platform.

'Do you go with Mark on many of these trips?'

'My first,' Louise acknowledged. 'We've always had children at home before but now they're abroad, so I'm free.' She made it sound as though she had been given wings.

Val immediately wanted to know all about the family and soon Louise felt she'd known her for years, she was so easy to talk to; interested, intelligent and sympathetic.

'Oh, how you must miss them,' Val said when Louise had finished telling her about the route the twins intended to take. 'Do you worry constantly about their safety?'

Everybody else had said she mustn't worry, that of course they were going to be all right. Louise was grateful for someone who seemed to realise exactly how she felt. 'I know it's silly, but I do.'

'I don't think it's silly at all. I'd be wanting them to call every day so I'd know they were OK.' She paused for a moment, her eyes warm. 'Have they called?'

'Yes, the night after they arrived. They're supposed to try and call every week, we gave them BT charge cards, but sometimes they won't be anywhere near a telephone. At least, that's what they said.'

'Funny to think of anywhere not near a telephone these days,' Val commented.

'Do you have children?'

'A hazard we have so far avoided,' Val said blithely, but something

55

in her eyes denied the insouciance of her remark. 'Actually, I'd love them and I don't think Neil would be against the idea but so far Allah has not willed and it looks as though the biological clock will run out. Ah, I think this means breakfast!'

A hostess was handing them menu cards.

'I'm going to enjoy this,' said Louise after they'd ordered. 'I can't remember when I last had a cooked breakfast.'

'Nor me! Now, tell me how you met Mark. You must have got married terribly young, or do you take some secret elixir? If so, I want the name of it immediately.'

Louise gave a little giggle. 'I was nineteen when we married and the twins came within a year. We met at a tennis club.'

'Sounds like something out of P.G. Wodehouse.'

'Where did you and Neil meet?'

'At university. But we lost touch after graduation. Too busy getting on with our careers. Then one morning we ran into each other at, of all places, Piccadilly underground station. With both of us on our way to important meetings. Neil insisted I gave him my telephone number and I knew, I just knew, I'd never hear from him again.'

'Instead of which?'

'Instead of which he called that evening and we never looked back.' Val glanced contentedly out of the window. 'Isn't that a sight? Where would you rather be? Apart from Paris.'

The train was dawdling through the Kent countryside where harvest was in full swing. Huge machines slowly traversed golden fields, cutting, winnowing and parcelling up the corn, leaving bleached stubble behind them. Despite the warm sun, there was an air of autumn. Trees and hedges bore yellowing leaves and brambles were loaded with rich, dark berries. Nature at her most fecund.

Louise admitted it was wonderful. Then breakfast arrived and if it hadn't been for the announcement over the loudspeaker system, she might have missed going through the tunnel altogether. It was all so smooth, breakfast was such fun and she was getting on so well with Val, she hardly noticed the sudden darkness outside the windows.

But she saw how scenery flew past as they drove out into the French countryside, as ripe and golden as in Kent but more open and not so picturesque. Even so it was a shock to hear an announcement that the train was now travelling at its maximum speed of 300 kilometres an hour.

'That's amazing!' said Louise. 'I can't believe we're going that fast.'

'Look at that autoroute.' Val gestured towards a road running beside the railway. 'Those cars have to be doing a hundred miles an hour, because the French always drive that fast. Yet they seem to be crawling.'

They looked like toys to Louise. She felt a surge of excitement. This trip was already proving an experience.

'Not a bad way to travel, is it?' said Mark happily, gathering together his papers as the train approached Paris. 'We certainly wouldn't have got three hours' concentrated work done if we'd gone by plane. Now, I think the best thing would be for Louise and Val to take the luggage and check in at the Hôtel Lancaster. That would leave us free to go straight to our meeting.'

'Happy with that?' Neil asked his wife.

'For heaven's sake, do you think this is the first time I've travelled?' she asked, jokingly.

'You like to think of us as fragile flowers when actually we're tough old weeds,' Louise said.

'Right, then. We'll all meet at the hotel about seven-thirty and decide what we're going to do with the evening.'

The Gare du Nord decanted the Eurostar travellers as efficiently as Waterloo had entrained them and Mark shepherded his little group towards the taxi rank.

'Freedom,' said Val with a smile as their taxi drew away. 'Paris is ours!'

Chapter Eight

The two women spent a happy afternoon lunching in a little bistro then enjoying the superb views offered by La Grande Arche, President Pompidou's white marble, visionary counterpart to the Arc de Triumph that dominated the skyscrapers of La Défense on the edge of central Paris. Then they returned to their hotel for an al fresco tea in its courtyard, the air still and quiet, all the noises of Paris muted and distant. The visit seemed ripe with promise.

'What about tomorrow?' asked Val as they sipped their tea.

'I want to save the Louvre for when Mark's free, so how about some window shopping? Mark hates that.'

'Neil too. And let's do more than *look* in the windows. I'd love to find a dress or a suit, something for autumn.'

'I've got loads of addresses we can try. Oh, isn't this fun?'

Val laughed at Louise's enthusiasm.

'And that reminds me – I promised to give Polly's friend Marie-Claire a ring. I don't think there'll be time to meet but Polly was very keen for me to make contact.'

'Why don't you see if this Marie-Claire could join us for coffee or something tomorrow? I'd love to meet a genuine Parisienne.'

Louise went up to her room feeling wonderful. Paris had such an air – insouciant would be the word, she thought – and Val was such an easy companion. They'd have fun tomorrow and then she and Mark would have nearly two days together.

She rang Marie-Claire's number.

The Frenchwoman sounded delighted to hear from her.

'But, *je suis désolée*, tomorrow morning Claude, my 'usband, and me go to friends in the country. When Polly ring, I do not know this and say I love to see you and show you something of Paris. Then this 'appen! I am so sorry. But my brother, Jean-Paul, 'oo is also friend to Polly, 'e say he would love to see you. I tell him where you are staying and he will ring, no?'

'No – I mean, that sounds lovely but I don't want to put him to any trouble . . .'

'Nonsense, 'e likes very much to meet the friends of Polly. What is your 'usband's name?'

Louise put down the phone and sat on the bed, dismayed. To see Marie-Claire for coffee was one thing, but she didn't want to share her time with Mark by meeting an unknown Frenchman. She'd have to find some way to put him off.

Decision taken, she started to undress. Just as she was about to enter a scented bath, the phone rang.

Louise ran across the room, sure it was Mark to say the meeting was going on longer than anticipated.

It was a man with one of the sexiest voices she had ever heard. She sat on the bed seduced by its liquidity.

'Marie-Claire tell me you ring her. I am very, very pleased to meet you and your 'usband. You can tell me news of Polly and life in England.'

Suddenly Louise heard alarm bells. As something in the timbre of that devastating voice struck home, Louise was quite, quite certain that it wasn't news of Marie-Claire Polly had wanted.

'It's terribly kind of you to ring but the weekend's a little complicated,' Louise prevaricated. 'Would you perhaps be free for lunch with Val and me tomorrow?' She held her breath.

'*Bien sûr*! It would give me enormous pleasure. I book a table at a little restaurant on the left bank. Not great, not grand, but it 'as a good ambience and the food is very good and very French. I meet you there at a quarter of one, yes?' He gave her the address.

'Yes,' said Louise, feeling a little faint. She gave a brief description of Val and herself, took a contact number, rang off and went back to her bath fizzing with excitement.

Later, thoroughly rested after a long bath, she slipped on a silky electric blue dress and redid her make up. She chose long silver twists for earrings and added a necklace to match. A touch of Calèche and she was ready. She looked at her watch. Seven o'clock and no word yet from Mark.

The telephone rang again.

It was Val. 'Any news?' she asked.

'No, 'fraid not.'

'Wretched fellows. Why don't we go downstairs and have a drink?'

'Why don't I get the drinks up here?' Louise suggested. 'We've got such a nice sitting area.'

'Great idea, I'll be right along.'

Louise rang room service and ordered a bottle of champagne. 'I thought we deserved a little spoiling,' she said when Val exclaimed at the extravagance.

'That's my girl! Oh, wonderful!' She settled herself comfortably, sipping happily on the sparkling wine. She'd put on a burnt orange long sleeveless tunic over matching loose pants.

'Listen, I've got us a date for lunch tomorrow.' Louise put the champagne bottle back in the cooler and pushed the freshly made potato crisps towards Val.

'Date?'

'With the most gorgeous-sounding Frenchman ever!' Louise gave her the details.

'He'll probably turn out to be short, stout and have bad breath.' Val helped herself to more crisps.

'Not if I know my friend Polly,' Louise asserted. 'I bet he's an absolute raver.'

'And you really think your friend's having an affair with him?'

'Oh, I don't know, it's just a gut feeling. Polly's husband told Mark he thinks she's involved with someone and when this Jean-Paul rang, everything suddenly sort of clicked together.'

'Fascinating. What's her husband like?'

'Willoughby? Pretty boring, really. Nothing in the looks line and totally immersed in business. Always asking Polly to host dinners and lunches for him, which she does brilliantly.'

'Sounds as though your friend needs a Jean-Paul in her life.'

'If his appearance matches his voice, Willoughby will need to start paying Polly a bit more attention.' Louise looked at her watch. 'And if those men don't come back soon, I shall seriously start thinking of finding a Frenchman for myself,' she laughed. 'Is Neil often late?'

'Often.'

'What do you do with yourself in the evenings? With no children?'

'I have a job,' Val reminded her. 'I also work late quite often. Or I have to bring papers home with me, so being on my own doesn't really worry me. I love it when Neil is home, of course. He often cooks the meal. I don't even help with the preparation, just sit in the kitchen drinking a glass of wine and watching him. We talk over what we've done with our day. Is Mark good at cooking?'

'Mark, cooking? You must be joking! Though he does burn a pretty mean chop on the barbecue. Funny how when it's outdoors the men don't seem to think of it as cooking.' She smiled as she spoke but in her mind's eye she could see Val and Neil talking in a kitchen together. Maybe if she left the cooking till he came back, Mark would have a glass of wine and chat to *her* in the kitchen?

'That's because barbecuing isn't cooking!'

'Where did Neil learn?'

'He just read books and started experimenting. Sometimes things don't come out quite as intended but it's usually very edible.'

'Mark's mother was one of the old-fashioned sort. He was brought up with the idea that men went out and earned the bread, women cooked and washed up.'

'Oh dear, that sounds as though he doesn't iron his own shirts, either.'

'Tell me about it! I've made sure that James does. He's rather better at it, in fact, than his sister. She irons the parts that show then leaves the rest. He's terribly particular, hates any sort of

61

crease.' Louise sighed. 'I don't really know what to do now that they've gone. My life seems sort of used up and empty. It's as though its elastic has worn out; instead of contracting nicely around me, it sags all over the place. I keep wanting to make everything bright and interesting again and instead everywhere I turn, I just think of them.' She gave a disgusted snort. 'Listen to me! Here I am in a five-star hotel in Paris for a long weekend and all I can do is whinge. I really don't know what's the matter with me.'

Val leaned across and put a hand on her arm. 'Don't feel guilty. I think it must be something like a bereavement.'

Louise stared at her. 'But the twins are still alive.'

'Yes, of course they are. But no longer with you as your children anymore.'

Louise blinked rapidly. 'I'm not sure I like that thought. Oh, where are those wretched husbands of ours? It's getting on for eight.'

On cue the telephone rang again and this time it was Mark.

'Darling, I really am sorry but we're still tied up here. It looks as though we shall have to have a working dinner. Could you and Val possibly amuse yourselves? Have dinner in the restaurant, maybe?'

'Indeed we will not!' Louise said robustly as she fought her disappointment. 'We'll go out and do the town. We may or may not be here when you return.' She put the phone down with an irritated click. Then regretted not being more sympathetic. He must be disappointed too.

When they got back to the hotel after a delicious meal, Mark and his colleagues were in the bar. They looked tired and frazzled.

Neil leaped up as he saw them. 'Thank heavens for some sane people who have no connection with wretched business.' He wrapped one arm round Val and gave her a smacking kiss.

Mark smiled warmly at Louise. 'I'll endorse that. How are you, darling? Did you find somewhere nice to eat?'

'Great! We had a marvellous meal. What about you?'

'Oh, we managed to grab a little something,' he said smoothly.

'Little something!' Robin laughed. She was looking the least frazzled of them all. The jacket of her attractive suit was now unbuttoned and hanging loose. The silk blouse clung to her curves and the skin of her cleavage was enhanced by the glow of a very good string of pearls. 'I'd always heard the French were serious about their food, and now I know. We had the most sensational meal.'

'Talking business all the way through,' Don said hastily, glancing from Val to Louise.

'Yes, don't run away with the idea we've been enjoying ourselves,' Neil agreed.

Louise looked at Robin and thought that here was someone who looked as though she'd had a really good time. Still was, in fact.

'Drink?' asked Mark.

'I think I've had enough alcohol for this evening,' said Val.

'Oh, come on! We haven't seen anything of you yet, and I want to talk to the beautiful Louise.' Neil drew out a chair.

'Yes, darling, sit down and tell us what you've been doing this afternoon and evening,' Mark agreed.

'In that case, it'll have to be more champagne,' Louise declared.

'Oho, *more* champagne, is it? Right, let's get a bottle'

Robin said it had been a long day and she was for bed. Don followed suit. But the two couples sat over their champagne and Louise felt very content. It was as though she and Mark had known Val and Neil for a long time.

'I hope you didn't mind too much not dining with us,' Mark said later as they were getting into bed. 'I thought all it was going to be was a bit of rubber stamping but the French lot have found something they aren't at all happy with on the American end of things so it's taking much longer.'

'Val and I are enjoying ourselves enormously,' Louise assured him. 'But I'm really looking forward to Saturday, when we can go off and do things, just you and me.'

Mark slipped into the large double bed and drew back the covers from Louise's side invitingly.

Her cleansing routine finished, she stood up.

'Wow!' he said as he saw what she was wearing. 'I haven't seen that before. It looks absolutely luscious and so do you. Come on, don't keep me waiting! We are on honeymoon, remember?'

'I have to clean my teeth first,' Louise said demurely. The new nightie had the scantiest of tops, all lace and chiffon, and it floated around her as she moved; it was just the thing for a second honeymoon in the Hôtel Lancaster, when half the fun of something like that was its removal.

A moment later she slipped into bed next to Mark and moved sinuously up to him.

Five minutes later, in the middle of saying her body was the most exciting of any woman's in the whole wide world, he fell asleep.

Chapter Nine

Next morning Louise and Val investigated some of Polly's fashion suggestions. At the third shop they visited, Val found a very smart dark brown gabardine suit together with a silky shirt in a geometric pattern, and bought both. 'Ideal for board meetings,' she said as the girl wrapped the items in tissue paper.

Louise tried on several things at each place they went to and bought nothing.

'I think that looks wonderful,' Val said as Louise slowly turned around in a red dress in front of a long mirror.

She gazed doubtfully at her reflection. 'I just don't know what sort of thing I want,' she confessed. 'Six months ago I'd have got those snazzy trousers and top we found in that other place. They'd have been ideal for going around with the twins. Now, I don't know. Mark likes me in something more classic.'

'He'd love that dress,' Val said positively.

'Maybe,' Louise said listlessly and went back into the changing room. No, she said to the girl afterwards, she was sorry but she didn't want it.

'What's up?' Val asked gently as they started walking towards the restaurant where they were to meet Jean-Paul. 'Come on, something's worrying you, I can tell. Is it that empty house you're going back to?'

How perceptive she was! Louise walked a little way in silence then said, 'It's like a sore, a wound that one can't leave alone. If only I could, I'm sure everything would be fine. But I have to keep picking at the scab and making it bleed all over again.'

'Or like digging up seeds to see if the roots are beginning to grow?'

'That's a much more positive way to look at it, isn't it? After all, I suppose this is my chance to do something completely different. I could get a job,' she added, and thought, Yes, that's what I'm going to do.

They stopped at some traffic lights and Louise consulted her Paris street map. 'The restaurant's just across the road and down that first left-hand turn. We've got about twenty minutes before we're due to meet Jean-Paul. Why don't we have a drink at that café on that corner?' She gestured towards a collection of tables and chairs with exuberant umbrellas, neatly corralled by a small white fence.

They found a table and ordered two glasses of wine.

'And a job,' Louise said as though there had been no interruption, 'would mean I'd have my own money as well.'

Val looked startled. 'Surely Mark . . .' she started a little hesitantly.

'He's very generous,' Louise said quickly. 'Anything I ask for, I can have. But I don't have a regular allowance of my own.'

'How do you manage?' Val looked at her in amazement.

'Oh, it's quite easy. In the old days I had accounts at all the local shops. Now I just have signing rights on his credit card. But Mark goes through the account each month and sees exactly what I've bought.'

'Then comes the big bad husband?'

'No, nothing like that! But there's the odd comment. "I thought you bought one of those only a couple of months ago." Things like that.'

'Bastard!' Val said with feeling.

The drinks arrived.

'It's not so bad.' Louise felt she'd been disloyal. 'But if I had an income of my own, then it would be entirely up to me what I spent it on. Imagine, I could blow the whole lot on a day at the races!'

'Is that your idea of a real treat?' Val looked amused.

'Not exactly, but Mark hates it. A friend of his once asked us to go to Ascot. They had a company box and I loved the whole experience. I even won a little. Mark said afterwards it was his idea of purgatory, watching expensive horseflesh forced into providing entertainment for people who should know better. And that gambling was the most pernicious of all activities.'

'My, he sounds puritanical.'

'He isn't really! He loves a good time, but racing isn't his idea of a good time.'

'As you've made abundantly clear!' Val sounded amused. 'I shall look at your husband with new eyes tonight. Well, I think a job sounds excellent. What sort are you thinking of?'

'Heavens, I've only just had the idea.' Louise began to feel excited and nervous at the same time.

'What qualifications do you have?'

'Not a lot,' she said cheerfully. 'I trained as a secretary when I left school. Then worked for a literary agent for about eighteen months, until I got pregnant. I was a very junior shorthand typist and most of my time seemed to be spent making tea and taking manuscripts round to publishers. Every six months I had to type masses of envelopes to send royalty statements and cheques out to authors. That was quite fun. I used to time myself and see how many I could do in an hour, whipping them in and out of the typewriter and making sure I had them absolutely right. Nowadays I suppose it's all done by computer.'

'Do you want another secretarial job?'

Louise looked doubtful. 'I'd have to do a word processing course, wouldn't I? My friend Nicky did one and she's just landed the position of secretary to the headmaster of one of our local schools.'

'But the idea doesn't appeal to you?'

Louise gazed dreamily at a poster advertising an opera. 'When I first started, I saw myself as personal assistant to some tycoon in industry, organising his life, being on the inside of mergers and takeovers, party to all sorts of business secrets.'

Val laughed. 'I can see you are exactly the right sort of wife for Mark. I bet he enjoys telling you what he's been up to, all the wheeler-dealing of share flotations and mergers.'

Louise looked appalled. 'He never tells me anything! Says it's more than his job's worth.'

Val opened her mouth then quickly closed it again.

'You mean, Neil tells you things?'

'Well, yes. Nothing terribly secret, I'm sure, but he knows he can trust me. And he likes me to share what's going on in his life, just as I do with him. You'd better not tell Mark, though,' she added hastily.

'On my honour, cross my heart, hope to die.'

'So what sort of job do you want?'

'I don't know, I'll look around next week.'

'Discuss it with Mark, he might have some ideas.'

'So he might,' Louise said doubtfully. She thought Mark giving her ideas for possible employment was as likely as the Eiffel Tower growing wings. He wouldn't want her anywhere but at home. 'I don't think he'll be too keen on the idea though.'

'Don't worry about that, he'll soon get used to it. After all, he wants you to be happy, doesn't he?'

Louise nodded.

Val looked at her watch. 'Should we think about moving? If we keep your gorgeous man waiting, he may think we aren't coming and take off!'

In the restaurant a well-dressed, well-upholstered Frenchwoman greeted them as they entered. 'Monsieur Hupel? He 'as arrived and waits for you,' she said with brisk efficiency and led them to a window table.

The man waiting there got up with a smile, took Louise's hand and bowed over it in true continental fashion. 'Madame 'Enderson, this is an honour,' he said.

Well, he certainly wasn't a pin-up but he wasn't short and stout either.

Jean-Paul Hupel was a medium height, medium build, dark-haired man with dark eyes, a very lined face and a mobile mouth.

He had an air of exuberance that was very engaging and a way of speaking that suggested everything was a most delightful surprise.

'This is most fortunate, that I should be able to lunch with two such charming Englishwomen,' he said after he'd ordered aperitifs and they were supplied with menus. 'I am hoping that I shall be able to show you and your husbands a little of my country tomorrow. We could drive out to Versailles or St Cloud, where there is a most interesting château with an English connection. Your King James Three is buried there.'

'James Three?' queried Louise. 'Oh, you mean the Old Pretender!'

'If the weather continues fine there is a wonderful park we can walk in.'

Louise could see that Val was charmed by the idea. 'Would your wife come too?' she asked, thinking there was nothing like a frontal attack for finding out what you wanted to know.

'Ah, alas, my wife died three years ago.' The twinkle disappeared from Jean-Paul's eyes.

'Oh, I'm so sorry!' both Louise and Val said, practically in unison.

'It is life, no? She was very young and very much fun. She was in a car accident.'

'Do you have children?' Val asked, a second before Louise could get the question in.

'No, we should have had our first. Arlette was three months pregnant when she died.'

Worse and worse! Once again Louise and Val expressed their regrets.

'But we shall not talk of such sad things,' Jean-Paul said firmly. 'Life goes on, yes? And now you shall tell me what of Paris you have seen.'

As they sat drinking Kir Royale and talking about Paris, Louise wondered how long it was going to take before Polly's name came up.

'And how is lovely Polly?' Jean-Paul turned to her after the waiter had taken their order. 'You must tell her we miss her very much here.' He spoke quite simply, quietly and in a tone that was very different from the lively one he'd used up until now.

Once again alarm bells sounded in Louise's head. This was a serious man, she realised suddenly. Oh, Polly, she thought, what are you involved in?

'She's very busy,' she said quickly. 'Settling back in England, you know? Pooh – that is, Caroline, her daughter – gets back from holiday somewhere in France today.'

'Yes, I know Caroline. She has been staying in the Loire Valley, with the Comte and Comtesse de Chambord. The Comtesse is friend to my sister, Marie-Claire. And does Polly like being back in England?'

'She misses Paris,' Louise said quietly, then added gaily, 'She was thrilled to hear I was coming over, gave me lots and lots of addresses and made me promise to ring your sister. I was so sorry she was going away for the weekend and we couldn't meet. Polly particularly wanted news of her.'

'Yes, they are close friends,' Jean-Paul agreed. 'But now you can tell Polly of me instead of Marie-Claire, yes?'

'And what shall I tell her of you?' Louise enquired mischievously while Val watched the conversation with an ironic smile in her eyes.

'Ah, that will be up to you.' The twinkle and the exuberance were back and the rest of lunch passed in the same spirit, talking about Paris and Jean-Paul's job in banking.

He refused to let Louise and Val contribute towards the bill, saying, 'Now, this evening I am engaged but you will ring me early tomorrow morning and say you and your 'usbands would love to come out with me, yes? Then maybe I let you take me out to lunch.'

They promised.

'Wow, what a charmer!' said Val as they resumed their shopping. 'Lucky, lucky Polly!'

'Do you mean that?' Louise hadn't thought Val the sort of woman who would condone adultery. But who really knew about people?

'I spoke too easily,' she said ruefully. 'You don't accept surface judgements, do you, Louise? You're right, of course. If Jean-Paul is as sincere as he appears, he could be serious about your friend. Is she serious about him?'

Louise dug her hands into the pockets of her tailored shorts and walked with her head down while she thought. 'I don't know. I'm not even certain anything is actually going on. Perhaps Jean-Paul is just hoping.' Louise saw again Polly's eager face as she talked about Paris. There'd been something else there, she realised now. Wistful yearning was the phrase that came into her mind but that was surely too fey for bright, cynical Polly. 'I'll know more after we get back and I tell her about meeting him. She's bound to say something then.' But would she? And what if this was as serious on Polly's side as both of them obviously thought it was on Jean-Paul's? What was going to happen then?

That night the working party got back to the hotel sufficiently early for them all to go out to dinner together.

Mark had booked a table at Joel Robuchon's restaurant. 'Wonderful food,' he said as they gathered in the lobby of the Hôtel Lancaster and Louise was slightly surprised to see that Robin and Don were still with them.

'Are you going to have the weekend in Paris, too?' she asked Don once they were all seated in the restaurant and Mark had ordered drinks.

'Ah, well, yes, I suppose so.' His face turned an embarrassed red, he dropped his napkin and bent to pick it up.

Louise looked across at Mark, chatting urbanely to Val. 'Tell me you're not working tomorrow?' she said in a pleading voice.

For a moment he, too, looked embarrassed. Robin, elegant as usual in a grey silk dress which showed off her pearls, broke off her conversation with Neil and reached for her wine. She, too, looked as though she wished she were elsewhere.

'Darling, I'm sorry, I was going to tell you later, I didn't want to spoil the evening. We've reached an absolutely critical stage in the negotiations. A few hours tomorrow should just about wrap it all up. The French were willing so what else could we do?' He spread his hands helplessly.

'So much for our second honeymoons,' Val said flatly. By now Louise knew her well enough to recognise the depth of her disappointment.

'In that case, we shall find ourselves an incredibly attractive Frenchman to take us out,' Louise said gaily.

'And don't think that's just a threat,' added Val. 'We had lunch with him today and he wanted to take us all to St Cloud or Versailles tomorrow. Now we can have him all to ourselves.'

'What do we say to that, Mark?' asked Neil with a grin.

'I say safety in numbers,' he replied. 'And let's make this a meal to remember.'

But despite Mark's and Neil's efforts, the evening still fell flat and no one wanted to stay up drinking after the meal.

'So it's Val and me on our own again tomorrow, is it? Apart from Jean-Paul, that is,' Louise said through her teeth as they closed the door of their room behind them.

Mark caught her in his arms. 'Darling, I really am very sorry, but there's nothing I can do. If I'd realised how these negotiations were going to go, I'd never have suggested you come along. I can quite understand how cross you must be.' He kissed her eyelids tenderly. 'But I hope you're enjoying seeing Paris with Val, not to mention this mysterious Jean-Paul?' he added before finding her mouth.

Louise felt herself melting into his arms. 'If you believe he's something we made up, think again,' she murmured. But Mark took no notice.

Jean-Paul was not at all unhappy to have just the women with him for the trip out to St Cloud.

It was a beautiful day again and after viewing the church where James II's son, the Old Pretender, had a star-spangled niche for his monument, and the austere château, the three of them walked in the park. It was on an escarpment and had a staggering view of Paris, or would have if the air hadn't been too misty to pick out details.

'Autumn is coming,' said Louise with regret. 'Look, the leaves are turning. Summer is almost over.'

'It is so important to make the most of everything while it is with you,' Jean-Paul said, drawing her arm through his. 'Now, I have booked a table at a charming restaurant behind the château. You will be happy with this, yes?'

At the end of the meal, Louise and Val skilfully managed to settle the bill before Jean-Paul could insist it was his treat again. He cast his eyes up to heaven with a look of resignation when he discovered what they had done and then thanked them charmingly.

Afterwards he drove them back to their hotel. As he said goodbye, Jean-Paul took Louise's hand in both of his. 'You will remember me to Polly, no? Tell her she must come and see us very soon. And that Marie-Claire joins me in sending love. You will tell her this?' He sounded anxious.

'I will,' Louise said gently. 'I will tell her exactly what you said. And that you gave us a wonderful time.'

She and Val went into the hotel and left him standing beside his car with a lost look on his face.

By the time the party got back to Waterloo via Eurostar late on Sunday afternoon, Louise and Val had managed to spend Sunday morning with their husbands. Not alone, though, Robin and Don had joined them. After all, Mark said, they deserved a little fun after the successful conclusion of the negotiations late on Saturday night.

Louise and Val, who had taken themselves off to the cinema that evening, followed by steak and chips at one of the fast food cafés in the Champs Elysées, agreed between the two of them that Don and Robin should have had the tact to go off sightseeing together.

But as the morning passed, Louise saw that Robin considered Don was definitely junior to herself. There was no way she would have wanted to explore Paris with him when there was Mark and Neil to go around with, even if it meant their wives came too.

Then Louise told herself she was being unfair. Robin was extremely friendly to both her and Val. In other circumstances, in fact, Louise thought she could have liked her quiet humour and enthusiasm for Paris, even if her sense of tact was definitely lacking.

'Some honeymoon that was!' Louise declared as they all parted at Waterloo.

'I agree,' Val concurred as they kissed each other goodbye. 'Now, you must come and have a meal with us very soon. After we've told our men exactly what we think of them.'

'Love that,' said Louise, thinking she hadn't met anyone she liked as much as Val for a long time.

Mark was very quiet in the train going home and Louise could see that he was exhausted.

'Early night,' she said as they retrieved her car from the car park.

71

'We won't want to eat anything anyway.'

'Not for weeks and weeks,' Mark agreed. 'Yes, let's go straight to bed and watch television together. Pretend this Paris trip never happened.'

But when they got back there was a message for Louise on the answering machine to say her mother had had an accident and was in hospital.

Chapter Ten

Polly Fawkes, dressed in a shirtdress that was understated but with a hemline well above her knees, waited in the Terminal One arrivals hall at London Airport, her stomach tight with tension. She'd eaten hardly any breakfast that morning and she could feel the caffeine from the three cups of coffee she'd had buzzing around her head.

It was ridiculous to feel so nervous about meeting her daughter. But these days she never knew how Pooh was going to react.

Typical teenager, said all her friends. She'll settle down soon enough, they added blithely. But either they were over that stage, hadn't met it yet or had boys who were so much easier than girls.

All Polly had was Pooh. Where had that silly nickname come from? It wasn't as though the girl had been christened Winifred. Polly stood and thought, sending her mind back to the days when Caroline had been three or four years old. It had had something to do with Christopher Robin, it must have done. Then she remembered: Caroline had loved honey, Willoughby had started calling her Pooh bear, it had rapidly got shortened to Pooh and somehow had stuck.

A new set of arrivals started streaming through the door from customs and suddenly Polly saw her daughter and felt torn between love and exasperation. Why on earth did the girl have to wear her rather nice brown hair in that silly plait? It hadn't an ounce of style, didn't even start at the top of her head and seemed to be finished off with nothing more than a rubber band. And why those dreadful wire frames for her glasses? No chic to them at all. If they'd been gold they might have had some sort of charm, but plain metal! And the way her shoulders slouched! And why did she have to wear that awful T shirt and jeans that didn't even fit properly, sagging like that, nobody could see that her figure was actually very good.

'Darling! Over here!' Polly waved to her daughter. Pooh, hiking a heavy bag higher on her thin shoulder, responded by holding up her right hand in a brief acknowledgement. She continued to go with the flow, not making any particular effort to increase her speed towards her mother.

'Hi,' she said in a dead voice as Polly gave her a hug and kissed her cheek. They were of a height.

'Darling Pooh, how wonderful to have you back.' Polly put all the enthusiasm she could muster into her voice. She looked at the bag. 'Is that all you've got?'

'You know it is, Mum, you saw me off on the train, remember?' Pooh had the worldweary tone of one who found having to deal with life's mental incompetents a sore trial.

Polly attempted to make up lost ground. 'Of course, darling. It's just that so much has happened since then.' She fished out the parking ticket and steered them both in the direction of the pay machines. 'I mean, packing up the Paris flat, moving back here and trying to get everything organised. But Daddy and I have managed to get your room sorted out.'

'Great,' Pooh said without enthusiasm.

'How was the holiday? Did you enjoy staying with Anne-Lise and her family? Who was it who told me their château is quite delightful?'

'Probably Anne-Lise's mother, she's the biggest snob ever! Even worse than you, Mum.'

'Did you do lots of interesting things?'

'If you mean did we visit the château of the Loire, no, we did not, thank heavens!'

Polly fielded the franked parking ticket and led the way to the multi-storey parking. Trying to get information out of Pooh was harder than cracking a Swiss banking code. 'So, what did you do? Lots of tennis and swimming?'

'Anne-Lise didn't like being beaten at tennis and I can't stand lying around a pool all day. Anne-Lise didn't rate any activity that didn't include boys and I found them all a load of nerds. So, yes, it was a brilliant holiday, thanks, Mum.'

Oh, dear! Polly had met Anne-Lise's mother at one of Marie-Claire's dinner parties, after which they'd lunched several times. Polly had enjoyed the other woman's wit and sophistication and when she'd discovered their daughters were of an age, it had seemed such a good idea for Pooh to go and stay with the de Chambruns this summer. It had been intended that Anne-Lise would come over to England and stay with the Fawkeses in the Easter holidays. Polly had promised tennis and swimming, lots of young people, and visits to London and around.

They reached her Mercedes coupé and deposited Pooh's bag in the boot.

Polly started the engine and engaged gear.

'The one good thing about the holiday,' Pooh said unexpectedly, slouching in the passenger seat, 'was that I told them my name was Caroline and I wasn't to be called anything else.'

'Did you, darling?' Polly concentrated on easing her car into the Heathrow one-way system and finding her way out of the airport.

'And now I want you and Dad to call me Caroline too.'

Polly bit back a hasty remark about its being a bit late for that now. 'If that's what you want, darling, then of course we'll try. But you know how difficult it is changing a name once everyone knows you by it.'

'Everyone doesn't know me by it. Nobody at school calls me Pooh.' Her tone of voice was scathing. 'Only you and Dad and your friends. I wouldn't have thought it was too much to ask.'

'I've said we'll try, darling,' Polly said in a placatory tone, trying to feel relaxed and happy but knowing that Willoughby wasn't going to find this at all easy. 'Now, what do you want to do for the final few days of your holiday? I thought we could go to London and get you some new clothes and perhaps see a show or something. Daddy wants to take us out for the evening. And perhaps we could have some of your old friends over for a barbecue round the swimming pool, if the weather lasts.'

'I haven't got any old friends here. All my friends are in Paris.'

'Of course you have, darling. What about Emma and James?' Polly almost bit her tongue as, too late, she remembered.

'They've gone to India, Mum. Don't you listen to what anybody tells you?'

'So they have. I saw Louise only the other day. She's in Paris with Mark this weekend. I gave her lots of addresses – I can't wait to hear all about it.'

'I bet,' Pooh said with a level of innuendo that Polly decided she wouldn't question.

During the rest of the journey home, Polly brought up several other names of local youngsters Pooh used to play tennis and go around with before they moved to Paris. Pooh killed each mention either by pointing out they, too, had left home or by saying she'd grown out of them.

Pooh had continued to attend her English boarding school and had spent the holidays in Paris. It had amazed Polly how well her daughter had got on with the French young, who all had a laid back savoir-faire that was distinctly unnerving. The first holiday, Polly had found several youngsters more or less Pooh's age and gave a couple of parties for them and their parents. The young had melted away immediately after the meal, off to some disco or film or café. Pooh's French rapidly acquired an idiomatic argot that made her practically incomprehensible to her parents and she had been absorbed into their culture without effort. Soon she was rarely at home. A relief in one way, if slightly worrying. However, beyond encouraging her to bring home as many of her new friends as possible, there hadn't been much Polly could do. Still, they seemed respectable enough underneath the surface grot. Sophisticated French grot but grot nevertheless with their extraordinary clothes, make up and air of debauched exhaustion.

'Perhaps you can invite some French friends over?' Polly suggested in a bright voice that was beginning to fray at the edges.

75

Pooh shrugged her shoulders in a way that suggested she didn't have the energy to counter such a stupid suggestion.

Polly parked outside Whiteways' three-car garage and released the boot. Pooh picked up her bag. 'Am I in my old room?' she asked.

'Of course, darling.'

Polly unlocked the front door and followed Pooh up the sweeping staircase, along the corridor and into the large room that she'd spent a considerable amount of time redoing ready for her daughter's return.

She knew as soon as Pooh opened the door that she'd done it all wrong. How could she have been so stupid? Buying that terribly expensive white four-poster bed with glazed chintz curtains, matching curtains at the windows and a white carpet. She had had to sweet talk Willoughby into agreeing the cost of it all, not that that had been difficult, he adored Pooh. But he'd been doubtful about his daughter's liking it.

Polly, remembering herself at that age, had thought her daughter couldn't help but adore it.

Now Pooh stood in the doorway looking with appalled fascination at the room.

Without a word she went into the one next door. 'I'll have this if it's all the same to you,' she announced baldly.

'But it doesn't have its own bathroom,' Polly said limply. It was the second best guest room with twin beds and quite ordinary mahogany furniture. But a nice view over the rose garden.

'There is life beyond the en suite.' Pooh went back into her own room. 'I like this desk, I'll move it into the other room with my computer.'

'Of course, darling,' Polly felt as though she'd been steamrollered. How was it that she, who managed to get on terms with everybody she met, failed so miserably with her daughter? 'Let me help you.'

Together they unplugged the computer with all its bits and pieces, took it next door, dumped it all on the bed, then followed with the desk and reassembled everything, moving the dressing table over from its position in front of the window to one corner. Polly, rearranging the mirror and other bits and pieces, made a note to herself to get some better lights for the room.

'That's a really nice desk,' Pooh said suddenly, after studying it for a few minutes. 'Thanks, Mum.'

Polly felt extraordinarily comforted.

The five days before Pooh went back to school seemed endless.

Polly couldn't think of her daughter as Caroline. For every time she remembered, there were four or five others she called her by her nickname.

And where Pooh had been difficult before, now she made the extra effort and was impossible. She refused to go shopping in London, saying she didn't need any more clothes. She didn't want to play tennis with Polly or anyone else. When her mother suggested they went and had lunch at the club and saw if there was anyone there Pooh, or rather Caroline, would like to get together with, it was as if she had suggested a visit to a zoo.

'I just can't do anything right,' Polly complained to Willoughby when he came home, late as usual, three nights after Pooh had returned from France. 'I really do try but I get nowhere!'

He sat down in his special chair, took off his glasses and rubbed his eyes. Polly brought him over his usual whisky and water and thought how tired he looked. 'Perhaps you try too hard,' he said. 'It's a difficult age.'

'That's what everybody says,' she burst out. 'But nobody tells you how to cope!'

The previous evening they'd had a sticky time going out to the latest musical – Willoughby said by the end of a busy day he couldn't concentrate on anything else – followed by dinner at Quaglino's. Caroline hadn't been quite so poisonous as she was with her mother on her own, but even so Polly had had to work very hard to get any sort of harmony going between the three of them.

'Where is she now?'

'Up in her room, playing with her computer. As usual. It's all she ever seems to do. They are the most diabolical things. What would you like to eat?'

Willoughby looked at her unenthusiastically. 'Have you had yours?'

Polly nodded. 'Pooh, that is, Caroline – oh, how I wish I could remember to call her that – said we should wait for you but I pointed out that half the time when you get back you've already had something. I served ours at eight o'clock. Not that we ate together. She took hers up to her room so I had mine on my own.'

'In front of the television?' Willoughby asked without much interest.

'Indeed not! The day that I have to eat in front of the box will be the day you can carry me out feet first.' Polly got herself a gin and tonic and sat at the opposite side of the fireplace from her husband. 'Picture me, if you will, with a nicely laid table, a glass of decent wine which Pooh refused in favour of Coca-cola, and the *Times* crossword.'

'What makes the crossword so much less contemptible than the box?' Willoughby asked with a faint smile.

Polly cheered up at this evidence that she had, even slightly, amused her husband. These days it was getting harder and harder to get a smile out of him. 'Why, interaction! Zee working of zee leettle grey cells, instead of a couch potato with a mind like a soggy mass of nothing. So, have you eaten or do you want something?'

Willoughby shook his head. 'Don't think so, thanks, darling.'

Polly sat back in her chair and put thoughts of microwaving frozen food from her mind. 'Well, tell me about your day. Are you getting to grips with the new company?'

Willoughby put down his glass. 'I think I'll just pop upstairs and see Pooh. We won't have her with us for much longer.' He left the room.

Polly switched on the television and watched the ten o'clock news.

After a while she heard her husband and daughter come downstairs and go into the kitchen.

The news came to an end. She switched off, got herself another gin and tonic and went into the kitchen.

Laughter greeted her as she opened the door.

Pooh was by the open microwave holding a plate of pizza. 'This is just gross, Dad. You can't eat it! There's hardly any topping at all.'

'But I like the base and I'm hungry!' He snatched it away and took it over to the table in the corner of the kitchen.

Polly felt a sudden bolt of jealousy at the obvious closeness of their relationship. On her own with her father, Caroline was a different girl. Was there something she wanted out of him? Polly wondered, then told herself she was being unduly cynical. 'Darling, I thought you didn't want anything to eat!' She came through.

Caroline's face was instantly wiped clean of laughter.

'I didn't until I started talking to Pooh,' Willoughby said apologetically. 'Last thing I wanted when I came in was food. I think it must have been the whisky, woke up my appetite.'

'And pizza! There's masses of other things.' Polly bustled over to the large upright freezer and opened the door. 'Look!' she said to her daughter.

Caroline shrugged her shoulders. 'Dad said he wanted pizza,' she said tonelessly.

'And you got it ready for him, Pooh – I mean, Caroline. That was kind of you. Shall I put some coffee on?'

Willoughby looked across at his daughter. 'I'm going back up to my room,' she said abruptly and left.

Willoughby sighed. 'We seemed to be having such a nice time.'

'Until I came in,' Polly said bitterly, switching on the kettle. 'What were you talking about?'

'Oh, I don't know. This and that.' He pushed away the half-eaten pizza. 'I find I'm not really very hungry after all.'

Polly picked up the plate and dumped its contents in the waste bin. 'What are we going to do with her?'

'Honestly, Polly, I think it's your problem. I don't have any trouble with her. No, don't do coffee for me, I think I'll go and have another whisky.'

Left to herself in the kitchen, Polly sat at the table, looked at her carefully manicured hands, and thought about her daughter.

★ ★ ★

The next day was Caroline's last before going back to school. Polly asked if there was anything special she wanted to do.

'Nah, nothing,' her daughter said briefly.

'Well, there's something I would like, very much. And that's for you to come out to lunch with me. We've had so little time together this holidays. It would be nice to have a chat.'

Caroline looked as though that was the way she'd wanted it but all she said was, 'Why can't we have lunch here? You can talk to me just as well as in a restaurant.'

But Polly knew that if they stayed at home, Caroline would just disappear to her room and there'd be no hope of a proper conversation. Neutral ground was what was needed.

'We could go to that little place next to the record shop. Then you could get some CDs to take back to school with you.' Willoughby had given Caroline a portable CD player for her previous birthday and it went everywhere with her.

'OK, I suppose, as long as lunch doesn't take too long.'

Polly said nothing about the disgraceful T shirt and jeans Caroline appeared in just as they were about to leave. Nor about the fact that her plait looked as though she had slept in it. Instead she kept up a steady stream of light conversation that didn't require an answer as she drove them down to the shopping centre of their little community and parked behind the library.

They walked to the restaurant Polly had selected. It offered reasonable food but wasn't too upmarket. She sometimes lunched there with friends. Today, she was happy to see, there was no one she knew.

She chose a table reasonably well tucked away and waited until Caroline had refused a starter and ordered chicken with chips. Polly chose a salad for herself and ordered two glasses of wine. 'I think we deserve a little alcohol, don't you?' she said.

Caroline made a face. 'What have we done that's deserving of anything?'

'Well, we've got all your clothes ready for school, sewn the tapes on to the new stuff, checked you've got the right number of pants and shirts. I think that's all very commendable.'

'You mean, you did it. I didn't help.'

'No, you didn't,' Polly agreed equably, delighted to be handed this perfect entrée into the whole purpose of the lunch. 'In fact, you're right, you don't deserve anything for the way you've behaved since you got back. What I would like to know is why?'

Caroline stared mutely down at the table.

'Well, I'm glad that at least you don't want to argue with me over that.'

The silence continued.

'You see, Pooh,' Polly hesitated for the briefest of moments then decided to carry straight on, 'I know we've had our differences but

79

things have never been this bad between us and I don't want you to go off to school without my knowing why.'

The glasses of wine arrived and Caroline immediately took a sip of hers then sat twisting the stem in her fingers, not looking at her mother.

The little restaurant was full now, mainly with women, a few businessmen and over on the far side one table of youngsters. The place buzzed with conversation and activity. Except at their table.

'I can't say I like you very much at the moment but I do love you, you know, a lot. And I think you're probably making yourself very uncomfortable by your attitude,' Polly continued quietly.

Caroline raised her eyes at last and Polly was shocked at the unhappiness she saw behind the metal-rimmed spectacles. There was a film of tears over the hazel eyes, so like Willoughby's.

Polly put her hand over her daughter's. 'Darling Pooh, what is it?'

'I can't stand the way you're treating Daddy,' she burst out.

Whatever Polly had expected, and perhaps she hadn't expected anything, it wasn't this. 'Whatever do you mean?' she gasped and clutched at her own glass of wine.

'You just don't care, do you? You never get him anything special to eat when he comes home. You're never interested in what he's done. You – you just treat him as a money bags.' Any suggestion of tears had gone now, replaced by spitting anger as Caroline found her voice. 'I think the way you're behaving is disgusting!'

'Darling.' Polly tried to gather her shattered senses together. 'It's not true, of course I care.' She had to lean back as their food arrived. 'Yes, I only do frozen meals when your father comes home late because I've grown tired of preparing food he doesn't eat.' She picked up her fork and started turning over the contents of her plate. 'You've seen how late he can be, though believe me he's been earlier than usual since you returned. When you're back at school, it'll often be eleven before he gets home.' She tried to keep her voice reasonable and controlled.

'No wonder,' spat Caroline as she jabbed her knife and fork into her chicken. 'I wouldn't want to come home to you either.'

Polly stared at her daughter. 'I do everything I can to make sure your father's life is as comfortable and happy as possible,' she said, wondering just how she'd managed to get into the position of having to justify her actions to Caroline.

'Oh, yes?' sneered the girl. 'So why are you having an affair then?'

Polly's fork clattered on to her plate. 'What do you mean?'

Caroline sat back in her chair and abandoned whatever interest she had had in her meal. 'Don't give me that, you know exactly what I mean. I saw you and that berk Jean-Paul whatshisname, holding hands as you walked down the Champs Elysées. Talk about young love! Except you aren't young and you've no business to be in love with anyone except Dad.' Tears were running down her

80

cheeks now. She jumped up. 'Oh, I don't know why I came. I can't bear to be in the same room as you.' She ran out of the restaurant, followed by the interested gaze of several diners.

For a moment Polly sat feeling as though the air had been knocked out of her. Then she gathered up her handbag, pulled out some notes from her purse, left them on the table and hurried after her daughter. She caught her up a little way from the restaurant.

Polly grabbed her by the arm. 'Now, young lady, we're going to go home and have this out. I am not having an affair, do you understand?' She forced the girl to walk in the other direction. 'But I'm not going to discuss it here or in the car. You will wait until we get back.'

Caroline said nothing, just stared straight ahead, her expression mutinous and disbelieving. But she offered no resistance.

They drove back in silence.

Polly left the car outside, unlocked the front door, marched into the small room where they normally sat in the evenings and indicated a chair.

Caroline slouched down in the seat, her legs stuck straight out before her. 'OK, you've got me here, now let's hear your feeble excuses,' she said. But behind the aggressive expression, Polly thought she could detect the merest hint of eagerness.

It gave her courage. She walked over to the fireplace and turned so as to look her daughter straight in the eye. 'I'm not going to say it wasn't me you saw with Jean-Paul,' she said slowly. 'I wish you'd told me, though, what you'd seen and thought.'

'So you could give me more of your lies?' Once again the words were spat out, but with less force this time. 'Like when you tell Dad you're going to meet one of your girlfriends and it's really Jean-Paul?'

Polly took the chair opposite Caroline's and leaned forward, her hands clasped together. 'I'll tell you exactly what happened that evening. In the mood you're in at the moment, I don't know whether you will believe me but this is the truth.' She took a deep breath. 'Marie-Claire and I had arranged to visit the cinema that evening. It was a film your father didn't want to see, and anyway he was going to be working late.' Polly paused. Caroline remained slouched in her chair but at least there was no angry interruption.

'Marie-Claire and I had said we'd meet at the cinema, that one on the Champs Elysées where they usually show *version original* films. I hate dubbed ones.' Again Caroline said nothing but her expression was scornful. 'Well, I got there and waited and waited. Then I found I'd left my mobile phone at home and couldn't ring Marie-Claire, nor could she contact me. Just as I was about to try and find a public telephone, Jean-Paul arrived and explained Marie-Claire's husband had rung while he was having a drink with her and said she had to join him and some business colleagues for dinner, it was really important. She couldn't raise my mobile so

Jean-Paul said not to worry, he would meet me instead.' There was silence as Polly stopped speaking.

'You expect me to believe that?' said Caroline scornfully. 'And even if it's true, what about the holding hands?'

Polly gave a light laugh. 'We just felt happy, that was all. We saw the film together, it was great fun, very romantic, and we came out talking about the first time each of us had fallen in love and what we'd done. And then, somehow, I don't know, it just seemed natural to hold hands as though we were back in that time. We went down to one of the cafés and had a drink together than I caught a taxi home and that was that. Wasn't I at home when you got back? Far too late, if I remember correctly.' She looked sternly at her daughter.

'Yes, you were,' muttered Caroline, easing herself up in the chair slightly. 'Talking to Dad as though nothing was wrong.'

'Because nothing *was* wrong,' Polly said persuasively.

Caroline's feet shuffled about in their trainers, turning first one way then another.

'Has your father suggested there's anything wrong?'

'Of course he hasn't.'

'Well, then?'

Caroline raised her head and looked at her mother. 'You swear that was all it was?'

'Darling, what else could it have been? I love your father, I always have.'

'You don't show it.'

'When you've been married for years and years, the way we have, you don't go around all lovey-dovey any more. What about Anne-Lise's parents? How did they seem to you?'

'Oh, each of them is having an affair with someone else,' Caroline said contemptuously. 'Anne-Lise told me all about it. She says it's the way they do things over there. I think it's disgusting.'

'So you thought that because I was in France, I was picking up French habits, did you?' Polly laughed lightly. 'Darling, it's not a case of when in Rome, you know.'

Caroline shuffled her feet some more. 'So you and Dad aren't going to get a divorce?'

At that Polly really did laugh. 'Good heavens, no. Is that why you've been so strange?' She went and sat on the arm of Caroline's chair and hugged her. 'Pooh, let's forget we ever had this conversation. We'll make a really nice dinner for your father tonight and be a proper family again, shall we?'

Suddenly Caroline buried her face in Polly's chest and burst into tears. 'Oh, Mum, I was so frightened.'

'Hush,' Polly soothed her. 'It's all right, we'll forget about it.'

Above Caroline's head she stared bleakly through the window at the garden where yellowing leaves were blowing down from the willow tree.

Chapter Eleven

When Louise rang the hospital, she found her mother was resting comfortably. 'A slight concussion, that's all,' the cheerful ward sister said. 'But if she's all right tomorrow morning, I should think Mrs Russell will be allowed home.'

'How did it happen?' asked Louise, not liking the sound of concussion.

The sister thought she'd fallen but didn't know the details.

'If Mother's able to come out tomorrow morning, I think I'd better bring her back here,' Louise said to Mark, who'd put the kettle on.

'Of course, darling,' he said, spooning instant coffee into mugs. 'She'll be company for you.'

Louise, hearing the silence of the house fold itself around her, agreed.

When she arrived at the hospital the next morning, her mother was already dressed and waiting in a chair in the day room. She looked tired, pale and hunched. There was a large bruise down the left side of her face.

'Mother,' Louise said lovingly, slipping an arm around her shoulders, 'how are you feeling?'

'I'm still alive,' she said wanly. 'But it's been a terrible shock.'

'I'm sure.' Louise sat down in the chair next to hers. 'What happened?'

'I was in my bedroom, sorting through my stockings. I thought I heard something.' Betty spoke as though fighting for breath. 'I went to the top of the stairs and shouted to see if somebody was there. I thought it might have been you.'

'But, Mother, I was in Paris.'

'So you were, darling. I must have forgotten.' Betty looked contrite.

Louise squeezed her mother's hand. 'So, you were at the top of the stairs?'

'And I thought maybe I should go down. I took a step and – and Purrfect leaped out of nowhere, straight between my legs, and I stumbled and fell.'

'All the way down the stairs?' Louise was appalled. 'That wretched cat!'

'No, just to the turn but that was quite far enough! I had the most dreadful pain, here,' she put a hand to her side, 'and trying to breathe was agony.'

'And no one was in the house! Oh, poor Mother.'

'Well,' Betty gave a brave smile, 'it was a bit of a business getting myself to the phone and ringing for an ambulance.'

'I'm amazed you could manage it! What a relief it must have been when they came. Now I'm going to take you home with me and look after you.'

Her mother immediately looked more cheerful, 'Oh, darling, will you? Won't that be a terrible burden to you?'

'Nonsense, I shall enjoy it.'

'And won't Mark mind?'

'He agreed with me you should come,' Louise said firmly. 'You know he enjoys your company.

It was true. Mark and Betty got on extremely well together.

'He's a dear boy. It'll be nice to see a little more of him.' Betty was looking better by the minute. 'Can we collect Purrfect on the way back?'

'Of course.'

'I'll need some things as well.'

'I can pack a case for you.'

Louise went and had a word with the sister and was told her mother should be fine. 'A few days' rest, a bit of TLC, and she'll feel a different person,' the nurse said.

'TLC?' Louise asked, wondering if she should stop at the chemist on the way back.

'Tender loving care,' the woman laughed. 'Best medicine there is.'

'Then I'd better stock up.' Louise grinned at her. 'But what about her ribs?'

'They'll heal by themselves. They're only cracked.'

'She seems to be in a lot of pain.'

'Most of that's bruising from the fall. She's got some pills that should keep it under control.'

Gently and carefully, Louise helped her mother out of the hospital.

Betty lived in a small house with a tiny garden on a nicely landscaped estate. When they arrived, Louise suggested her mother remain in the car while she checked everything was in order, packed a small bag and collected the cat. As she opened the door, the telephone started to ring.

It was her sister-in-law. 'Just one of my routine calls,' Jemima's cheerful voice said. 'You visiting Mum for coffee?'

Louise explained.

'Oh, my,' Jemima exclaimed. 'Should I come over?'

Louise's brother Tom lived in Essex with his family. A civil servant at one of the ministries, he worked in London.

Tom was not the easiest of people to talk to. A sentence of more than three words was dangerously loose language to him. Louise often wondered how he'd managed to summon enough words to ask Jemima to marry him. She, on the other hand, spoke enough for two. Mark had once suggested that was what had attracted Tom because she had little else to recommend her. No looks, no background, no brains.

Louise, who was very fond of her sister-in-law, had flared up in her defence. 'You only think she's plain because she's uninterested in clothes. And she does have brains; I've heard her discuss art in a very knowledgeable and interesting way. If you bothered to talk to her properly, you might find out things that would surprise you!' Louise realised that if Mark had a fault, it was taking people at face value. And when it wasn't a particularly interesting face, he couldn't be bothered to look any further.

When the children were small, she used to drive them over to Tom and Jemima's for a couple of nights twice a year. The Russell children were three and four years younger than the Henderson twins, two girls as quiet as their father. Sally and Sue, all large grey eyes and heavy dark fringes, adored their much larger and more voluble cousins. Emma and James took a kindly interest in them but once they'd grown beyond being enthralled by the Russell livestock – four guinea pigs, two goats, a dozen bantam hens, two dogs and one cat – and walks in the nearby wood had palled, the visits had become difficult.

For the last six years, Louise had taken Emma and James over for the day. It was always a weekday because Mark refused to go as well. 'Tom's OK,' he said, 'I always enjoy having a chat with him about what's going on in the government, but Jemima and the girls bore the hell out of me.'

Twice a year Tom brought his family to stay with his mother in her tiny house, Betty had bought bunk beds to put into the third bedroom that was no larger than a sizeable cupboard. Louise always had them over to her for at least a couple of meals.

'It's much too far for you to come,' she told Jemima now. 'Mother doesn't seem too bad. Of course we'd love to see you if you want to come over this week, but don't feel you have to. Give her a ring later today at our place. How are the girls?'

Hearing about Sue and Sally brought back to Louise just how much she was missing Emma and James. Where were they now? Up near Nepal? Could they see the snow-capped Himalayas soaring up to the roof of the world? Visions of Emma and James towering over tiny Ghurkas filled her mind as she packed a suitcase for her mother.

She found the cat in the living room, sitting in Betty's special chair: a huge pile of fluffy fur as white as the snow on the Himalayas. She scooped up the outraged animal and took him out to the car. 'Here he is. I'm afraid I've affronted his dignity.'

'Oh, Purrfect, have you missed me?' Betty asked caressingly, settling the cat on her lap and running a hand over his white fur. Two enormous bright blue eyes fixed themselves on her face, then blinked twice before closing.

Louise went back for Betty's case and a couple of tins of cat food in case she didn't have time to go shopping later, then locked the door. When the children had been growing up, they'd had a dog. Rosie the yellow labrador was adored by everyone. When, two years ago, she'd finally had to be put to sleep, the twins had pleaded for another. But Mark had pointed out that with their leaving home in the near future, this was not the time for their mother to saddle herself with a demanding animal.

Louise, who had always hated taking Rosie to the very expensive but beautifully run local kennels at holiday times, watching her head turn to look mournfully back as she was led away, had agreed. But now seeing Betty stroking Purrfect, she wished she, too, had an animal waiting for her at home.

Driving back, Louise remembered how she used to take Rosie for walks when the twins had been more than usually difficult. She'd talk to her, imagine she could hear Rosie giving her the reassurance she needed: that it was only growing up that made Emma shout at her or James lock himself in his room; give it an hour or two and they would be all right again. And Rosie would trot on ahead, looking round every now and then to make sure Louise was keeping up, before diving off to investigate some particularly interesting smell, her furry hindquarters trembling with excitement. Sometimes they'd run together, Louise working out her frustrations in exercise, Rosie panting happily beside her. The only love money can buy, someone had once cynically said. Go to a pet shop and there it is, sitting in a cage waiting for you to pick up and take away. I'll have that one, the one with the perky ears and brown eyes.

Was that what Polly had done when she'd seen Jean-Paul? Said to herself, I'll have Gallic love with dancing eyes and a liquid voice?

'I hope Purrfect won't sulk,' Betty said, giving the cat another stroke. 'I once took him with me when I visited my friend Daphne in Sussex. He went right off his food. Even when we got back it took days before he was himself again.'

On their arrival, Louise took the cat from her mother and carried him into the house. Purrfect shook himself, looked around with disdain, then stalked into the drawing room and claimed the most comfortable chair, settling down and staring at Louise with huge sapphire eyes, as much as to say, Try to move me if you dare.

She left him in possession and went to help her mother from the car.

Jemima rang that afternoon and, much to Louise's surprise, the

86

next evening saw her brother arrive.

'Thought I should come and see how Mother is,' he said abruptly as Louise opened the front door.

'Come in, how nice to see you.' Louise stood back. She had given up kissing her brother many years earlier when she'd realised it only made him pricklier than ever.

'All right, is she?' He stood awkwardly in the hall.

'She's fine, watching the news while I get a meal ready. There's more than enough for you as well. I'm afraid Mark won't be home tonight, he's staying in town. Did you drive here?'

'Came by train.'

'You should have let me know, I'd have met you.'

'Prefer to walk.' Tom made it sound as though being met at the station was tantamount to riotous living.

Louise led him into the room where they watched television. 'Mother, look who's come to see you.'

Betty's face lit up. 'Tom! How lovely!'

'Mother,' he said dutifully, and went forward to peck her cheek.

'Now sit down and tell me all about yourself.' She switched off the television and looked expectant.

Momentary panic crossed Tom's face and he glanced beseechingly at his sister.

'What would you both like to drink?' she asked cheerfully.

Louise settled them with a sherry for her mother and a whisky for Tom then disappeared into the kitchen to cook supper. When she went back a little later, Betty was in the middle of a long story about the hospital and Tom was looking bored to the back teeth.

Things got better over supper as Louise encouraged her brother to tell them how his daughters were doing and how Jemima's pottery business was going.

As Tom outlined Sally's tussle with O levels and Sue's despair over her inability to get to grips with maths, he visibly relaxed. Listening, Louise realised just how deeply fond of his daughters he was.

'What a pity they haven't inherited your brains, darling,' Betty said, pushing the rest of her chicken breast to the edge of the plate and placing her knife and fork together. 'That was very nice but I don't seem to have much appetite, I expect it's the pain.'

Louise opened her mouth to ask if she should get her mother some Panadol but was prevented by Tom's saying fiercely, 'They're very bright, particularly Sue. She's got a real feel for languages and with my help she's getting over her problem with maths.'

'Oh, that's wonderful, darling. I'm sorry if you thought I was accusing them or something. It's just that I've never seen any sign of great intelligence, though they are dear girls, both of them.'

'What's Jemima working on at the moment?' Louise asked hastily, deciding Betty would ask for a pain killer if she needed one.

Tom's expression cleared. 'She's started a new casserole design. Really beautiful. The pots have the swell and curve of a pregnant woman and the colour is a most wonderful grey with flecks that swim through the glaze like schools of tiny fish in clear waters. Then they're finished with small swirls of a soft blue round the top and the lid. I can look at one for hours.'

Louise stared at him. She'd never heard Tom put so many words together or use such poetic language.

'Are they useful?' asked Betty. 'That's what I think a pot should be, useful.'

Louise braced herself but Tom suddenly gave a wide grin. 'If the stew we had out of one the other night was anything to go by, they certainly are! You'd better come and stay with us when you're better, Mum, and then you can see for yourself.'

'I'd like that, Tom.' Betty looked so delighted, Louise felt like awarding her brother some sort of medal.

He looked at his watch. 'I'd better be off, have to catch the last train from Liverpool Street.'

'Why not stay the night?' For once Louise felt real warmth towards him.

He considered the question.

Betty put her hand on his arm, 'Do, please, then I could see you in the morning. I think I'll have to go to bed now. I'm really very tired.' She looked exhausted, Louise realised.

'I'll do coffee while you help Mother,' Tom said, getting up.

He was obviously going to stay.

'You'd probably like to ring Jemima,' Louise suggested as she assisted Betty to rise. After she was tucked up in bed with the portable television playing and Purrfect beside her, Louise returned to the kitchen. 'My, you are house trained,' she said as she took in the fact that the dishwasher was stacked, the table cleared and pans washed up.

'Can't stand men who expect their wives to do everything.' Tom frowned as he opened a cupboard. 'Where do you keep the coffee?' He'd already found the cafetière and filled it with hot water.

'Here.' Louise fished out the canister of coffee beans and poured some into the grinder. 'Can I get you a brandy?' she asked as he poured away the hot water and she tipped in the freshly ground coffee.

'Maybe a bit more of that whisky.' Tom added freshly boiled water from the kettle on to the coffee grounds.

'How about a malt?'

'Great!'

When they were settled in the small television room, Louise said, 'It was very good of you to come. Mother really appreciates it. Did Jemima mind your not going back this evening?'

He shook his head and relaxed into his chair. 'Expected it.' He glanced at his sister. 'Her suggestion I came.'

'I thought it might be,' Louise said, rather dryly.

Tom looked a touch resentful. 'I'm not unfeeling.'

'But not the first to rush round if something's wrong with Mother.'

He swirled his whisky round in the glass, watching the way the deep amber liquid clung briefly to the sides before sliding back. 'You remember how hot the old man always was on telling the truth?' he suddenly asked.

Louise flushed slightly. The memory of the way she'd lied that night with the Americans was still with her. Back came her father's voice.

'Sign of inadequacy,' he'd told them whenever they'd been caught out in some fib.

'Yet he lived the biggest lie of all.' Tom's tone was bitter.

'What do you mean?'

'Trying to hide the fact that his marriage was a disaster.'

'A disaster?' She put down her coffee and looked at him as if at a stranger.

'Oh, come off it! You must have known!'

'As far as I know, they were both very happy.'

'Happy!' Tom rose, his tall, thin body tense. He walked over to the window and stood looking out at the garden. 'You were only seventeen when he died but I gave you more credit for intelligence.'

Louise felt stung. 'What do you know about me? When have you ever talked to me? I've always been your little sister, six years younger, beneath your notice.'

He paid no attention, continued standing with his back to her.

'Talk to me, Tom. Tell me what you mean.'

He turned round slowly and half sat on the window sill, nursing his drink. 'Did you never wonder why he wasn't at home more often?'

'But he was busy! A doctor is always having to go out.'

'Not so much as Dad. And did you ever wonder about Barbara Wright?'

'You mean his receptionist?'

'Receptionist? She was more than that.'

Louise couldn't believe what he was saying. 'You mean, Dad was having an affair with her? You can't be serious!'

'Believe it.'

Louise desperately cast her mind back. 'But she was always so nice! I really enjoyed talking to her.'

'She is. An intelligent, warm, loving woman who gave Dad comfort.'

Louise's eyes narrowed. 'What do you mean, *is*? Do you still see her?'

Tom nodded. He drank some of the whisky and then looked down at his shoes.

'Don't you think that's rather disloyal?'

His head jerked up. 'Disloyal? You mean to Mother?'

Louise nodded.

'I feel no loyalty to her. She stifled Dad. Ate him up.'

'Tom!'

'She did. When did you ever hear them have a conversation? Discuss anything other than us children, what the neighbours were doing or who they should have for dinner?' The malt seemed to be loosening his tongue.

Louise helped herself to more coffee as thoughts frantically zigzagged around her mind. 'But she devoted herself to him. To him and to us.'

'Too right! That's all she was fit for.'

'Tom, she's a good woman.'

'God preserve me from good women!' he said savagely. 'Look at what she did to you.'

'Me?'

'When Dad wanted you to try for university, she said it would be a waste of time. Right from the start she brought you up to think looking after a man and raising a family was the only thing for a girl to do.' He gave her a straight look. 'Dad suggested I had a talk with you about it but she said it was none of my business.'

'I've never known you to listen to anything Mother said.' A touch of bitterness laced Louise's voice.

'Oh, I had a go all right. You've obviously forgotten. I tried to tell you how stimulating I'd found Oxford, and all you could say was that university was for the bright ones and you weren't bright. I knew then that she'd brainwashed you and there was no point in my saying anything more.'

'But I'm not bright!' Louise said faintly.

'You got your A levels, didn't you?'

'Only because I worked hard.'

'What do you think I did?' Tom burst out.

Louise sat with her mind in a whirl. Her brother had never talked to her like this before. The revelation he had made regarding their father was extraordinary. Louise remembered Barbara Wright, a quietly attractive woman who'd run the surgery in a self-effacing way. Always there with her calm voice and pleasant manner. Louise had never been able to understand why her mother hadn't liked her. 'That Barbara,' Betty had said once, 'never knows her place.'

Tom tossed off the last of his whisky. 'I'll have another of those,' he said bluntly. Louise refilled his glass. He came back to his chair, sat down and leaned forward. 'Listen,' he said urgently, 'never let anyone tell you you're not bright. Especially Mother. You just haven't had your mind trained. You need to find something you can

90

do. Don't get like her, always waiting for the next visit, the next telephone call from one of us. Always resentful there aren't more.'

'That's unfair,' flared Louise. 'Mother has a full life, lots of friends. She's always going somewhere, doing something . . .'

'When Jemima and I got married,' Tom continued as if she hadn't spoken, 'I told her never to give up her career. I said I'd help in any way I could to ensure she had time to continue her pottery.'

'And you have,' Louise murmured.

He looked across at her and his thin, intense face softened. 'I love you, Lou, you know that? You give so much to everyone, but I'm worried you never seem to take anything for yourself. Now the children have left home it's time you branched out, looked for something you could be interested in. You've got to stop being a doormat.'

'I'm not a doormat!' she said fiercely. Tom said nothing. After a moment she added, 'I think you've said more to me tonight than over the last ten years.'

He looked down at his glass. 'Yes, well.' Then glanced up at her, his eyes serious. 'Jemima and I have been talking. She's worried about you and made me promise I'd say something.' He rubbed a hand over his mouth and chin. 'I don't think she actually meant me to sound off in quite the way I have, though.' His voice was rueful. 'When I go home and tell her, she'll say I've put my great big foot in it as usual.'

'You mean, it's only with me and Mother you act like a Trappist monk? I've watched you talk to Mark and thought it must be because we were so stupid that you never had anything to say to us.'

'Don't say that! I've always cared for you. It's just I knew if I once started, I'd not be able to stop saying what I think.'

'Well, now that you have got going, I shall expect you to keep it up,' she told him. 'I like hearing you talk, even if I can't agree with everything you say.'

'Just think about it,' he urged.

Chapter Twelve

Nicky hovered over the chilled food cabinet and debated whether Colin would prefer chicken Kiev or fish pie for supper. Then she picked out two of each. He could choose and the others would go into the deep freeze. The packets joined the salad items in her basket. She felt a moment's guilt about the cost of the meals she'd chosen. If she made cottage pie, it would be cheaper – and Colin would enjoy it more. But when did she have time to make anything other than the beds these days?

Nicky carried on through the aisles, adding bread, butter, eggs, tins of baked beans and sardines, dried pasta and long-life milk, then she went on to toilet rolls, soap powder and all the other basic items the household needed to keep running smoothly. An internal calculator kept a rough total of the cost of the trolley's contents and by the time she came to the instant coffee and biscuits, warning bells were ringing. Regardless, she added a jar of their favourite coffee granules and a packet of Darjeeling tea. Then she headed for the wine department.

'Nicky!' a familiar voice called.

'Louise, shopping on a Friday evening? I thought that was just for the workers.' Nicky swung her trolley round as her friend came up behind her then wondered if she'd been rude.

'Not my usual time,' Louise sunnily agreed. 'But Mark's back from Hong Kong early tomorrow morning, I had my mother staying for what seemed weeks and we've run out of everything.'

Her trolley was indeed laden. 'Oh, it's nice to see you!' she added, giving a big smile to Nicky who was slightly taken aback by Louise's warmth.

'Have you got time for a drink or do you have to dash back and cook for Colin?'

Nicky looked at her watch. 'He won't be home until later. Look, why don't you come back and have a drink at our place? In face, why don't you eat with us?' That would mean opening both packets of either the chicken Kiev or the fish pie, but what the hell? They owed Louise a meal. Except, would this count as a return of hospitality if Mark wasn't included?

'Are you sure that wouldn't be a nuisance?' Louise looked doubtful.

'Not at all. It's all precooked.' Nicky waved a hand insouciantly at the boxes in the trolley. 'All I have time for these days.' She reached for a couple of bottles of her favourite Australian Chardonnay, noticing with dismay that it had gone up in price.

'I'm longing to hear about your job.' Louise added several bottles to her trolley without seeming to look at how much they cost, then moved on to the red wine section. Nicky followed. 'There, I've done! No, Mark's out of whisky . . .' She darted off to another section and returned with two bottles. Nicky recognised a malt and a bottle of The Famous Grouse, Colin's favourite. They only had the supermarket's own brand these days.

'Have you got everything?' Louise asked.

Nicky nodded. 'Let's go.' She headed for the jammed checkout section.

Outside in the car park, Nicky found Louise was parked not far from her. They loaded up their vehicles, then Nicky led the way out.

The Webbers' drive was clogged with dead leaves that scrunched under the car wheels. Nicky sighed as she drove into the car port. Autumn was having its usual ball unloading the old before the process of regeneration began again. She bet Louise's drive and garden were well-swept. Her own weekend's activity was clear.

'Give me some of those bags.' Louise was out of her car, standing waiting.

'Put them on the table,' Nicky said as she unlocked the back door and let them into the kitchen. The stale smell of a house left locked up with dirty dishes by the sink hit her.

'I'll get the rest.' Louise had dumped her load and gone back to the car before Nicky could say anything.

She opened the windows, letting in the crisp evening air, and dumped the remains of breakfast and the previous evening's supper into the sink. 'We were really tired last night,' she excused herself to Louise as her friend returned with the rest of the purchases. 'I wouldn't let Colin clear up and then we both overslept. Dreadful!' She wrinkled her nose fastidiously as the soapy water started to soak away the clogged remnants of beefburgers and tomato ketchup.

'Let me do that while you put away the shopping,' insisted Louise, taking off her jacket and gently moving Nicky from the sink.

She started to protest then thought, Well, why not? Louise has all that help in her house, she probably finds doing someone else's washing up a treat. 'Did you say you'd had your mother staying?' she asked as she started to unpack the plastic bags.

'Yes, poor thing, she fell downstairs and cracked her ribs.'

'That sounds dreadful!'

'Not really serious, she just needed looking after.'

'So that's what you've been doing?' Nicky thought for an instant, decided on the chicken Kiev for that evening and flung the fish pies into the freezer.

'I thought it would only be for a week or so but she seemed to be in a lot of pain, and then she got a cold, and then whenever the idea of going home was suggested, there was always some reason why she wanted to stay a little longer.' Louise gave a big sigh. 'It was very nice to be able to give her a bit of cosseting but it did seem to go on for an awfully long time.'

'Began to think she'd moved in with you?' Nicky giggled, putting the dry goods in the cupboard.

'Mark did. He's always got on with Mother very well but just before he went off to Hong Kong, he did say it would be nice to have me to himself when he got back. So I took a deep breath and told Mother I thought it was time she went home.'

'Did she put up a fight?' Nicky opened the cupboard by the sink and stuffed in the cleaning materials.

Louise put the last clean dish on the draining board and reached for a drying up cloth. 'Not a murmur. I think she was really quite glad to get back to her own place again. Purrfect had a fit of the sulks, though. I think he liked our sofa, and the garden was marvellous for mousing. He left three heads in our bedroom – a sign of great favour, Mother said.'

'I'd have gone doolally, I hate mice.' Nicky shuddered theatrically as she folded up the last plastic bag and put the little pile away in the drawer where they were kept ready for the waste bin under the sink. 'There, that's done. Do you want to wash this lettuce and make the salad while I lay the table? We're only having fruit for pudding, is that all right?'

'Wonderful! I've had four weeks of producing puddings every day. Mother doesn't think a meal is a meal without one, and I'm bursting out of my clothes.'

'That'll be the day.' Nicky eyed Louise's trim figure in its grey flannel trousers, silk polo top and suede waistcoat.

'So, tell me about the job?' Louise started tearing lettuce leaves into a bowl of cold water.

All of a sudden, Nicky felt the traumas and strains of the day lift from her shoulders. 'Oh, Louise, it's wonderful! I can't tell you what fun I'm having.'

Louise glanced round from the sink. 'What was it Mark said when you told us about the job? You looked like a child at a pantomime? Well, that's just about it.'

'But I never imagined it would turn out so well!' Nicky exclaimed as she arranged the chicken pieces in a dish. She decided to leave all four in; the portions weren't all that large and Colin might be hungry.

'Where's your salad basket?' Louise started tipping water out of the bowl of torn leaves.

95

Nicky found it then gave her a bunch of spring onions and an avocado pear. She'd been going to keep that for tomorrow but the salad seemed a bit poor without it.

'I'll peel it and leave it on the top, shall I? Then I can cut it up just before we eat.'

'Oh, Louise, you always know how things should be done!'

Nicky hadn't meant to sound envious and was relieved when Louise pulled a small face and said, 'If only you knew! But, come on, tell me more about the job?'

'Why don't we open a bottle of wine and go through? I can lay the table when I put the chicken in the oven and you can keep Colin entertained while it's cooking. There's no point in doing anything more until he's back.'

They took the wine into the front room. A nice size, it had a beamed ceiling and an inglenook fireplace. Nicky liked to think it had all the charm of a country cottage without the inconvenience.

'So?' prompted Louise as they sat down and Nicky poured the wine. 'You're not finding it all too much?'

'I love it.'

'What do you have to do?'

'Well.' Nicky straightened her back and put down her wine. 'I manage all the appointments with the parents and the staff. Do the head's correspondence, of course, and keep track of his schedule. Then I seem to be the front man, the conduit for all the staff to reach the head. He seems to rely on my judgement as to what's important and what's peripheral.'

'You must have picked up an awful lot in a short time?' Louise looked fascinated.

Nicky laughed. 'Oh, you don't know the half of it! What a hot bed of politics that place is! But everyone talks to me and I've made it my place to listen to them all and say nothing. I've had the Head of English tell me what a disruptive influence the junior maths master is and the music teacher complain about lack of finance because science takes it all, and the chemistry master try to mark my card over the spiteful way the Head of English tries to do him down.'

'Good heavens! It sounds like the United Nations!'

'Much, much worse,' grinned Nicky. 'But they all think I'm wonderful. At the moment anyway.'

'You seem to be the lynchpin.' Louise sounded really impressed and Nicky was pleased because she, too, felt she wasn't doing badly. 'And how are the boys liking their new school?'

'Loving it,' her friend said promptly. 'For the first two weeks they rang every night asking to be taken away, saying it was like some sort of prison. Then Riff got picked for the junior rugger team and Raff landed a part in the school play, and now they're both sublimely happy. They seem to be able to come home most weekends and then all they want to do is rush up to their rooms and play with their computers or listen to pop music. They don't seem to miss us at all.'

'I'm glad,' Louise said, but there was a lack of expression in her voice and Nicky looked at her more closely.

'What are you getting up to these days?' she asked. 'Now that you no longer have the twins at home.'

Louise's face fell and she twisted her glass by its stem. 'Nothing much,' she said finally and Nicky realised she had lost some of her usual sparkle.

'Of course, you've had your mother. You can't have had time to think about anything else.'

'It's not that,' Louise burst out. She put the glass on a small table and leaned forward. She looked tired and, Nicky was amazed to see, depressed. She had never known Louise to be depressed, no matter what she had been going through with the twins. 'Ever since Emma and James left I've had this dreadful feeling that I'm no use anymore. It was almost a relief to have Mother with us because then I didn't have to wonder what I was going to do with my time.'

Nicky was shocked. Louise had always been so resilient, so resourceful. Now she sounded defeated. 'I bet Mark doesn't think that!'

'Oh, Mark!' Louise sounded exhausted. 'He keeps telling me to snap out of it. Reminds me that I've got a lovely home and quite enough to do making sure he's comfortable.'

'I thought you were going to go abroad with him? What about Hong Kong, why aren't you with him now?'

'Well, there was Mother.'

'But surely you could have sent her home in time to go off? She would have understood.'

Louise looked even more defeated. 'I know. But I thought about what happened in Paris, how I hardly saw Mark, and though I had a great time there, it was because Val was in the same boat – her husband was the lawyer who went out with Mark and, well, and his team. Val and I were able to do things together. In Hong Kong there wouldn't have been anybody else and somehow I just didn't feel up to wandering around on my own. Polly said when she went with Willoughby, the only things she found to do were shop and eat.'

Nicky felt almost angry. 'But you could have gone for a trip into China! Looked at the markets, explored the Peak District and Kowloon . . .'

Louise smiled weakly. 'You should have gone with him. You'd have known exactly how to amuse yourself.'

Nicky drew a sudden deep breath as the ridiculous suggestion hit her like a sledge hammer. She and Mark in Hong Kong, amongst all the oriental mystery, exploring the fastest moving city in the world . . . Then she remembered what Louise had said about his not having time for anything but business. But there would be evenings, surely? 'What you need,' she said bracingly, 'is something to occupy you. A job, voluntary work, that sort of thing.'

Louise looked up with a hint of eagerness. 'I know! And I've been thinking about possibilities. An interior decorator came the other week to look at the house. We're having it redone.'

How she threw the line away! Nicky rapidly computed what it would cost to have the Hendersons' home refurbished and mentally reeled at the total.

'I'd been dreading her arrival. I thought she'd make fun of what I'd done, like a new hairdresser. You know the way they pick up your hair and ask who cut it as though it was something a gardener had taken shears to?'

'But she wasn't like that?'

'No, she was charming. Said I had a real flair for decoration and we had a lovely chat about what to do with the house. So I asked her how one became an interior decorator.'

'You think it's something you'd like to do?'

'Well, I really enjoyed decorating the house when we first moved in there, working out the colour schemes and all the accessories. And I've always liked searching out antiques and bits and pieces, you know?'

Nicky did know. She'd long envied the way Louise could find exactly the right piece to set off a room or part of one – and the money that enabled her to buy it, seemingly regardless of what it cost. Louise always claimed anything Nicky admired hadn't been at all expensive. Nicky never knew if that was true or if Louise was trying to spare her feelings because the Webbers had always been on a tight budget. 'So, what did she say?'

'Oh, she was a bit evasive. Said there were lots of ways in but she'd worked for one of the top London interior decorators for years before she set up on her own. The important thing, she said, was that you needed contacts.'

'Clients?'

'That and trade contacts. You had to know what was available, what the new trends were, where to go, all that.'

'Well, you could learn.'

'If anyone would take me on. It's not the best of times and Marsha – that was her name, Marsha Reading – said there were always loads of people applying. She seemed to think I should start by studying for a fine arts degree.'

'That would be interesting.'

Louise looked gloomy. 'I want to *do* something, not study it. You must understand that, Nicky? Look how much you're enjoying your job! I know you got it because of needing the money with Riff and Raff's schooling, but it's giving you something, isn't it?'

Nicky grinned. She couldn't help it. Life in the school was stretching her mind, honing her skills, making her realise she had something to contribute.

Then the grin disappeared. 'I never have time for housework,' she said. 'Colin has had to start pushing the vacuum cleaner around on Saturdays and the dirt is gradually silting up the skirting boards. And I seem to have to spend so much money,' she added gloomily. 'My salary isn't going nearly as far as I thought. What with having to wear decent clothes all the time and buying time-saving items.' She suddenly grew impatient with Louise. 'Look, you don't need the money, why not do charity work? They're always looking for volunteers.'

Her friend's expression became obstinate. 'You don't understand, I need to earn money of my own. I can always do good works later on, when I'm older. Now is when I need an identity.'

'That's ridiculous.' Nicky grew crosser. 'Of course you've got an identity.'

Louise's face crumpled. 'I don't know who I am at the moment,' she whispered. 'The twins are gone, Mark is away so much, and I spend my days trying to work out what to do that will make some sort of sense.'

'Well, take up golf. Didn't you always say you wanted to play?'

'Golf?' said Louise blankly. Then smiled determinedly. 'You could be right, Nicky. Perhaps I should enrol for some lessons and see how I get on. At least it would get me out of the house.'

Nicky had a nasty feeling that she'd failed her in some way. 'Why don't you get a job in one of those smart dress shops? You've got such good taste, I'm sure they'd take you on. Then, after a bit, you could open a boutique of your own. Have you discussed all this with Mark? I bet he'll have some good ideas.'

She never knew how that went down because Colin entered the room.

'Louise, how nice!' he said, but Nicky wasn't sure he'd meant it. He'd looked tired and dispirited as he'd entered and she was sure what he'd really wanted was to collapse into a chair and have a drink instead of having to make conversation.

In the end, though, the evening went quite well and by the time Louise left, having insisted on helping to wash up, it was still not ten o'clock.

Colin shut the door behind her. 'How about a whisky before bed?'

Nicky was instantly alerted. Colin only ever drank after a meal when he was stressed. He could not have unwound enough during the evening, even though Louise had seemed to realise he needed cheering up and had managed to get him talking and even laughing.

'Great,' she said. 'Nice to have a bit of a chat. We don't seem to have much time for that these days.'

'Too right.' He reached into the back of the cupboard for the whisky bottle, poured two generous measures and handed one to her. 'Have you thought about half term?'

'We really should visit Mum but, I don't know . . . what with the boys being away all the time, it doesn't seem right somehow.'

'Is she expecting you?'

'What's this "you" business?'

'I can't take time off at the moment, too much going on at the office.'

'Colin!' Nicky wailed. 'What'll Riff and Raff say? And, anyway, I was looking forward to us all being together.' She felt really deflated. Every evening Colin was buried in paperwork while she tried to keep up with the housework, the washing and the ironing. Every weekend seemed to be spent driving to and from school, in between attempting to keep up with the gardening and entertain the kids! She'd thought maybe this half term they could go bowling, play some tennis, knock the odd ball about in the garden with the boys or go to the cinema.

Colin looked grim rather than guilty. 'I've been doing my damnedest to get more work into the practice and suddenly several new clients have appeared. So I'm sorry but I can't take the time off. Anyway, you'll be all right. Go and stay with your mother. You know she'll be upset if you don't, and the kids like it.'

'Not these days they don't,' Nicky objected. 'Last time they said how boring it was.'

Colin gazed silently at his whisky.

Nicky fidgeted in her chair, got up abruptly and went into the kitchen to splash water into her glass. She really didn't like spirits. But it had seemed unfriendly not to drink with Colin and unfriendly was the last she thing she wanted to appear.

She went back into the living room, half expecting to find that he'd turned on the television. But, no, he was still sitting, studying his whisky as though it was some legal conundrum he had to puzzle out.

'Good news about the business,' she said cheerfully. 'You must have worked really hard! Anything interesting?'

'One conveyancing job, a will that involves setting up a trust, and a company merger. Nothing that's going to tax my legal skills too far.'

'No need to sound so dismissive. You've said yourself that quite ordinary things often lead to much more interesting cases. And a trust could involve a trusteeship, couldn't it? And who knows where the company merger will lead.' Nicky worked hard at trying to sound positive and upbeat. She didn't like to see Colin looking so depressed. 'And it's all going to help the partner shareout at the end of the year, isn't it?' That was the best bit.

Colin put down his drink. 'Darling, I've been thinking.'

100

Nicky's heart sank. He looked so solemn. Whatever was going to come now, she sensed it was something she wouldn't like.

'Even with your salary, we're only just managing to pay the school bill.'

It was something that had been occupying her mind for the last few weeks too. She'd thought they were going to be so well off with two salaries, but the money she earned seemed to melt away.

'You know how much this property is worth,' Colin continued. 'It's even more now than in the late-eighties when we thought it made us seem really rich.'

Nicky said nothing but her mouth grew very dry.

'If we sold it and I got a partnership in a country practice, well, we'd be able to buy something reasonable, probably bigger than this, for less than half the money, then we'd be able to invest the rest and increase our income.' He looked hopefully at her.

For a moment Nicky couldn't speak. Colin sounded as though he'd sorted out the whole thing in his mind. He wasn't asking her opinion, he was telling her this was what they were going to do. She remembered the bitter way Polly had spoken to Willoughby that night they'd all had dinner at the Hendersons'. He'd uprooted her from Paris just when she was beginning to enjoy herself. Now it seemed as if Colin was about to do the same to Nicky.

She wanted to scream that he couldn't do this to her. Instead she said, steadily, 'Where were you thinking of going?'

His face cleared, as though this meant she was going along with his plan. 'Somewhere like Somerset or Devon. I know you've always liked the country down there. Remember that camping holiday we had when the boys were young?'

It had been a good holiday. The weather, for once, had been fine; the field they'd pitched their tent in was right by a farmhouse and the boys had had a great time helping with the harvest and feeding the animals. Raff still talked about it and declared he wanted to become a farmer.

'It was lovely,' Nicky agreed. 'But how easy would it be to buy into a practice that would give you the same level of income as here?'

Colin fiddled with an ashtray on the table beside his chair. 'Well, I'd have to look into that. But I don't see why it should offer any great problem. I mean, we aren't City types. The work would probably be much the same.'

'How about having to drive so much further to take the boys to and from school? They seem to come out most weekends.' She was very proud of the way she steadily brought up all these points.

'We might have to move them.' Colin tilted the ashtray and let it go so it banged on the table.

'What, after they've only just settled in?' Nicky couldn't help some of her outrage showing at this.

'Better now than after they've got really stuck in,' he said obstinately.

'And what about my job?' she said tightly, coming at last to what seemed to her the most important aspect of the whole project.

'Well, it's only a job, isn't it? I'm sure you could get another one somewhere else. And if we got a good enough price for the house, perhaps you wouldn't need one with the extra income we'd get.'

Nicky got up. She couldn't stay listening to this any longer. 'I think you've gone stark staring mad,' she said. 'You know how expensive it is to move house! Anything we bought would be bound to need things doing to it. You talk of something bigger than this. Well, what about the running costs? Are electricity and telephones going to be any cheaper in Somerset? We'd use a good deal more petrol, that's for sure, wherever the boys went to school. And I bet you wouldn't get an income anywhere near what you're getting at the moment. As for my finding another job, you have no idea how lucky I was to get this one. There were masses of people after it.'

'But they chose you,' Colin said. 'You're good, we both know that. Look at the jobs you held down before we were married.'

'That was then, this is now,' she said furiously. She picked up their empty glasses and swept out to the kitchen. If she remained any longer with Colin she'd say something she'd regret.

Chapter Thirteen

The first question Mark asked when Louise met him on his return from Hong Kong was, 'Is your mother still with us?'

She shook her head.

He gave a big grin. 'I like her very much, don't misunderstand me, but I was beginning to wonder if we'd turned into an old people's home.'

'Well, I took her home yesterday,' Louise said shortly.

'She's all right now, isn't she?'

'Oh, fine.' She turned away.

Mark pulled her back to him. 'Darling, I haven't upset you, have I? It's so good to see you again, I missed you very much, you really should have come to Hong Kong with me.'

Louise allowed him to kiss her, conscious both of the stiffness he must sense in her and the crowds of people surging around them. 'Let's get home, darling, you must be exhausted,' she said.

'Could do with a short rest, if you came and rested with me.' He grinned at her and Louise felt her heart do a flip.

''Bye, Mark. See you Monday,' said a voice behind them. Louise didn't have to turn to know who it was.

'Hello, Robin, did you enjoy Hong Kong?' she asked smoothly.

'It was great!' Robin gave her a wide smile. 'I bought some wonderful silk shirts and got Mark to order some for you as well. Hope you like them.'

'Damn!' he said softly as Robin's elegant back disappeared in the throng. 'I hoped you wouldn't know they weren't all my own idea! But I chose the silks,' he added.

'Then that's all right,' Louise told him sweetly.

The shirts were, in fact, beautiful and Louise couldn't help but say so.

'I thought the colours were just you.' Mark fingered the rich red, vibrant blue and emerald silks. But fabulous as the shades were, the chief beauty of each, slightly different shirt, was its cut. You couldn't fault Robin's sense of style, thought Louise with a faint feeling of despair as she tried one on and admired the way the material draped itself.

'Why don't you have a shower while I make you some breakfast?' she suggested, taking off the shirt and reaching for the sweater she'd

103

been wearing before. She waited for Mark to pull her down on to the bed and insist they had that rest now but instead he yawned and started unbuttoning his shirt.

'Good idea. Then I think I'll ring Colin and see if he'd like a game of squash, I need some exercise and you can unpack my things.'

He wandered off to his dressing room and Louise tugged down her sweater.

After his game of squash, Mark crashed out. Louise went upstairs with him and lay beside him while he snored heavily for two hours.

Then he woke and reached for her. The next half hour was highly satisfactory.

As she lay with her head on his chest, breathing in the smell of him, feeling relaxed and fulfilled, she said, 'Darling, I think I'd like to get a job.'

She'd thought he might be indulgent or cross or surprised. She hadn't really expected him to take her seriously or to be helpful but neither had she expected him to fling back his head and roar with laughter. 'A job? You, darling? You can't be serious.'

Louise felt annoyed. First Nicky didn't seem to understand what she needed and now Mark was treating her as a joke. 'What's so funny?' she asked stiffly, rolling on to her side of the bed.

He put an arm around her and pulled her back. 'I'm sorry, darling, I didn't mean to be rude but you must see the funny side?'

'I'm afraid I don't.' Louise refused to relax against him again.

'Oh, don't get on your high horse, it's not worth it.' He sobered up and looked at her more closely. 'Oh, oh! I've hurt you, haven't I?' He gave her a gentle kiss. 'You know, as far as I'm concerned you're the most wonderful woman in the world. But what sort of job do you think you're qualified for?' He seemed to be having difficulty controlling his amusement. 'And why on earth do you want one anyway?'

The second question was easier to deal with than the first. At least, Louise thought it was until she started to explain how she felt now that the children had left home.

'Come on now, darling,' Mark said with a reasonable attempt at patience as she faltered to a stop, realising there was no way she could get him to understand. 'This is just a phase. It won't last. Emma and James will be back. They're going to need you as their mum for a good many years yet.'

'It won't be the same.' Louise felt near to tears. 'They'll never be at home again in the way they were. Yes, of course they'll need me, but in a very different way. If I try and hang on to them, I'll lose them.'

Mark shook his head. 'Not our two. I know there've been slight problems, times when we haven't seen eye to eye, but considering everything, I think we have a pretty good relationship going there.'

Louise gave up. This was useless. She levered herself on to one elbow so she could see his face and tried a different angle. 'Also, I don't have enough to do. I need something to occupy my day.'

Mark pulled at one of her curls, eyes scanning her face as though to discover what she was sickening for. 'I've suggested you come around with me a bit more. I'm sorry Paris was such a let down but that won't happen every time.'

'Oh, no?' Louise couldn't help sounding cynical. 'How much free time did you have in Hong Kong that wasn't occupied by Robin?'

His eyes opened wide. 'Heavens, darling, you're not jealous, are you?'

Funnily enough, until that point Louise hadn't identified her feelings as jealousy. She had never had any cause to doubt Mark's love for her. Now, for a first fleeting moment, she wondered. 'Of course I'm not,' she asserted. 'It's just that I don't exactly fancy the three of us going around Hong Kong together. Or anywhere else for that matter. I'm sure Robin's a great person but you would be talking shop, or wanting to. And you don't always want to be worrying about whether I'm getting pissed off because your meeting is going on longer than you thought.'

Mark stretched one of his arms then hauled himself upright. 'Don't think I'm not interested, darling, but I'm dying for a cup of tea. We couldn't continue this discussion in the kitchen, could we?'

Louise tried not to feel diminished. Any urge to stay in bed vanished. She scrambled up and slipped into a wrap.

'The thing is, darling,' said Mark as she put the kettle on and got out the tea, 'I can see you're awfully keen to do something, and heaven forbid that I should put anything in your way, but what are you qualified to do?' He stretched out his long legs as he lounged on the banquette, watching her heat the teapot.

'Nicky suggested I get a job in a dress shop, you know, selling designer clothes, and then maybe I could work towards opening one of my own.'

'No wife of mine is going to be a shop assistant.' Mark brought his hand down on the table. 'You can forget that idea for a start! Everyone would think I was about to be made redundant!'

'If all you can think of is your own position, I'm not sure I want to go on discussing it with you,' Louise said unsteadily, ignoring the fact that the electric kettle had boiled.

'Oh, for heaven's sake! I'm only trying to be helpful!'

'Well, think of something, then.' She turned her back on him and spooned out Lapsang Souchong, spilling dried leaves on the work surface. She brought the kettle back to the boil, poured the water into the pot and took it to the table. Typical of Mark, he hadn't even got out the mugs. She went and fetched a couple, banging them down unnecessarily hard, found a lemon, sliced it, put the slices on a small dish and put that on the table as well.

105

'Any biscuits?' he asked as she sat down.

Louise got up again and found the tin, decided against putting the biscuits on a plate and banged the tin on the table.

'Now, now, no need to get into a state!' Mark said as she started pouring the tea into the mugs. 'Look,' he said peaceably, 'I don't think you've really thought this through. The twins aren't going to be away all that long, there's your mother liable to need you again, the redecoration of the house to oversee, and me. Don't I count for anything in your life?'

Instantly Louise felt guilt-stricken. 'Of course you do, darling. But that's part of it, don't you see? I'd be a much better wife to you if I were doing something fulfilling instead of just waiting around for you to come home.' She just prevented herself from saying that that was a fairly useless occupation half the time. She didn't think it would help the present situation one little bit.

'Do you know, darling, that does sound just a bit like Emma trying to wheedle something out of me.'

She gazed speechlessly at her husband then got up and went upstairs to dress.

'What an absolute bastard,' Val said. 'What did you do then?'

Louise laughed. 'I went round to see how my mother was. She was delighted, of course, until she realised that I'd left my husband all alone when he'd just returned from the other side of the world. So I went to the library and looked in the careers section to see if I could get any ideas about what I could do.'

'And did you?'

'No,' Louise said sadly.

She and Val were lunching in a small restaurant just round the corner from Val's office.

'And how did the rest of the weekend go?'

'By the time I got home, Mark was deep in work and seemed to have forgotten we'd ever had a discussion or that I'd got upset.'

'Oh, dear.'

'And now I don't know what to do. But that's enough about me. How are things in your world? I've been really disappointed we couldn't get together again before this, I enjoyed our time together in Paris, but with Mother needing so much attention, it's been impossible.'

'I quite understood. Only, I've been dying to know, did you find out what the situation is between your friend and that gorgeous Jean-Paul?'

Louise sat back and allowed the waiter to pour her a glass of wine from the half bottle they'd ordered. 'Not really,' she said regretfully. 'I rang Polly and suggested we get together for tennis or coffee so I could tell her all about Paris. But it was strange, she didn't seem to want to talk about it at all. Most unlike her.'

'A bad sign, do you think?'

Louise sipped her wine. 'It's difficult to tell. I said it was unlike her not to want to talk about things, but it's two years since we spent much time together. She may have changed.'

Val looked doubtful. 'A mature woman? Unlikely, isn't it? That is, unless she's been through some profound emotional experience?'

'Or is going through one? When I said we'd met Jean-Paul, Polly hardly said anything. I told her he said she must return to Paris very soon and that he as well as Marie-Claire sent their love, and she just laughed and said, "That's the French for you, always two kisses when one would do".'

'I bet you wished you weren't talking to her on the telephone!'

'Did I ever! For the life of me, I couldn't tell if she was just being flip or if she was hiding something deeper. When I tried to fix a game of tennis, she said it would have to wait, she had a lot to do with the house and Caroline. Then there was a long story about how Caroline didn't want to be called Pooh anymore and how difficult it was to remember. She didn't seem to have any difficulty when talking to me.'

'I think we were on the right lines,' Val said wisely.

'I agree. Except the old Polly would have wanted to tell all. I'm going to drop round on her soon, try to take her unawares, and see if I can find out some more.'

'But if she doesn't want to tell?'

'I'm sure she can't have changed *that* much. Deep inside she needs to confide in a friend.'

'If that's what you think, I'm sure you're right,' Val said as their food arrived. 'I trust your judgement on people, you're very perceptive.'

'Am I?' Louise was startled. Nobody had ever said that to her before. And she didn't think she was all that perceptive where her husband was concerned. For a moment she wanted to ask Val what she thought about Robin and whether she suspected something might be going on between her and Mark. But putting such a thought into words would somehow make it seem more possible. Louise preferred to tell herself she was being ridiculous. She picked up her knife and fork. 'Now, that's quite enough about me and about Polly. How're things with you?'

'Oh, fine. There's nothing much to tell. Neil works, I work, we get together every now and then, and that's about it.'

'That's the story of your life. I want to hear the story of your days. Seen any good films or plays recently, read any good books, seen anyone interesting?'

Val laughed. 'We've hardly had time for any of that. Well, actually, I've just finished a book I think you'd like.' The conversation quickly turned into a literary discussion.

'Oh, this has been fun,' Louise said when it was time for Val to return to work. 'We must meet again soon. Perhaps you and Neil could come to supper at the weekend?'

Val pulled out her diary. 'Seems to be clear. I'll have to check with Neil but otherwise we'd love to.'

Mark seemed pleased Louise had asked the Lewins. 'That's what you need, darling, a little entertaining.'

'Going to be difficult with the builders starting next week,' she retorted tartly. If this was Mark's way of saying she'd been bloody difficult, she'd have appreciated a more up front approach.

'No need to snap my head off,' he said mildly. 'Will you ask anybody else?'

Louise thought for a moment. 'I think I'd like to have them on their own, as it's the first time.'

The evening, she thought afterwards, had gone well. The four of them had enjoyed each other's company and when Mark had tried to keep Neil behind at the dining table for port, he had laughed the suggestion away. 'Miss a moment of our lovely hostess's company? Not on your life. Not that I wouldn't like the port as well, but can't we all drink it together, Mark?'

'Well done, Neil,' Louise said gaily as they went into the drawing room where she had a fire blazing away against the chill of the late-October evening. 'I'm always telling Mark it's too old-fashioned to split the men and the women.'

'It's what my mother and father always did and I think it's nice for the women to have a chance to gossip together.' Mark stood by the drinks table, back straight, face good-humoured but unapologetic. Not for the first time Louise thought how classic the lines of his face were, those hard, high cheekbones, the strong nose, the firm, inflexible mouth.

Neil sank on to the sofa beside Val and took her hand in his. 'Girls' gossip is for lunches and morning coffee, not for convivial evenings like this.' His monkey face was alight with mischief and delight that he'd got his way, but love for his wife was also plain. Val was a lucky woman was Louise's opinion as she started to pour out the coffee.

Later they all played snooker together and Neil was delighted that he and Louise beat Mark and Val. 'I like a girl who knows her balls,' he joked, as she shot the black neatly into a bottom pocket to end the game.

'Set up as a snooker coach,' Val suggested. She had obviously hardly ever played the game.

'Don't encourage her,' groaned Mark, chalking the end of his cue. He arranged the reds for another game.

'I like the idea. Who knows? She could end up on television.' Neil placed the colours on their spots.

'I've told Lulu, she's got plenty to do looking after things here. All right, Neil, let's us take the girls on.' Mark removed the wooden

108

frame from the triangle of red balls. 'We'll break first, give them a chance.'

Neil hesitated and Louise could see he didn't think this was going to be a fair competition; he was almost as good as she was. But Mark was much better than both of them and if Neil now partnered Val, the Hendersons would undoubtedly trounce their guests. 'I think we ought to be thinking of going,' Neil said gracefully.

'You're not going to chicken out now?' Mark insisted, and sent the white ball spinning down the table, just nicking one of the reds and hardly disturbing their formal arrangement.

Neil glanced at his wife.

'Come on, Val,' said Louise with a laugh. 'We ought to be able to give them a run for their money.'

After the game was over Neil flung an arm around Louise's shoulders. 'Val's quite right, you could earn a mint of money coaching. I never thought my wife would be able to pocket a ball but you had her sinking them with the best of us.'

It was an exaggeration, of course. But Louise had, by dint of gentle advice, helped Val to improve her game and it had by no means been a whitewash.

'An excellent evening,' Mark said as he helped stack the dishwasher. 'We should see more of them. I've always got on well with Neil and Val is charming even if rather too dauntingly intelligent for me. I like my women full of fun, like you.' He dropped a kiss on Louise's neck as she bent over to fit in the last of the glasses. 'When did you say the decorators were starting?'

'Monday.'

'Well, that'll give you something to occupy yourself with,' he said with satisfaction.

'You are a wretch.' She flicked a tea towel at him. 'You just think I need a new toy and the house is it.'

Mark held up his hands. 'Pax! I won't say another word. You want to go and get a job, you do it. I don't have to like it but if that's what you really want, I'll learn to live with it. You'll have to wait until the house is done, though. We don't want the job bodged.'

On Monday Louise waited for the work on the house to start. Nobody arrived.

'Typical,' said Mrs Parks. 'Like policemen, never there when you want them. Still, it means I can get on.' Then she stood stock still in the middle of the kitchen. 'Except what's the use, if there's going to be dust and mess everywhere?'

'We'll start stripping all the kitchen cupboards,' said Louise. 'They're not going to begin the refit of this for another couple of weeks but we might as well get the job under way. I'll just ring Marsha first and let her know the bad news.'

'Oh, dear,' the designer said. 'I'll get on to the builder.'

By the end of the morning, the contents of all the kitchen cupboards were either in the larder or on the dining-room table. Louise and Mark had supper that evening on their laps in front of the television. 'This had better not take too long,' he said, channel-switching glumly. 'Otherwise I shall stay at the flat.'

On Tuesday, a small army arrived. Louise went off to shop and came back to find the house full of dust sheets, step ladders and men stripping wallpaper. Marsha was just leaving. 'They're all organised. I'll pop in next week to see them safely started on the painting and check that the builders have managed to change those doors as we decided.' She had pointed out that the kitchen would be much more efficient if one door were blocked up and the remaining one moved. 'You don't need an entrance from the drawing room as well as the hall and the dining room,' she'd said during her initial discussions with Louise. 'And since we're taking out all the fitted cupboards and putting in new ones as well as an Aga, it won't cause much more chaos.'

Louise hovered between being grateful to Marsha and wondering whether she was going to like living with her proposals. However Mark had had no hesitation in agreeing with her on everything. So that had been that. After all, he was paying for the work.

As Louise spooned instant coffee into mugs for the builders, the telephone rang.

'Neil! How nice to hear you,' she said in surprise.

'That was a great evening we had with you on Saturday.' His voice was full of enthusiasm. 'But this isn't really a thank you call, I know Val has written to you.'

'So what brings me the pleasure of hearing your voice?' Louise watched the kettle turn itself off, tucked the telephone under her chin and started pouring hot water into the mugs.

'Val told me on the way home about your really wanting some sort of job?'

'Mmm,' Louise murmured, wondering what was coming next.

'And she said you were worried because you couldn't think of anything you were qualified for? Well,' he sounded pleased, 'I think I may have something that could interest you.'

'A job?' squeaked Louise. She put the kettle down and transferred the telephone from her shoulder to her hand.

'Don't get too excited, it's only something very temporary, but it might get you into the swing of things, reintroduce you to office life, you know?'

'What is it?' Louise couldn't help but be excited.

'Some clients of mine, a medium-sized firm of lawyers, have recently taken over another firm and they need someone to check through some ancient files and note names and addresses. It's nothing very difficult but they can't afford to take any of their staff off what they're doing and they've got to use someone who can be relied upon not to talk about any of the names involved. You do type, don't you?' His voice was suddenly anxious.

'Yes, but I can't use a word processor.'

'Don't worry, at this stage all they want is a list. The thing is, can you come up to London for an interview tomorrow?'

'Tomorrow?' She looked at the chaos around her in dismay. Then thought that she would be better off out of it all. 'Yes, of course. Tell me where and when?'

The address Neil had given her was not far from Mansion House. Louise signed in at the smart reception area on the ground floor then took the lift to the fifth with her heart beating fast. She stood alone, staring at the metallic grey walls and discreet lighting, trying to control her nerves.

She was met by a woman so like Mark's secretary, June, that Louise had to hide a smile. The June clone accompanied her along a corridor and showed the way into the office belonging to Neil's contact. Louise quickly took in her surroundings. The decor here was subdued and efficient but, also like Mark's offices, redolent of success. The carpet was either antique or very good modern and the paintings on the walls were original oils and watercolours from the nineteenth century. Men in shirtsleeves hurried by looking sleek and purposeful. It was one of those offices that had secretaries working in bays and she could feel eyes assessing her as she walked by.

Harry Smythe was a man in his fifties, overweight, genial and sharp-eyed. 'Come in, come in, Mrs Henderson. Delighted to meet you. Neil says you could be just what we need. Take a seat, won't you?' He drew out an armchair deeply upholstered in leather.

Louise was aware of the way he took in every detail of her appearance as she sat down. His own suit was of excellent cut, as was his shirt, and his tie was silk with an expensively ebullient pattern of pink elephants.

'Well now, let me tell you what we need.'

The interview wasn't long but she was given a quick resumé of the job, which seemed simple enough, while he skilfully elicited her background and pitifully small previous experience. 'Don't worry about that,' Harry Smythe said comfortably as she made a small joke about giving up being an office dogsbody to become a home one instead. 'The important thing is that you can be discreet, and I think I've satisfied myself on that point. Your husband will have made you well aware of the importance of keeping business private.'

He certainly had, if only by the way he kept it so intensely private himself.

'And anyone who can run a home the way you obviously do has to be good at attending to detail. The only other requirement we have is typing skills and you say you are happy on that point?'

'I've always typed my personal correspondence. So many people complained my writing was difficult to read,' Louise said. Then wondered if that wouldn't disqualify her after all.

It seemed not. Harry Smythe told her what they were willing to pay for the three weeks it was thought the job would take and it seemed a great deal of money to Louise. 'So, start on Monday?' he said hopefully, standing up and extending his hand.

'Monday?'

'Tomorrow would be even better but you will probably need a day or two to get organised and the start of the week is tidier, isn't it?'

It hadn't occurred to Louise she might be needed immediately but that made the job even more exciting.

'That'll be fine, Mr Smythe. Nine o'clock?'

'Most of us are here by eight-thirty but nine, at least for the first day, will be fine.'

Louise left the office floating on air. She was so thrilled, she hardly took in what an eight-thirty start would mean in terms of leaving the house.

'Good heavens!' said Mark when she told him. 'Who's going to look after the builders?'

Chapter Fourteen

'I don't know why you don't find yourself something to do!'
Willoughby said irritably.

'You mean a job, darling?' Polly took out her number three wood
and approached her ball. It was lying on the fairway of the third
hole, a par five. 'Don't you want me to have time to play golf with
you?'

In fact, no one could have been more surprised than Willoughby
when she'd suggested they have a game together this weekend.

'But you've complained for weeks that there's nothing for you to
do in England,' he said as Polly carefully lined up her shoulders
towards the hole.

She addressed the ball, drew back the club then brought it down
and followed through with a fluidity that sent the dimpled little
white sphere in a low arc straight towards the hole.

'Oh, good shot,' he said involuntarily.

'Thank you, darling.' Polly thrust the club back into her bag and
took hold of the trolley's handle, following Willoughby to rough
well ahead of her lie and helping him search for his ball.

It took them a few minutes to discover it, lying in a small nest of
leaves.

'I'll give you a free drop,' she offered.

'For heaven's sake, Poll,' he said irritably. 'I have to play it from
here.'

'Don't want to develop bad habits, you mean,' she said with
composure and stood back to watch him take a mighty swing with a
six iron that lofted the ball straight into a bunker. 'Oh, bad luck.'

It took him two attempts to get out of the bunker but the second
shot landed the ball on the edge of the green. Polly's was some six
feet from the hole.

'Give you that hole,' Willoughby, now two shots behind, said
ungraciously.

'How kind of you, darling, but I want to put in a card. Don't feel
you have to finish the hole, though.'

Willoughby flashed her a bad-tempered look and approached his
ball, hunkering down behind it to judge the lie of the green.

Polly stood quietly by as he took an age to line up his shot then
breathed a small prayer of thankfulness as the ball curved

113

eccentrically towards the hole and dropped in. 'Brilliant shot, darling.' That meant she wouldn't have to miss her putt deliberately. She hated doing that; it not only went against all her competitive instincts, she was also very bad at making it look natural.

She was beginning to think it hadn't been the best of ideas to suggest this match.

For the last four weeks or so she'd hardly seen her husband. He'd been up in the Midlands somewhere trying to sort out the firm he'd been brought back to England to manage. He'd come back each weekend exhausted and bad-tempered. Only taking out Caroline from school seemed to relax him.

Polly had suggested they did some entertaining. 'We could ask Louise and Mark, we owe them after all. Or catch up on some of our other old friends,' she'd coaxed him.

'God, not a dinner party,' he'd groaned. 'I can't stand the thought of people. Not even Louise and Mark. If I want to talk to him, we can have lunch.'

'But you adore Louise,' Polly said in surprise.

'I'm too involved to adore anyone at the moment.'

That was certainly true where she was concerned. The harder Polly tried to make Willoughby's life brighter, the more surly he seemed to become.

She sank her putt, checked he'd filled in her score card then walked with him to the next tee.

It was a glorious autumn afternoon, the late-October air crisp and sunny, exactly the sort of weather that usually lifted the spirits.

Polly sank her tee into the ground, balanced her ball on top, hesitated over the choice of club then drew out her trusty two and a half wood. The ball soared cleanly away towards the hole. Why was it when you weren't really trying, things seemed to go so much better than when you gave all your attention to playing?

She stood to one side of Willoughby's tee and prayed that he would play an equally good shot.

The ball hooked badly into a copse of trees and they had to let a couple and a foursome through while they searched for it. Luckily, when they eventually found the ball, it was sitting in long grass on a tiny mound that made a natural tee and Willoughby had no trouble in reaching the green from there.

Polly had, as she'd intended, overshot it into some nasty rough from where it took her three shots to hole out. That made them all square.

Her next drive went straight down the middle of the fairway. Willoughby ended up in a bunker. He didn't say anything but jerked his golfing trolley into motion and set off angrily. Polly followed. Really, she thought, here they were, on a beautiful day, Willoughby wasn't two down as he might easily have been, so why couldn't he try to enjoy himself? And what the hell was she doing trying to keep him in the game?

Coming level with her ball she selected a five iron and aimed for the green. Not caring if Willoughby lost the hole, she put everything she had into the stroke; the ball landed four feet from the hole.

Willoughby took three to get out of the bunker and another two to get down. As he marked her card, his face twitched: a bad sign. It twitched like that when he had to fire someone, or the garage revealed that Polly's Mercedes had some expensive fault, or his favourite shirt was unironed.

There was a short walk to the fifth tee.

'What sort of a job do you think I ought to look for?' Polly asked pleasantly as they crossed a path that wound through the golf course.

'I can't imagine,' he said curtly. 'Anyone who'd hire you would want their head examined.'

'Oh, I don't know.' Her tone was blithe and carefree. 'I'm very good at organising, I speak excellent French and quite good Spanish, my people skills are often envied. I can imagine a number of organisations could make use of me.'

Willoughby said nothing.

Golf had seemed such a good idea to Polly when she'd suggested it. Walking companionably round she would be able to charm her husband out of the scratchy mood that seemed to be a constant with him ever since they'd returned from France. And perhaps she'd be able to find out if it was the new job or something else that was making him such a trial to live with.

She hoped it was the job.

But if this mood of his continued for much longer, she wasn't sure she cared.

Teeing up with some care, Polly hooked into the rough and watched Willoughby drive straight down the fairway. 'Oh, good shot!' She put as much enthusiasm as she could into her voice.

'What I should have been doing from the start,' he said grimly.

It took them a little time to find Polly's ball. 'I thought you said your golf was improving,' he snapped as they had to let another couple through before she spied it nestling in a small dip. She chipped out on to the fairway. 'You know what golf is,' she said through gritted teeth as she took out her three iron for a shot at the green. 'Just as you think everything might be coming good, your whole game goes to pot.' She took a swipe at the ball without thinking and it flew low but straight towards the green, gradually losing its impetus some six feet from the hole. 'There, that was better,' she said after it became clear that Willoughby wasn't going to praise the shot.

'Constancy is not one of your virtues,' he said.

'You mean consistency,' Polly corrected automatically.

'Do I?' He stalked off towards his ball.

Her heart in her mouth, she followed him.

He put his ball on the green, then they both watched it bounce over the back.

Polly decided to change the subject. 'How did things go at work this week?' she asked as they walked towards the green, Willoughby's whole body rigid with a bottled-up emotion she didn't want to guess at.

'There's absolutely no point in my discussing business with you. You haven't the faintest idea what it's about and couldn't begin to understand any of the problems I have to face every day.'

That got to her. As though she didn't have enough to contend with, considering his temper, his demands and Caroline's sulks.

She helped Willoughby find his ball in dead silence, watched him chip on to the green, too far to the right, then take two more to hole out.

She sank her putt in one.

They walked to the next tee in dead silence. The sixth was a short hole. Polly just knew as she took her five iron that she was going to land on the green.

Willoughby took two to reach it but only one putt. Polly took two.

From then on the battle grew grimmer and grimmer. Willoughby's game started to improve, Polly's to unravel as his snide remarks got to her.

Whatever she did, she couldn't recapture the accuracy of her earlier play, while Willoughby's got better and better. So did his temper. As they approached the eighteenth green, he was whistling tunelessly.

'For heaven's sake,' Polly ground out, 'can't you make a better noise than that?'

He said nothing but the unmusical whistling grew louder.

Shaking with anger, she lofted her approach shot over the green.

Willoughby laughed.

Polly flung down her wedge and strode off to the club house, leaving him on the fairway.

'Hey,' he called. 'I'm not taking your clubs, you'd better come back for them.'

She took no notice.

Just before she reached the club house, she turned round. Willoughby had chipped on to the green and was calmly lining up his putt. Still standing on the fairway was her trolley loaded with her clubs.

'I'll get them,' said a quiet voice at her elbow.

'Louise!'

'Mark's in the club house. Go and join him when you're ready.' Louise set off towards the trolley.

Polly went into the ladies' changing room, shaking. She'd ruined everything she'd tried to achieve. Willoughby's behaviour might have been reprehensible, but hers had been unforgivable. Flouncing

116

off in a temper like that! How could she have done it?

She stood under the shower and let the hot water lash on to her body.

Then with damp hair, dressed in a tartan skirt with toning shirt and knitted jacket, she went through to the bar. Willoughby, Mark and Louise were sitting at a table drinking tea.

'Well, who made an idiot of herself, then?' she said cheerfully as Mark stood up. Willoughby didn't move. 'Are you sure you want to take up this dreadful game, Lulu? I warn you, it brings out every worst instinct.'

'The only benefit is the exercise,' Mark agreed, holding out a chair for her. 'At least, that's what I try to tell myself when my play is even worse than usual. But I'm trying to persuade Louise that it is the best game in the world, never the same, always a challenge.'

'It could provide more excitement than I can cope with at the moment,' she said, smiling.

Polly tried to put her own misery behind her. 'You look extremely happy, Lulu, anything happened?'

'She's only gone and got a job,' Mark said with mock despair.

'No, really?'

'Temporary, for three weeks, but I shall be working in an office.' Louise sounded really excited by the prospect.

'Handing over the supervision of the builders to the interior decorator!'

'That's all part of her job, darling,' Louise said sweetly – too sweetly, Polly thought. 'Part of what we're paying for.'

'We should still have someone on the spot checking everything is going smoothly. Anyway,' Mark said to the others, 'by the sound of it, the job Louise has been hired to do will be so boring, I'll bet money she'll be wanting to give it up by the end of the first week.'

Polly hated the pompous way Mark spoke.

'There can be satisfaction in doing even a boring job properly, especially if it's only for three weeks,' she said. 'Willoughby wants me to get a job.'

'No!' Louise looked amazed.

'Oh, for heaven's sake, I meant you should find something to occupy your time, not go and join the office brigade. Find a charity that needs your skills or work for the Conservatives.' Willoughby sank back in his chair, thick lower lip pushed out sulkily. He'd changed from his golfing clothes into cavalry twill trousers with a tweed jacket and check shirt. Somehow he managed to look like a private apeing an officer in civvies.

Polly turned towards Louise. 'We've never really talked about how you enjoyed Paris, was it enormous fun?'

She noted the way Louise darted a look towards Mark before turning her attention back to Polly. 'Val Lewin and I had a great time. You remember I told you Val's husband was part of Mark's team?'

As Louise started to detail which of the shops Polly had recommended they'd visited, Mark and Willoughby struck up a conversation about who was going to be the next captain of the club.

Then Polly heard Louise say quietly, 'And we really loved meeting Jean-Paul. He – well, he was something special.'

'He is rather, isn't he?' she said casually. Over the other side of the table, Willoughby was filling Mark in on the finer points of his round. 'And you say he and Marie-Claire missed me?' Still that casual tone.

'Yes,' Louise stated simply.

Polly couldn't stop herself. 'Tell me where he took you? What you did together?'

It was sweet agony to listen to details of gorgeous French meals, exploring St Cloud, walking in the park with its view of Paris. After a little Polly had to stop her. 'Well, you certainly seem to have had a good time, even if Mark did have to work more than you'd hoped,' she said with a note of finality. Then she ignored Louise's look of surprise and tuned in to what Willoughby was saying. He was describing the company he was trying to rescue.

'The worst of it is, the workforce lacks any sort of morale,' he was saying to Mark. 'Don't seem able to believe we can make the company profitable. The foreman told me bluntly the other day that they're just waiting for us to pull the plug and sell off the assets. That's why they think we've bought it.'

'And have you?' Mark asked.

'That's the infuriating thing! We actually think the company's got a future.'

'Have you tried explaining that to them?' Polly asked before she could stop herself. At times Willoughby could overlook the obvious.

'Of course!' His irritation was plain. 'I've had meeting after meeting with the shop foreman and the representatives of the white-collar union. Trouble is, so many of the workers today don't belong and the unions are desperate to demonstrate they can take a tough line with management, so there's no trust anywhere along the line.'

'Tricky, that,' Mark murmured.

'Why not call all the workforce together and explain exactly what you have in mind for the firm?' continued Polly. In the old days she used to enjoy talking about business to Willoughby and he'd often asked her advice when it came to man management. It had never failed to amaze her how top management could ignore the commonsense approach when it came to dealing with their workers. 'They're probably desperate for accurate information and really worried about their jobs. If you can see how to turn the company round, why not explain it to all of them? With charts, slides and profit forecasts. Most of them won't be dummies. They'll be able to take it on board!'

Willoughby opened his mouth and for a moment she thought he was going to demolish her with one of his cutting remarks.

'Sounds good advice,' Mark put in as Willoughby hesitated, his pale hazel eyes suddenly thoughtful.

Slowly he nodded. 'You might have something there,' he agreed reflectively.

Polly gave a small sigh of relief.

Mark plunged into an account of some industrial dispute one of his clients had recently been involved in. Polly watched Willoughby listen but could see he was still turning her suggestion over in his mind.

'Do you think I'll ever be able to think like that?' Louise suddenly asked her.

'Of course!'

'Somehow I don't think I've got a business brain.'

'I'm not sure I have either. But I can see what makes people tick, and you're very good at that. Much better than me, actually, because you really care about them.'

'And don't you?' Louise asked, sounding surprised.

Polly shook her head. 'I get irritated by the way they can't see the most obvious things. It infuriates me how people dither about what to do or where to go.' She was suddenly conscious of the way Louise was looking at her.

'Do you always know exactly what you should do?' she asked.

Polly looked away and reached for the teapot. She waved it around the table but the men had moved off to consult a competition draw the secretary had just pinned on the notice board.

'Well?' Louise insisted.

'Damn it, of course there are times one doesn't know what's the right thing to do. When I lie awake at night torn apart by not knowing.'

'By really not knowing or by not being able to face making the right decision?' Louise asked gently.

Polly filled her cup. 'Oh, right, wrong . . . who's to say which is which?' she said bitterly. 'All I know is, if it weren't for Caroline I'd be off tomorrow.'

Louise's eyes widened. 'Bad as that?' She was clearly shaken by Polly's intensity.

'I couldn't begin to tell you the half of it!'

'Oh, poor Polly! I'd hate to be in that position.'

Polly looked across at Mark returning to the table with Willoughby. 'No chance of that, Lulu. Not while you've got that lovely man in tow.'

Louise followed her glance. 'I can't imagine loving anyone else,' she said quietly.

119

Chapter Fifteen

Mark drove Louise into the City on her first day. 'Remember, I won't be home this evening,' he said as she got out of the car. 'Staying in town. Got things to do at the office, and with the house the way it is at present, it's better if I spend the night at the flat.'

'That's fine, darling,' said Louise as she got out of the car, wishing she could stay at the flat with him and not have to go back and check on the builders. She glanced back inside. 'Have a nice day, I'll look forward to seeing you tomorrow night?'

'Probably.' Someone honked a horn. Mark put the car into gear and zoomed off.

Louise squared her shoulders and looked up at the tall building where she was going to work. It seemed to loom over her. She hitched her bag a little higher on her shoulder and walked in. It was only a quarter past eight and she wouldn't have been surprised if she'd had to wait outside the doors for someone to come along and open up.

But no, like Mark they appeared to start early. Mr Smythe's secretary, the June clone, came out to see her. 'Ah, Mrs Henderson. Brenda Reeves – we met the other day. I wasn't expecting you until nine.' She sounded a trifle harassed.

'If you're not ready for me, I can sit in reception and read the newspaper,' Louise offered, feeling wrong-footed.

'No, of course not. Your office is all ready but I shan't have much time to show you things.' Brenda Reeves was already walking fast down a corridor. Not the one where Harry Smythe's office was. Louise followed. 'Here we are.' A door was flung open on a small office.

There was a desk with a typewriter under a cover, a stationery box and a typist's chair. Set against one wall were two tables laden with dusty-looking files. A stack of storage bins against another wall held more. Finally there was another table with a collection of empty bins set on it.

Brenda took a file off the top of one of the piles. 'It's all quite simple. You find the client address in each file and type it on an index card, just like this one.' She opened a drawer in the desk and took out a card. 'There should be enough in here.' The stationery box was opened and Louise could see it was stacked with packets of more cards. Brenda laid the file on the desk. 'Then you note down the first date in the file, the last one, and the name of the lawyer who dealt with the client. Some of them have more than one file. Don't worry about the file contents, all you need to note down are the first and last dates. That's all. Then put the file in one of these bins.' Brenda touched one of the empty storage containers. 'When all these empty ones are filled, let me know and I'll organise a porter to take them away to storage and bring you another lot.'

'Do you want them in alphabetical order?' Louise asked brightly.

'No, that'll be done down in the storage room. Now, if you think you'll be all right, I'll let you get started.'

Brenda Reeves was almost out of the door.

'I'll be fine,' Louise asserted.

The door closed and she was on her own. Only then did she realise the room had no window and she would be working the whole day by artificial light.

Louise slowly took off her trenchcoat and looked around for somewhere to hang it. Failing to find a hook of any sort, she laid it across one of the filled storage containers. Then she picked up an armful of files and took them to the desk.

She sat down and investigated the typewriter. It was electric and must have been around some time because she found it not much different from the one she used at home. It took her a little time, though, before she got the hang of all the keys and the correcting tape, and a couple of cards had to go into the waste paper bin.

Then she settled to work in earnest.

Louise soon discovered why the job was considered confidential. A goodly proportion of the files seemed to belong to members of the aristocracy or eminent people. The firm that had been taken over appeared to have enjoyed a star-studded list of clients, though all the files seemed to have become inactive at least ten years previously. But no doubt inside many of the files there were still sensitive details pertaining to the clients.

At the interview Harry Smythe had told Louise that any other records of these old clients had been lost in the handover. 'We don't need to enter them on our computer records, it's highly unlikely we shall ever need them again. But we do need to know who is there.'

Indeed! Louise could see that if only a few of these inactive accounts could be revived, some interesting business could come the firm's way. She started carefully entering names, addresses and dates.

The files were all old and dusty. Soon the cuffs of her silk blouse were grimy and her fingers filthy. The dust also seemed to have entered her lungs.

At twelve-thirty Brenda popped her head round the door. 'How you doing? Good, glad you're OK. How many bins have you filled? Only two? Oh, dear. Well, I expect you'll get faster as you go along.

122

You can take an hour for lunch, any time between now and one.'

Louise eased her back, unaccustomed to sitting in one position for so long. 'Where's the best place to go?' she asked, hoping Brenda would suggest they lunch together.

'I generally get a sandwich at a little place just round the corner. Turn right as you leave the building then right again, you can't miss it.' And Brenda disappeared.

Louise looked at the closed door and decided she would go and get some sandwiches then bring them back to her desk. It was obvious she had to learn to up her production rate. She wondered how many more bins there were to be brought up.

By five-thirty, Louise's eyes were aching from working under the artificial light, her back felt as if it could be breaking and, despite frequent visits to the cloakroom, her fingers were ingrained with dirt. Brenda had not appeared to tell her when the day was considered officially over and it was a detail Louise had omitted to find out during her interview. Just as she was deciding that enough was definitely enough for her first day, the door opened and Harry Smythe entered.

'Thought I'd come along and see how you're doing.'

Louise managed to conjure up a bright smile. 'I've made a start anyway.' She picked up the pile of cards she'd typed that day and gave them to him.

He flipped quickly through them, pausing every now and again, then leaned against the table holding the finished files and went through them once more, slowly. 'Excellent, excellent,' he murmured as he got towards the end.

Louise had decided not to start on another but sat patiently waiting for him to finish.

'Splendid work, Mrs Henderson. Are you enjoying it?' Then, as if he realised that was an inane question, he added, 'I hope we've made you welcome.'

'Brenda Reeves has been very helpful.'

'Splendid, splendid. You off home now?' he asked as if noticing for the first time that Louise was sitting with her handbag on her knee, the cover on her typewriter.

'When do you normally finish?'

'The junior staff usually leave at five-thirty, many of the secretaries stay later, and few of the lawyers leave before around seven.'

'I think I'm probably junior, don't you?' Louise said firmly.

'Oh, quite, quite. We'll see how you get along. This what you've done today?' He turned and looked at the filled bins on the table he was leaning against. It was difficult to tell whether he thought the amount satisfactory or not.

'It took me a little time to get a system going,' she murmured. 'I should do more tomorrow.'

'Excellent, excellent. Well, we'll see you then.' And he was gone.

Louise picked up her coat, brushed off the dust, put it on and left the building. Her first day at work had produced a distinct feeling of deep anti-climax.

On Friday she had a quick lunch with Val Lewin.

'How's it all going?' was Val's first question.

'Stupefyingly, devastatingly, disastrously boring!'

'Oh, dear!'

'All I do is move a pile of files on to one side of my desk, type details on cards, moving each file in the process to the other side of the desk, then walk them over to the other side of the room. How I'm going to last out the three weeks, I don't know. The only way I can keep going is by timing the number of cards I type in an hour. Except I keep losing count!'

'You need an abacus,' Val laughed.

'And travelling to and from London is costing an absolute packet. I had no idea how expensive it was. If it weren't for Neil recommending me and Mark saying I'd pack it in after a week, I'd be sorely tempted to tell them to keep their job.'

'You won't be trying for something permanent there, then?'

'You know, I don't really think I'm cut out for office life.'

Louise picked up her fork and hungrily attacked the salad that she had ordered.

'Surely you can't judge every office by what you're experiencing in this job?'

Louise arrested the progress of a prawn-laden fork to her mouth. 'I'm not that stupid. No, it's the thought of having to go into an office every day, at the same time, to spend the whole day typing out letters or filling in cards, answering the telephone and maybe, just maybe, organising someone's diary for them. Forty-eight weeks of the year.'

'Ah, you wouldn't feel like that if it was something you really enjoyed.'

'Then there's Mark. He'd go bananas if I wasn't able to go with him on a particular trip. And what about the twins' vacations?'

Val looked amused. 'It's what I said when we first met: you don't really want a job at all. You have your home and your family.'

'I never realised what variety there was in my day before. But it's not enough,' Louise burst out passionately. 'Not now, not with the children gone.'

'Have you heard from them again?'

She nodded, pushing salad around the plate; her appetite seemed to have disappeared. 'We actually had a letter from James. They're up in Nepal at the moment. He says it's wonderful. They love the Indians, James said they are so warm and open. Apparently they're eating nothing but vegetarian food and he says they've never felt healthier. You can imagine how that made me feel!'

124

'Better practise some vegetarian dishes for when they return,' Val said dryly.

Louise said nothing. Blowing up like this to Val had made her feel even more confused and depressed.

'What does Mark say about it all?'

'I haven't seen him since Wednesday morning when he went up to Birmingham. With Robin,' Louise added casually. 'He seems to be going around with her an awful lot.' What she wanted was for Val to say it was only natural, Neil had said how closely they were working together, or something like that. Anything to suggest Louise's suspicions had no foundation.

'Robin, eh?' Val looked thoughtful.

Louise forced herself to look up. 'He's never liked working with women before. I mean, on the same sort of level. Secretaries are a different matter, of course.'

'Of course,' Val echoed ironically. 'Neil is wondering just what her arrival in the department is going to mean to Mark,' she added thoughtfully.

'What do you mean?'

'Whether he'll be ratified in his position as acting head of the department or whether the advent of Robin could mean they aren't so happy with Mark. Apparently she's very bright.'

Louise gazed at her open-mouthed. It had never occurred to her that Robin could be threatening Mark professionally.

'Oh, I'm sure Neil must have got it wrong,' she declared. 'Mark would have told me if that were the case.'

'Of course,' Val agreed hastily.

Louise had no trouble rejecting Val's suggestion. She had unassailable confidence in Mark's ability and business skills. His position in the firm, as far as she was concerned, was impregnable. His upward progress ever since they'd married had never faltered and it had never occurred to her that it might. Nor could she even begin to imagine that Robin Howard would be a threat to that progress, however bright Neil thought she was.

'He's in Birmingham at the moment but he'll be back for the weekend, thank heavens,' Louise continued. 'But he says next week he'll stay mostly in the flat. The decorators are all over the house, and anyway he will be working late.' She hoped she could get him to come home on Wednesday; she wasn't sure there were enough clean shirts to see him through to the end of the week.

'I don't really get this flat business,' Val said thoughtfully, finishing her salad. 'Neil wouldn't dream of having one in London and it takes just as long to get back to Hampstead as it does for Mark to get home.'

'The flat's for the twins, when they need a place in London.' Even as she said it, Louise began to wonder exactly what Mark's motivation had been.

125

'Uh huh!'

'I trust Mark,' Louise said angrily, suddenly feeling out of sympathy with her friend for the first time.

Val stretched out a hand and laid it briefly on Louise's. 'I'm sorry, that was out of order. Of course you do.'

Louise felt there was something more Val could have said, maybe how much she liked Mark, how much Neil admired him. She looked at her watch. 'We'd better ask for the bill. I've got to go, I daren't be late.'

That night Louise hurried to catch the train so she'd be back before Mark. She had deliberately not asked him to pick her up.

She drove from the station to the supermarket and picked up the same ready-made chicken dish that Nicky had fed her with the other week and did her shopping for the rest of the weekend. At least if Mark were staying in the flat she wouldn't have to think about cooking beyond Monday. As she reached into the chill cabinet stacked with inviting-looking packages of ready-prepared meals, she thought again that if only she didn't have to monitor what the decorators had done each evening, she could have joined him there. But if the decorators hadn't been in possession of the house, Mark would be coming home. Wouldn't he?

He arrived back just before eight, looking tired. He toured the house, seeing what had been achieved during the week, and expressed himself dissatisfied. 'I can't think what they've been up to. You better get on to Marsha whatever her name is and raise stink.'

Louise immediately felt put on the defensive. 'I think they've done more than it looks like, darling. Preparation work always takes forever. What counts is whether they are still on target for finishing everything by Christmas.'

'They'd better be!'

When Louise produced supper, Mark ate half his portion then pushed the rest away. 'I don't know what this is but it definitely isn't one of your better efforts.'

'I'm sorry, I didn't have time to cook properly, this is ready-prepared. I thought it tasted all right when I had it at Nicky's.'

'Think again,' he said briefly.

Louise remembered Colin complimenting Nicky on the meal she'd got together so quickly.

She simmered like a pan being brought to the boil, anger bubbling away beneath the surface.

'The trouble is,' she said as she brought in cheese, 'I've spoilt you.'

That startled him. 'Spoilt? Me?'

'Yes.' She banged the cheese board on the table. 'Always making sure I cooked you something delicious.'

She sat down and the absence of James and Emma filled her with

126

physical pain. Now, more than ever, she missed them. The house, full as it was with decorators, seemed empty to her and she longed for their presence. Emma could have got Mark out of his sulks, or James would have provided a diversion. Even if it had made the tension worse in one way, it would have given her something else to think about, allowed her to put into practice her well-honed ability to mediate and interpret her two men to each other.

Mark frowned as he inspected the piece of Cheddar she'd offered.

'That's farmhouse cheese, non-pasteurised,' she told him.

'Looks good,' he said absently, and helped himself to a large chunk.

Louise looked across the table at her husband, eating cheese with the sort of attentiveness he gave his papers. She'd thought she knew him through and through. His ambition, his zest for life, his impatience with James's moodiness and involvement with music, his enjoyment of her and Emma's sportiness, the way they were attractive to men, his trust in both of them.

What had happened? How had he changed so much? Become so careless of her feelings, so selfish? He couldn't have been like this always, could he? Was it that without the children to involve her so completely, she saw him in a different light.

How could she be so understanding of her husband when he was at odds with their son and find him so opaque when they were on their own together? Was it the advent of Robin Howard or was it that her perception of him had changed? She tried to put such thoughts behind her. This was her beloved husband. If anybody had changed, it had to be her.

'Oh, by the way,' Mark said, putting two oatcakes on his plate with more cheese, 'I'm off to Denmark next week. You'd better make sure I've got enough shirts and underpants to take. I'll probably be gone at least ten days.'

'When are you off?'

'Tuesday,' he said briefly.

That meant Louise would have to catch up on the ironing over the weekend. And that there'd hardly be time to try and get their relationship back on its previous footing before he was off.

'Is it an interesting job?' she asked. When they were first married she'd tried to involve herself with his work. But he'd always told her it was some boring auditing job and he'd rather not talk about it. Which had set a pattern. Even when his work had become more interesting and he'd started bringing papers back in the evening, then spending the weekend working, he'd never wanted to talk about what he was doing. It hadn't taken long for Louise, who'd easily persuaded herself she wouldn't have understood even if he had told her, to stop asking questions.

'New clients, came to us out of the blue. It's a major new account,' Mark said briefly.

She braced herself to ask the only question that really concerned her. 'Robin going as well?' she asked as casually as she could.

'Yes, damn it!' Mark snarled at her. But his anger was obviously directed against the absent Robin.

Louise's heart leaped with hope. 'That's a bit of an extreme reaction. I thought you liked her?'

'Nothing against her as a woman but I can't see why Douglas wants her on this account as well as me. It's a departure from our normal practice and I'm perfectly able to look after the situation.'

Did he protest too much? 'Ah, well, darling, Douglas probably thinks she'll disarm the clients with her charm.'

'What a crass remark! You know nothing about the situation.'

'No need to snap my head off, Mark. I'm only trying to show an interest in what your work involves.' Louise got up and started collecting together the remains of their meal.

He looked slightly shamefaced. 'I suppose I ought to be grateful for it but you really don't understand anything of what goes on and it's been a tough week. By the way, how's your job going? Bored with it yet?'

'It's not a barrel of laughs but I'm satisfied with my progress.' She stalked out of the room with immense dignity.

Mark spent the weekend immersed in papers, his only exercise a round of golf on Sunday morning. The weather continued bright and sunny but there was a bite now to the air. Louise, missing her twice-weekly tennis, rang round a few friends trying to find either a partner or a four. It was hopeless. Everyone was already organised for the weekend. Polly sounded breathless as she said they would be away. 'Pooh – Caroline, that is – has an exeat this weekend. We're taking her to stay with my mother-in-law.'

Willoughby's mother was a matriarch of the old sort. He was terrified of her but Polly had taken her measure during their engagement and enjoyed their battles. Mrs Fawkes lived in a large, draughty house in Cornwall. Heaven in the summer, Polly said, but hell in the winter. 'Can't think why Cornwall is said to be such a mild climate,' she always said when facing a trip in the cold weather, 'I never have enough clothes and always have to take a hot water bottle.'

'Packed your thermals?' asked Louise now.

'What? Oh, yes, thermals. Got them for us all. But I held a gun to Ma's head last winter until she bought electric blankets for each of the beds. I told her otherwise we'd only come in the summer. So I shan't need the boogly.'

'How are things?' Louise probed tentatively as Polly seemed to recapture some of her old verve.

'Things? Oh, things are fine,' she said brightly. 'Just coming, Willoughby,' she called. 'Sorry, Lulu, have to go, Willoughby's waiting. We're picking Pooh up on the way. Talk to you soon.'

Nicky sounded even more distracted. 'The house is a pit, I've just got to do something to the kitchen. And we're taking the boys out tomorrow. Why is every weekend such a rush? Every Friday evening I feel like Montgomery facing Alamein.'

'You'll win. You've got everything going for you.'

'You think so?' Nicky's voice was odd. 'Look, can't talk now, I'm in the middle of defrosting the freezer.'

'I'll give you a ring next week, see if we can get together then,' Louise promised. She looked in on Mark, frowning over a stack of papers in the study. 'Want a quick game of tennis?'

'Not a chance,' he said without looking up.

'All work and no play, Jack. Don't want to get dull around the office, do we?'

It was the wrong angle. He glanced up, his face unreadable. 'Let me say it once and for all, Louise. I HAVE TO WORK! Work to keep the house over our heads, the kids swanning round the world and you in designer clothes. If I don't get my head round this lot, we can say goodbye to all that.'

She went to put on trainers, feeling frightened. This wasn't a Mark she knew. What did he mean, keep the house over their heads? It wasn't as though they had a mortgage. James and Emma were travelling on their own savings and when had she ever demanded designer clothes? She would be perfectly happy shopping at Marks and Spencers. Oh, Mark could really be a sod at times.

She put on a track suit and went for a run round the neighbourhood, pounding out her frustration, feeling her lungs expand and her body pushing itself in physical activity. Lately she'd had too little of this. Gradually she put Mark's odd mood out of her mind but deep inside herself she was terrified they were drifting apart.

Gradually the pressure involved in combining a job and keeping in touch with the refurbishment on the house began to tell on Louise. Marsha visited the house twice a week to check on progress but rang her every morning so any problems could be discussed.

When Louise had started her job, she'd told Brenda Reeves that she would have to take a personal call each morning; she didn't want Brenda walking into her office while she was on the phone and then have to apologise for taking the time, and for once Brenda had appeared thoroughly understanding.

On Wednesday Louise arrived at work earlier than usual. Mark had gone off to Denmark in a foul mood and she had felt herself gradually relax with the realisation she had ten clear days ahead of her. By the time he returned, she would have finished the job and could regain control of the house and, hopefully, her marriage.

The sight of the now familiar table with its load of files for once was welcoming. This was work she understood now and was in control of. All right, it was repetitive and boring, and didn't occupy her mind in any way; in fact it had a disconcerting habit of wondering just what some of the files contained. But she was whipping through the work now. Filled containers continued to arrive. She was quite friendly with the porter who brought fresh boxes and removed the completed ones.

'More from beyond the grave,' Peter would remark, hauling a box off a trolley load and banging it on to the table. 'Don't know what they're worried about. The tax man can't reach you there, can 'e?'

'Ours not to question why,' Louise would answer sententiously, then give him a smile. 'How's the squash going, then?' She'd found out not only that he played every weekend but that he wasn't married and lived on his own. Liked it, he said, partners were only a problem. But he belonged to a sports club and spent a lot of time there. Had to keep in trim. It was important, wasn't it?

'Certainly is, especially when you have to haul loads like this around,' Louise had said.

But the cheerful exchanges with Peter were small compensation for the loss of her relationship with Mrs Parks. Louise treasured the notes her cleaner would leave after she'd finished work. Tuesday's had said, 'Cleared out boxroom today. It's history up there, it is. Suggest discard old tennis stuff and take jumble to Oxfam. Could make use of that cradle for a bit, Karen's expecting her first. Any ideas what I do Friday, seeing as how dusting is redundant?'

Louise longed for the day when she could talk to Mrs Parks about becoming a grandmother. She started typing her cards on Wednesday wondering whether she should recover the old cradle or if Mrs Parks would prefer to do that herself.

Marsha rang and Louise gave her daily report. 'They really do seem to be getting a move on now. It's exciting getting home and seeing what they've done. Look, do you think they could manage to do our bedroom and bathrooms over the next ten days? It would be wonderful for Mark to return and find them ready.' The drawing room was completed and so was the dining room. If he didn't have to move out of their bedroom, it would surely put him in a better temper.

'I'll make sure it's done,' Marsha said equably. Louise liked the way nothing seemed to put her out.

On Friday morning, on her way to the little coffee room to make one of the interminable cups that kept her going, Louise met Brenda Reeves.

'Mrs Henderson, so pleased to see you. I was wondering, could you spare me a few moments in my office?'

Had she transgressed some company code of practice? Well, only a few more days and she'd be finished with this place.

'Of course, Mrs Reeves.'

Louise followed the senior secretary back along the corridor.

130

Mrs Reeves enjoyed a spacious office well-furnished with an L-shaped desk equipped with word processor, printer, several telephones and trays for papers. A junior was arranging a large blotter book on the front of the desk as they entered.

'I've done the letters, Mrs Reeves,' she said. A mouse of a girl who hid behind a fall of brown hair, she waited nervously.

'Thank you, Jenny. Here's the report Mr Smythe has amended. Please correct and print it off for me. We need six copies by this afternoon.'

'Right, Mrs Reeves,' the mouse said and scuttled out of the office clutching a pile of papers.

Mrs Reeves sat down behind her desk and waved Louise towards a chair on the other side. 'Do sit down, Mrs Henderson. Or may I call you Louise?'

'Mrs Henderson always makes me feel I'm something out of the ark,' Louise giggled, sitting down.

Perhaps it wasn't the best thing to have said.

Brenda Reeves considered the remark then seemed to decide she had better let it pass. She sat back in her chair and bestowed a benevolent smile on Louise. 'I have to tell you how impressed we have been by the way you have tackled this job.'

'Really?' Louise was astonished and pleased.

'Not easy. Confidentiality required but also,' Brenda hesitated while she searched for the word, 'stickability!'

Louise could think of nothing to say.

'I must tell you that when you started, I gave you two days.'

'Why?'

'Couldn't see why you would want to stick it. It didn't look as though you needed the money. I reckoned you'd got bored at home and didn't realise what you'd let yourself in for.'

How right she'd been! Had it not been for the fact she didn't want to let Neil down, and Mark's attitude, Louise might well have proved her right.

'But now, well, we can see you have stamina and dependability and are meticulous. Your cards are a pleasure to scan!'

Louise was overwhelmed.

'Tell me, my dear, what is your shorthand like?'

Louise laughed. 'Never been one of my strong points, Brenda.'

'Usually I am known as Mrs Reeves but I see no reason why we should stand on ceremony, at least inside my office. Hmm, pity that.'

'Luckily I don't need it most of the time.'

'Yes, well, I am going to need another junior. I was wondering whether you would be interested in the position? You would need to do a word processing course but that should not be difficult for you. As a trained typist you will pick up the threads very quickly. I would, though, have to test your shorthand.'

131

'Brenda, I'm overwhelmed, of course, but I'm afraid I'm not interested in a permanent job.'

'You aren't? Then what, pray, are you doing working on our files?'

'You see, I'm looking for something and I thought an office job might be it. But, well, now I see that I couldn't commit myself to the hours. My husband and family, you see,' Louise tried to explain.

Brenda Reeves looked considerably put out. 'Well, you might have said!'

'I didn't realise it was important. I want to finish the job I was hired for, and this is obviously a very good company to work for,' she added hastily, 'and I'm very grateful that it's shown me I need to look for something with more flexible hours.'

'I see.' Brenda Reeves said slowly, studying her even more intently. Then her manner changed completely. 'Well, now, why don't we look at what your strengths and weaknesses are? Maybe I can propose something that would suit you better . . .'

Chapter Sixteen

'Oh, good shot!' Colin called as Mark whipped a ball from the back of the court at an unplayable angle.

Mark served hard and watched in satisfaction as Colin failed to get anywhere near the ball to return. 'My game, I think. Shall we have another?'

Colin shook his head, panting. 'You've played me out. Let's go and get a beer.'

As he showered and towelled his hair dry, Mark congratulated himself on his game. He could feel every muscle in his body loose and limber. Forty-four, huh? It wasn't any different from thirty-four. He ran a comb through his curly hair then pulled in his stomach under his Daks turquoise sweat shirt and dark blue trousers. 'Right, let's hit the bar,' he said.

Colin was still pulling on a jumper that had seen better days. He hurriedly stuffed his squash kit into a bag and ran a hand over his still wet, thinning hair. 'What are you doing for Christmas?'

Mark shrugged as he placed his sports bag in his locker. 'Usual, I suppose. Eat and drink too much, get fed up with my mother-in-law, bawl out the kids and return to the office as quickly as possible.' Then he remembered. 'Except we shan't have James and Emma with us this year. Or Dad.' He'd been with Mark and Louise last year, this Christmas would be spent with Fiona or Patricia.

They reached the bar and Mark ordered two pints of bitter. He still hadn't got used to the fact that the twins had left home. But at least he hadn't gone overboard about it.

'Thought you might be going away, seeing as how you didn't have the family with you?'

'Funny, Lulu suggested something like that but I don't know. It's too late to get in anywhere good and we'd have to take her mother and, well . . .'

''Nough said,' Colin remarked dryly.

'Not that I don't get on with my mother-in-law but there are limits.'

'Quite!'

'Then we have my sisters and their families coming to us on Boxing Day, plus Dad. But without the kids it hardly seems the same. Still, it'll be an ideal time for them to see the house. Only right they should check what we've done to it.' Mark had a feeling of deep satisfaction at the thought of how good the house was beginning to look. Marsha had done a first-class job and was talking about a feature on the decor in one of the glossy magazines. One should never alert burglars but Mark rather liked the idea of his home featuring amongst those of the beautiful people.

'Decoration finished yet?' Colin made it sound as though they'd just slapped some new wallpaper on, Mark thought, then realised as his friend settled down in one of the club's comfortable chairs that he looked tired. Needed to play squash or tennis more regularly; it had been weeks since they'd had a game together.

'Nearly there. Since Lulu gave up spending every day in London and could get behind the builders, things have moved more quickly.'

'Not working anymore then?'

'Not exactly. She's found some sort of Orphan Annie establishment to work for.'

'Orphan Annie?'

'You know – want your child collected from school and put on a plane, your dog walked or house sat, you get in touch with this lot.'

'And Louise is working for them?'

'Says it gives her something to do but doesn't commit her to a nine-to-five job. So far she's escorted three young monsters from Paddington to Heathrow, taken an old duck to hospital for a small eye operation then home again, driven two dogs from quarantine in Dover to their elderly owners in Wales, and grandfather-sat from ten till four for a curmudgeonly old sod in Berkshire. He spent the whole time telling her how his son and daughter-in-law abused him, and suggesting they go away together. Beats my why she feels she has to go and do anything like that. I mean, there's the Conservatives, they'd be delighted if she could give them some of her time, not to mention any number of charities. She doesn't seem to see that it demeans me, her going out to work in this way. Makes it look as if I can't earn enough to give her what she wants.'

Colin's pale grey eyes flickered. He ran a hand over the bald part of his head and, too late, Mark remembered. 'Nicky still enjoying her job?' he asked, unable to think of a tactful way of repairing his error.

Colin took a deep draught of his bitter. 'Loves it,' he said briefly. Then he put his glass down on the small table between them and leaned forward. 'Thing is, Mark, I've been meaning to tell you – I'm thinking of moving out to the country.'

Mark stared at him, for the moment lost for words.

'We could sell the house, you see, realise some capital and set it to work to produce income.'

Mark saw immediately what Colin meant. 'What are the chances of a worthwhile country practice?' he asked shrewdly.

'Still looking into it but I've heard of one in Exeter which sounds very promising.'

'Nicky keen on the idea?'

Colin's gaze dropped again and he drew a finger through a little pool of spilt beer on the table. 'She'll come round eventually,' he said lamely.

Mark wondered about that.

'Of course she will,' he said heartily. 'She knows what a wife's place is. After all, there's a job market in Exeter, right?'

'Right,' Colin said miserably.

'Mark, Colin! Mind if I join you?'

Mark looked up to see Willoughby hovering uncertainly beside them. As always, he looked out of place in the club, his tweed jacket too hairy, his tie too formal, his trousers too dark, his eyes too wary.

Mark grabbed a nearby chair by the arm and dragged it towards their table. 'Sure, take a pew. How's things?' He was delighted to see Willoughby. They'd had lunch a couple of times since the Fawkeses had returned from Paris and he had high hopes of securing the account of Willoughby's new company. Which could give him an entrée into the group – rumour had it the holding board was dissatisfied with their current accountants. That would be the sort of coup Mark desperately needed. Robin Howard had brought in three big accounts since she'd joined the department. He had a sudden, unsettling vision of her announcing her latest triumph, svelte and charming in her usual uniform of grey suit and soft cream blouse, her crisp tones contrasting with the femininity of her appearance.

Willoughby sat himself down heavily, put his glass on the table, spread his knees and dropped his big hands between them. 'Could be worse, I suppose,' he said gloomily.

'Polly giving trouble?' Mark angled cheerfully. Another remark he regretted as he watched Willoughby's expression close down, eyelids hooding the sharp hazel eyes.

'She's fine,' he said curtly.

'And Pooh?'

'Enjoying school, she says.' He seemed to relax slightly. 'We're both looking forward to her coming home for the holidays.'

'What are you doing for Christmas?'

Willoughby's expression became hunted. 'Polly keeps on talking about going to Paris.'

'Too late now, old boy, everything will have been booked,' Mark offered jovially. 'Just been talking to Colin about our plans. Lulu's not at all keen on just having the family on Boxing Day so why don't we make it a proper party and have both of you over as well?' He glanced from Willoughby to Colin. 'After all, it could be the last time.'

'What do you mean?' Willoughby ground out in tones of deep

suspicion. 'Has Louise said anything?'

'I've just told Mark I'm thinking of relocating to Exeter,' Colin said quietly. 'But nothing's settled yet. I'd be obliged if you didn't mention anything to Polly, or to Louise,' he added, switching his attention back to Mark.

'Won't Nicky have told her?'

Colin shrugged his shoulders. 'Maybe. But if not, don't, OK?'

'Of course, of course. So, how about Boxing Day? Lunchtime together with kids. It'll be stand and fight for your food but should offer a bit of relief from the all-family syndrome. You both on?'

'Hadn't you better check with Louise first?' offered Colin. But Mark could see he looked pleased at the suggestion. And Willoughby's face had lightened. 'Oh, she'll think it's a great idea,' Mark said confidently.

Going home, he began to have second thoughts. He could never tell how Louise was going to react to anything these days. And she'd shown an unnerving ability to keep on about Robin. Take the night he'd got back from Denmark the other week.

He'd no sooner got into the house, tired and frazzled by the way things had turned out, than she was on at him, asking how things had gone.

'Oh, the job went extremely well,' he had said shortly, unable to forget how Robin had taken command and proved she could handle matters every bit as well as he could. He'd collapsed into his usual chair and flicked on the television. Normally Louise would have taken this as a sign he didn't want to talk.

Instead, 'How was Robin?'

He'd flicked the remote control rapidly through several stations then allowed the set to remain on Channel Four News. 'She was extremely effective.' He'd given his attention to the newscast and after a few minutes Louise had departed in a huff to the kitchen.

He couldn't imagine how Louise had somehow got it into her head that he was attracted to Robin. That she had seemed undeniable. But, really, Robin was the last woman in the world with whom he would think of having an affair.

Now Mark parked his car and went into the kitchen. He felt deep satisfaction as he looked around at the carefully orchestrated old dressers and cupboards that had been fitted around the new Aga and the old island unit. The eating area was much the same but the table had been changed for one of antique pine. When Louise had protested that she didn't want to have to keep polishing it, Marsha had said she should keep a cloth on it for everyday use. The banquette covering had been changed from leatherette to a heavy duty cotton in a vaguely ethnic print in bright colours. The same material had been used for Roman blinds at the windows and a laminated cloth for the table. Mark considered the final effect striking but easy to live with. Yes, Marsha had proved a real find.

Louise was taking a quiche out of the Aga. 'How was Colin?' she asked as Mark dumped his sports bag on the floor.

'Fine. Want a drink?'

She shook her head, slipped the quiche on to a plate and took it over to the table. 'Has he found a country practice yet?'

'So you know about that?'

'Nicky told me. She's devastated, hates the very thought of it and doesn't think moving's going to raise their income much anyway.'

'Colin sounds pretty set on the idea.' Mark eased himself on to the banquette behind the table.

'So I suppose that makes it all right?' Louise enquired, bringing over a salad.

Mark decided to ignore this. 'Willoughby was at the club. He says Polly wants to spend Christmas in Paris but he's against it.' Too late he saw where that had led him and plunged swiftly on as he cut into the flan: 'I thought it would – might,' he swiftly corrected himself, 'be a good idea if we widened the Boxing Day party, as the kids won't be with us, and asked the Fawkeses and Webbers as well. What do you think?' He added salad to the plate of quiche.

'So they can all admire the new decor!' Louise's tone was caustic.

'It will be finished in time?' Mark was suddenly anxious. There seemed an awful lot to do upstairs still, though it had been a great relief to return from Denmark and find their bedroom and his bathroom and dressing area had been done. He'd not been looking forward to sleeping in a strange bed and having his clothes all over the place.

'It will,' Louise said wearily. 'Marsha and the builders have promised and I'm not doing anymore Orphan Annie jobs until after the New Year so I can keep right on top of the situation and make sure Christmas goes well. Though without the kids it really hardly seems worth decorating, let alone cooking a turkey.'

'But I love turkey!'

Louise gave a big sigh as she took a small slice of quiche and added a spoonful of salad. 'And turkey you will get, I promise.' She gave him a quick smile that looked as though she'd dragged it up from somewhere deep inside her, where it was kept for emergencies.

'So, what do you think about Boxing Day?'

'I suppose it might be a good idea.'

Where was the Louise who used to pounce on this sort of suggestion with enthusiasm and immediately start turning it into something even better?

'That is, unless they're doing something else?'

'No, neither of them is,' Mark said thoughtlessly.

'You mean, you've asked them already? Really, you might have discussed it with me first!'

'I only mentioned it as an idea! Promise! I said you had to be consulted first.'

'And what will I look like if I say no?'

'We can always say the family wanted it kept just for family. Come on, darling, isn't it a good idea? You know it's always sticky having Fiona and Patricia and their families, and with Emma and James away it'll be even worse. This way it'll be something new. We could ask some other people as well, make it a real thrash.'

'I don't know if I've got the energy to cope with all those people.' She did look tired.

'Get caterers in.'

'Three weeks before Christmas? Honestly, Mark, you have no idea about this sort of thing. Boxing Day parties have to be booked months in advance.'

'Bet you could find someone if you really tried.'

'No, we'll keep it to thirty maximum and I'll be able to cope.' Louise got up and brought some cheese over to the table, her face thoughtful. 'Actually, you're right, it could be quite fun. We could organise some games . . .'

'No games!' Mark said firmly. 'The young can play snooker and the rest of us can be civilised in the drawing room.'

'Civilised? On Boxing Day?'

Christmas did not work out happily for Mark.

Christmas Eve should have started well. In the late afternoon there was a telephone call from Emma and James. They took it in Mark's study using his conference facility.

James came on first. 'Hi, son,' said Mark.

'Hello, darling.' Louise sounded unbelievably happy.

'Hope you and Emma are all right, and haven't got Delhi belly?' Betty asked anxiously.

'We've having a fabulous time,' James said. 'And we're in China now. It's cold but fantastic.' He sounded happy and mature.

Mark relaxed and felt that maybe the trip had been a good idea after all.

Then Emma came on. 'Hi, gang! You all set for Christmas?'

'Your mother's done a fabulous job on the house. Huge great tree in the hall, swags of greenery and gilded doodads in the drawing room and dining room, Christmas cards everywhere,' Mark assured her. He didn't say that tears had streamed down Louise's face as she'd hung the tree with all the favourite bits and pieces they had collected over the years.

He had wanted to go to her, take her in his arms and say that it was all right, they had each other and Emma and James would soon be back. But something had prevented him. Perhaps it was that Louise had been in tears too often since the children had left. Perhaps because he himself felt their loss and his wife didn't seem to realise she wasn't the only one affected by their absence.

'The house has all been redecorated,' Betty said. 'It's looking quite gorgeous. You won't recognise the place.'

'You might have a bit of trouble recognising *me*,' Emma said, her voice sounding distant for the first time. 'I've had a nose job.'

'Nose job? What does she mean?' gasped her grandmother.

'Your nose has always looked great,' Mark shouted.

'Looks even better now,' Emma said gaily from all those thousands of miles away. 'I've had it pierced and your Christmas present to me has been a diamond. It's on the left nostril.'

'Looks great.' James was suddenly back on the line. 'Don't worry about her, you'll like the result.'

Easy enough for him to say. Mark was outraged. 'You'll have it taken out the moment you get home, you hear? I won't have you wearing it here.'

'Hush,' Louise hissed at him. 'Darling, it sounds sensational, try and send us a photograph,' she said to the telephone. Mark said nothing more during the call.

'How could you say that to her?' Louise stormed when the connection had been severed. 'When she's so far away?'

'What on earth is everyone going to think?' Mark ground out through clenched teeth.

'There's nothing we can do about it,' Louise insisted. 'It's her nose and her decision as to how she spends the money you sent her. Now, what time would you both like supper? I thought we shouldn't eat too early, not if we're going to the midnight service.'

It was a long-standing tradition that they went every Christmas Eve. Not only did they all like the atmosphere and coming back in the crisp night air knowing Christmas had actually arrived, but Louise appreciated having Christmas morning free for the final preparations.

'I don't think I can manage midnight this year,' Betty said plaintively. 'Since my fall I don't seem to have as much strength. I'd been hoping we could go in the morning. Such fun with all the carols.'

'They have carols at the midnight service too,' Mark said stiffly.

'Well, it wouldn't hurt us to make a change this year,' Louise put in quickly. 'Everything else is so different, why not church as well?'

'Why don't you and I go?' he suggested, straightening his desk, not looking at Betty, ensconced in the chair on the other side, her expression gloomy. It would be good to have Louise to himself, for them to take Communion and experience the Christmas spirit together.

'Would you go in the morning as well?' she asked, her head on one side, glancing from her mother to her husband.

'Once is quite enough for me but you two go.'

'It's no fun if we don't all go together,' Louise said firmly. Mark realised she wasn't going to leave her mother on her own. He sighed heavily. It seemed it would have to be the morning service. To try

139

and help Louise, he suggested they ate in the evening instead of lunchtime.

Once again it was Betty who objected and Louise who sided with her mother, with the result that Mark entertained his mother-in-law after they all got back from church while Louise banged pots in the kitchen, working desperately to get everything ready.

As Betty droned on about some neighbour of hers and the cavalier way she'd behaved over some problem with the cat, Mark wondered what had happened to the delightful habit she'd had of asking his opinion about matters such as the government and how the economy was doing. She'd never showed any sign of understanding what he told her, but at least it had created the warm feeling that she was interested in him and his views and wanted to share in his life.

Now it appeared that all she wanted was for Mark to be interested in her.

It was too much to ask. When, after the meal, the rest of the day slid into television watching with the choice of programme dictated by Betty, Mark took himself off to his study and occupied himself with computer games.

Finally bored with that, he found his mother-in-law had gone to bed and Louise was clearing away the debris of the light supper she'd served earlier.

'Christ, your mother's turned into a drag,' he said, leaning against the island unit and watching her. 'How long is she staying?'

'It would help if you'd jolly her along. What's happened to you? You always used to be so good with her.' Louise sounded stressed. She stuffed glasses into the washing-up machine without her usual care.

'Well, Christmas used to be a fun time. I can't say today has been any fun at all, not for me,' he said, thinking of previous years, with Emma and James excited over their presents and all of them singing to James's guitar: Emma in her contralto, Louise in a clear, true soprano and him off-key. It was the only time Mark felt easy with James's obsession with music. He remembered the way they used to sit round the Christmas table after the meal had finished, drinking port, paper hats on their heads, reading silly mottos and cracking jokes with the nuts. Betty had joined in all that, singing along with them, telling not unfunny anecdotes – very different from the dampening influence she'd been today.

'I'm sorry.' Louise's voice faltered but she straightened herself and looked at him. Her eyes were angry, her mouth tense. 'Mother's feeling her age. This evening she was wondering what she'd done to upset you.' Her voice strengthened as she spoke. ' "Mark always used to be so nice to me," was what she said.'

He felt unpleasantly like a heel.

'So I'd be grateful if you could do a little more to help things

140

along tomorrow.' Louise scratched at the bottom of the scrambled egg saucepan, her movements jerky. 'After all, the party was your idea.'

'I know,' he ground out. 'You don't have to remind me.'

They went up to bed out of charity with each other. Mark undressed in his bathroom, regretting the days when they'd shared facilities. He'd always enjoyed watching Louise undress, seeing the layers come off and reveal her sleek little body. He'd enjoyed the jostling for position at the basin, the way she'd help hang up his clothes. It had all been part of their togetherness.

By the time he was ready to slip into bed, Louise was already there, hunched over under the duvet, her steady breathing suggesting she was fast asleep. Mark put a hand firmly on her shoulder and ran it down her arm then felt underneath for her breast, feeling if only they could share physical passion, it would bring them closer together.

Louise hunched some more and made protesting noises.

All the frustrations of the day rose in him with the bitterness of gall.

He flung back the duvet angrily. 'Since you obviously don't care to have me in the same bed, I shall spend the night in my dressing room,' he said, and marched off there.

The effect of outraged dignity he felt he'd created was somewhat spoiled when he found that, underneath its heavy brown cover, the bed was unmade. He toyed with the idea of going to James's room, then decided that sleeping on an underblanket with a naked duvet couldn't be too bad for one night.

The makeshift accommodation proved sufficiently comfortable for him to oversleep the following morning. By the time he woke, Louise had already gone downstairs.

As he showered and dressed, he found the events of the previous day replaying themselves in his mind like the video of a programme it had been a mistake to record.

By the time he reached the kitchen, he had an uneasy feeling he should apologise to Louise but the sight of her preparing to take breakfast up to Betty brought back his resentment. 'Make her too comfortable and she'll never leave,' he muttered. Louise picked up the tray and swept out of the kitchen with her expression thunderous.

Mark helped himself to breakfast then tried to make himself useful setting up the table in the hall beside the Christmas tree for the champagne and other drinks, filling large buckets with the ice he'd stocked up on before the holiday and inserting the already chilled bottles. At least, he thought, putting a lump of sugar in each glass then adding a couple of drops of Angostura bitters, his family were going to be impressed by the house. He was really looking forward to showing his father and sisters what had been achieved.

141

He went and took a last look around the drawing room, admired its deep terracotta walls, the sumptuous Italian upholstery and the restrained splendour of the curtains. He particularly liked the collections of cushions on the sofas and chairs. In a variety of contrasting and toning materials, they really made you want to sink into the comfort they promised. A huge wood fire was blazing in the fireplace, where Mrs Parks had polished the brass fender until it rivalled gold.

'Have you got the drinks ready?' Louise asked, coming in with bowls of crisps and home-made cheese straws.

'Are you changing?' Mark countered.

'I've told everyone it's casual,' she replied. 'Anyway this is smart enough, isn't it?'

'If you say so.' He eyed the leopard print top and deep brown trousers doubtfully.

'And I would be grateful if you could manage not to criticise my efforts until everyone has gone.' She put down the bowls and left without waiting for an answer.

Mark's sister Fiona was the first to arrive for the party with her husband Geoffrey Franks, the gynaecologist. With them were their three children, two grown up and an after-thought, Jeremy, aged sixteen.

Fiona, masterful and magnificently dressed in a two-piece that had 'designer' written all over it, her hair bronzed and lacquered into place, swept over the threshold. 'Goodness,' she said, looking around her, 'isn't this fantastic? Geoffrey, don't you think it looks fantastic?'

'Very nice,' he said in a colourless voice. Geoffrey reserved his charm for his patients. Mark had a theory that his brother-in-law only ever noticed other people when they were in his surgery. He kissed his sister, turned to his two nephews and niece and discovered there were four young people instead of three.

Charlotte, a young Valkyrie who showed every sign of maturing into as majestic a woman as her mother but at the moment was simply enormous fun, had in tow a vapid-looking youth she introduced as, 'Chris, who's staying with us for Christmas.' Mark wondered where she had picked him up.

'Found him at Reading, he's reading agriculture,' her brother John told him. Equally tall, John was as self-contained as his father but wasn't afraid of displaying charm. He'd just finished university and was now articled to a firm of solicitors. 'Charlie is currently enamoured with the environment and feels Chris can educate her on organic farming and similar issues. Ah, here's my lovely aunt!'

Louise had appeared from the kitchen and was greeting Fiona with enthusiasm.

'My dear Louise,' Fiona said, 'what a triumph!' She swept her

142

hand round in an all-encompassing gesture.

Louise blushed, obviously pleased. She went and kissed her brother-in-law. 'Geoffrey, how lovely to see you. And Charlotte and John!' Louise was very popular with Mark's nephews and nieces. 'But where's Jeremy?'

'Here, Aunt Louise.' He had been standing a little apart from his family. Mark often wondered if he were a changeling. Small and dark, awkward of manner, glasses constantly falling off his nose, hair over his eyes, he lacked the overwhelming confidence of his parents and siblings.

'Jeremy, you've grown!' Louise gave him a big hug. 'You used to be one member of the Henderson family I didn't have to look up to. Now you tower over me.'

He flushed happily. 'Not quite, Aunt Louise!'

Indeed, he was only just taller than her now. Mark threw an arm around the boy's shoulders. 'Have you playing basketball in no time,' he said heartily. He never really knew what to say to Jeremy. 'I found a new computer game the other day, really taxing. Perhaps I can show it to you later on?' The boy was mad on computers.

Jeremy brightened, then faded into the background again as Mark's other sister, Patricia, her husband Matthew and their four offspring arrived.

Mark considered that Patricia and Matthew had managed things rather better than Fiona and Geoffrey. Their two daughters, Veronica and Carol, were three years younger than John and Charlotte. Then there was a four-year gap before Charles, now fifteen, had come along and they'd followed up two years later with Stewart, thirteen. With Patricia and Matthew was Mark's father, Victor.

More greetings, more admiration for the new decor.

'Hardly recognise the old house,' Victor said quietly, rubbing his hand lightly up Mark's arm, his way of saying how pleased he was to be with him.

'Great to see you, Dad,' he said, thinking that the old man looked pale and drawn. He hoped Patricia and Matthew hadn't been overdoing the celebrating with him. 'Now, what about some champagne? John, you want to help opening a bottle or two?'

'Not a champagne cocktail for me, Mark. I'd prefer it straight – if it's a halfway decent cuvée, that is,' Fiona said imperiously.

'I think you'll be amused by its impertinence,' Mark told her, thinking that she didn't change. Always the bossy elder sister, she never seemed able to acknowledge that he'd grown up and was making a success of his life.

'Still travelling to Manchester, Leeds and other romantic cities at a moment's notice, leaving Louise a grass widow?' she asked, accepting a glass of champagne.

'Oh, he goes to much more romantic places these days,' Louise said. Mark was pleased to see that she seemed to have lost that edge to her voice. 'Paris and Hong Kong and then three weeks ago it was Copenhagen.'

'Bet it's Manchester in the New Year,' Fiona riposted.

'Actually, it's back to Copenhagen,' Mark said without thinking.

'Really?' Louise said, sounding startled. 'You never said.'

He cursed himself. He'd been meaning to tell her but these days they hardly seemed to talk. 'Only just been decided.'

'When are you going?'

He nerved himself. 'New Year's Eve.' It was tradition that he and Louise went to a local New Year's Eve party known for its entertainment and bonhomie.

Now everyone was looking at the two of them.

'Oho,' said Fiona. 'No wonder he hasn't told you.'

Mark saw Louise pull herself together and give them all a big, bright smile. 'That's OK with me, I'll go to Copenhagen as well! Now, everyone, let's go through to the drawing room, Mother is in there already.' The double doors leading into the main room were open and Fiona, as always, took the lead, commenting enthusiastically on the decor to Patricia, a willing accomplice in all her sister's activities.

Mark grabbed Louise as she made to follow them. 'Look, darling, it's sweet of you to say you'll come with me but it's not going to work.'

She didn't seem to understand at first. 'What do you mean? The house is finished and Orphan Annie's won't mind if I'm not available for another ten days or so.'

Mark drew a hand across his brow and wondered how to get himself out of this mess. 'I mean, it won't work your coming to Denmark. I'll be working all the time, it'll be worse than Paris.'

The hurt in her eyes was such he almost went back on his words and said he'd love to have her along. But he couldn't, not with having to work so hard and watch what Robin was up to; it was vital he manage to counter any move on her part to take over from him entirely.

'But I wouldn't get in the way! We could surely have the odd evening together!'

Mark felt frustrated. Why couldn't Louise realise his whole future with the firm depended on how this job went? 'Look, I can't explain now, we'll talk about it later, after the party is over.'

The doorbell rang. The Webbers had arrived.

Louise welcomed them heartily but Mark could see she was still smarting under his rejection.

Cursing himself, Robin, Douglas, the firm, Christmas, the whole damned shooting match, he opened another bottle of champagne.

'Happy Christmas, favourite man!' Nicky, looking exceedingly fetching in a very short shocking pink dress, laughed up at him.

144

Mark gave her a kiss. 'What a little Christmas cracker you are!' he exclaimed, then smacked hands with Colin and ruffled the hair of the two Webber boys. At thirteen and fourteen they were still as short as their mother but Mark could see from the size of their feet that they'd soon shoot up to their father's height. 'How's the new school?'

'Brilliant,' said Riff, the elder. 'I'm in the junior rugger team. We're unbeaten this year so far.'

'And they've brought home the first halfway decent reports in history,' Nicky said with pride.

'Have a Coke, kids.' Mark handed over a couple of glasses. 'If you look under the tree you could find something to your advantage.'

With identical squeals of delight, the boys plunged beneath the tree and started tearing paper off the two packages waiting for them.

'Do you know what Colin wants us to do?' hissed Nicky with an outraged look at her husband as Mark handed her a champagne cocktail. 'Only yank them out of that place and go down to the West Country! I won't have him even discuss it with Riff and Raff. They've been mucked about enough.'

Mark glanced at Colin, who shrugged his shoulders in a resigned way.

'To say nothing of my job! Now, where's this party? Come on, boys, let's go and see who we can find for you to tell tall tales of your rugby prowess.' Nicky bustled her sons ostentatiously into the drawing room, followed by Louise, saying she'd introduce them to Charles and Stewart.

Mark silently handed a champagne cocktail to Colin and took one himself. They drank and Mark topped up each glass with more champagne. 'Christmas – peace, joy and understanding, eh?'

'Whoever thought up the idea should be shot!'

The doorbell rang again and Mark welcomed some neighbours with a son and daughter of Riff and Raff's ages. Louise came into the hall, made them all welcome and led them into the drawing room.

'Is it really a good idea, moving them from their school?' Mark ventured. 'They do seem to have settled down well.'

'Don't you start.' Colin looked tortured. 'I've been through the whole thing with Nicky. It's taking her a long time to accept that the figures do seem to add up. We may well leave them where they are and put up with the driving. You have no idea how expensive private education is, you lucky sod.'

Mark reflected that he could well have afforded to send both Emma and James to public school. He'd tried it with James and it hadn't been a success, but he hadn't even considered it for his daughter. Because she'd settled down so well at the grant-aided school where she'd been accepted? Because he'd so enjoyed having

145

her at home? It was too late to decide now. 'I suppose we should go and join the others,' he ventured to Colin. Neither of them moved and after a moment Mark topped up their glasses again.

Patricia came out into the hall. 'Mark, it really is divine. Louise has done a dramatically wonderful job.'

Mark wondered if it was being married to a barrister that made her so effusive.

'I just must see the rest. Do you think Louise would do us a guided tour? Not everybody, of course, just me, or perhaps Fiona and me.'

'I'm sure she would, all you have to do is ask,' he said blandly. 'But later, I think?'

'Of course, darling boy. And remind me to have a word with you about Father.'

Mark remembered Victor's pallor and felt immediate alarm. 'Is something wrong?' he asked, as Colin melted away towards the drawing room.

'Not wrong, no. But haven't you noticed how frail he's getting?'

Mark couldn't say he had, not before today. But then he saw much more of Victor than either Patricia or Fiona did. Victor lunched with Mark and Louise nearly every weekend and every now and then Mark visited him on his way home.

Patricia glanced towards the Christmas tree and said, 'I really think the time is coming when he'll need some looking after. That sheltered housing he's in doesn't offer much, you know?' She focused again on Mark. 'Don't you think you should ask him to come and live with you?'

Mark was taken aback. The thought had never occurred to him. 'Isn't it daughters who look after their parents?'

'With four children, you can't expect me to be able to do much. And it was you to whom he gave the house, don't you think you owe him something?'

Mark was stung. It wasn't his fault Victor had wanted him and Louise to have the house. 'I hardly think you need take that attitude, Pat. Whatever needs to be done to look after Father, Louise and I will of course do.'

His sister hated being called Pat. Her expression showed she was torn between annoyance at that and relief that he'd agreed to take their father in.

The front door bell went again.

This time it was the Fawkeses and Mark's heart sank as he welcomed them in. Things mightn't be good between him and Louise, but it seemed war had broken out between Willoughby and Polly.

Chapter Seventeen

Louise handed round the brown bread squares that Betty had spent the morning loading with smoked salmon, hardly noticing to whom she was speaking.

Her soul felt as if it had been blasted and seared by a bitter wind straight from Siberia.

What had happened to Mark? She could do nothing right for him these days. It couldn't just be that wretched job she'd taken, or her involvement with Orphan Annie's. They barely talked anymore. Every time she tried to find out what was wrong, he snapped her head off.

This Christmas was a nightmare, in fact. Betty was upset and taking it out on Louise. She considered that it must be her daughter's fault that Mark was being so difficult. She hadn't said so in as many words but Louise knew that was what she was thinking.

And when Louise had said she'd go with Mark to Copenhagen so that they could spend New Year's Eve together as they always had, he'd rejected her. It had felt as though she'd been kicked by a vicious horse. And in front of his family!

Louise couldn't deal with the implications of this. Not until all these people had left. For the present she tried to push the hurt deep inside and concentrate on being a good hostess.

'Darling, what a success the house is,' Fiona said with delight. 'When I think how you came to me for advice when you and Mark first moved in here, and now look what you've achieved!'

She sounded genuinely admiring and Louise felt flattered. If her sister-in-law felt the decor hit the right note, it could be deemed a success.

'It's been amazing the way it's all come together,' she said to Fiona. 'All due to Marsha, of course. The best ideas were hers.'

'But I recognise your touch everywhere,' Fiona said generously. 'The colour schemes, the way it's so stylish and yet comfortable as well. If you hadn't told me, I would have thought it was all your own work.' She gave a little laugh. 'You've always been too honest for your own good! Look, there's your mother and my father together. Isn't it nice they get on so well?'

Betty and Victor were having a desultory conversation over by the doors to the garden. Did they get on well?

147

Louise often had them over together for lunch or supper; it was convenient and they seemed to accept each other's company. But underneath the social ease, Louise sensed they had very little in common. If she hadn't married Mark, Louise doubted Betty and Victor would ever have become friends.

'Such a relief for you.' Patricia joined her sister and sister-in-law. 'It would be so awkward if they hated the sight of each other. Especially now Father is deteriorating.'

'Deteriorating?' Louise asked sharply. 'I know he's getting older but he seems to manage very well.' She looked again at Victor, more closely this time. He seemed tired, no doubt of that, he was perching on the arm of a chair now and Louise doubted he was listening to whatever story it was Betty was telling him.

Patricia followed her gaze. 'Yes, well, he's had a week of being looked after. You know he didn't want to drive over to us?'

That wasn't like Victor, who valued his independence. 'No, I didn't realise,' Louise said slowly.

'Well, when I collected him, he was so short of breath I thought he was going to collapse.'

Louise was really worried now. 'Did you get him to see a doctor?'

'I wanted to but he refused. Said it was just the effort of getting everything ready to go away, presents, his clothes, checking the fridge, you know?'

'I wish he'd told me,' Louise said, 'I could have gone over and helped him. I didn't realise he was finding it all such a problem.'

'I think it's just increasing years,' Patricia told her gently. 'He soon perked up. But Fiona and I are really relieved Mark has agreed that you will give him a home.' She exchanged a glance with Fiona and smiled affectionately at Louise.

Give Victor a home? What was this? Either Patricia or Fiona or both, Louise realised, must have spoken to Mark. And he had agreed to have Victor come and live with them without saying a word to her.

A white heat of fury hit her that had nothing to do with her father-in-law; nor with Fiona or Patricia.

'Mark and I are both very fond of Victor,' she said steadily. 'He's a lovely man. Forgive me, I must check on something.' Somehow she managed to give them a smile as she turned and walked away. 'Here,' she said to Nicky, thrusting the plate of smoked salmon canapés at her, 'take these round, will you?' She couldn't trust herself to say more, she had to find Mark. The fact that they were in the middle of a party was not going to prevent her from having it out with him. This time he'd gone too far!

But the hall was full of people.

Automatically Louise welcomed the Fawkeses and another set of neighbours who had just arrived. The neighbours were no trouble. They picked up champagne cocktails and moved into the drawing room with the minimum of fuss. But when Louise saw Polly and her daughter, she forgot her grievances against Mark.

'Aunty Louise!' Pooh flung her arms around Louise and promptly burst into tears.

Louise held the distressed girl and looked enquiringly towards Polly.

Her face was white, eyes huge, as she stared back in a desolate silence.

Willoughby accepted his champagne cocktail from Mark, his expression set and hostile. 'Never should have come,' he said abruptly to his host. 'Told them but they insisted.'

'Come into the kitchen,' Louise said to Caroline soothingly as she led her out of the hall.

She sat the girl down on the banquette and put the kettle on. 'I think a nice cup of tea, don't you?'

Caroline hiccuped as she tried to control her sobs. Her long hair was held back with a black velvet Alice band that contrasted oddly with the owl look of her metal-framed glasses, and plain, unmade-up face. Her smock-style denim dress was worn over a lace-collared blouse that clearly belonged to a classier outfit. Opaque tights and Doc Marten boots completed an ensemble that was an obvious compromise between her taste and Polly's.

'Mummy's going away! She's leaving Daddy!' she cried.

Louise put the kettle down on the Aga hotplate with a thump. 'Oh, darling! Are you sure?'

Stupid question. How could Caroline not be sure?

The girl nodded miserably. 'She promised me she wouldn't. She promised me!'

Louise didn't know what to say. She came and sat down beside Caroline and placed an arm around her thin shoulders. 'Darling, I'm sure she's as wretched about it as you are.'

'She's not!' Caroline suddenly flared. 'She's selfish! She doesn't care about Daddy or about me. All she cares about is herself.'

'Have you talked to her about it?'

Caroline shook her head. 'She told us this morning. She and Daddy had a terrible row last night. It was awful, even worse than the rows they've been having ever since I got home for the holidays. I locked myself into my room and wouldn't come out. Then, this morning, she said she was going, that she couldn't take it anymore. But why couldn't she?' wailed the girl.

'What about you?' Louise asked her, trying to be calm, stroking back stray wisps of hair from Caroline's forehead.

She gave another hiccup. 'Mummy wants me to go with her, to Paris. She said we'd get a flat there together. But I know what it'll be like. That man will be with us!'

'What man?' But Louise knew.

'Jean-Paul. It's disgusting and I won't live with him,' Caroline

149

said passionately. Her tears had dried and her small face was set now.

'Well, perhaps she won't go. And even if she does, you'll be back at school soon, you won't have to make any decisions until much later,' Louise tried to soothe her. Inside she felt intense anger and sadness. How could Polly do this to her family, no matter what she felt about Willoughby and Jean-Paul?

The door opened and Jeremy came in. 'Aunt Louise, may I play with Uncle Mark's computer? He's got a new game he said he'd show me.' He saw Caroline and flushed bright red. She looked down at her hands and laced them together awkwardly.

'I'm sure you can but why not ask him?'

'He's disappeared!' Jeremy's face gradually regained its normal colour but he remained staring at Caroline, who was starting to look more composed now.

Louise sighed. 'He can't be far away,' she said brightly. She rose and looked at Caroline. 'You're a bit of an expert on the computer, I hear. Why not see if you and Jeremy can crack the new game together?'

Caroline looked back at her doubtfully then at Jeremy, at his glasses and thin, dark face with its wary expression. 'OK,' she said, getting up with the air of one who doesn't expect much but can't think of anything better.

'Right,' Louise said briskly. 'The computer's in Mark's study and I don't suppose it'll be difficult to find the game.'

It was on top of a box of discs, almost as though it had been deliberately placed there. For Mark to play with that evening?

Jeremy picked up the disc eagerly. 'Gosh, that's great!' he breathed. 'Thanks, Aunt Louise. Do you know how it works?' He turned to Caroline in a kindly way.

''Course I do,' she said and sat herself down, switched on the machine and took the disc from him. 'Do you want to mess about with the first level or shall we go straight to third? The third's the most fun.'

'Oh, the third then,' he said happily, sitting himself down beside her.

Louise pressed a hand gratefully on his shoulder. 'Well, I'll leave you two to it, then. Coke's in the hall, Jeremy. Can I rely on you to look after Caroline?'

'You bet,' he said distantly, his attention all on the screen which had come alive with rapidly moving, highly coloured figures that looked to Louise like nothing so much as gremlins, accompanied by hectic music backed by explosive sound effects.

She left them to it and went in search of Mark.

She found him in the snooker room, half sitting on the table and listening to Willoughby, who was saying, 'It's been hell these last few months, ever since we got back from Paris.'

Mark saw Louise. 'How are things going with Pooh?' he asked.

'She's in your study with Jeremy, taking him through some new computer game you apparently promised to show him.'

'Should I go to her?' asked Willoughby. The knot of his tie had slipped, as though he'd tugged at it, and one end of his collar had flipped up. 'The trouble is . . .' he ran a hand hesitantly through his thinning hair . . . 'I don't know what to say to her.'

'It really is true then, that Polly wants to go back to Paris?' Louise asked him.

'It's what she says,' he answered distractedly. 'And to tell you the truth, the way she's been these last few weeks, I really think it would be for the best. She's quite impossible – ranting at me, snapping at Caroline, bursting into tears at the slightest provocation – I tell you, most of the time I haven't wanted to come home. Thank heavens there's been plenty at the office to keep me late.'

'What about Caroline?' asked Louise grimly. Hard as it was to forgive Polly for her behaviour, she could see only selfishness in Willoughby's attitude. 'She says Polly wants her to go to Paris as well.'

'Caroline doesn't want to,' he said, suddenly grim, 'and I've told her she's staying with me. There's isn't a judge in the world would award Polly custody. She just can't get away with this behaviour.'

'Can you look after Caroline?' Louise asked.

Willoughby's distracted look came back but he said, 'Don't see why not. Got the house, get a housekeeper. Simplest thing in the world.'

'That's right,' said Mark encouragingly. 'You show her, old boy.'

It was too much for Louise. 'Look, Willoughby, I'm sorry but we've got a house full of guests. Mark needs to look after drinks and I think it would do you good to chat to other people, get away from it all for a bit. Caroline is fine with Jeremy.' She left the room without a backward glance.

She went through the hall where Riff and Raff were playing carpet bowls with the three neighbouring youngsters and having a great time. In the drawing room the party was in full swing. Nobody seemed to have noticed her absence. Betty had fetched another plate of smoked salmon from the kitchen and looked happy to be of use, chatting animatedly as she worked her way round the room. Victor had also found a job. Together with John, his eldest grandson, he was taking champagne round. Louise went and took a dish of bacon-wrapped smoked oysters out of the warming oven of the Aga and started to work the room.

'Thanks, Dad,' she said quietly in Victor's ear as their paths crossed. 'Mark's dealing with a small crisis in the snooker room.'

'Reckoned it was something like that,' he said equably, pouring champagne into Nicky's glass. She was flirting with Fiona's husband, the gynaecologist. Over the other side of the room Polly

151

was deep in conversation with Patricia. Louise felt no inclination to go and talk to her but watched Victor work his way over towards them. He did look frail, she realised, and there was a slight tremor to his hand as he held the heavy champagne bottle over Polly's glass. Not seeing him for ten days or so made her realise how much he'd aged recently. Moving over with her dish of smoked oysters to a couple of the neighbours who were talking to him, Louise worked out how old her father-in-law was: eighty-four. He'd been forty at the time of Mark's birth, late to take on a child. She wasn't at all sure, though, that he'd want to give up his independence and come and live with them. She and Mark would have to approach the matter very carefully. For the moment Louise forgot how angry she was with the way her husband had taken her approval of the plan for granted.

Back in the kitchen she checked the huge venison casserole she had prepared together with red cabbage and mashed potato. There was a lot to be said for the capacity and steady heat of the Aga.

'Thanks for taking care of Pooh.' Polly came up behind her. 'Is she all right?'

'She and Jeremy are playing with Mark's computer. He's a kind boy and will look after her.'

Polly took out a cigarette and lit it. Her fingers shook. 'God, it's all so dreadful,' she said and sat at the table. There were dark rings under her eyes and the whites were bloodshot. 'I don't want to go but there isn't any alternative.'

Louise turned round and leaned against the rail of the stove, her hands still in oven gloves. 'Caroline thinks you're going to live with Jean-Paul.'

Polly's face became transformed. 'I never imagined anything like this could happen to me. Oh, I've had the odd affair . . .'

'Have you?' Louise asked, astonished.

'You don't imagine I could live all these years with Willoughby without a fling every now and then, do you? Get a life, Lulu!'

Ash was lengthening at the end of Polly's cigarette. Louise jerked one hand out of its oven glove, crossed the kitchen, snatched the cigarette away and ground it into the waste bin. 'I don't like people smoking in my kitchen.'

Polly gazed unblinkingly at her. Then her hand reached for her bag and fished out the pack of cigarettes. She drew one out and put it into her mouth, saw Louise's expression then replaced it in the pack. 'Sorry, Lulu, I wasn't thinking. I spend the whole time smoking at the moment.'

'Why did you marry Willoughby?' Louise asked through gritted teeth.

Polly picked up her champagne from the table and finished it off. 'Usual story, darling. Got me pregnant.'

'I thought shotgun marriages belonged to the past?' Louise

couldn't believe what she was hearing. Was this independent, strong-minded Polly speaking?

She fiddled with the stem of her wine glass. 'Easy enough to say, darling. Willoughby had chased me like a hound after the season's first fox. I suppose I was flattered and, yes, interested. He was so different from the other men I was involved with. So single-minded, never gave a damn what anyone thought, did his own thing. In a strange way his looks turned me on, you know?'

Louise didn't.

'Then, when the wretched curse didn't come and I went through the tests, I thought, why not? Everyone else seemed ordinary beside Willoughby. I certainly wasn't having an abortion and I thought, yes, I can make a go of this.'

Louise crossed her arms, leaned back against the Aga again and looked sternly at her. 'And you have. You've made him a good wife.'

'*Bloody* good wife!' Polly exclaimed. 'When I think of everything I've done for that sod . . . And what has he ever done for me?'

'Loved you, given you everything you wanted?' suggested Louise.

Polly waved a hand dismissively. 'He's pleased himself the whole time. If he's wanted to work late, he's worked late. Sent abroad? Polly will make a home. Don't want to go to a party? Won't go. Does want to go? Never ask Polly if she wants to. Any time I've wanted anything, I've had to fight for it. And fight I have, darling. But there comes a time when you just get tired of the bloody battle. And then along came Jean-Paul.' Once again a glow lit her face.

'But what about Caroline?' Louise demanded. 'Doesn't she deserve to have her parents stay together? How can you just walk out?'

The glow faded. Polly's glance fell to her hands, still fiddling with the wine glass. 'I hope she'll understand eventually,' she said quietly.

Louise gave a snort of impatience.

The door to the kitchen burst open and in came Nicky, her face flushed with wine, her eyes sparkling. 'Your mother's wondering when we're going to eat. I said I'd come and find out,' she announced. Then took in the atmosphere. 'Oh, have I interrupted something?' She looked from Louise to Polly uncertainly.

'You might as well know,' Polly said bleakly, 'I'm leaving Willoughby.'

'Good for you!' Nicky came over, sat beside her and put an arm around her shoulders.

'Nicky!' protested Louise.

'Well, he's a bastard! He tried to touch me up that supper we had here in the summer.'

But Polly said lightly, 'That's Willoughby for you! I hope you told him where to get off.'

'You bet.' Nicky sat back on the banquette and gave her a straight

153

look. 'Does he do that sort of thing often?'

Polly shrugged. 'As far as I know, he doesn't put a great deal of effort into his seductions, not like business. Sees a chance and takes it, I think. I remember one time we went on a picnic with another couple.' She glanced away from Nicky and Louise. 'I was rather attracted to the husband and we went for a little walk, with Pooh and their daughter, took them to see some swans I seem to remember, and had a delightful conversation. When we came back I could see immediately that Willoughby had made the most of his opportunity – his flies were still undone! She, of course, looked cool as anything.'

'What did you do?' breathed Nicky.

'What could I do?' countered Polly. 'Told Willoughby to take a load of picnic stuff back to the car and followed him with the rug. Then suggested he zip up. His morals as well as his flies. He didn't speak to me for two days! Combination of guilt and anger at being discovered like that, made a fool of by me.'

'Colin wants to remove us to Cornwall,' Nicky said gloomily.

'I thought it was Exeter?' Louise said.

'Well, it might just as well be Cornwall. No consideration for what I want, or whether the boys will be better off.'

'But if you can't afford the fees?' offered Louise.

Nicky's face crumpled. 'Oh, don't tell me. I'm sick to death of having it all flung in my face. If only he'd really consult me, ask my opinion, instead of telling me what has to be.'

Louise remembered that supper in the summer. She'd been devastated then by Emma and James leaving home. Now she looked back and it seemed that that was when everything had started to go wrong. For all of them. She'd floundered along trying to sort things out and only getting into deeper trouble. Mark acted as though the whole summer was her fault. That if only she'd give up any idea of doing something for herself, everything would get back to where it was before.

But she didn't want it back there. Not without the twins at home. 'You're both so lucky to have children still in your lives,' she said suddenly. 'They are the most important thing.'

'Oh, Lulu, I've been trying and trying to hold on to that, believe me,' Polly sighed. 'But there comes a time . . .'

'Yes, children are important, but you can't do your best by them if you're not at ease with your husband and yourself.' Nicky raised her glass and saw that it was empty. 'Shall I go and tell your mum we'll be eating soon?' she asked, getting up.

Louise couldn't have been less interested in feeding a host of people. What was going on here seemed much more important. 'You're not telling me you're thinking of leaving Colin?' she demanded.

'Heavens, no, then we really would be up the financial creek

154

without a paddle!' But Nicky didn't look as certain as her words sounded.

'You want life too simple, Lulu,' Polly said. 'The nice husband, the two children, the pretty home and everything happy ever after. Life isn't like that.'

No, it wasn't, Louise decided. It certainly wasn't. All her anger against Mark and her frustration with life surged back. At that minute she could almost understand Polly and Nicky.

'Tell Mother I'm taking everything into the dining room now,' she said decisively. 'Polly, can you help carry this food through.' Louise handed her an oven cloth and indicated the venison casserole. 'Put it on the hot plate. Everyone's going to serve themselves. Salads and puddings are in there already. Nicky, after you've told everyone to go through, you could come back for the red cabbage.' She bent and got the dish of mashed potato out of the bottom oven and tried to put her problems aside for the moment. Get on with life, she told herself. Everything will sort itself out.

But would it?

Once people had served themselves with food, Louise moved around the main rooms, assessing the state of her party. With satisfaction she noted Caroline chatting happily with Jeremy, and with a certain unease she saw Riff and Raff being exuberant with their new friends. If they didn't calm down, there could be trouble there. She noted Polly carefully avoiding Willoughby, and Colin trying to talk to an unresponsive Nicky; there was nothing she could do about them at the moment, and perhaps never. She saw Mark's sisters sitting talking happily together, ignoring their families, and thought that at least they appeared to be enjoying themselves. Victor had helped Betty to food and was now seeing her nicely settled at a small table in the drawing room. The old liked to be properly comfortable to eat. Her father-in-law seemed fine at the moment. She wondered whether Patricia was overstating the problem with his health. Mark was chatting up the attractive girl who lived two houses down and appeared to have forgotten about filling people's glasses. Well, no point in trying to bring him back to his duties.

Louise got John and his sister's boyfriend on to opening bottles of wine and going round with it. The young liked making themselves useful at this sort of party. Then she went back to the kitchen.

'Are you all right, Louise?' asked Victor as she was taking mince pies out of the warming oven.

She smiled brightly at him. 'Fine, thanks, Dad.'

'You don't seem yourself somehow.' He hovered by the side of the Aga.

Looking at him with newly opened eyes, Louise realised that his tall, elegant figure had shrunk recently. Why hadn't she noticed this before? She smiled at him. 'Strain of Christmas and all that.'

The intelligent grey eyes under their dark brows surveyed her. 'Without the children? Christmas a strain? You never found it so before, my dear.'

'Perhaps that's the strain,' Louise acknowledged, placing hot mince pies on two large serving plates. 'I miss Emma and James, you know?'

Victor leaned against one of the cupboards and watched her, his expression alert. 'Of course you do. How's the job coming along?'

'Orphan Annie's?' Louise gave him a wide, genuine smile. 'I've enjoyed the few things I've done for them so far but it's far from regular. I think as they get to know me, the work will increase. I hope so.'

'Yes, you need something to do now the children have left,' he agreed. 'I think you should consider starting a business of your own.'

'You do?' asked a startled Louise.

'You're intelligent, enterprising and full of energy. I'm sure you'd make a success of the right thing.'

What a different attitude from his son, thought Louise. She wished Mark could be so interested in her. 'Ah, well, there's the problem – I haven't any ideas for starting a business.'

'You will have,' he said calmly. 'I think you're being very sensible, branching out, trying different things and not rushing into major decisions. You've got time. Then, when you're sure of what it is, you can put everything you've got into it.'

Louise went and gave him a kiss. 'Thanks, Dad, it means a lot your saying that.'

He gave her a quick squeeze. 'Mark's a lucky man and you can tell him I said so!'

Regretfully she watched him leave the kitchen. Victor's support was very valuable to her. She put the kettle on for coffee, picked up a plate of mince pies and longed for the party to be over.

The telephone call came when most of the guests had left. The Fawkeses had been the first to go, Caroline looking miserable, Willoughby defiant and Polly exhausted. They'd been followed by the Webbers, Nicky still not talking to Colin but Riff and Raff energetically arguing over who had been better at carpet bowls. Then the neighbours had left with enthusiastic thanks, followed at last by Mark's sisters and their families, Jeremy shyly telling Louise that he had really enjoyed himself. 'Caroline's a real whizz on the computer,' he'd said.

'He wants me to invite her over,' Fiona told Louise. 'Could you let me have her mother's telephone number?'

Louise scribbled it down, debating whether to say anything about Polly's leaving for Paris. But she couldn't go, surely, before Caroline went back to school?'

That left just Betty and Victor.

156

'I'll drive you back, Dad,' said Mark.

'Oh, no, stay until this evening,' pleaded Louise. 'We haven't had a chance to talk to you yet.' She was almost sure now that Patricia and Fiona were worrying unnecessarily. Victor had undoubtedly aged a lot in the last few months but he seemed a long way off not being able to look after himself. And he was going to be insulted by any suggestion that he couldn't.

'We could play some bridge,' suggested Betty.

'Why not?' Louise agreed. She saw Victor hesitate and look at his son. 'You'd like Dad to stay a bit longer, wouldn't you?' she asked Mark.

That was when the telephone rang.

Mark answered.

'It's for you,' he said, handing the cordless receiver to Louise. She took it into the kitchen.

When she rejoined them five minutes later, the three of them were still standing by the drinks table, now scattered with dirty glasses and empty bottles. Mark had his father's coat in his hand.

'That was Orphan Annie's,' Louise announced. 'They've got an emergency and wondered whether I'd be prepared to accompany an eighty-year-old woman to Florida the day after tomorrow and stay there with her for two weeks.'

'What a pity you can't go,' Betty said, sitting on the corner seat by the front door. 'Florida at this time of the year must be wonderful.'

'I told them I'd discuss it with my family and ring them back,' Louise said expressionlessly, her eyes on Mark.

'But you can't go to Florida!' Her mother sounded shocked.

'Why not?' Louise looked at her husband. He was standing still holding Victor's coat, and looked at her as though she'd taken leave of her senses.

'Come off it, darling, of course you can't!'

'Why not? You're off to Copenhagen. You've just told me you won't be here for New Year and that I can't go with you, so why shouldn't I take this woman to Florida?' Louise asked in tones of utter reasonableness. Inside she was pleading with her husband to see things her way for once. Because until he did, their marriage didn't stand a chance.

Mark looked exasperated, the way he did when James proposed doing anything unconventional. 'Well, apart from anything else, the whole thing sounds distinctly dodgy. What on earth is an eighty year old doing making up her mind on the spur of the moment to travel the Atlantic?' He held out the coat to his father. 'Come on, Dad.'

'Just a minute, Mark,' said Victor quietly. 'I think I agree with Louise. If you're off to Denmark on business, why shouldn't she go to Florida?'

157

'Because I'm not going to be in Denmark much longer than a week, and anyway, Louise's mother is staying here.'

'I'm sure Betty was thinking of going home in a day or so anyway,' Victor suggested gently.

She looked bewildered.

'Dad! Don't *you* think it's odd, all this coming up at the last minute? Wouldn't *you* be worried if your wife told you she was off at a moment's notice?'

'It's only a last-minute arrangement,' Louise said, 'because the carer who was going with Mrs Toler has fallen and broken her leg. So Orphan Annie's has to find someone else. I consider it a compliment they've contacted me.'

'I suppose it could be difficult to find someone free to go at this time of the year,' Betty suggested, her expression puzzled and upset.

'I find this incredible! Dad, I can't believe you really think Louise should abandon all her responsibilities here and go.'

Victor hesitated. He looked at Louise.

Her heart thumped in her chest. As she'd expected, Mark was dead against the idea and her mother obviously felt she should do what her husband said. Louise didn't consider either of these reactions valid but she did care what Victor thought.

'Louise should do what she thinks is best,' he said gently. 'And best not for you, Mark, but for herself.'

Mark tried to control himself. White patches flared by his mouth as he compressed his lips. 'Well?' he demanded, looking straight at her.

'I'm going,' she told him.

Chapter Eighteen

For a moment there was silence in the hall. Then Mark said in a dangerously quiet voice, 'We'll discuss this later. Come on, Dad.' Once again he held out Victor's Crombie.

Victor, looking very tired, stuck his hands into the sleeves and allowed his son to help him on with the coat.

Louise came and kissed him goodbye. 'You stick to your guns,' he whispered in her ear as he hugged her. 'I'll try and talk some sense into Mark on the way home.' He released her and stepped back. 'Goodbye, my dear,' he said in normal tones. 'Give me a ring tomorrow.'

'I will, Dad,' she said then watched Mark stride out of the house and bang the door behind Victor.

'Oh, darling,' said her mother, 'are you sure you're doing the right thing?' She, too, looked exhausted.

'I'll make us a cup of tea,' Louise said, 'and we'll talk about it. You go and sit by the fire and I'll bring it in.'

She put the kettle on, knowing that if she had to fight her mother as well as Mark, it could be too much.

But Victor was backing her decision to go.

'Darling,' Betty started as Louise put down the tray in the drawing room, 'Mark works so hard to keep you and this lovely house going.' She looked around the refurbished room. 'I can't think what all this must have cost.'

'So you think I owe it to him to do exactly what he wants?' Louise asked her gently. 'Don't you think I have some rights as well?'

'One has to keep men happy,' Betty said.

'Is that what you tried to do with Daddy?' Louise handed her a cup of China tea.

Betty put the cup down on a little table beside her chair and smoothed the skirt of her jersey two-piece. 'Men can be very demanding,' she said obscurely. 'It's important you make them realise they are the most important thing in your life. That everything revolves around them. Your father knew he meant everything to me, that without him I'd be bereft. He would never have left me.' Her lips closed stubbornly and her eyes were fixed on the fire.

Louise remembered what her brother had said.

She had a sudden vision of her mother and father locked together

159

in a barren marriage, neither able to fulfil the other, her mother determined to hang on to what she had and her father feeling unable to break free and claim the happiness that waited for him.

Louise shivered.

'Mummy,' she used the old name without thinking, 'I do love Mark, really I do, but he's been so difficult recently.'

'I think it's been difficult for both of you since the children left,' Betty said gently, and picked up her cup of tea.

'I've realised I can't just sit in this house waiting for him to come back from wherever he's gone to. He's always going to have to spend a large part of his time away and, without the children to look after, what am I going to do?'

'There's bridge, coffee mornings, lunches . . .' Her mother's voice trailed away. 'But, no, I can see it wouldn't be enough for you.' Louise almost cheered. That was a considerable concession on her mother's part. 'But what about voluntary work?' Betty continued, looking brighter. 'I'm sure Mark wouldn't object to that.' Still on what mattered to Mark.

'I need to prove I can earn my own living, however humble. I can't explain it but it's important to me.'

Betty looked alarmed. 'You're not thinking of leaving him?'

'No, Mummy, I'm not.' Louise felt she could be quite positive about that. However difficult Mark was, and at the moment he was being impossible, she was sure she would never be able to walk out on her marriage the way Polly seemed to be planning to do.

Betty sighed. 'Well, I can't pretend to understand any of this, darling. I just hope you're doing the right thing. Now, shall we finish the clearing up? Then I'll go and put my things together. We never discussed when I was going home but I think it should be tomorrow morning, don't you?'

Louise kissed her. 'I don't want to chase you away.'

'Don't be ridiculous. I have a life of my own, you know. And I can always come again!' Betty put her cup and saucer back on the tray and busily started to add dirty ashtrays.

They'd just switched on the first load in the dishwasher when Mark returned. He looked thoroughly out of temper, said he didn't want anything to eat that evening and went straight through to his study. Louise knew he was going to switch on his computer and start playing one of his games.

He stayed there all evening.

Betty and Louise ate cold turkey and salad, watched television and centred their conversation on what was showing on the screen. Only when she said she was going up to bed did Betty add, 'Never let the sun go down on your wrath, that's what I always used to say.' She picked up her book and a glass of lemon barley water, kissed Louise and went up to bed.

160

Louise went to the study. Mark was hunched over the screen, his eyes intent on the hand of cards shown there, a large glass of whisky at his elbow. He didn't look round as the door opened.

'Mother's gone to bed and I'm going up now.' There was no point at this moment in raising the matter of Victor's coming to live with them. 'Is there anything I can get you? There's plenty of leftover turkey.'

The tension in Mark's shoulders seemed to increase. 'Women,' he said loudly to the television screen. 'No sense of loyalty, that's their trouble. Take Polly. Willoughby's given her everything and look how she's repaying him.' He swung round in his chair and looked straight at Louise. 'And now you're doing the same to me.'

She looked at him. 'I am not leaving you, I'm taking a job for a couple of weeks, that's all,' she said slowly and distinctly. 'One week of which you are not going to be here for anyway.'

'Don't talk to me as though I'm a child!' Mark was suddenly furious.

'And don't you treat me as though I am one,' she flared at him. 'I have a life of my own, I'm not your slave to be ordered around!'

The anger that had built up during the long, long day spilled over. 'Haven't you any idea how you're behaving?' she demanded. 'You've been like a bear all over Christmas and today you told your sisters we'll have your father to live with us without even asking if that's all right with me. I don't know you anymore, Mark.' Her energy suddenly ran out. 'What's happened to you?' she added in a whisper.

Mark reached for his drink and swallowed half. 'I thought you loved me,' he said pathetically.

'Oh, for God's sake!' Exasperation replaced the anger. 'Love isn't the issue here, it's respect. Your respect for me and what I need from life.' She stopped abruptly as she realised that the whisky on top of the champagne Mark had drunk so freely this morning meant he was in no condition for this sort of discussion.

'I do love you, I've always loved you,' Mark insisted, his voice now slurred. He reached out for his glass again and knocked it to the floor, splashing the amber liquid over the pale newness of the carpet. 'Oh dear,' he said with a hiccup. 'Oh, dear, that was me! Now you'll be cross.'

'Oh, go to bed,' Louise said wearily. 'We can talk in the morning.'

In the morning Mark didn't appear.

Eventually Louise took a cup of black coffee upstairs. He grunted painfully and hunched himself under the duvet as she drew back the curtains. Louise put the cup on his bedside table and went downstairs again.

'Don't disturb him,' said Betty when she was ready to leave. 'Give him my love when he surfaces. I remember your father being just

161

like that.' She looked concerned for a moment, then smiled reassuringly at her daughter. 'You mustn't worry about me, I've had a lovely Christmas, it's really put me on top of things again. I'll give you a ring in a day or so.' Then she remembered. 'Oh, but you're going away tomorrow, aren't you? Well, I'll ring this evening.'

Louise kissed her warmly, took her case out and put it into the back of the little Metro. Betty got in, started the car, clashed the gears, jerked it into reverse and skidded backwards into a flower bed, yanked it into first gear and then set off down the drive.

Louise stood and watched her go, then walked round to the back, shivering from the cold. It was a dark, dank and dreary day. The red hips on the shrub roses were shrivelled and the few leaves left on the trees hung limply as though they couldn't summon the energy to fall.

Inside, a wealth of sorting out and packing for Florida awaited Louise. She couldn't afford to waste a moment. She stood, shivering, and watched the birds attacking the crumbs she'd thrown out for them earlier.

With a ring of her bicycle bell, Mrs Parks arrived. 'Too cold to be in the garden,' she tutted as she alighted. 'Are you checking the veg?'

Louise shook her head. 'We had the last of the sprouts on Christmas Day. Nothing now until the spring.' She rubbed her arms to get the circulation going. 'It seems to be getting colder. Do you think we'll have snow?'

Mrs Parks leaned her bicycle against the kitchen wall. 'Nah, it needs to be warmer. Just more of those danged old frosts.'

Both women went into the kitchen. 'Had a nice time, have you?' asked Mrs Parks, looking about her. 'House still standing, I see. Party went well?'

'Not without its little dramas but we managed to finish without blood on the floor, just. And how was your Christmas?' Louise put the kettle on the Aga.

Mrs Parks hung up her coat and stood arrayed in a very short skirt and what had obviously once been someone's best shirt. She had had a splendid Christmas, she told Louise, three of her children had popped in over Christmas and Boxing Day. 'Of course, Kev couldn't come, not with being in LA as he is. But he rang, said the weather's lovely out there.' Mrs Park looked out of the window at the desolate scene outside. 'We could all do with a bit of that sunshine, couldn't we?'

'And I'm going to get it,' Louise announced. She talked about the Florida trip while she made them both a cup of coffee without asking Mrs Parks if she wanted one.

'My,' said Mrs Parks admiringly, stacking Louise and Betty's breakfast things in the dishwasher. She accepted the mug without comment. 'That's the ticket, isn't it? Good for you, dear. You need

162

a bit of cheering up, what with the twins not here and Mr Henderson always being away like he is. 'Course, I know it's a job and not a holiday but no reason why you shouldn't enjoy it as well, is there?'

'No, Mrs Parks, there isn't,' Louise said determinedly. 'Mrs Toler sounds interesting and I think I shall enjoy being her companion. And Mark's off again. To Copenhagen on New Year's Eve.'

'Never know what they're up to, half the time, do you?' Mrs Parks observed with perfect equanimity. 'Well, if he's back before you, I'll make sure he's all right.' She rolled up the sleeves of her too-large silk shirt and reached underneath the sink for the bleach. 'I can always go to M & S for some of their nice meals and put them in the fridge for him.'

Louise took a gulp of her coffee, feeling the caffeine ricochet round her body. Deep down she was incredibly weary. 'Oh, would you, Mrs Parks? I don't think I'm going to have time to do any shopping before I go. He'll be all right until he leaves, there're masses of leftovers.'

But Mark would probably spend his days in the office. It would be open even over the weekend. No doubt he'd be having discussions with Robin Howard about the Danish trip, not sitting at home all alone, wondering where his wife was.

She drank more coffee and went over to the tin where she always kept some housekeeping money. 'I'll tell Mark to ring and let you know when he's coming back, then if you could get some milk and bread and stuff, I'd be very grateful.' She handed over a crisp note.

Mrs Parks stuffed it into her gaily coloured leather bag, brought back by one of her children from Morocco. ''Spect there'll be mutterings about you going off on your own but we'll pay no attention to that, will we?' Her bright eyes fixed themselves on Louise's face and she beamed warmly.

Louise thought about Mr Parks and his weak back. Not much support there for his family. Yet his wife went on cheerfully with her life and never said a word against him.

'How long is it you've been married now?' Louise opened the fridge and started checking its contents.

'We'll have our thirtieth next year,' Mrs Parks declared with pride. She advanced on the Aga with a damp cloth and wiped down its gleaming enamelled surface. 'What about you?'

'It'll be our twentieth in July.' Nearly twenty years they'd been married. For a blinding moment Louise remembered their early days: so much fun, so much hope, so much togetherness.

'That's nice. It's awful the way so many marriages just don't last these days.' Mrs Parks turned her attention to the island's surfaces, skilfully tidying the assorted pepper and salt mills, knife blocks and other impedimenta that found a home there.

Louise started slicing up the remains of the turkey and ham.

163

She'd put some in the deep freeze then leave the rest for tonight's supper and for Mark before he left for Copenhagen. 'What do you think makes a marriage last?' she asked as she hacked away at the ham.

'Oh, now that's a question!' Mrs Parks continued to wield her cloth. 'I reckon it's determination, that's what.'

'On one person's part or both?'

'Ah, well, takes a bit of effort from both but I always think there's one what has to do more of the giving than the other.'

'Then there comes a point when that one isn't prepared to keep on giving any longer, I suppose?'

'More than like,' Mrs Parks agreed.

The kitchen door opened and Mark stuck his head round. 'I'm off for a game of squash with Colin. Don't know when I'll be back.'

'That's all right,' Louise said steadily. She wondered when she'd see him again.

When Mark was still not back by five-thirty, she rang a local taxi firm and ordered a cab to take her to the airport the following morning. If Mark did want to take her, she could always cancel.

She had just put down the phone when the door bell rang.

It was Victor.

'Dad! Come in. How lovely to see you. But you shouldn't be out on such an awful day, especially in the dark.' The lights from the house illuminated a driving sleet which had started an hour earlier.

'Brrr – dreadful weather! The sooner you're in Florida, my dear, the better.' Victor hustled himself inside, taking gloves off hands that were obviously frozen despite the protection. 'Now, is Mark taking you to the airport, or can I do the honours?'

Louise took his coat, rain glistening on the heavy material, and hung it over the newel post. 'You are sweet but I expect Mark will take me.'

Victor gave her a keen look. 'I tried to talk some sense into him last night but the last thing he wanted was to listen to his old father. I'm afraid the chauvinistic instinct lives in my son. Don't think he gets it from me, though. His mother was a wonderful woman but old-fashioned in many ways.'

'Believed in a woman's place being in the home?' Louise grinned at him. Victor was a very comfortable person to be with. 'A cup of tea or something stronger?'

'Since I have to drive back and the night being what it is, I think it had better be tea.' He took something out of the pocket of his coat and followed her into the kitchen. 'I've got you an extra Christmas present,' he said and put the packet on the island.

'Dad! You shouldn't have, you gave me that lovely cashmere sweater.' Louise looked at the oblong parcel curiously.

'Open it,' Victor said, sitting down on the banquette.

Again Louise noticed the slight tremor in his hands. The effect of the cold? She sat beside him and put a hand on his. 'You all right, Dad?'

'I'm fine,' he said cheerfully. 'Cold gets into one's bones, though. Penalty of old age, I suppose.' He glanced at her sharply. 'I'm not ready for the scrap heap yet, though.'

'You know, Dad,' she said gently, still holding his hand, 'Mark and I would love you to come and live with us.'

She'd startled him, she could see that. An unreadable emotion crossed his face then he seemed to gather himself up, sit taller. He returned the pressure of her hand then gently removed his. 'That's sweet of you, my dear, and I appreciate the thought. But I hope you're not suggesting I'm not capable of looking after myself?' His voice was very steady and so was his gaze.

Louise felt reassured. 'Of course not, Dad. We'd enjoy having you here for your company, that's all. It has to be your decision, just think about it.' She got up and put the kettle on then unwrapped the gift.

It was a mobile telephone.

'I know you've always said you didn't need one,' Victor explained. 'But you can use this to phone from the US, or the children can ring you from wherever they are. There's a charger as well, works off any voltage.'

Louise looked at her father-in-law, touched beyond anything. 'That's the nicest present you could have given me. I shall ring you as soon as I get there. How on earth did you manage to get it today?'

'That's modern life for you. Anything can be obtained at any time, provided you have credit. You don't even have to have cash. Just let your fingers do the walking.' He looked very pleased with himself. 'Didn't like to think of you off there without being able to touch base, as you might say. Know how difficult it can be using someone else's phone to make international calls. You'd better see if you can work out how to use it. Chap showed me and I might just be able to remember if you can't understand the instructions. The battery is all charged, I insisted.'

Louise made the tea, brought it over to the table and they sat together working out how to use the phone. Then she rang her mother on it.

Halfway through the call, Mark came in.

'Dad?' he said questioningly.

'Sorry, Mother, have to go now. Ring you soon.' Louise switched off the phone. 'Look!' she said, glowing with pleasure. 'Look what your father's given me.'

'You never wanted a mobile phone,' Mark protested.

'But it means I can ring you from the States, and Mother – and Dad, of course – and the children can ring me. And so can you,' she added quickly. 'I'll write the number down for you.'

'You'll spend more on phone bills than you'll earn,' he said sourly.

She got up and fetched a mug then poured out some tea for him.

'I'll take this into the study,' he said. 'You don't mind, do you, Dad?'

'I do, actually,' said Victor quietly. 'I'd prefer it if you'd snap out of your childish sulks and behave properly, both to your wife and to me.'

Mark glowered at him.

'I can't take this,' he said simply and left the room.

Victor followed him.

Louise waited, her mind a blank, and played with the telephone.

After a little Victor came back, his expression dismayed. 'I can't get through to him,' he said despairingly. 'My dear, I'm so sorry. Are you sure you wouldn't like me to take you to the airport tomorrow morning?' His eyes were worried. 'I don't like you to go off on your own and it doesn't look as though Mark is going to.'

It was a gallant offer. This eighty-four-year-old man had preferred not to drive himself to his daughter's, a journey of less than thirty miles, and now was offering to do more than twice as much for Louise.

'It's very kind of you, Dad, but I've ordered a taxi. I'd prefer to go on my own.'

'He'll come round, you know,' Victor said, sounding none too sure. 'He's just never had to deal with a situation like this before.'

'On a steep learning curve, isn't that what the jargon is?' Louise gave a small smile. 'Well, I'm on a learning curve, too. I wonder where it's going to take me – and Mark,' she added.

166

Chapter Nineteen

'Where did you say that girl was going to meet us?' Gladys Toler demanded of her son as he steered the luggage trolley towards the check-in desks.

'By Virgin Airways,' he said imperturbably. 'She's going to be carrying a copy of the *Independent*.'

'Lot of nonsense! I'm perfectly capable of looking after myself.'

'Of course you are,' he agreed. 'It's just to keep us happy. Now, do you need your other stick as well as that one?'

Gladys controlled her impatience with her infirmities. It wasn't Michael's fault she hated not only the pain she continually suffered but also the way it made her dependent on others. All her life she had been independent; had fought for that independence; it was very hard now to have to admit she needed others. 'I can manage, thank you, darling,' she said, some of her frustration coming through despite herself.

He looked at her closely then seemed to decide to take her statement at face value. 'Right,' he said and continued pushing the trolley.

Gladys gritted her teeth and swung her painful knees in a jerky action behind him.

It seemed a long way to the check-in desk and she began seriously to consider calling a halt so she could pull out her collapsible stick from the small haversack she wore on her back. But that would be a sign of weakness. She struggled on, grimly determined.

'How you doing, Ma?' Michael Toler stopped and allowed her to catch up with him. She suddenly realised how tired he looked. And no wonder. He'd been on call Boxing Day and had spent most of the time visiting patients, dealing with a premature baby, two heart attacks and several minor ills. People shouldn't need medical attention over the Christmas period, it was inconsiderate. Then he'd had to stand in at surgery yesterday for a partner down with 'flu. This evening he'd be back there.

'I'm fine,' she puffed, 'nearly there. You shouldn't have brought me. Joyce said she could easily do it. Or I could have got a taxi.'

'But I wanted to,' Michael told her gently. 'I wouldn't have been happy unless I'd seen you off.'

'Unless you'd checked out the new carer, you mean,' Gladys

167

gasped, trying to get her breath back. 'It's all a load of nonsense. I didn't mind Shirley. Even though I didn't need her, she was company. But I'm too old to start getting to know someone else. Not too old to get myself to Florida, though,' she added hastily.

'Of course you aren't, you're just indulging your family,' he said with a smile.

Gladys let this go, she needed all her energy to keep moving her knees along. This, she swore, was the last time she'd do this trip, with or without a minder. Michael was trying to persuade her into a wheelchair but she was damned if she was going to give up her independence one moment sooner than she had to. It was bad enough having to take all the pills he prescribed.

At last the Virgin Airways check-in desks loomed into view.

Gladys looked around. 'Can't see any *Independent*s,' she said with satisfaction. 'Good, she hasn't come. I can go on my own.'

'Don't get your hopes up.' Her son grinned at her. 'She'll be along any minute.'

Gladys leaned against the luggage trolley while Michael checked her into the upper-class section. Her minder would be travelling economy. Mary, her daughter, had offered two upper-class return tickets but Gladys's independent streak wouldn't let her accept them. She was able to afford upper-class on her own account and liked being able to set a little distance between her carer and herself. Shirley was such a fusser while they were travelling, she hoped this woman wasn't going to treat her like an outsize infant.

'Hello, are you Mrs Toler?' asked a voice.

'Yes, we're the Tolers,' Michael said eagerly.

Gladys swung herself round and found she was facing a slight woman with dark hair and large grey eyes who looked younger than the late-thirties they had been told was her age.

She was flustered. 'I'm so sorry I'm late. My taxi took me to the wrong terminal.' She held out her hand. 'I'm Louise Henderson, Mrs Toler. What a shame about your other carer, it must be such a nuisance to have to get used to someone new.'

Well, she seemed to have a certain amount of sense. 'You won't have much to do,' Gladys said with a dry laugh, shaking the woman's hand and feeling the youthfulness of its skin. Her own was mottled with liver spots and dry with age. 'We'll rub along well enough, I'm sure.'

Michael gave Louise her ticket and nodded apologetically towards one of the economy queues. 'That one's the shortest, I think.'

Gladys watched while Louise took her place at the end of the line. They'd arrived early so there weren't many people ahead of her.

Gladys's two suitcases vanished on to the conveyor belt behind the check-in desk. 'Here are your boarding card, return ticket and passport,' Michael said, handing the collection to her. 'Do you feel strong enough to go and get to know Mrs Henderson now? Or would you rather I found you somewhere to sit?'

'I can always sit on the baggage trolley,' she said, leading the way over to her new carer. She looked curiously at the small case on Louise Henderson's trolley. 'Is this all your luggage?'

Louise hefted a holdall that hung from her shoulder. 'I've got this as well. I didn't think I'd need a lot of clothes and summer ones don't take much room, do they?'

'Good, someone who can travel light.' Gladys thought of her own two large bags that had disappeared into the baggage system. She never knew what she'd need and was always terrified of running out of reading material. Not being very mobile had many disadvantages, chief of which was having to spend so much time sitting around when there wasn't a car she could drive. Such a weight, books were, but she knew she wouldn't have to carry her own luggage.

'Now, Ma, are you sure you don't want a wheelchair to get to the plane? It's not too late to arrange one. You know the miles you have to walk.' Michael looked worried.

'I'm not a cripple,' Gladys said, more than a little impatiently, annoyance at his suggestion fighting with her desire to remove the frown lines from his forehead.

'Of course you aren't,' he said hastily.

'Oh, please say you want to be taken,' Louise Henderson put in. 'I've always wanted to travel on one of those people carts. They look such fun.'

Gladys eyed her suspiciously. The large grey eyes regarded her with a lively air, the mouth curved into a winning smile. Louise Henderson was hard to resist.

'Fun, eh? You think it'll be fun?'

'Oh, yes. Leaving all the pedestrians behind as you swish along.'

Gladys was far too canny to fall for this approach but her knees were paining her even more than usual and there was a long trip ahead. For once it seemed that playing along with someone else's ideas could be justified. 'I suppose if it'll give you a treat,' she said, somewhat grudgingly, then decided that Michael's look of gratitude was worth the concession. He went back to the upper-class desk to make the necessary arrangement.

Then, after Louise had been booked in, they were shown to a little enclosure where they had to wait for the transport. Once there Gladys reached up and kissed her son. 'Go now, Michael, please. Joyce is at home and your grandson will be there by the time you get back. You know you don't want to miss a moment of him,' she said gruffly. She was sorry not to be there herself. She'd gone over to Michael and Joyce for Christmas Day but had missed all their three children. The two younger ones had gone skiing and the elder girl, her husband and nine-month-old baby boy, were arriving today from Scotland to stay until the New Year. Gladys hadn't seen her great-grandson yet. Yes, she decided, this really would be the last time she flew off to Florida, there was too much going on here.

Michael looked as though he were going to argue, thought better of it, kissed Gladys and was gone.

'Now, Louise,' she said, 'you'd better tell me about yourself.' She scrutinised her companion carefully and was puzzled to find her first quick impression confirmed. Gladys didn't know much about fashion but Louise's clothes looked expensive, as did the gold chain round her neck. Her shoes were good quality, too, as was her casual-looking shoulder bag. Why was she doing this job? Suddenly lost all her money? Husband left her? Young widow? She looked strained, as though life was not easy for her at the moment. Yes, some crisis had taken place in her life, Gladys was willing to bet on it.

Louise sat quietly but, despite the air of tension, her eyes were alive with humour and she appeared to be studying Gladys as closely as Gladys was scrutinising her.

'Hmm, so what do you see?' she asked imperiously. She liked to rattle people with unexpected demands and comments. It cut through a lot of the flim-flam, enabled her to assess their true quality, and she wanted to get on terms with her companion quickly.

Louise smiled. 'Someone with a lot of character who likes her own way, and a person who is damned if she's going to give in.'

Gladys was delighted. 'Right! Now tell me why you've agreed to come with me? You're not intending to spend your time sunbathing, are you?' She regretted suggesting this as soon as she'd said it; she didn't want Louise to think she had to dance attendance on her charge.

'I don't think you'd mind if I did,' Louise said, and met Gladys's fierce gaze with dancing eyes. She suddenly looked even younger. 'I think you hate the idea of a carer, Mrs Toler.'

'Gladys, please, don't make me feel any older than I already do. And you can leave me and my feelings out of it. I want to know what you're doing here.'

She watched the delight fade from Louise's expression, the tension return.

'Need the money, do you?' It was an impertinent question but Gladys felt her age and position gave her certain privileges and was determined to take advantage of them.

'Not exactly,' Louise said with a trace of reluctance. Then she looked Gladys straight in the face. 'I want to do a job.'

'You do, huh? This sort of job?'

'You see, I don't have any real qualifications,' she confessed, her eyes wide and serious.

Gladys gave a shout of laughter that had the infirm and aged passengers also waiting for transport looking round at her. 'So that's what I've become, is it? An opportunity for employment for those unfitted for anything else?'

'We all have our uses,' the girl shot back with an enchanting smile.

'Do you have family?' Gladys demanded, beginning to feel distinctly hopeful about this new relationship.

'An accountant husband who spends half his time travelling and twins who are now on a trip around the world.'

'And you want to prove you can hold down a proper job, is that it?'

'Right!' Louise looked delighted to have been understood so quickly. 'What was your career?'

'You mean, I obviously have some fellow feeling for you?' Gladys had forgotten her aching knees. 'I was an engineer.'

'Really?' Louise was impressed. 'You must have had a tough time qualifying? There can't have been many women taking engineering then.'

'I was the only one on my course,' Gladys acknowledged. 'Everybody expected me to give up in the first few months. It took a long time to convince them that I both could and would make it.'

'You still practise?'

'No,' she had to acknowledge. Even after ten years it was distressing to wake each morning without an office to go to, problems to solve, projects to supervise. Gladys's family were fond of telling her that, now she was retired, she looked on people as engineering problems. 'You want to adjust their gearing, alter their energy sources, discover their breaking points and find out how they can avoid reaching them,' Michael had once said. 'You don't seem to understand that humans can't be treated like mechanical devices. One of these days you'll interfere too much and then you'll be sorry.'

Now Gladys reached out and patted Louise's hand. 'You and I will have lots to talk about later. Have you got all you want for the journey?'

Louise laughed, the look of tension once again dissolving. 'I should be asking you that. Do you want a magazine or a newspaper?'

'I have everything I need.' Gladys felt a positive fizz of anticipation.

'The agency said you were going to stay with your daughter. Can you tell me something about her?'

'Good question. Why does a daughter need a carer for her mother, eh? That's what you really want to know, isn't it?'

'You obviously have difficulty in getting about,' Louise said gently.

171

'Oh, that!' Gladys was dismissive. 'I manage. But Mary's terrified I'll fall while she's out, or get bored when she's working.'

'Is she an engineer as well?'

Gladys chuckled. 'No, she channelled her creativity into quite a different direction, much to my surprise. I could understand Michael's becoming a doctor – medicine and engineering are not so far apart. But Mary's a writer. Specialises in television: soap operas, weepy dramas, that sort of thing. No use to anyone,' she added cheerfully.

'That sounds fascinating! I love a really soppy play.' Louise's sincerity was patent.

'You do?' Gladys was interested. 'Why?'

'It's relaxing, like a warm bath. You don't have to think, just lie back and enjoy.'

'Humph! Give up thinking and you might as well give up living.'

'But isn't it exhausting when you do it all the time?'

'I wouldn't know, I don't know how to stop.'

Louise looked at her with interest. 'Does your daughter take after you?'

Gladys thought about Mary, the constant battles they had had as she grew up. Michael had been relatively easy, Mary had been the one who challenged everything.

'Yes, she said slowly. 'I think she does.' It was a great pity that she had gone off to the States after graduation and then married an American just as she was maturing. She and her mother might have become friends then. Two weeks once a year wasn't enough to forge a proper relationship.

'And what do you do together when you visit?' asked Louise.

Gladys gave a little grunt, somewhere between exasperation and acceptance. 'Mary always has great plans that are constantly defeated by the fact she has to work. According to her, she tries to arrange things so she's free when I'm there but the unexpected insists on coming along. She's even been known to fly off for overnight meetings. Last year, I'd no sooner arrived than she announced she had to go to Los Angeles, leaving me on my own for three days!'

'What a shame, you must both have been very upset.'

'I know I was and I think she was too. But she still went,' Gladys said sadly.

'Is your daughter married?'

Gladys sighed. 'She's divorced. Twice. Neither husband seemed able to stand the fact that she earned more than he did.'

'I think husbands often find it difficult to accept that wives can have jobs that matter,' Louise said quietly.

Gladys looked at her with renewed interest; that comment sounded heartfelt. 'Your husband one of them?'

From the expression on Louise's face, Gladys knew immediately

172

she had put her finger on the problem. 'He doesn't think I'm capable of holding down a job that matters.' Then Louise thought for a moment and added, 'No, that's not quite right. He thinks I should be content with the job of being a wife and mother.'

'But you've lost the children and don't have your husband half the time, is that it?' Louise didn't say anything, just looked as though she'd rather she hadn't spoken.

'Of course you want some other interest,' Gladys said gently. 'I found the housewife bit the most boring job in the world. Luckily I was married to a man who agreed with me. We made a good partnership. Lewis was an engineer as well, we built our own consultancy together. He died fifteen years ago. I've missed him every day since.' Her voice trailed off.

'I'm sorry,' Louise said gently, losing her look of introspection.

'I survive,' Gladys commented gruffly.

'I'm going to enjoy getting to know you. This won't be a job, it'll be a holiday! And think of all that wonderful sun instead of this wretched weather we've got here.'

Gladys laughed again. 'You'll be tired of me long before the fortnight is over.'

'Want to bet? Oh, I think they've come for us,' Louise said as their names were called out.

Louise saw Gladys nicely settled in her seat then made her way to the rear of the plane. She didn't appear at all disconcerted by her inferior seating, though Gladys would have been willing to wager a large bet that it had been a long time since Louise Henderson had travelled anything but first-class. Now, instead of being able to continue their increasingly interesting conversation, Gladys had to assess the potential of her neighbour in upper-class.

He turned out to be a monosyllabic businessman who refused all refreshment, donned eye shades, swallowed two pills and settled himself for sleep as soon as they were in the air. Which meant Gladys was thrown back on her own resources. But at least the food was excellent and the wine palatable. After a while she began to relax. She put back her head, closed her eyes and thought about her new companion. Louise Henderson was a sweet young woman who obviously had problems. Reading between the lines, Gladys decided that her relationship with her husband was under severe strain.

The man hadn't driven her to the airport and the way she'd talked about him, trying so desperately to be fair, probably meant he was a sod. What was it she'd said – he was an accountant who spent half his time travelling?

Gladys only knew two accountants: the one who'd been financial director of her and Lewis's engineering company and the one currently looking after her financial affairs. Dry sticks both of them. Only interested in figures and what was referred to as 'the bottom line'. They didn't mean bikinis either!

It was going to be New Year's Eve in a few days yet the Hendersons were going to be apart. Whose decision had that been? Gladys didn't think it had been Louise's. No, she'd taken this job because her husband wasn't going to be around. Gladys remembered New Year's Eve when Lewis had been alive. They and a group of close friends had always taken it in turns to host a dinner party. Always lots of fun. But the best part had been Lewis and her on their own afterwards, talking over the evening that had just passed and outlining their hopes for the year to come. Gladys couldn't imagine anything that would have taken her away from him at such a time.

As the grinding pain in her knees gradually eased, she concluded that Louise's marriage was in deep difficulties and she was preparing to embark on a life of her own. Gladys decided that while they were in Florida, she would help Louise achieve her independence.

Gladys found this decision immensely stimulating. It gave a sense of purpose to her trip that would help if Mary became caught up in her work as usual. Yes, Gladys should be able to teach Louise how to wave goodbye to this obviously unsatisfactory husband of hers and find something else to do with her life.

Mulling over the possibilities occupied Gladys quite nicely for the rest of the trip. But it was a long time to be cooped up in a steel torpedo hurtling through the atmosphere and she gave a sigh of relief as their arrival was announced.

The businessman next door to her woke up, stripped off his eye shade and adjusted his watch. 'Soon adjust to the new tummy time,' he announced to her blandly. 'Great secret is not to drink while in the air. Eating's no good either.'

Gladys wasn't interested in his personal anti-jet lag philosophy. She was exhausted and her knees were once again aching badly. She called the stewardess for a cup of water and swallowed some painkillers. She was damned if Mary was going to see her at anything less than her best.

Emerging from the relative calm of the international section into the mayhem of the general concourse of Miami airport, walking independently but with Louise close beside, Gladys looked for her daughter.

No sign of Mary Baxter.

'Look,' said Louise, and pointed towards a tall man waving a piece of cardboard at them on which was printed: Gladys Toler.

Gladys was surprised by the depth of her disappointment; she had been counting on seeing her daughter in the flesh after what was nearly a year.

Louise was waving to the man who was already advancing towards them. No doubt Mary had described her crippled mother accurately enough. Gladys threw herself into a rapid stagger, using both sticks in a way that cleared a path through the jostling crowds with miraculous efficiency, left Louise behind and had the man fielding her as she staggered over a small child who had strayed into her path.

'Mrs Toler, this is a pleasure!' he said as he courteously helped her to regain her balance. 'Mary is so sorry but she's been called to New York today. She couldn't get out of it – a meeting of people from all points of the compass, the only day the majority could make it. I'm Jake Muller. I'm staying with Sam. He couldn't come either so I volunteered.'

Sam Stahl was Mary's new beau. At least, that was the way he'd been described to Gladys by Beth, Mary's grownup daughter. 'Mom has this absolutely delicious man,' she had said six months ago. 'He's just so dishy, such a beau! I only hope she doesn't bawl him out like all the other men in her life. I'd like to see her happily settled.' It had sounded a little strange coming from a twenty-four year old, but this particular twenty-four year old had just finished medical school and was heavily into maturity. She had had the same boyfriend for the last five years, another medical student, and they planned to marry when each was properly set on their career.

And this was Sam's friend. While she thanked him for coming to meet them, Gladys took stock of the unexpected arrival.

Tall and spare, with a shock of dark hair, Jake's looks would never sell menswear. His hawk-like nose had a Wellingtonian authority. The rest of his face was equally bony but his eyes were dark and sparkled with intelligence and humour. His mouth was wide and slightly lopsided and his ears were big. It all added up to a face that commanded attention and suggested warmth and humour. Maybe not a beau but definitely the sort of man Gladys had time for.

'Now, ladies, let's find the car,' he said after he'd shaken hands with them both. 'Can I give you a hand here?' He offered an arm to Gladys, who for once was happy to hand her collapsible stick to Louise and hang on.

'You staying long with Sam?' she enquired as they engaged the services of a redcap to deal with the luggage. Miami airport didn't seem to offer baggage trolleys.

'Undecided at the moment. Sam and I go way back,' Jake volunteered.

'I think Beth told me he was a graphic designer. That your line as well?' Gladys probed.

Jake seemed amused by her curiosity. 'No, ma'am, I'm an historian, professor at one of our colleges over here. Oh, and I write, like Mary. Well, not quite like Mary. I write historical books, and no one pays me a fortune for them.'

'Fact or fiction?' asked Gladys, liking this man who seemed to have a sense of humour and a degree of intelligence.

'With history it's not always easy to decide but librarians place them on the non-fiction shelves. Watch yourself crossing this road.' He grabbed Gladys's elbow at the edge of the pavement outside the main building. Cars, coaches and taxis whizzed along between them and the car park. 'Mary would never forgive me if I lost you before she'd even had a chance to say hello.' He carefully guided Gladys across, glancing back to see that Louise was managing on her own, and then led the way to a comfortable-looking Buick, still talking easily.

Jake had a nice deep rumble for a voice. Gladys could imagine a class of students listening entranced.

He opened the car boot, helped the redcap load in the luggage, then tipped him and settled Gladys in the front and Louise behind.

As he drove them out of the airport, Gladys said, 'We do appreciate your meeting us like this, Jake. I hope we're not taking you away from a family?'

He whipped the car into the flow of swiftly moving traffic. 'No, ma'am, I'm not encumbered with that sort of baggage. My wife and I divorced some years ago.'

'Sorry to hear that,' Gladys said gleefully. 'Do you have children?'

'Two, both in college.'

'I have two children as well, they're starting university next year,' Louise volunteered from the back of the car. 'They're twins.'

'Twins, are they?' Jake looked in the rear-view mirror to catch Louise's eye. 'That must be really interesting.'

As she started to chatter about Emma and James and Jake drove skilfully through the maze of Miami traffic up towards Palm Beach, the tiny seed that had planted itself in Gladys's mind while they waited for the luggage began to sprout into a fully fledged idea.

What Louise needed was a man like Jake!

Chapter Twenty

The train rushed through the flat French landscape. Thick clouds pressed down from the sky, the fields were dark, frost-rimed, winter-gripped. Polly, too, felt frozen, outside and inside. The train was warm but she shivered as she shrank into the depths of the seat, making herself small, pulling up the collar of her Armani jacket.

She had the Eurostar compartment almost to herself. Apparently not many people wanted to visit Paris in early January. There was no chance of striking up a conversation with someone else to help pass the time and divert her from the implications of her journey.

Polly glanced at her watch. Another hour before they arrived at the Gare du Nord. And there Jean-Paul would be.

She closed her eyes and tried to summon the delight that normally rushed through her at the mere thought of his name. Now that she had at last taken the decision to leave Willoughby, that delight should be magnified a thousandfold. Soon she and Jean-Paul would be together. No need for anymore subterfuge, snatched meetings, messy partings. No more uncertain joy. Now the sweetness they'd found together would contain no bitterness. All she should be feeling was ecstasy and joyous anticipation.

Instead, Polly felt empty. She had slammed the door behind her that morning with a sense of overwhelming relief that all the agonising was over. In the taxi going to Waterloo she hadn't dared to think of Paris; instead she'd sat going over all the little things she'd had to do before leaving. Collecting Willoughby's cleaning, arranging for her daily to provide him with meals, cancelling her fitness training, her hair and beauty appointments, two dinner parties they'd been invited to – the list had seemed endless.

But everything had eventually been done. The last task had been the hardest of all: taking Caroline back to school. Willoughby had insisted on coming too. 'She's my daughter as well,' he'd grated at Polly when she'd pleaded to take her alone.

Perhaps, though, it had been for the best. Caroline had refused to speak to Polly for the last three days – ever since Boxing Day morning when she'd come into the cosy little room where Willoughby and Caroline were playing cards and announced she was going to Paris and wouldn't be coming back.

It had been while clearing up breakfast that she had actually come to her decision. She'd dropped one of the bowls that had been a wedding present. The gold-rimmed porcelain had bounced once on the Provençal tiles of the floor then broken into several pieces. Polly had picked up the bits and tried to fit them together on the work surface, her mind rapidly running through her list of repairers. Someone must be able to glue it together, the pattern had been discontinued. Why on earth had she been using the best china today anyway – still trying to impress Willoughby with her efforts after all these years?

For a long moment she had stood there, the smallest piece still held in her hand, while a rapid series of scenes from her marriage unspooled before her mind's eye.

Finally, with an impatient gesture, she had swept up the bits from the work top, dumped them in the waste bin, gone through to her husband and child and launched into her bald statement.

Caroline had gone quite white, her eyes enormous behind the wire-framed spectacles, her mouth pinched. Suddenly Polly could see what she'd look like at forty if life were unkind to her.

'You've told that Frenchman, I take it?' Willoughby said stiffly, not looking at her.

'No,' Polly said tensely. She hadn't spoken to Jean-Paul for several days. She'd said then she wouldn't ring again until she'd made her decision. Their conversations were tearing her apart.

'You know I want you more than anything,' he'd said quietly. 'But I will respect whatever you decide.'

'You're a liar!' Caroline burst out passionately to her mother. 'You swore you weren't having an affair with him.'

'I'm sorry, darling,' Polly had said to her, ignoring Willoughby who sat, eyes downcast, face stony. 'I thought I could make it true. If anything could have kept me here, it was you. But I want you to come to me in Paris for your holidays. Don't say anything now,' she rushed on, 'it's too soon, too difficult. Think about it at school. Come over at Easter and just see if you like it. If you don't want to stay with Jean-Paul, I can get us an apartment on our own. You can see all your Paris friends.' She was gabbling now, clasping her hands together. She forced herself to stop. 'Forgive me,' she finished abruptly and left the room. Her husband and daughter watched her go silently.

Caroline had worn the same haunted expression until she'd gone back to school. She'd avoided Polly, leaving a room the moment her mother entered it. She'd spent most of the time in her bedroom with her computer, taking her meals up there as well. Willoughby went straight up the moment he returned from work, not even bothering to greet Polly.

Getting together Caroline's trunk, efficiently and ruthlessly making the arrangements for her own departure as well, packing away personal belongings ready for despatch at a later date, had kept

178

Polly from thinking anymore about her decision. She had bottled up all her feelings, kept going like an automaton.

Now, at last, on the train going to meet Jean-Paul, she could release everything she had kept dammed up.

But all she could feel was emptiness.

Even the thought of Jean-Paul waiting for her at the Gare du Nord couldn't light the flame of anticipation, of surging joy, that it should.

For one horror-stricken moment, Polly wondered whether she was doing the right thing. Should she stay on the train when it reached Paris and return to Waterloo? Go back to Willoughby so Caroline could still have her parents living together?

There flashed before Polly a vision of all the evenings she'd waited alone until Willoughby returned home; the weekends she'd done her own thing while he played golf or squash, went to the pub with 'the boys', worked on reports and projects. Other times when he'd dragged her to boring company dinners. The number of evenings she'd chatted up men and tried to make them forget they'd rather be talking business, and many times succeeded, making them receptive to another evening with the Fawkeses and the idea of getting closer to Willoughby. Oh, she'd been a good wife all right. But Willoughby hadn't seemed to realise she'd needed more in return than expensive birthday and Christmas presents and a more than comfortable lifestyle.

If only he'd involved her more in what was going on in his mind, made her a partner rather than a personal assistant. If only he'd sat down with her when he had come home and told her what he'd been up to, asked her opinion of things, instead of asking for a drink and then sitting moodily, ignoring all her attempts to draw him out. If only he hadn't forgotten all about making her feel desirable almost as soon as they were married.

The real mistake had been hers, she'd finally admitted, and if it hadn't been for Caroline in her womb, she would never have made it.

Caroline was the one saving grace in the whole sorry mess. Polly had loved her daughter with all her heart from the first moment she'd been placed in her arms. She was nothing like the child she'd imagined she would have, shared none of her mother's interests and Polly found it hard to understand her. But none of that mattered. Caroline was hers and she loved her. For her sake Polly had made the very best of her marriage she could. But now she couldn't continue any longer. More than that, she was convinced that Caroline would fare worse if her parents went on living together than if they parted. Polly could remember growing up in a house where her mother despised her father but couldn't bring herself to leave him. She remembered the arguments, the fights, the tensions, the way each parent had tried to enlist the support of the children.

179

Polly didn't want Caroline to remember her parents like that.

No, she couldn't go back. Once she was in Paris, everything was going to be all right.

Jean-Paul would fold her in his arms, she'd feel the thud of his heart as he kissed her, her body would respond as it did only to his, she would look into his dark eyes under their lazy lids and know that at last she was home.

By the time the train pulled in to the station, dead on time, Polly could hardly wait to catch up her luggage, pile it on a baggage cart and fly down the platform, through the brief formalities, down the escalator and on to the concourse, her eyes eagerly seeking Jean-Paul's slight and dapper figure.

He was not there.

She hung on to the baggage cart, weak with disappointment. Then found a corner in which to wait for him.

Half an hour later she pulled out her mobile phone and rang his apartment. Only to get the answering machine.

It had been the answering machine to which she had given her arrival details. Even after she'd made her decision, she'd waited, to be absolutely sure, before ringing Jean-Paul on the evening of New Year's Day to tell him she was coming to Paris for good.

There'd been an intake of breath from the other end of the phone. Then: 'Ah, *chérie*, you are certain?' he'd asked.

'Of course,' she'd said. 'I can't wait to get to you. I'd come tomorrow if I could but there's Caroline to get back to school and a thousand and one things to do here.'

'I understand,' he'd said gently. 'Come as soon as you can. I will be waiting. Just let me know the details.'

Polly had wanted to stay on the phone, asking for reassurance, for Jean-Paul to tell her again and again how much he loved her, how much he wanted her, but Caroline had walked into the bedroom and stood implacably waiting for her to finish the call, her stormy eyes daring her to continue talking. 'I'll ring you back, Polly had told Jean-Paul, put down the phone and stretched out her hand to her daughter. 'Come and sit with me, let's talk,' she'd pleaded.

'I hate you,' her daughter had said, not moving an inch towards her. 'I won't come to Paris, the only place I'll ever see you is here.' Then she'd left the room.

Polly had sat on the bed and restrained herself from running after her. She'd rung Jean-Paul back and then burst into tears. 'I can't talk to you now,' she'd sobbed finally. 'I'll ring you in a couple of days. By then I'll know when I'm coming.'

'I'll call you tomorrow,' he'd said.

'No,' Polly had told him. 'It's too difficult.'

He'd understood and hadn't rung her.

Now Polly waited at the Gare du Nord and started to wonder. He couldn't have got cold feet, could he? It was no use ringing

180

Marie-Claire, she was off skiing with her husband.

Polly opened her Filofax and looked up Jean-Paul's office number. She hated ringing men at their offices, listening to secretaries say with chilly politeness that they weren't available. But what other option did she have?

A few minutes later Jean-Paul's secretary told her he wasn't available, could she help?

At least she sounded reasonably friendly. 'Will he be back soon?' Polly asked, feeling a stab of fear. Perhaps Jean-Paul had been involved in an accident on his way to meet her.

'Not for another week,' the secretary said, her voice unconcerned.

'A week?' Polly's own voice rose uncontrollably. 'Where's he gone?'

'New York. You did not know?'

'No,' she whispered. 'When did he leave?'

'Two days ago. It was very sudden.' The girl's voice became confidential, almost conspiratorial. 'There is a small crisis in our office there, no? M. Hupel had to go without ceremony, immediately. He tells me he thinks he returns in one week. I give him a message for you?'

Polly shook her head then said, 'No, I will ring him when he returns.'

'Perhaps your name, I can tell him you rang?' the secretary probed, now patently curious.

'No, thank you, it was nothing.' Polly rang off and stood for a moment blindly surveying the busy scene, taking in nothing. Not even the fact that Jean-Paul appeared to have left the country without telling her.

Slowly some sort of automatic control clicked in. She wheeled her luggage to the taxi rank, waited her turn then told the driver to take her to a small, exclusive hotel Willoughby had used to put up business friends when they were in Paris.

She was welcomed at reception with flattering cordiality and given a good room.

She tipped the porter who'd carried up her luggage, watched the door close behind him and sank down into a chair. After a moment she took her phone out of her bag again and rang Willoughby.

'It's me,' she said imperiously. 'Did you wipe any messages from Jean-Paul off my answering machine in the last few days?'

Willoughby sighed. 'Is that what you think of me?' he said in a superior tone. 'That I could be that petty?'

It had been a possibility, Polly acknowledged to herself. 'You've changed so much, I wouldn't put anything past you these days,' she said stiffly, hating herself for having rung him.

'What's happened – lover boy not there? I've always said you can't trust the French.'

How she hated that sneering tone.

'A business crisis. *You* can understand that, can't you, Willoughby?' she retorted.

'And I thought he was different from me, that that was the whole point of this escapade!' Oh, how she'd like to be in the same room with him, so she could wipe that look off his face.

'So where are you staying then?' he asked, his voice almost friendly now.

She told him.

'I've cancelled your credit cards, you'd better come home,' he said briefly and rang off.

Polly put down the phone slowly. She looked round the room, at the toile de Jouy wallpaper and curtains, the matching cover to the bed, the antique furniture, the porcelain bits and pieces. She calculated the cost of staying here. The total without benefit of plastic credit was horrifying.

But she was too tired to find somewhere else tonight. Tomorrow she'd think of something.

Chapter Twenty-One

Mark looked at his watch. Eight o'clock. He suddenly felt hungry. Around him the empty expanse of the office seemed to stretch into infinity. No, not quite empty. From the room next door he could hear Robin speaking. For a moment he tensed, wondering exactly what she was up to now. Afraid that she was working to undermine him in some subtle way.

Abruptly he saved his work on the computer and rose, reaching for his jacket. He knocked lightly at Robin's door, then stuck his head round. 'Still at it?'

'What? Oh, hello, Mark, did you want something?' Robin sat in her chair, the soft ruffle of her chiffon blouse spilling over the dark severity of her jacket. A voice issued from the telephone. She smiled at Mark. 'I'll be with you in a minute,' she told him. 'Come in, why don't you?'

As he sat in a chair before her desk, she turned her attention back to her call. 'Sorry, Denis, slight interruption. Yes, I've got that. I'll consider the situation and give you a ring tomorrow. OK?'

She listened for a moment, and picked up a pencil to scribble down a note on her pad.

'Probably in the afternoon, I've got a conference in the morning.' She severed the connection without further ceremony.

Not pleasure, thought Mark, business. 'I wondered if you'd like a bite to eat? We could discuss where we are with the Danish deal.'

An expression of surprise flitted across Robin's face, usually so composed, then a rueful smile lit her large brown eyes. 'Louise not back from the States yet?' she enquired astutely.

Mark was uneasily aware he'd been put at a disadvantage. 'The house needn't be empty before I suggest we have a meal together,' he said boldly.

Robin brought the pencil to the coral fullness of her lips as she considered him for a moment. Then: 'Why not?' she decided. 'It's time for a break.' She flung the pencil on to the desk and got to her feet. 'Give me a moment and I'll be with you.' She swept out of the office, presumably to go to the ladies' cloakroom.

Mark went to get his coat, wondering exactly what he'd let himself in for.

Life had been hard for him since Christmas. He still hadn't got over the shock of Louise's actually taking the Florida job. Until she had got into the taxi that morning, he'd really believed she'd change her mind. Or, at the very least, plead with him to understand why she wanted to go.

Instead she'd acted as though it was the most natural thing in the world for her to be abandoning him. If she'd ranted and raved again, the way she had on Boxing Day, maybe he could have understood. And maybe he would have admitted that his own behaviour had left a lot to be desired. But when she just ignored him, behaved as though he didn't exist, he'd been left not knowing how to react.

In all the twenty years of their marriage, Louise had never questioned his judgement in anything more than the choice of a holiday location or what colour her car should be. All right, maybe she'd sometimes disagreed with the way he dealt with James's intransigence, or nagged him into going to see Victor, but always he'd been confident he had her respect. He was master of the house and she understood that.

Now everything was different.

How could she just go off like that? Leaving him to do his own packing for Denmark, find his own way to the airport? Leaving him an empty house to come back to after what, as he'd expected, had been a very stressful trip?

All right, she'd rung him several times from America, short calls that said she was fine, the job was fine, the weather was fine, everything was fine. Everything but their relationship.

At the end of each call he had been left with the uneasy feeling she'd been expecting something from him. An apology, he supposed. But, bloody hell, how could he apologise with her on the other side of the Atlantic?

Robin came into his office as he was angrily flinging papers into his briefcase, standing beside the desk, the photograph of Louise and the twins gazing at him with what he fancied was an air of reproach. He'd already put on his overcoat. Robin was snuggled into some voluminous grey garment with soft fur at the neck. 'Ready?' she asked brightly.

They went to Chez Gerard at the bottom of Chancery Lane. The restaurant was buzzing, noisy with young professionals enjoying the French atmosphere. Mark was reminded of the Paris trip. 'Let's find somewhere quieter,' he said abruptly.

Robin followed him out unprotestingly and stood quietly as he hailed a cab and helped her in. 'The Connaught,' he told the driver.

In the peaceful surroundings of the panelled dining room the head waiter settled them at a discreet table for two. Robin looked around with frank curiosity. 'I'd never have thought of coming here, I've always considered it boring. It's not, is it?'

Mark felt better. 'This place is one of London's best kept secrets.

The food's wonderful, the service impeccable, and as you can see it's incredibly pleasant. What will you have to drink?'

'I'll stick to wine, I think,' she said, opening the heavy menu card.

'Then shall we have some champagne while we're considering what to eat?'

Robin raised an eyebrow. 'Pushing the boat out?'

'Why not?' he offered lightly after ordering a bottle of Bollinger. 'Copenhagen was a triumph. You heard Douglas yesterday. The contract is ours and it's going to put jam on an awful lot of bread and butter.' He hesitated for a nanosecond then added, 'We make an excellent team.'

She smiled, her manner relaxed. When she'd first joined the department, she had appeared reserved, glacial almost. Always concentrating on business, never allowing herself the luxury of a personal comment, impatient of any tendency to lighten proceedings with a joke or some innocuous comment, not the easiest of companions.

But now it was as though Mark was dining with someone he could well have chosen for her charm and the warmth of her personality as well as the looks he had always recognised as stunningly attractive. More, he realised with a touch of surprise that for the first time since he'd met Robin, he felt in total command of the situation.

The wine waiter arrived and poured their champagne. His place was taken by another waiter who asked if they had decided what to eat. Mark suggested he return a few minutes later and any thought of business was forgotten while they discussed the menu.

Left on their own again, Mark raised his glass to his companion. 'Here's to our continued teamwork.'

Robin sipped her wine, looking at him over the top of the glass with frank interest, her manner once again alert and focused. 'Forgive me for saying this, Mark, but I thought you resented my presence?'

'Not at all,' he said suavely. 'To have had the benefit of your intelligence and experience has been illuminating and constructive. I hope we can work together on many more equally lucrative projects.'

'Hmmm. I accept the intended compliment but none of that means you weren't resentful, at any rate when I first came back to London.'

He took a moment to decide on the exact nature of his response. 'It's always tricky when someone new joins a well-organised team,' he started.

'Especially when that someone is a woman,' she shot back.

Now it was Mark's turn to raise an eyebrow. 'That sounds a little sensitive to me,' he suggested urbanely.

'Does it?' Robin asked, and her eyes sparkled dangerously as she raised her glass once again.

'Can you cite anything that suggested I regarded you as in any way different from a male colleague? Other than my admiring your looks,' he added with what he confidently assumed was flattering gallantry.

Flags of red suddenly flamed in Robin's cheeks, offsetting the severity of her short blonde hair and increasing the femininity of her face. 'You've just demonstrated exactly what I resent,' she said in a low, clear voice. 'Those little remarks about my looks. When would you ever tell a male colleague how masculine or attractive he was looking today?'

Mark felt he was being attacked unfairly. 'Don't you like being admired?'

Robin took another sip of her champagne. Her eyes seemed larger than ever. 'Suppose I told you I really liked the way the colour of your shirt brought out the blue of your eyes?'

Louise had given him the shirt and that had been precisely what she had said as he'd opened the present. He remembered her smoothing the collar the first time he'd worn it and the look in her eyes as she'd straightened the paisley tie he'd picked to wear with it as they dressed to go out to dinner with friends. The shirt had had to be changed for another, uncreased one before they'd finally left the house, late to the point of rudeness.

'What you mean is,' he said deliberately, moving the champagne glass in small circles on the crisp, damask cloth, 'that you find me patronising.'

'In a word, yes,' she flashed at him. 'But don't take it personally. You merely react like most men to my presence in what they have been brought up to consider a male environment. Despite equal opportunities and a female presence in many a boardroom, you and others only really feel comfortable working alongside your own sex.'

If she had been more aggressive perhaps Mark would have reacted differently. But the little flash of spirit had given way to her usual calm and she spoke in a quiet, amused voice that made him consider her words.

'I may have thought that when you first joined us,' he said eventually, leaning back in his chair, carefully choosing what he said. 'But in Copenhagen – well, this may sound a little odd, but I forgot you were a woman there. You just fitted so well into the team.' He could have added that for the first time, during those negotiations, they'd worked together as though they knew each other's minds intimately, picking up on the merest hints, acting as a partnership. It had been an exhilarating experience.

The Copenhagen project had kept them in Denmark for five days – a shorter stay than he'd expected. They hadn't had much time for socialising, everything had been focused on the discussions, and any moments spent alone together had involved assessing progress and deciding on tactics. They'd returned two days ago. Back in the

186

familiar surroundings of the office, more at ease than he'd been during the Danish discussions, Mark had found himself uneasily aware of Robin's femininity.

She smiled gently at him. 'Forgot I was a woman? I'm not sure that isn't as patronising as your previous attitude.'

'For heaven's sake,' he said in exasperation. 'You're beginning to sound like Louise! What exactly *do* you want?'

Their food arrived and he had to wait while napkins were snapped open and plates arranged. He feared she would take the opportunity to change the subject. He found he really wanted to hear her try and explain.

'Tell me, Mark,' Robin said, picking up her fork after they'd been left alone, 'do you actually like women?'

He felt impatient. 'What on earth do you mean? Of course I like women!'

'Are you sure?' she queried calmly. 'Do you like talking to them? I mean a proper conversation, not paying them compliments and making jokes? What happens when you entertain at home? Say there are six or eight of you. Do the men talk together and the women chat amongst themselves? Or do you find yourself discussing things with a woman as often as with a man?' She started on her food, as though she knew what his answer was going to be.

Mark opened his mouth, closed it again, pushed a piece of smoked salmon around on his plate then ate it. The question made him feel uncomfortable. 'Louise and I are always talking,' he said belligerently.

'Good,' Robin said brightly. 'What about?'

'Oh, lots of things. The children, of course. What we're going to do . . . our parents . . . you know.'

'Yes,' she said lightly. 'I think I do. When was the last time you discussed what the government was doing, or a book either of you had read, or found yourself involved in a philosophical debate?'

Mark gave a shout of laughter. 'I'm sorry, but really! The government? Philosophy? Louise? You've met her. She's enchanting, of course, but she doesn't know the first thing about politics or anything cerebral.' A vague feeling of disloyalty began to trouble him and he tried to backtrack. 'Quite apart from being beautiful, Louise is a wonderful wife and mother,' he added. 'I've never looked at another woman from the day we married. I don't want an intellectual for a wife. They can be very uncomfortable in bed.'

Robin did not appear at all disconcerted. 'Your wife strikes me as an intelligent woman. I seem to remember she and Val Lewin having very interesting conversations in Paris?'

Had they? The only interesting remark Mark could remember Louise making was that ridiculous pretence of being a magazine editor the night they'd gone out with Robin and the Americans. He felt it was time to move on to more comfortable areas. 'Why don't we talk about you for a moment?' he suggested, restraining himself from adding the sort of joking remark he'd normally make to a woman, something along the lines that her eyes would make anything sound interesting. 'What made you become an accountant?'

She gave him another of those straight, assessing looks. Then seemed to make up her mind about something. 'Power,' she said simply.

He was taken aback. 'Power?'

She nodded. 'I've always wanted to be where the action is. In the engine room, so to speak. Not tending the boilers but directing the engineers. I've always had a feeling for figures, but it's what they represent that determined my choice of career. It's economics that makes the world go round. Any company, any country, is only as strong as its balance sheet. I decided that my most direct route to anything worthwhile was through accountancy. What decided you?'

Mark felt a curious empathy. 'Exactly the same things as you.'

Robin smiled, genuine warmth in her eyes. 'So we have something in common after all.'

'And where do you see yourself ending up?' he asked deliberately. Now was as good a time as any to get her to admit what he knew had to be her aim: to topple him and take over his fast track to the top.

She looked at him for a long, heart-stopping moment. Then dropped her gaze. 'I'm not sure,' she said at last.

For the first time that evening he knew she was evading him.

'Come on,' he urged. 'We're friends, aren't we? Even if you want to be head of department, I won't hold it against you.' That had to shake her into a confession.

She looked startled. Her face held slightly to one side, a pose that somehow emphasised the brilliance of her eyes and the slender curve of her neck, she surveyed him. 'It's a typically male attitude, to stress the title on the door. I prefer to remember our equality in the general scheme of things. I think Douglas prefers to view things that way too.'

A faint echo in Mark's mind replayed Douglas's message during their last lunch together. Anger flooded through him but it was directed at the Senior Partner, not the attractive woman sitting opposite.

'I think,' he said, 'we should talk about something other than accountancy and the office. Tell me,' his tone deadpan, 'what do you think about the cabinet reshuffle?'

There was a brief pause while she inspected his face warily then, apparently reassured by what she found there, laughed. It was a genuine laugh, amused and understanding. 'Now you're getting the idea,' she said.

Chapter Twenty-Two

Rather to her surprise, Louise found she was greatly enjoying her
Florida trip.

It had taken one and a half hours to drive from the airport to
Mary's home and they'd arrived in the late afternoon. It was a large,
modern house on an estate tastefully filled with similar houses. The
estate itself was only one of a number, each built in a different
architectural style, that had been sited between several golf courses
that formed a skilfully designed and sizeable complex.

Jake brought in their luggage, refusing to let Louise help. Gladys
showed him where to put the cases in the luxurious accommodation
known as the 'guest suite', two larger bedrooms that shared a bath
and shower room with separate loo. The suite was on the ground
floor. Mary's accommodation and that of her now grownup daughter was upstairs.

'There now,' said Jake after placing the cases in the right rooms.
'Mary won't be long. I'll bet you'd like a cup of coffee? Or seeing as
how you're English, should that be tea?' He gave them one of the
smiles that warmed his rather serious face and made him seem
immensely approachable.

'If she's flying in so soon, couldn't we have waited for her at the
airport?' Gladys asked. She seemed understandably tired and
tetchy.

'Ah, well now, she's not flying in to Miami but to Palm Beach. It's
about fifteen minutes away,' explained Jake.

At that moment the front door opened and a small woman flew
in, flung a large briefcase and a padded down jacket on to a chair
and wrapped Gladys in a warm embrace. 'Mums, will you ever
forgive me?' she said as she released her mother but kept her arms
on Gladys's shoulders, eyes searching her face. 'I begged and
pleaded but television has no heart, and you don't know how tight
everything is on this production. The best I could negotiate was a
nine o'clock start to the meeting, which meant going up yesterday.
But it's so exciting! We think the series is going to be really big and
could take us right to the top. Just think, you might even see it in
England!' She guided Gladys to a chair. 'I was out of there the
moment we'd covered the script. Told them they didn't need me
any longer and I had a plane to catch. Just made the lunchtime

flight. Now you sit there and I'll make us some tea. I'm the only person in the US who knows how to make it properly.'

'I've brought you Earl Grey from Fortnum's,' Gladys said, inserting the words quickly as though she mightn't get another chance. She sat stiffly in the chair, her bright eyes following Mary as she rushed from the living to the kitchen area.

Apart from the bedrooms, the house was all open plan, the different activity areas flowing into one another with any culinary disorder shielded by a wall three-quarters the height of the ceiling between the kitchen and living areas, topped with an array of plants which formed a living screen of green.

'Mums, that's wonderful! You know how I love it and I'm almost out of my current lot. Jake, you are an absolute doll to have met them. Did you have any trouble with customs or luggage or anything?'

Mary stood in the entrance to the kitchen area, holding a tea canister. She looked to be in her late-forties, was wearing jeans, a T shirt and a blazer-type jacket, trainers on her feet. Superficially there was a strong resemblance to Gladys. Neither seemed to have much interest in fashion. They were both about five foot four in height, with neat figures; both had high foreheads and big noses that were only noticeable when you caught them in profile. Then what had seemed a straightforwardly attractive face turned out to be more quirky and interesting. Both had brown eyes that looked everywhere, saw everything. Neither wore make up beyond a brownish lipstick. But Mary's hair was blonde, drawn back into a workmanlike pony tail secured with a rubber band, while Gladys's was cut short into dazzling white curls that almost managed to soften her strong facial bones.

'I'm sorry.' Mary's dancing eyes lit on Louise and her face took on an expression of distress that was almost comical. 'I'd forgotten you weren't bringing Shirley this time.' She came forward, still holding the tea canister in her left hand, her right outstretched to Louise. 'What must you think of me? I'm Mary Baxter, and I'm so grateful to you for taking on looking after my mother at such short notice. Did I ever know your name?' She paused for a microsecond before giving Louise a wide smile. 'I'm sorry if I did because I've forgotten it.'

'Louise Henderson,' she said. Her hand was taken and quickly squeezed. The dark eyes looked deep into hers then Mary gave a small nod which seemed to indicate approval of what she saw before she was back in the kitchen again, taking china out of a cupboard.

Jake had sat himself down in a corner of one of the living area's deep sofas. He didn't seem at all disconcerted by this whirlwind of activity but watched it all in a relaxed manner.

Louise sat herself down in another of the chairs and attempted to melt into the background. In a few minutes Mary brought in the tea

190

tray. As she poured, her non-stop conversation barely slowed. Louise rose and handed cups to Gladys and Jake, who received his with a graceful smile of thanks.

'That's better,' Mary said after she'd drunk some of her tea. She sat back and smiled at her mother. 'Sam's coming over for supper this evening, I thought you'd like to meet him as soon as possible. The worst thing for jet lag is not to follow local time, but perhaps you'd like a couple of hours rest?' Her voice was gentle, ending on a questioning upward note. 'I won't let you sleep any longer, promise.'

A look of relief came into Gladys's eyes. She put down her cup and immediately started to struggle to her feet, gnarled fingers grasping the cane and trying to lever herself upright.

Louise was beside her in an instant, pre-empting Jake who was also offering help.

'Thanks, Mary, that seems sensible,' Gladys said briefly. Louise wondered if she would have managed to bring herself to say she needed a rest if one hadn't been offered.

Gladys turned in the direction of her bedroom then paused in front of her daughter. 'Thanks for hurrying back from New York, I do know just how far it is.' Her gruffness hid emotion, Louise realised.

She followed Gladys to the bedroom and helped her to take off trainers and tracksuit. 'Would you like me to unpack?' she asked, looking at the two large suitcases.

'Later, later,' she said curtly.

'Then I'll leave you to rest.' Louise gave her a smile, saw her draw the coverlet up to her chin, and let herself out of the room.

She then felt at a bit of a loss. She preferred not to take a rest herself but she wasn't sure Mary would want to entertain her. She, too, must be tired.

Louise went into her room, unpacked the few clothes she'd brought with her then had a shower in the magnificent guest bathroom. After a little thought, she put on a pair of cotton trousers and a T shirt. She hadn't been at all certain how a carer was expected to dress and had finally packed an assortment of simple casual clothes. If they wanted her to wear an overall, she was sure it was possible to buy one locally.

Then she left her room and went through to the living area again.

For a moment it seemed empty. Jake had disappeared and Louise wondered if Mary had gone up to her room, then saw she was in the kitchen area. Caught unawares, she looked tired and very different from the vivacious woman who had greeted them. The next moment she caught sight of Louise and her smile reappeared.

'You look like a new woman! Is my mother sleeping?'

'I hope so. I left her snugly settled down. I think she's very tired.'

Mary nodded. 'The trip always takes a lot out of her.' She lifted saladings out of the sink into a colander. 'There, that's the evening meal more or less taken care of. I hope you like steak?'

Louise nodded. 'Love it. Is there anything I can do? Lay the table or something?'

'Sweet of you. We can do it together.' Mary seemed genuinely pleased by the offer. Louise wondered how Shirley had seen her duties.

'I'm here to help in any way I can,' she said as Mary got out silver and mats and they started to lay places at the glass and chrome dining table.

All the furniture in the house was modern: simple shapes and the very best quality. The deeply comfortable chairs and sofas were upholstered in cream. The only colour was provided by a stunning collection of modern paintings.

'Sam says I know nothing about art – but I know what I like,' Mary said after Louise had commented on them. 'I like landscapes and still lifes and figurative paintings, but paintings that make me question what I see. I think it's a reaction against my parents' home. The only picture they had on the wall was a reproduction of that dreadful Asian beauty. You know: head on one side, glossy dark hair and a greeny-yellow cheongsam. I thought anything had to be better than that. I bought my first picture when I sold my first television screenplay. Now I go regularly to galleries and add to my collection.'

'What does your mother think of them?' Louise laid cutlery round the mats that had been placed on the table.

Mary smiled. 'She thinks they're a waste of money but if that's what I'm interested in, she's willing to give them a cursory glance from time to time.' She paused, scanning Louise's face. 'My mother and I have very little in common but, despite appearances sometimes, we are actually very fond of each other. Especially if we don't spend too much time together.' She looked at the table. 'Glasses, that's what we need, and napkins.' She opened a cupboard at the bottom of the dividing wall between dining and kitchen area and handed out some cut glass goblets to Louise. Another cupboard yielded striped cotton napkins and a set of rings.

Louise carefully rolled each napkin, placed it in a ring and laid one beside each place.

'There, that's done!' said Mary with an air of relief. 'I think we deserve a drink, don't you? My usual tipple is a whisky and soda. Will you join me or would you prefer wine or something soft? Americans seem to drink fewer and fewer spirits these days. Sam says I should break myself of the habit but I don't see why I should.' Another bright smile.

'I'd love a glass of white wine.'

'Good, I hate drinking on my own, makes me feel totally decadent. Mind you, feeling decadent every now and then can be a good thing, don't you think?'

192

'I don't think I've ever felt decadent in my life,' Louise confessed, following her to the kitchen and watching her hostess open a bottle of Californian Chardonnay.

'Oh dear, haven't you?' Mary looked at her with wide eyes. 'And there was I thinking it was pretty tame only to have felt it. I've never really kicked over the traces in real life. That's one reason I enjoy writing my silly dramas so much.'

'Living vicariously, you mean?'

'Right! That's something else my mother can't really understand. I show her tapes of my efforts when she's here and she sits watching as though they're some form of space-age technology she's trying to get her mind round. Then she gets bored.'

'I'm sure your mother understands,' Louise offered, not at all certain this was so.

'Actually, she does,' Mary said unexpectedly. 'The great thing about Mums is that she understands careers.'

All at once, against her initial expectations, Louise felt very comfortable with this woman who was as straightforward as her mother. 'So how do I entertain Gladys?' she asked a trifle anxiously.

'Now, the secret to keeping my mother happy is lots of variety. She has a very low boredom threshold. But she's adept at finding her own amusements.'

Louise looked apprehensive and Mary gave another whoop of laughter. 'You'll enjoy yourself, promise! Do you play cards? Good, she loves that. And doing jigsaws, as long as they aren't too large and don't take too long. I've got a stack of new ones in.' She nodded to a pile sitting on a glass shelving unit. 'She usually likes to interfere with the housekeeping too. You won't mind if she suggests a little cooking?' Mary looked anxious, as though Louise might start declaring demarcation lines for her job.

'I'll be happy to help with anything,' Louise assured her.

'Then we're all going to have a great time. Now, tell me a little bit about yourself?'

Without quite knowing how, Louise found herself telling Mary far more than she'd intended about her family and her desire to find some sort of job.

'I do understand what you mean.' Mary leaned forward companionably. 'I'd have hated it if I hadn't had my work during all the various crises of my life. Not to mention the fact that I'd have found things pretty difficult financially without it. Both my husbands were artists, never knowing where the next commission was coming from, one a musician and the other a sculptor. Thank heavens Beth takes after my side of the family. Highly practical, and just imaginative enough to make a first-class physician.'

'Did you never wish you could just be a mother?' Louise found herself asking.

Mary appeared to consider the question seriously. 'No,' she said

193

eventually. 'But I was lucky, I was able to work from home most of the time.'

'And I suppose you were following your own mother's example?' Louise suggested.

Mary looked interested. 'Do you know, that's something I've always taken for granted? She and Father had a wonderful marriage and always managed to be there for us when we needed them. I missed out on the wonderful marriage bit but I've tried to make sure I was always there for Beth. And she's never seemed to resent my work. As for me,' Mary gurgled with sudden laughter, 'I can't tell you how grateful I was Mums had her career, otherwise I think she and I would have come to blows, we thought so differently about things! As it was, I knew if I could only deflect her attention for long enough from whatever escapade I was busy with at the time, she'd get involved again with her current project and I'd be able to do what I wanted.' Mary pursed her mouth like a naughty child then chuckled.

Louise laughed with her. There was an amazing lack of tension about this woman. She looked forward to seeing what Mary's boyfriend was like.

Sam and Jake arrived while Louise was helping Gladys unpack and find something suitable to wear that didn't need a press. Eventually Gladys pounced enthusiastically on a scarlet suit and found a dramatic jet necklace to wear with it. As she saw her pleasure in dressing up, Louise realised she had underestimated Gladys's interest in fashion.

'Do you think I should change?' she asked, looking at her own pink trousers and green T shirt in the full-length mirror.

'Nonsense, you look like neapolitan icecream,' Gladys asserted, picking up her stick. 'Come on, I want to meet this Sam.'

Louise followed but Gladys's remark had brought Mark vividly back to mind. That's what he had said once when she'd worn the trousers and shirt at home. Both home and Mark now seemed a very long way away.

Sam and Jake jumped to their feet as Gladys entered the room. Sam was a corpulent man, not nearly as tall as his friend, with twinkling eyes, a deeply lined face and sticking out ears. He obviously paid as little attention to fashion as Mary. His jeans were badly cut and were topped by a shapeless sweat shirt. Both, though, were clean and looked as though they'd just been put on, and a subtle hint of some expensive aftershave hung around him.

'So this is the famous Gladys Toler,' he said, advancing towards her with a warm smile. 'You're going to have to work hard at living up to your advance publicity.' He surveyed her with a frank interest that she returned.

'If only we were dogs,' Gladys said with a lift of an eyebrow, 'we would sniff at each other.'

'Ah, but I have,' he said, taking her hand. 'You are fragrant with some fantastically costly aroma that my highly tuned nose recognises as Diorama. A sophisticated choice for a sophisticated lady.'

'Mary,' Gladys said severely, 'I hope you don't place much trust in this man. He sounds like a boulevardier and looks like . . .' She put her head on one side and surveyed him again. 'Well, he looks like a home-loving body. That's a dangerous combination.' She was obviously delighted with him.

Mary came to Sam's side, the top of her head on a level with his ear, and put one hand on to his shoulder as he drew her close to him. 'You don't want to pay any attention to what Sam says,' she said dryly.

'Thank you, my angel.' He dropped a kiss on her ear, then gave her rear end a light pat. 'How about some chips, or should I say crisps? What's your poison, Gladys?'

After she'd settled herself with some difficulty in one of the low chairs and announced that a whisky and soda would hit the spot, he turned to Louise. 'And you have to be the beauteous Louise. I recognise Jake's description which, at the time, I put down to some unexpected fever contracted in that hell hole of an airport.'

'Sam, stop wittering and attend to your duties,' Mary said cheerfully.

Their relationship seemed casual but from the looks they gave each other, Louise could see they were deeply committed. As the evening wore on she realised that they had settled into an easy acceptance of each other that suited them both.

'Why don't we sit outside?' asked Gladys while Sam was getting the drinks. 'You've got lights on the terrace, haven't you?' The sun had already set and it was dark. 'After the dreadful English weather, I can't bear to pass up this warmth.'

'Oh, that would be lovely,' agreed Louise immediately. She found the air conditioning chilly and outside she could hear cicadas singing.

'OK, if that's what you want.' Mary slid open the large patio door and led the way, switching on outside wall lights. 'Bring the cushions, Jake, will you? They're in that cupboard by the windows.'

Louise helped him fit them on to the rattan furniture that stood on the terrace. As they did so, she realised that the area was completely enclosed in a cage of fine mesh netting.

'Why,' she said, 'it's just like an aviary.'

'The mosquitoes aren't too bad at present,' Mary explained apologetically, helping her mother get settled. 'But in the summer they eat you alive and you can't sit outside without this sort of protection. I can't imagine how the early explorers survived.'

'Now Jake can tell you all about that,' Sam said immediately. 'He's a historian and Florida is one of his specialities. He's going to write a book on it.'

Jake looked embarrassed. 'Now, Sam, I don't know that's so at all.'

'Haven't you told me you're on sabbatical to do just that?'

'Write a book, yes. On Florida? Well, I don't know that yet.'

'But you must have an idea or two,' Gladys said brightly. 'This will be great, you can take us around and fill in the background for us.'

'Mums!' Mary protested. 'Jake probably has other plans.'

'Nothing that doesn't pall beside such an attractive prospect as driving the two of you around,' he said gallantly.

'Good,' Gladys said complacently. 'I promise we'll keep you amused.'

Sipping her white wine, Louise saw what Mary had meant about Gladys being good at finding her own entertainment. How good was Jake going to be at coping with her commando tactics?

'Well, you can take us to the supermarket tomorrow. I'm taking over the cooking then Mary can get on with her work.'

'Thanks, Mums, but don't you really mean you prefer your own cooking?' she asked cheerfully.

'Now, that's not very gracious, darling,' objected Sam, laying a hand affectionately on hers.

'I do have to admit, my ears show a distinct tendency to lengthen when fed too often by Mary. She's far too fond of the rabbit food. How about it, Jake? You can taste our efforts.' Gladys gave him a dig in the ribs as he sat beside her on the rattan sofa.

'That will be ample repayment,' he assured her with a smile for Louise.

He was as good as his word. They soon settled into a routine whereby Jake spent either every morning or afternoon with Gladys and Louise. He drove them around, played cards, helped with a jigsaw or produced some board game he thought might amuse Gladys. And he was willing to be quizzed endlessly.

Louise found herself relaxing in an atmosphere that was always stimulating but totally free from tension.

Gradually the situation with Mark at home drifted to the back of her mind. It was too easy to tease Gladys and Jake, become interested in their discussions, beat them at cards, then enjoy helping to cook the evening meal. Gladys turned out to be an excellent cook, far more interested in food than her daughter was, and Louise was happy to take orders, assist with the preparations but leave the actual cooking to her. Gladys never seemed to mind any difficulties involved in standing at the stove.

Suppertime was equally enjoyable, with Sam and Mary both relaxing after their work was over for the day and Gladys drawing Jake into elaborating on some point that had come up earlier.

Louise began to worry that they were taking advantage of Jake's kindly nature. He must, surely, have other things to do.

196

She raised this point with Gladys.

'Don't see what else he would be doing if he wasn't with us,' she retorted. 'Sam works as hard as Mary. Coops himself up in his studio, bent over that drawing board, leaving his guest to fend for himself. If you ask me, as far as Jake's concerned, we're a belated Christmas present.'

Louise had to admit there was a certain amount of truth in what Gladys said. But she couldn't help remembering he'd come down here to decide what sort of a book he wanted to write. What if he really wanted to get on with research for it?

Much as she realised she would miss having him around, Louise began to look for an opportunity to get Jake on his own so she could find out exactly how he felt about the situation.

Chapter Twenty-Three

Geoffrey Barnes, the headmaster, came into Nicky's office shrugging off his overcoat, its shoulders wet from the heavy rain that was coming down outside. 'Brrr! Winter's arrived with a vengeance! Still, I suppose we have to be grateful it isn't snowing. Morning, Nicky. Sorry I'm late, car wouldn't start. The wife had already left and I had to get the AA. Any disasters?'

Nicky smiled at him. She relished the sense of being on top of things. 'Not really, Headmaster. But Bob wants you to go and inspect the tuck room. He says last night's storm brought down a branch on to the roof. Several tiles have gone and the snow's coming through.'

Geoffrey groaned. 'More expense! Still, the insurance should cover most of it. Better get on to the builders and organise some sort of roof covering.'

'Already done, Headmaster. By the time you get down there, they should have arrived.'

'Excellent, Nicky. What did I ever do without you?' The question was rhetorical but nonetheless pleasing. 'Did your boys get back to school all right?' he asked, making no effort to go through to his office. That was one of the things Nicky really liked about her job: how Geoffrey Barnes always seemed to have time for the personal details. He hadn't minded at all her taking the previous day off so that she and Colin could drive Riff and Raff back to their school.

'It went fine. They seem to love it there, they've settled in. The moment they arrived, they were greeting this boy and that as though they'd been apart a year instead of a few weeks.'

'Happy with the staff, are they?'

'Housemaster's really nice. Seems to have got their measure!' Nicky grinned at her boss. 'We wondered whether they should be in the same house. They tend to egg each other on, you know?' Geoffrey nodded and smiled. Nicky liked his smile, which lightened his heavy-jawed face. When he was giving a telling off to boys or staff, he could look really grim. 'Well, Mr Long, the headmaster, talked to them both when we took them for the interview and said that as they were such late entries, it would probably be better if they were in the same house. They wouldn't feel so adrift then. Anyway, so far it seems to be working.'

199

'Well, that's good.' Geoffrey Barnes looked at his watch. 'Better get over to the other side of the playing field and see what's happened to that tuck shop.' He started to work his way back into the damp overcoat. 'Any time bombs waiting in the mail?'

Nicky shook her head. 'All pretty much routine stuff. But,' she flicked open the master diary, 'Mr and Mrs Thomas are due here at eleven.' Five days after term had started, Dave Thomas, terror of 3C, was already in trouble. His parents held the school to blame; his form master said if only he received some discipline at home, perhaps he'd be able to accept it elsewhere. Whatever the rights or wrongs of the matter, Dave Thomas's father was far too ready to bully and threaten.

'I'll be back by then, I won't leave you unprotected!' He gave her another of his cheerful smiles and vanished through the door that led into the school's main hall.

Nicky pressed 'Save' and scrolled back to check the timetable she'd been entering into her computer. Half her mind was on her work, half on the battle she'd had with the builders. When the groundsman's call had come through, she'd already been in the office an hour, making up for having had the previous day off. The mail had been sorted, the letters Geoffrey Barnes had left on her desk with brief notes had been answered, she'd entered several appointments he'd made into the diary, and had started to sort out a new timetable from the rough notes that had also been on her desk.

Nicky had listened to Bob then offered to ring the builders immediately.

'Oh, would you, Mrs Webber?' Bob sounded highly relieved. 'I'm that pushed this morning.'

The builders had been reluctant to come round immediately; the school wasn't the only place that had suffered damage the night before. Nicky pleasantly reminded the person she was speaking to of the ongoing contract the firm had with the school. By the time she'd finished, she was confident the men would be there without serious delay. The confrontation left her with a feeling of triumph. Still checking the timetable, she allowed her mind to return to her conversation with the head. Yes, the boys really were happy at that new school. As they'd driven home, she'd said as much to Colin.

'Uh huh!' was all he'd said, pushing the old Rover to greater speed. 'Weather looks dreadful. Like to get home before it breaks if we can.'

Nicky had felt a familiar frustration. Why wouldn't he admit that the best thing for the boys would be to remain where they were? 'Why can't you . . .' she started, her voice rising. 'I've something to tell you,' he said at the same moment.

'Don't,' Nicky had said. 'Don't tell me anything now, wait until we get home.'

She hadn't felt up to coping with Colin and his plans at that moment.

He'd glanced at her, eyes worried but steely as oncoming headlights caught them.

'Keep your eyes on the road,' she'd suddenly screamed at him. 'Do you want to get us killed!'

That had kept him quiet until they were back in the house. She'd regretted her outburst the moment she'd made it. Colin never took risks driving. But it was too late by then.

'I suppose it's to do with that firm in Exeter?' she said as she put the kettle on for coffee and Colin hung up their coats.

He nodded, leaning against one of the kitchen cupboards and keeping his eyes on her, a frown creasing his high forehead. 'While I've been home these last few days' – he had taken some overdue leave and looked after the boys while Nicky went back to work – 'I rang them. They're really very keen to see me. Us, in fact. I said I'd try and get down there at the end of this week or next.' He waited.

Nicky hadn't known what to say. 'Are you telling me that's what you're going to do or asking if I approve?' She kept her back to him, fighting tears. Was her whole life going to fall apart?

She'd heard him sigh.

What she'd wanted was for him to come and take hold of her, wrap his arms around her and tell her she was the most important thing in his life.

'I can't discuss anything with you in this mood,' he'd said and left the kitchen.

Panic had set in then. She'd taken him a mug of coffee. The fire wasn't lit in the living room so he'd gone into his tiny study, switching on the electric fire and the small television set in there.

Nicky set the mug on the corner of his desk. He didn't look round from his chair. She looked at the slumped shoulders, his head thrust forward, the news programme chattering away in the corner. 'I'm going to bed,' she said abruptly. 'I must be in early tomorrow.' By the time he'd come up she'd been asleep. She'd set the alarm for six o'clock and he'd merely hunched his shoulders under the duvet when it went off. So they hadn't spoken again.

Now she continued to gaze at her screen and tried to get her mind back on her work.

The door to her office opened and in walked Theresa Pratt, face glowing.

Theresa was French, a voluptuous girl with a mane of dark hair that was always escaping from the clips she used to hold it back from her high cheekbones.

'Is Mr Barnes in?' she asked.

Nicky jolted herself back to the present. 'Not at the moment, Theresa. Anything I can help with?' A French teacher, Theresa was not one of the troublesome ones and Nicky liked her very much.

201

Once they'd gone and had coffee together at the end of the day and talked French.

'No, thanks, Nicky.' Theresa beamed again. 'I just wanted to tell Mr Barnes – I passed my Social Sciences course.'

'No wonder you're looking pleased! Congratulations!' Nicky gave her a wide smile then asked, 'Exactly what course did you take?'

'Open University, foundation course. I did a French course as well.'

'You'd have no trouble passing that!'

'No,' Theresa acknowledged, looking a little smug. 'It was what you call an easy option, no?'

'Yes!' They laughed together. 'Do you want me to tell Mr Barnes when he gets back or do you want the pleasure of giving him the news yourself?'

'Oh, I must tell him myself. He has been very good, encouraging me. If I get a degree, you see, I can look for a job with more money. Perhaps in the state system. At the moment I cannot work there.'

'We'd be very sorry to lose you,' Nicky told her. 'I know your work is valued.'

'That is good to hear,' Theresa said simply.

'Tell me,' said Nicky suddenly, 'is the work very difficult?'

'Oh, I hated the Social Sciences – all that jargon! But I didn't feel I could handle arts and maths and science. Pouf, they are impossible!' Theresa gave a little toss of her head and click of her fingers to demonstrate just how impossible she found them. 'But you, Nicky, you would have no trouble. And you could take the French just as easily as I.'

Nicky flushed with pleasure. 'You think so?'

'*Bien sûr*! You do not have a degree already?'

Nicky felt like asking if she looked as though she had a degree, then realised how silly that would be. She shook her head.

'You would like to teach?'

'Me?' Nicky hadn't even considered the possibility. 'Good heavens, no,' she said.

But as the day wore on she found herself coming back to the idea which had been so unexpectedly placed in her head by Theresa.

That evening she could hardly wait for Colin to get back.

'I've got something I want to discuss with you,' she said eagerly the moment he came in the door. 'Don't look like that, I'm not going to slag you off or anything. Go and get yourself a drink then come and talk to me while I'm cooking.'

'You mean listen to you,' he said with a grin that for a moment brought back a trace of the old Colin.

He went and poured them both a whisky and brought the glasses back to the kitchen. He put one on the side of the stove where Nicky was making a cheese sauce and sat down at the table, already laid for supper, with the other. 'OK, fire away.'

So she told him about Theresa and her one and a half credits towards a degree. 'She thinks another three years at most and she will have it. And that I could get one too. It's too late to apply for this year, apparently, but I might be able to start next January,' she finished excitedly as she poured the sauce over the cooked cauliflower, placed it in the oven and switched on the grill.

'And that's what you'd like to do, is it?' he asked, looking bemused. But not, Nicky was pleased to see, doubtful.

'Theresa showed me the units she's going to be working on this year. They look terrifically interesting and I think I could manage them. I mean, it would take a lot of work,' she added hurriedly, 'but they weren't too intimidating. And Theresa says I'd walk the French courses that are available. Don't you think I could?' she added anxiously as Colin still didn't say anything.

'Of course,' he assured her robustly. 'I've always had great respect for your brains. It was a thousand pities you didn't go to university when you left school.'

Nicky felt a jolt of pleasure go through her. He'd never told her that before! 'Yes, well, you didn't do that sort of thing in my family.' She reached for the kitchen scissors and started to take the rind off slices of bacon. 'My parents regarded qualifying as a secretary like yours did becoming a lawyer.' She got out the grill pan and lined the rack with foil. Maybe Colin was going to be all right over this. Maybe he'd see the sense of her plan. 'You see, if I was qualified, I could get a job as a teacher. Then it would be all right to move down to the country.' She turned and faced him. 'Don't you see? Going now is all wrong! The boys only have another one and a half years or two and a half years at that school, then they'll be moving on. That's the time to leave.'

Colin's face tightened. 'And how are we to manage in the meantime?' he asked heavily.

Nicky turned back to the bacon, finished taking the rind off the last piece and laid all the slices on the grill pan. 'Can't we hang on?'

Then she abandoned her cooking, came and sat down opposite her husband and looked at him pleadingly. 'Colin, don't you see how important this is to me?'

Chapter Twenty-Four

Mark spent weekdays up at the flat. Home was depressing without Louise. The first weekend he was there on his own, the splendid decor seemed to mock him as he wandered from room to room, a glass of whisky in his hand, wondering what he should do with himself. He had more than enough work to occupy him, there was the billiard room to amuse himself with, not to mention the golf club and squash. None of it had attracted him one little bit.

In the flat at least, Louise's continued absence didn't constantly taunt him. What did was the memory of her casual mention of a fellow who seemed to be squiring her and her employer around.

'An elderly admirer, eh?' He'd tried to make light of the information.

Louise had laughed. 'He's no more than a few years older than you, Mark.' Which had aroused such a raging jealousy in him that he'd hardly been able to speak to her.

Perhaps it was that which had sent him into Robin's office with nothing very much in mind but a bit of a chat.

Since their dinner at the Connaught, he'd fallen into the habit of dropping into her office at odd moments, suggesting they have lunch together or a drink at the end of the day.

They often discussed work. But more and more their conversation ranged wider. Politics, literature, music, sport, even philosophy – Mark was constantly amazed at the unexpected courses their discussions took. There didn't seem to be anything on which Robin wasn't able to contribute an interesting viewpoint and often he found himself debating things in a way he hadn't done since university.

But when he caught the fire of enthusiasm in her big eyes, that tantalising shade that was not quite grey, not quite green, saw the light catch the gold of her hair, or the way her finger would sometimes press itself against her mouth when she hadn't a pencil to hand, then something in him responded in a way it never could have done to Colin or any of his university pals. It was beginning to be deeply disturbing.

That morning, however, there was little time for chatting because Robin immediately raised the subject of the audit she was overseeing.

'There's something wrong somewhere,' she said. 'I can't see what but I just don't like the feel of the figures.' The account had been brought in by Mark and, the regulation number of years for him to handle it having passed, was now being handed over to Robin to oversee. 'Have you time to go through one or two areas with me?'

He was flattered she'd asked for his help, but worried too. There'd been nothing in the previous years' audits to cause concern. But two years ago the management had undergone considerable change and new policies had been implemented. He looked at his watch. 'I've only got thirty minutes before a meeting that's scheduled for most of the day.'

She tapped her pencil against her teeth and looked at him, a frown creasing the smooth skin of her forehead. 'I'm really worried, Mark.'

He could see she was. 'Why don't I make sure tomorrow's free? Can it wait that long?'

She laid the pencil carefully on the desk. 'Of course.'

The next day they spent together in her office, hunched over piles of computer print-outs.

At half-past seven they still had a fat pile awaiting attention. 'What shall we do?' asked Robin. 'Get sandwiches in or break for a quick bite?'

'I've got a better idea,' said Mark. 'Why don't we take it all over to my flat and pick up a takeaway? This place is beginning to get me down.'

He caught a quick glance from Robin and knew she was assessing the wisdom of this move.

'OK,' she said after a moment's pause. She started separating out the papers they hadn't looked at yet. 'I'll find a box for these.'

'Have you got a car?' asked Mark, assembling the notes they'd been making and disconnecting his laptop from its desk wiring.

She shook her head.

'Well, I've got mine, so that's all right.'

Still talking about the audit and the possible discrepancies they needed to check out, Mark followed Robin out of the office, carrying a large box laden with the papers they needed. She had charge of his laptop and a bulging briefcase of her own.

Mark loaded everything on to the back seat of his BMW then helped Robin into the passenger seat. As he fastened his seat belt and checked hers, he caught a subtle hint of scent – musky, sophisticated and teasing.

The traffic was light and it wasn't long before they were driving round Sloane Square. As they entered the King's Road, he said, 'I've a better idea than a takeaway. I'll pick up a couple of steaks and a salad at the supermarket.' Robin said nothing.

The parking area was full but just as Mark thought he'd have to find somewhere else, a car left and he was able to nip in. 'Stay there,' he ordered as he got out, 'I won't be a moment.'

Rather to his surprise, she made no demur, merely took some papers out of her briefcase and switched on the interior light.

As he headed towards the supermarket, he glanced back and saw her blonde head bent over her work in fierce concentration.

It didn't take long to snatch up the meat, a bag of assorted saladings and a couple of bottles of Burgundy. Checking out took longer.

'Sorry,' he gasped as he raced back to the car and placed the plastic bag with the box of papers on the back seat. 'Half Chelsea seems to be in there tonight.'

Robin said nothing, merely made a note in the margin of the top piece of paper and slipped the file back into her briefcase.

'You're staying up in London these days, are you?' she commented as they arrived at the flat and he loaded himself up with the supermarket shopping and the box of papers.

'Not much point in going home to an empty house,' he said crossly, balancing the box as he activated the locking device on the car and juggled to get the key to the flat ready.

'But the flat's empty as well, isn't it?' Robin murmured, not making a move to help.

'Not the same,' he grunted, putting a knee up to support the box as he inserted the key in the front door. His flat was on the second floor and the box grew increasingly heavy as he led the way up.

At last he got the flat door open and stood aside to let Robin go first.

In she went and deposited her briefcase on the only chair in the small hall. She started taking her coat off.

Mark staggered through to the living room and dumped the heavy box on the sofa. He went to help her with her coat and hung it up.

In the living room she looked curiously about her. 'Not quite what I expected.'

'What was that?' Mark picked up the shopping bag and took it through to the tiny kitchen, feeling he'd let himself down in some way.

'Oh, I don't know.' Robin wandered over to the back wall and studied two framed concert posters that hung there. 'Something a bit more classic, I suppose.'

'Mozart and Albinoni not classical enough for you?' Mark came back with one of the bottles of wine and an opener.

She laughed, a pearly, musical sound that was very appealing, and waved a hand at the room, a comprehensive gesture that managed to encompass the stripped pine furniture, the Indian throws decorating the calico-upholstered sofa, the two modern armchairs that looked like a collection of beige bolsters tied together with tape and the huge coffee table, made from a sheet of

207

glass balanced on two stone lions, one of them with a broken tail. The room had a cheerful, informal look, enhanced by the dirty plate and empty glass Mark had left there the night before.

He drew the cork from the bottle, placed it on the front of a large shelving unit running down one wall and picked up the dirty crockery. 'Louise furnished it for the kids. It's supposed to be for them when they eventually hit London. You want to see how I really live, come and visit our house. I promise you classicism there.' He dumped the plate and glass in the kitchen and came back to pour them both a glass of wine.

'Your answering machine's blinking,' Robin pointed out as she accepted her drink. She took a seat in one of the chairs, looking relaxed yet somehow formal.

Mark glanced over at the machine. 'Nothing that can't wait,' he said smoothly. If it was another message from Louise telling him just what fun she was having with her new friend, he didn't want to hear it, especially in front of Robin. 'You want to eat now or later?'

'I think later, don't you? We need to get our heads round those figures.'

Mark put his glass of wine on the table then started unpacking the print-outs from the box. When he had everything sorted out, Robin leaned forward and picked out one of the sheets. 'Now, look at these figures here.' She pointed at one of the columns. 'How do they strike you?'

He sat at the end of the sofa nearest her and tried to look where she was pointing.

'I think I'd better come and sit beside you,' she said and moved on to the sofa.

Half an hour later, with a sense of mounting excitement, through some cross-checking of the figures, Mark discovered the first discrepancy. Then the real paper chase began.

Two hours later they reckoned they had it cracked. 'What a stupid bastard,' Mark breathed as they finished highlighting the relevant figures. 'Thought he could get away with it. That we wouldn't notice a little leakage from the pension fund.'

'And we nearly didn't,' Robin pointed out.

'No, if you hadn't sniffed at the figures quite so hard, the audit would have been agreed and that would have been that. Until next year.' He leaned back on the sofa and stretched his arms, loosening the tension in his shoulders. He caught sight of his watch. 'Hey, look at the time! If we don't grill those steaks now, we'll be having them for breakfast!'

Robin flipped her highlighter on to the table. 'You one of those men who always expects the female to do the chef bit?'

'Am I hell! I can grill a steak like you've never eaten before.' Mark stood up. 'Just let me know, rare, medium or well?'

'Rare side of medium for me.' Robin picked up her glass and

drank the last few drops. 'Can you also do refills?' She held out the glass.

Mark fetched the second bottle of Burgundy, opened it, recharged both their glasses then took his into the kitchen. Robin stayed in the living room. While the grill was heating and he prepared a dressing for the salad, he heard a Mozart piano concerto drifting through. The precise beauty of the music suited his mood of elation and seemed to intensity it. He took cutlery and table mats through. 'Want to make yourself useful?' He grinned at Robin as he placed them on the round pine table in the corner of the room.

She abandoned her scrutiny of the CDs stacked beside the player, mostly chosen by Louise, and came across willingly enough. He switched off the bright standard lamp that had illuminated their paper chase as he went back to the kitchen. He'd thought she might say something but there was no comment.

Supper was eaten hungrily and happily, as they discussed what had to be done next. When they'd finished eating, Robin raised the last of her wine in a toast. 'Compliments to the chef,' she said. 'I'll be happy to eat your steak any time.'

She helped him clear the table and stack the dirty things in the kitchen but made no move to wash anything up.

'Coffee?' asked Mark.

Robin looked at her watch. 'That would be nice,' she said, and returned to the living room.

A stickler for freshly ground coffee at home, Mark never bothered with anything but instant when he was on his own. He took two filled mugs through to the living room, hoping that Robin would have had enough wine not to notice the difference.

She was putting another CD on the player. Brahms this time, he thought, not at all certain he was right. But the passion running through the music had to be nineteenth-rather than eighteenth-century and Brahms did fit the bill. He'd liked the Mozart, as beautiful and clean as an arithmetical progression, but the flowing, pulsing force of this was more exciting.

He put the mugs of coffee down on the table and took the same position as during their audit examination. He didn't realise he was holding his breath until Robin came and sat down beside him. Much earlier in the evening she had slipped off her jacket and now he noticed that the straps of her slip and bra were visible through the silk of her blouse. As she reached forward for the mug of coffee, he saw outlined the little clips that held the bra together across her back.

Mark leaned back against the sofa and closed his eyes, letting the music weave its spell. Beside him he sensed Robin relaxing too.

Moving to kiss her wasn't a conscious decision. It was, somehow, all part of the atmosphere that had been created between them: her nearness, that subtle, teasing scent that had filled his nostrils the whole of the evening, the passionate music that was filling the room.

So it seemed entirely natural to him to remove the mug of coffee she was holding, run his hand up her arm to cup the back of her head, and bend his own so that their lips were brought into contact.

For the briefest of moments he felt her respond, then she jerked herself away.

He opened his eyes to meet her reproachful gaze. 'To think I was fool enough to imagine we could be friends,' she said sadly. 'I really thought you wouldn't be like all the rest.'

That stung. Mark had always considered himself unique. 'Don't you think you gave me reason to consider you felt – well, shall we say, a little more than friendly?'

The reproachful expression disappeared to be replaced by one that was infinitely cold. 'Are you suggesting I led you on?'

The contempt in her tone got to Mark. 'Coming to my apartment, taking off your jacket and sharing the sofa . . . what else was I to think?'

Anger sparked in her eyes. 'Honestly, Mark! Were you brought up in the dark ages or something? What if I'd refused to come here? Wouldn't you have suggested I was reading an ulterior motive into a perfectly normal suggestion? Are we or are we not colleagues? As for removing jackets, I notice you aren't wearing one either! The heating in this place was either designed by Don Giovanni or you are a masochist when it comes to paying for energy.'

He sought refuge in anger. 'It was just a kiss. You're an attractive girl, you must realise the effect you have.'

The ice in her eyes showed no sign of melting. 'I thought we'd been through all this before. I thought I'd made it plain that I despise men who try to combine business with a little light lechery. I thought you'd know better than to call me a girl.' She paused for a moment then added, 'And apart from anything else, I never, never have anything to do with married men. I don't care if their wives don't understand them or what they have to put up with. In your case, I think your wife understands you very well and if there's any putting up with to be done, I reckon it's *she* who does it.'

Beneath his anger, Mark felt inadequate.

Robin rose, picked up her jacket and put it on. 'If you will call me a taxi, I'll be going.' She went out into the hall and he could hear her opening the coat cupboard.

Cursing himself, Mark called the cab company.

While he was on the phone, Robin returned to the room wearing her coat and stood watching him.

'One will be along shortly,' he told her stiffly.

She regarded him steadily. 'Poor Mark. You really don't understand very much, do you?'

He shrugged. 'I think you're making far too much of a small

misunderstanding. But then, that's what women so often do. Blow things up out of all proportion.'

'Oh, dear,' she said. 'It's Louise I feel sorry for.'

In the background the Brahms reached a shattering finale. Mark strode over and switched off the CD player. 'Don't worry about the papers, I'll bring everything into the office in the morning,' he said curtly, his back to her.

She came over and laid a hand lightly on his shoulder. 'I expected nothing less. And don't worry, tomorrow it will all be forgotten. We shall be colleagues again.'

He turned, a debonair smile on his face. 'Just mark me down as another of the scalps to be hung on your office wall. We'll laugh together at the folly of men.'

Her expression relaxed and a trace of the warm smile he'd grown to expect from her returned. 'I'll drink to that,' she said quietly.

There was the sound of a cab stopping outside the building. Mark went across, opened the curtain and looked through the window. 'Your cab's here.'

He saw her downstairs. As the cab drew away, he went back into the building, shut the front door and leaned his head against the cool wood. What a fool he'd made of himself!

He dragged himself up the stairs and went back into the flat. The first thing he saw was the still blinking light of the answering machine.

Chapter Twenty-Five

Five days into Gladys Toler's holiday Jake didn't seem to have tired of driving her and Louise around.

He enlivened the trips along the dead straight roads lined with shopping malls and light industry parks, interspersed by residential areas, with a running commentary on the scenery. 'And there you have modern man's greatest centre of entertainment, the Gardens Shopping Mall. Over here, you can bank without getting out of your car. Now here's where you buy your gourmet food. They stock more varieties of olive oil than Mother Hubbard had children.'

'I've noticed you like your food,' Gladys said with a knowing wink at him.

'Sure. We all have to eat, don't we?'

Louise was reminded vividly of the American to whom she'd told that outrageous lie. But the episode had finally lost its sting. Jake was nothing like Roy. Here was an amusing, sophisticated man who appeared to enjoy her company as much as she was enjoying his.

For the first time since she'd been married, Louise was made to feel that her contributions to a discussion or participation in a game were valued.

At parties at home, Mark would steer Emma and James away from games that required any sort of brain power. 'We'll play charades, don't want to show up your mother,' he'd say. Or he'd lead the way to the billiard table, where Louise quickly showed she could almost match his standard. It was good to feel she could hold her own there and on the tennis court though she had been the first to laugh and agree that intellect was not her strong point.

Now it was unexpectedly satisfying to find she wasn't looked on as an idiot. It was another thread in the weave of this increasingly enjoyable interlude.

One morning Gladys announced she was going to produce her special dish for lunch, that she didn't need anyone in the kitchen nosing out her secrets, and pushed Louise and Jake out on to the terrace.

'Dare I ask what we'll be having?' he enquired, putting his Coke down on the table.

Louise laughed. 'I think it's some sort of stirfry. She picked over

213

the vegetables this morning like a diamond merchant selecting jewels.'

'Great.' He rubbed his hands together. 'Stirfry'll just hit the spot.'

Louise sat back in her chair with a glass of mineral water. At last she had Jake to herself. She surveyed him. 'Gladys can be a bit of a bully when she puts her mind to it,' she started.

'Hold on there a moment. Not quite accurate, are we? "Bit of a bully?" And "when she puts her mind to it?" You mean, don't you, that Gladys Toler is the biggest bully either of us has ever met!'

Louise had to laugh, his tone was so serious yet his eyes were dancing.

'She means well.' Louise thought he might come in there with another of his little comments but he continued to sit quietly nursing his Coke, regarding her with amusement. 'But what about your idea of a history of Florida? Don't you need to do research? Find out whether you want to write a book on it or not? You must have places to go, people to see. You can't allow us to hog all your time. We are well able to look after ourselves,' she added hastily.

'I have to say I'm disappointed in you, Louise.'

'Disappointed?'

'I hadn't realised I came over as quite so spineless.'

'Spineless?' she gasped.

'Well, here you are, trying to protect me from myself. The poor provincial who can't hack it against little old ladies from England. It's a long time since anyone felt they had to do that.'

'Jake, you're impossible!' she spluttered.

'That's better,' he said approvingly. 'Now perhaps we can admit that I know my way around, and if I'm driving you and Mary's mom it's because I want to and not through some misplaced idea of being a gentleman?'

'You're right, Jake, I'm an idiot!'

'Never that! An unusually thoughtful woman would be more accurate. Now, I think it's time I heard about your family, I know all about Gladys's. Tell me more about your twins.'

Jake appeared impressed as she described the time they were having in New Zealand with distant cousins.

'Sounds a hell of a trip!' he said.

'It is, and I don't mind telling you that I worry about them all the time.' Louise worried about Mark as well but didn't want to mention that to Jake. 'Do you have children?'

He nodded. 'Two, girls, twenty and twenty-two. Lovely, both of them.' He felt for his back pocket and brought out a wallet. A photograph was pushed across the glass table towards Louise.

The girls were indeed incredibly attractive in a very American, open-air way with clouds of fair hair, wide laughing mouths and long, rangy bodies. They had their arms around each other and looked exceedingly happy together. 'What are their names?' asked

214

Louise as she handed the photo back.

'Kate and Amanda.' He looked down at the two girls, a small smile on his face as he inserted the snapshot back in his wallet.

'Are they at college?'

He nodded. 'Both English students. Good, too. Kate graduated last summer and is working on her master's now.'

'Academics, you think?'

He shrugged his shoulders. 'I'd like it if that happened but the competition's pretty tough out there. How long have you been in the companion business?'

Louise felt a lurch of dismay. Here was where she had to admit what an amateur she was at everything. Just a wife and mother with nothing to say and no other role in life. She gave Jake one of her best smiles. 'It's almost my first job. Apart from a stint sorting out some old records for a law firm.'

'Looking to occupy yourself now the parenting bit is coming to an end, huh?'

She drew a deep breath of relief.

'What does your husband think about it? I'd be more'n a bit peeved to have my beautiful wife take off with a geriatric to the other side of the Atlantic.'

'I don't suppose he's noticed I'm not there,' she said without thinking. Then quickly added, 'No, I shouldn't say that. But, well, the thing is, he has a very demanding job and it means he's away a lot of the time and works late when he's in London.' She stopped abruptly, aware of how pathetic her words sounded. 'But he's loads of fun and we have some great times at the weekends.'

'What an idiot he sounds,' said Jake. 'But then, I'm the last one to talk. That's how I ruined my marriage. Spending too much time with my head in books. How could I blame Bonny when she took it into her head to start another career?'

'What sort of career?'

He put down his empty glass carefully on the table and appeared to distance himself from Louise. 'She was a model when we met. The girls look very like her, except at their age she was twice as beautiful. The poor things have my genes mixed in there as well. After we married, she continued to model for a bit, sometimes with the kids. They were a help, you know?'

Louise nodded. She could see that two beautiful babies with a beautiful mother would have terrific drawing power with advertisers in the family market.

'Then the girls grew up and she got older and jobs became more and more difficult to come by. And, well, I didn't help any. Always teaching, researching, writing.'

'At least you were at home,' Louise couldn't stop herself saying.

Jake seemed to see her again and gave a grim smile. 'To hear Bonny, that was worse than if I'd gone away. 'Your body's here but

215

your head is somewhere else,' she'd tell me. So finally she went back to school.'

'School?'

'What you call college in the UK. She took a law degree then got a job in a law firm. The same time as Kate started university.'

Louise was impressed. 'Your wife must have worked very hard.'

'Yup! Never realised what a good mind she had in that beautiful head. 'Nother mistake of mine. We never talked enough. And by the time I saw what was happening it was too late, she'd fallen for one of her tutors. Now he's working in the same firm as her.'

Jake looked down at his hands, lying loosely in his lap, the long, strong fingers interlaced. 'She left me two years ago. The decree came through last Christmas. Not a good time to be on your own. Kate and Amanda and I spent it together with my mom, she lives not far from us, then we all went to the Caribbean. I had a lot of fun watching the girls in action amongst the young turks down there.'

'You couldn't do that this year?' hazarded Louise.

His face grew bleak. 'This year they told me they were going to join Bonny and Ned, that's her new husband, skiing at Aspen for New Year. All of a sudden it just hit me how I'd thrown happiness down the plug hole.' He picked up his glass and downed the last of the Coke. 'I had to take off, do something new. The dean didn't like it when I wanted a sabbatical at such short notice but I was due and I just told him I wouldn't take classes.'

For the first time Louise recognised that underneath the balanced, amused exterior here was a man in danger of losing control. 'I told everyone I had a book to write and rang Sam, asked could I take up the rain check, the invitation he'd always said was mine.' Jake gave a self-deprecating grimace. 'When he said he'd be all tied up during the day, I told him, fine, I'd be able to do my own thing, nose around to see if I wanted to write something on Florida.' He looked rueful. 'I hadn't been here two days before I was at my wit's end. No way could I even think about writing. All that was on my mind was the mess I'd made of my life. So when Sam and Mary were trying to sort out how to meet you and your mother, I couldn't wait to volunteer.'

'White knight stuff?' Louise suggested, torn between sympathy for this man's pain and amusement at a picture of the distinguished academic leaping at the chance to collect an unknown geriatric and her companion from Miami airport. He must have been desperate indeed!

He smiled awkwardly back at her. 'Something like that,' he acknowledged.

'Thanks for telling me all this.' Louise paused for a moment then felt compelled to add, 'I'm really sorry your marriage broke up, it must be hell.'

216

'You can say that again.'

'And maybe I can see how Gladys and I could be some sort of diversion rather than a millstone round your neck.'

'Never that! More like a lifebelt.'

For a little while they sat in companionable silence, Jake slowly revolving his empty glass on the table.

Then Louise took a deep breath and said, 'You shouldn't blame yourself entirely for Bonny's leaving you. I'm sure it wasn't all your fault. It takes two to break a marriage, just as it does to make one.' She thought of Polly and Willoughby. Where did the blame lie there?

Jake sighed as he raised his head and looked at her with unhappy eyes. 'My brains tells me you're right, but I still know that if we put the various wrongs in the balance, mine would weigh the heavier. Hey, I didn't intend to burden you with all this. Forget everything I've said!' He made an obvious effort to look cheerful.

'You two happy together?' Gladys poked her head round the terrace door. 'I hope not because lunch is just about ready and I want you to lay the table out there.'

'Your timing is impeccable,' Jake said, standing up, 'I was just about to seduce this lovely lady.'

After that, Louise didn't worry about Jake's being taken advantage of. Anything that kept his mind off the failure of his marriage had to be a good thing.

Even when Gladys suggested a few days later that he come with them to Orlando and the Disney World Resort, all Louise thought was that it would be a pleasant distraction for him.

The visit was definitely a success. Gladys was unexpectedly enchanted by the whole Disney experience, and Louise was impressed by Jake's smooth and efficient organisation of their trip.

Jake and Louise took it in turns to push the wheelchair and help Gladys on to the various adventure rides at EPCOT, a sister adventure to Disney World that focused on technology and foreign lands. She wanted to see and do everything. 'It's like being a child again,' she said, eyes glowing after a 'trip into the technological future'. 'Everything is so simplistic and yet there's real imagination at work here. I suppose one can only call it a touch of magic.'

Louise breathed a sigh of relief. When they'd started the trip, she'd wondered if it might turn out to be a big mistake. Why hadn't she realised the engineer in Gladys would revel in the audacity of the undertaking, the sheer size of it and innovative use of scientific principles? Louise hadn't expected her to succumb to the Disney vision. But by the end of the first ride she realised the tough former engineer had done just that.

It was only towards the end of the day, watching an English family with two young teenagers shrieking with joy at taking a trip in 'Norwegian fjords' that Louise was vividly reminded of the time

217

Mark and she had brought the twins here.

Suddenly the years rolled back and it was as if she could hear Emma and James shrieking in just the same way. It had been such a happy holiday. For once James hadn't annoyed his father. Even when he'd got into conversation with a group of musicians playing in the French village, Mark had been tolerant, suggesting they went into the café for a cup of coffee and a croissant until James had finished. He had come to join them twenty minutes later, his face flushed with pleasure, full of how he'd been allowed to play something with the group on a borrowed guitar. And the only thing Mark had said was, 'Well done, son.' It seemed the magic of Disney had touched them all then.

All at once Louise longed to speak to Mark, to hear his voice. She felt certain that if she could, everything would suddenly be right between them. She thought of the mobile telephone in the small haversack she'd taken to carrying for Gladys. It would be the middle of the evening in England. Mark should be back from the office. They'd had a brief conversation the previous weekend, Louise trying desperately to sound relaxed and as though she was enjoying talking to him, Mark stilted and monosyllabic. He'd told her then he'd spend next week in the flat.

'Why don't we have a break?' she suggested to Gladys and Jake. They were by the lake, a open-air café to hand, and the suggestion met with immediate approval. Once Gladys was comfortable, Louise said she'd be back in a few minutes and to please get her a coffee, and left the two of them settling at a table.

Out of their sight, she took out the telephone and punched in the number. There was something about the ringing tone that told her almost immediately that Mark wasn't there. Stupid to think so, but there it was. She leaned back against a convenient wall and looked out over the lake with its small islands and couple of cabin cruisers on the calm waters and heard the answering machine kick in. 'Hi,' she said after the long tone, 'it's me. Just giving you a ring from EPCOT. I'm here with Gladys and Jake. We're having a lot of fun but I can't help remembering that week we spent here with Emma and James . . .' She wanted to say she wished Mark was here with her but found she couldn't continue. 'Speak to you soon, darling, don't work too hard,' she managed to get out before finishing the call.

She couldn't bring herself to go back to Gladys and Jake immediately so found the nearest restroom and tried to recapture her previous happy mood.

It was so stupid to be upset Mark wasn't here! Even more stupid to find herself wondering just where he was. Probably having supper with Neil and Val, or some other friends. Louise dashed cold water on her face, renewed her lipstick and went back to the café.

Jake put a cardboard cup of coffee in front of her. 'I'm assured that's Disney's best.' She gave him a smile she couldn't help feeling was slightly watery but he said nothing.

Then Gladys raised her cardboard cup. 'My dears, I want to tell you I'm having the best time I can remember for years. It's as though I've been allowed to step aside from life for a day, forget my age and just enjoy.' She smiled wickedly at Jake. 'That's what you Americans say we should do the whole time, isn't it? Enjoy!'

'Why not?' He smiled easily back at her. 'It's one of our Constitutional rights: life, liberty and the pursuit of happiness.'

Louise found that remarkable. The guiding principles she'd been brought up with were duty, honesty, probity, and the importance of looking after others and not putting yourself first. 'What other nation puts such a high priority on selfishness?' she asked.

'Ah,' said Jake, 'that's not what the Constitution says. Everyone has their own idea what the pursuit of happiness is. For you, I doubt that it's looking after number one.'

'Though maybe you'd find life easier if it was,' Gladys interpolated gently.

Louise felt warmed by their obvious concern for her. She stretched out her arms and put back her head so she could feel the sun on her face. 'The pursuit of happiness,' she repeated. 'My own happiness.' Then she sat up straight and looked at them. 'Right now I feel happy to be here with you both. I don't want to think about anything else.'

Chapter Twenty-Six

Polly passed a wretched night in her luxurious Paris hotel room. Round and round her mind went Jean-Paul's disappearance, Caroline's anguished expression as she was left at her school, and worry about how she was going to pay her hotel bill. How much for granted one took credit cards these days!

By eight o'clock Polly felt she'd aged several decades. She ordered continental breakfast to be brought to her then tried to look at her situation realistically. Jean-Paul would be getting in touch with her within the next few days. He had to! It was just a matter of finding somewhere to stay until then. But where? The first thing any hotel asked for these days was your credit card number. If that bombed, she could whistle goodbye to a room. So what was left?

Buoyed up by the caffeine – such a relief to get real French coffee again – and the really excellent croissants, she reached for her Filofax. Surely if she rang around her old friends, someone would offer her hospitality? That's what she would do if they rang her in England. But the French were different, Polly knew that. Oh, if only Marie-Claire weren't skiing!

Half an hour later she ended her series of calls in despair. She'd been welcomed back by several old friends, all of whom sounded delighted to hear she was in Paris and pressed her to make a date for lunch. Could she get back on that? she'd asked each time. She had one or two business arrangements to make first but she was dying to see them. She'd known the moment she'd mentioned business no one would offer her a bed. Business meant an expense account and a good hotel. Even when she'd just said she wasn't sure exactly where she'd be staying, no invitation was forthcoming. But they did take her mobile phone number.

Polly reflected gloomily that no doubt Willoughby would cut off that account too when he thought of it.

She thumped the pillows into a more accommodating shape (might as well make the most of their comfort while she had it) then had another trawl through her Filofax. This time she stopped at the number of an English girl she'd chummed up with a few months before her departure from Paris.

'Polly, darling!' Mitzi screamed when she got through. 'You're actually in Paris? How divine! I can't wait to see you. Is Willoughby

221

with you? No? Then why not come and stay? Arthur's away in the Middle East and I'd adore to have you. I'm going out of my mind here, my French is still abysmal and since you left there's no one to talk to.'

Mitzi Paton was younger than Polly, the third wife of an international businessman who had, Polly suspected, chosen her for her inability to understand exactly what he was up to. Shortly after meeting him, Willoughby had suggested Arthur was too sharp an operator and he wanted nothing to do with him. 'I can't afford to be associated with someone who could end up in any one of a number of jails,' he'd said.

It hadn't worried Polly. Mitzi Paton was amusing, determined to have a good time, dedicated both to making the most of her considerable personal charms and to enjoying Arthur's money. Polly and she had spent several enjoyable shopping trips together, Mitzi delighted to find someone who could take her to all the right places, each session always ending with a gossipy lunch.

Perhaps she wasn't the companion Polly would have preferred right now, someone like Louise Henderson was what she really needed, but Mitzi offered a haven she couldn't afford to pass up.

She checked her small supply of francs, unchanged from when they'd left Paris (you always lost on foreign exchanges, far better to keep the currency for your next visit, Polly always considered, secure in the knowledge that there would always be another visit), then informed the hotel reception that the bill should be sent to Willoughby's company for settlement. She waited with her heart in her mouth while they checked the details. Had he cancelled the arrangement he'd had with them?

Not yet, it seemed, though there was a bad moment when they said that usually they required company confirmation of any reservation. But as it was Madame Fawkes herself, the manager said with a gracious smile, they were happy to make an exception.

She'd got away with it. But Polly reckoned that before the bill arrived in Willoughby's office, he would have stopped this loophole.

Trying not to remember just how few francs were in her purse, she took a taxi. How long was it going to be before she heard from Jean-Paul? Surely he must ring her soon? She'd left the number of her mobile phone on his answering machine, then had added that of the Patons and their address. Would he access the messages from New York? She felt if he didn't ring soon, the uncertainty would kill her.

The Patons rented a splendid house not far from the Champs Elysées, set within its own garden. No sooner had the taxi drawn up on the entrance drive, than the front door was opened by a manservant. Polly handed over the fare and congratulated herself on making the right decision concerning her arrival.

The taxi driver helped the servant take her cases into the grand hall. Then she was shown into the drawing room, where Mitzi sat working on a tapestry. The embroidery was flung aside and Mitzi rushed at her, two small dogs yapping at her heels. 'Darling! You don't know what this means to me. It's just too wonderful you said you could stay, we can have lots and lots of seriously intimate chats. Let me show you to your room. Maurice, bring us some champagne, please, immediately.' The servant gave a nod of his head and left the room. 'It's the only thing for this time of the morning, isn't it?'

Mitzi was tiny and curvaceous, dressed in a tiger print silk dress that nipped in her waist and displayed her bust. The expensively blonde curls were elegantly casual, her pekinese face was skilfully made up, and the amount of gold she was wearing would have done credit to a Maharani.

Polly hoped her Armani suit didn't look as rumpled after her trip as she feared it did and followed her up the curving marble staircase.

She was allowed a brief look at an ornate suite in which a florist's arrangement of expensive blossoms perfumed the air, then Mitzi dragged her downstairs again.

The champagne was in place and Mitzi lost no time in opening and pouring it. 'I don't need a man to open my champagne and we don't want Maurice hanging around,' she said. 'I can't wait to hear all about everything. How long are you here and what are your plans?'

Polly relaxed in a well-upholstered Louis Quinze-style chair with her glass of champagne and raised an expressive eyebrow. 'Who knows?' she said airily. 'London is just too desperately dull. Suddenly I longed for Paris. As for plans? Well, what can you suggest?'

It was enough. Mitzi launched into a veritable barrage of ideas. Shopping, of course; the opera – she was dying to go but needed company; there was a dinner party she'd been asked to but without Arthur hadn't felt she could accept. 'But now you're here, I'll ring and say we'll go together. You'll be able to translate and everything. And I've got to do something about this room. Well, look at it, darling? Isn't it the worst?'

Polly looked round the reproduction eighteenth-century French furnishings heavy with ormolu, gold leaf and embossed damask. Crystal chandeliers coruscated from the elaborately moulded ceiling and there were mirrors everywhere. 'Overpowering,' she murmured.

'I want to get rid of everything, but everything! Modern, don't you think? Pastels and light woods and durrie rugs. Oh, Polly, it's wonderful you're here. We'll go shopping as soon as we've had lunch. But I must tell you about the Mediterranean cruise Arthur has organised for Easter . . .' Mitzi launched into what sounded like something copied from a Greek shipowner's social calendar. Polly

223

relaxed and listened with half an ear.

Lunch was taken in a plant-filled conservatory, pale winter sun maximised by central heating. A little fish, salad, mangoes carefully sliced and served with fromage frais. Mitzi was on a diet.

Halfway through, the phone in Polly's leather handbag rang. She snatched it up with indecent haste and answered with the eagerness of a child. Only to lose her sudden exhilaration at the sound of one of her Parisian friends phoning back with an invitation to dinner. Numbly she negotiated the inclusion of Mitzi and signed off as enthusiastically as she could manage.

Mitzi eyed her with the curiosity of a horse dealer surveying an unknown filly but appeared delighted by the invitation.

She and Polly then spent an energetic afternoon exploring interior decor showrooms. By the time they returned home, Polly felt exhausted.

'Tiny little zizzies now, don't you think, darling?' suggested Mitzi. 'Come down about seven-thirty, right? Maurice will have the cocktails ready and dinner will be superb, I promise you. And guaranteed not to add one single, teeny-weeny ounce. Or, as I suppose they say over here, *un gram*!'

Polly undressed to her slip then flopped on to the huge guest-room bed. She felt as though she was coming apart at the seams. The luxury of this house was oppressive; Mitzi was exhausting, her tinkly chatter devoid of interest but demanding of attention. And what was draining Polly above all was the silence from Jean-Paul. She picked up her mobile phone and stared at it. It remained obstinately silent. Then she closed her eyes and tried to sleep. The prospect of an exhausting evening loomed before her.

As on the previous night too many thoughts were buzzing round in her brain for her to sleep but she must have catnapped because when she opened her eyes a couple of hours had passed.

She slipped quickly from the bed, had a shower, renewed her make up and changed into silk trousers and a cashmere sweater with a large, flattering collar. She checked her appearance in the mirror and decided she looked almost a new woman.

Mitzi was waiting for her in the drawing room, working again on her tapestry, a pair of light-framed glasses with narrow lenses perched halfway down her nose. A completely unnecessary fire, given the efficiency of the house's central heating system, blazed in the hearth. Mitzi was dressed in a long velvet housegown, with the most superb double row of baroque pearls Polly had ever seen around her neck.

'Darling,' she said, putting aside her tapestry, 'do hope you're rested? So selfish of me to rush you off your feet like that. Now, I've got the most divine cocktail I've only just learned how to do. Maurice has set out all the makings and I insist that you are going to enjoy this.'

By the time dinner was over, Polly was feeling adrift on a sea of alcohol and low-fat food.

'Now, angel,' Mitzi said as they settled again in the drawing room. The fire had been stoked up in their absence and a coffee tray placed ready with two brandy snifters and a bottle of cognac. 'Why not tell me everything?' She sloshed brandy into one of the snifters and held it towards Polly with a smile.

'I'm sorry?' Automatically she took the brandy, looked at it, then placed the glass on the table beside her.

'Darling, I know you. You would never have accepted my invitation unless there was something seriously wrong.' Mitzi calmly poured out coffee and offered Polly a cup. 'I'm not a complete idiot, you know?'

'I should never have imposed upon you,' Polly said stiffly.

'No, don't say that.' Mitzi looked distressed. She put down the coffee cup. 'It was just lovely you called me. No one has ever wanted to be my friend before and I adore having you here. Please, won't you let me help?' It was said gently and sweetly and all at once Polly found tears streaming down her face.

'That's better,' Mitzi said with just a touch of complacency. 'You've had a shell round you as tough as a tortoise's ever since you arrived. You need to tell someone, don't you?'

It was true.

Slowly, haltingly at first, Polly began the story of her affair with Jean-Paul. She left out nothing, including her present financial difficulty.

Mitzi tucked her feet beneath her, cradled her brandy glass in her hand and listened, large cornflower blue eyes gazing unblinkingly at her guest, all artifice vanished now. 'Oh, darling, how dreadful,' she said as Polly stumbled to a finish. 'Do you really think Jean-Paul has got cold feet?'

Polly wiped at her eyes with a tissue handed her by Mitzi at an early stage of her tale. 'No, I don't, I really don't,' she said, then started to pull the tissue gently apart. 'I don't know what's happened but I believe in him. I have to.'

Mitzi gazed pensively at her guest. 'I'm sure you know best on that,' she said finally. 'Give it another few days and it'll sort itself out. Jean-Paul will be back and all will be explained.'

Polly wished she could feel as confident as Mitzi sounded.

'What's much worse for you is Willoughby cancelling your credit, the sod!' Mitzi said with unexpected vehemence.

Polly shrugged her shoulders. 'I'm the idiot. I should have foreseen something like this. After all, why should he finance my running away? I just never thought.'

'You don't, do you? One hands out these bits of plastic without thinking. I mean, Arthur's always telling me the well isn't bottomless but that's what it seems like, doesn't it?' She widened her eyes disingenuously. 'What's much more important, though, darling, is that you shouldn't have left home. Not without having nailed Willoughby.'

'What do you mean?' Polly stared at her.

Mitzi leaned forward confidingly. 'You have rights, financial rights. Even if you want to leave, you still have rights. But once you leave home, darling, well, you've handed the advantage to the enemy. Who knows what Willoughby's doing? I bet he's got his money man working on shaving your share down as far as he can go.'

It had never occurred to Polly to think this way. For over sixteen years Willoughby had taken care of the financial aspect of her life. He had been generous, no doubt of that, but she had kept within his budgets. And the funds had never failed to be there. What had she thought, that Jean-Paul was going to support her from now on so she'd have no need to think about money? How could she have been so stupid?

'I helped him build his career,' she said in a low voice. 'That must be worth something in this modern world!'

'Of course it is, darling,' Mitzi said eagerly. 'And if you get a good lawyer, you'll receive a reasonable settlement. But not for ages. You wouldn't believe what the law can put between a girl and her rights.'

Polly suddenly became alert. 'You sound as though you have a degree in divorce proceedings, Mitzi.'

The blonde curls bobbed as she nodded vigorously. 'I went through it myself, darling, long before I met Arthur. I was just a little blonde bimbo with a diploma in how to make men feel good. I'm very, very good at that. And eventually I became good at looking after myself. Arthur has no idea how good I am at looking after myself.' There was an unexpectedly steely edge to her voice. 'I learned my lessons, the first of which is: never leave home, darling. Always make the man go.'

Fascinated by the change in her hostess, Polly gave a little shrug. 'Too late for that, sweetie.'

'You could go back?' Mitzi suggested.

'No!' Polly baldly stated. 'I'll do anything but that.' Just the thought of creeping home to Willoughby made her break out in a cold sweat. She'd see him with Caroline there, was willing to try and show their daughter that they could still be friends as long as Willoughby played ball, but that was all.

'Well, as long as you know what's involved,' Mitzi said equably. She set off on a new tack. 'Have you money of your own?'

'Some. Father left me a little and under the management of Willoughby's investment adviser, it's grown very nicely.'

'Enough to give you a reasonable income?'

Polly shook her head. 'Pin money, sweetie. But I should be able to access some funds in a few days.' She felt it was important to let Mitzi know she wasn't trying to move in on her.

226

'Darling, you can stay here as long as you want. And I can lend you taxi money but nothing more. Arthur has that sort of thing all tied up.' The cornflower blue eyes gazed at her candidly.

'I wouldn't dream of asking you for a loan,' Polly assured her. 'It was bad enough accepting your invitation to stay.' She glanced down at the still-untouched brandy. 'It wasn't just a free bed, you know, I needed your company.'

'Darling,' Mitzi said quickly, 'I understand. And I know you'd have done the same for me.'

Yes, Polly knew she would have.

'So, you're going to need a job.'

She realised with a sense of hopelessness that Mitzi obviously thought that Jean-Paul didn't want Polly around on a permanent basis. Could he be that devious? 'You can't trust the French,' Willoughby had said, and it was a sentiment she'd heard voiced by others as well.

'Do you have qualifications?'

Polly wondered whether Arthur had any idea how practical and focused his bimbo bride could be. 'I was a very successful public relations executive before I married.'

'Have you kept up your contacts?' Mitzi shot at her.

'Not really, we've moved around too much. But there are a couple of old colleagues I still send Christmas cards to.'

'Hmm. In London, I suppose?'

Polly nodded.

'You should probably go back there and lunch them, sound out the possibilities.' Mitzi gave a little laugh. 'Listen to me! I'm talking as though your gorgeous Jean-Paul isn't going to come back from New York. When you know, and I know, that in a few days this is all going to seem like a bad dream. Come on, drink up your nice brandy, it'll help you to sleep.'

'I don't think I need any more help to sleep,' Polly objected. But she sipped the intoxicating liquid anyway, letting the warm fumes drift up her nose as she lifted the glass to her lips. As the smooth fire slipped down her throat, her mind seemed to detach itself from her skull and float up to the ceiling, letting her observe the two of them sitting beside the fire in this overdecorated room.

'Whatever happens, I want to stay in Paris,' she said dreamily. 'I feel at home here – and who knows? I might find a job.'

'Of course, darling,' said Mitzi, her voice coming from a long way away.

Polly carefully placed the brandy balloon on the table and stood up. 'I think I'll go to bed now,' she said, and was mildly shocked to hear how slurred her voice was. 'Thanks, Mitzi darling, thanks . . .' She drifted off, holding hard to the door handle as she opened it, using the curved banister to haul herself up the marble staircase to her bedroom.

227

Polly woke to find herself in bed still dressed in her undies, her trousers and sweater in a heap on the floor.

She should have had the mother and father of hangovers but, amazingly, her head was clear. She looked at her travelling clock and was astonished to see that it was nearly lunchtime. She must have slept for twelve hours.

The door opened very softly and Mitzi peered round, then came in as she saw Polly half sitting up in bed. 'You're awake!' She clapped her hands in pleasure. 'I thought you were going to sleep forever!' She came and sat on the end of the bed. 'Do you feel any better?'

'Much better,' Polly assured her, wondering if it was true. Yes, she was rested, yes, her head was clear, but where there should have been feeling there was nothing but emptiness.

'Wasn't I awful giving you all that alcohol last night? Arthur's always telling me it's a depressive and no help to anyone. But I don't know, sometimes it really makes you relax and forget all your worries, and that's what you needed last night. Now, it's much too late to give you breakfast. Would you like lunch in bed or shall we go out somewhere?'

Polly managed a smile. 'What would you like to do?' she asked, then watched with distant amusement as Mitzi carefully considered the question.

'I think,' she said, eyes wide and candid, 'lunch at a simply superb restaurant and then there's a wonderful antique shop I love to explore whenever I'm feeling really extravagant.'

'And you're feeling really extravagant now?'

Mitzi nodded, blonde curls bouncing. 'Oh, yes. Arthur never seems to realise I spend much more on furniture and porcelain than I do on clothes. But their resale value is so much higher than suits and dresses, even haute couture.' She gave Polly a smile full of complicity.

For two days she tried to forget Jean-Paul as she accompanied her hostess to restaurants, antique shops, a fashion show and the dinner that had been arranged at the start of her visit. She was in limbo, a walking zombie. If only there was something she could do! If only she could see him, speak to him even. If only she could hear from his own lips that he no longer wanted her then, she felt, she would be able to face anything else that life had to throw at her.

But as the hours passed and no word came, something, some faith Polly had in her own judgement and her love, seemed to die.

Then on the third day as they returned from a shopping expedition during which Mitzi had bought a Vincennes tureen and three Sèvres candelabra, Maurice opened the door to them, his eyes alive with interest.

'Madame has a visitor,' he said to Polly. 'I showed Monsieur into the drawing room.'

Mitzi gave a little cry of delight. 'Oh, Polly, this is it! Go and see him.' She gave a little push to Polly's rigid back. 'I won't interrupt you, promise, even though I'm just dying to know everything!'

Propelled by her push, Polly found herself walking across the marble floor towards the tall double doors. But Maurice was before her. He opened them with a perfect butler's flourish. 'Madame Fawkes,' he announced.

Polly entered with every emotion held in check. She was unable to feel anything. It was as though she had been thrust into a deep freeze but left with the power to move. Behind her she heard the salon doors close.

Jean-Paul was standing by the conservatory window. He turned as Polly entered, his face strained and taut.

She found her legs wouldn't carry her any further. She stopped halfway across the room and a small suppressed moan escaped her.

Then Jean-Paul was beside her. His arms came around her, his mouth was in her hair. 'My darling! Oh, my darling!' he said, and he was speaking English. 'Can you ever forgive me?' Then he was kissing her and the ice started to melt from Polly's veins.

Her arms crept round Jean-Paul's neck and she strained against his body, unable to believe that it was really him, that he was holding her as though he'd never, never let her go again.

After several hundred years had passed, he drew gently away.

'Where were you?' she asked softly, holding back her head so she could see his face. 'Why didn't you meet me?'

He led her gently to one of the deep-cushioned sofas then sat down beside her and held her hands tightly. 'My darling, I was sent to New York by my bank. It was a crisis, I had to go. I didn't know when you were coming so I rang you. You weren't there but I left a message on your machine not to come until I telephoned you. It wouldn't be more than a week, I said. I rang again after I reached New York. Again, nothing but the machine. The third time I tried, your 'usband answered and he tell me you are out shopping. So I leave no message. I think you must 'ave my others.'

'Willoughby,' Polly murmured, never taking her eyes off Jean-Paul, drinking in the sight of his lined face and dark eyes, so dark she could see herself reflected in them, a miniature Polly. 'He wiped the tape.' He would never admit it, of course; he'd swear the machine must have been faulty, and if she challenged him about telling Jean-Paul she was out shopping, he'd bluster and say there must have been some misunderstanding. But she knew. She would always know what he had done to try and get her to return to England.

'I worked so hard in New York, frantic to get back so we could be together.' Jean-Paul had switched to French now and his hand was caressing her cheek, playing with her hair. 'I tried to access my machine, to see if you'd left a message, but something had gone wrong. All I received was bleeps! Then, this morning, I arrived and went straight home, instead of to the office as I should. Just in case there was word from you. And there were your messages. Oh, my darling.' He drew her to him again, holding her tight against his beating heart. 'I nearly died. To think you had arrived and no word from me! What you must have thought! So I came straight here.' He drew away again and looked down at her. 'Can you ever forgive me?'

'What is there to forgive?' Polly laughed, her heart light once again. 'I knew you would come back to me.'

Chapter Twenty-Seven

On Saturday morning Nicky dumped a horrendously expensive collection of supermarket goods on the kitchen table and started to sort out her weekly shop. First the perishable food was slammed into the fridge, then the groceries into the storage cupboard. Finally she turned her attention to the cleaning and toiletry items.

As she stuffed the economy-size bag of toilet rolls into the back of the cupboard under the stairs, the telephone rang. Nicky stumbled over the vacuum cleaner and several brushes as she fought her way out. 'Hello? Oh, hi, Mark.' Her voice suddenly became more cheerful.

'Hi, Nicky, is Colin there?'

'Sorry, Mark, no.' Her brief enthusiasm leaked away.

'Will he be long? I was hoping we could have a game of squash sometime this afternoon.' Mark's voice was full of determination.

'He's in Exeter, not coming back until tomorrow,' she said curtly.

'Oh.' Mark sounded deflated. 'You mean, he won't be available for a game at all?'

Mark wasn't usually so slow. Nicky leaned against the kitchen cupboard beside the wall telephone and spelled it out. 'No, sorry, he won't be. You at a loose end or something?' She couldn't imagine him at a loss for a squash partner – or anything else, come to that.

He laughed. To Nicky, over the telephone, it sounded hollow. 'No, no, I'm fine. Just thought it would be good to get together with Colin, you know.'

In Nicky's experience, Mark contacted Colin when he needed to let his hair down or had some sort of problem. When things were going swimmingly, he let their friendship drift. 'Come on, Mark, I know you better than that. What's up?' Before she'd started her job, Nicky would never have dared say anything like that to Mark for fear he'd take it the wrong way. Now daily experience in dealing with a wide range of personal problems, anything from dissatisfaction with another teacher's attitude to the impossibility of coping any longer with the little sod in 4C, had given her more confidence.

A long sigh came over the phone. 'Louise isn't coming back until next weekend.'

It was news to Nicky that she had gone anywhere. She hadn't had any contact with the Hendersons since that extraordinary Christmas party, though that was nothing unusual. Sometimes months went by without her seeing or speaking to Louise. 'Where's she gone? Not out to see the twins?' It would be just like the Hendersons to feel they had to make sure their children were all right when they were supposed to be going round the world on their own.

'No, nothing like that. She took a job – companion to some old biddy visiting a relation in Florida.'

'Good heavens,' Nicky said weakly.

'As you say, good heavens,' agreed Mark dryly.

'How long for?'

'That's the thing of it. I was all lined up to meet her at Gatwick this morning. Instead she rang me the day before yesterday and calmly announced they'd decided to stay another week.'

'Good heavens,' said Nicky again. Now she could see what this call was about. Mark was all alone, rattling around in that big house with nothing to do. She looked at the last of the shopping sitting on the kitchen table, the remains of her breakfast beside the sink, the floor that needed washing. 'Well, as we're both on our own, would you like to come round here for supper? It won't be much but it would be fun to see you.' Again, it would never have occurred to the pre-job Nicky to issue such an invitation, or if it had, she would have firmly squashed the idea.

'Supper?' Mark did appear a little startled.

Nicky started to backtrack. 'If you've something else to do . . .' she started.

'No, nothing. That's extremely nice of you, Nicky. Yes, I'd love to accept. What time would you like me?'

'Half-past seven suit?' she suggested. 'OK, look forward to seeing you then.' She put down the telephone and told herself she was out of her mind. She had enough to do today without worrying about having Mark to supper. But as she started to wash the floor, there was a pleasurable flutter in her breast.

He arrived at seven-thirty-five, clutching a bottle of wine.

'How kind,' she said, accepting his customary kiss on the cheek and catching whisky fumes on his breath. 'It looks good,' she said, studying the claret label. 'We're having chicken, will it be all right with that? I've got a white in the fridge but it isn't nearly as good as this looks.'

'I'm sure it'll be excellent. Why don't we start on that and then go on to the claret while we eat? If I open it now, it'll have a chance to breathe.' Mark headed off in the direction of the kitchen. 'Where do you keep your corkscrew?'

Nicky opened the drawer and took out the Screwpull she'd put in Colin's stocking.

'Oh, good, these take all the effort out,' Mark said approvingly as he slotted the device together and drew the cork.

232

A few minutes later they were sitting in the living room with glasses of white wine. Nicky smiled brightly at Mark. 'Hope you're warm enough? I lit the fire early but it doesn't seem to have made much of an impression.'

'With this weather, what do you expect?' he said a little bleakly.

It had frozen every night for the last week and today the cold had hardly let up at all. The forecast was for more cold, followed by snow. Colin had rung and said that in Exeter the temperature was well above freezing.

Mark pulled his roll top a little higher round his neck and hunched his shoulders inside his ornately patterned sweater. Nicky poked at the fire and added more wood. She was wearing leggings under a very loose knitted top that came halfway down her thighs. She balanced herself on a pouffe near the flames and cradled her wine. She couldn't remember ever being on her own with Mark like this and found it, despite her newly discovered confidence, a little unnerving. He looked so *very* attractive, lying back in the armchair with the blue of his sweater picking up his blue Robert Redford eyes and that straight patrician nose.

'So, what's Colin doing down in the West Country then?' he asked, his gaze fixed flatteringly on Nicky, long legs clad in blue jeans stretched out, feet towards the fire. Nicky loved the little leather tassels on his loafers. She bet herself the shoes were genuine Gucci, not a cheap imitation.

'Checking out a firm that's interested in taking him on as a partner. You remember I told you at Christmas he was thinking of it.'

Mark raised an eyebrow. 'So you did. You sounded as though it was bad news.'

Nicky gave another impatient poke to the fire. 'You mean, you think it's a good idea for us to up sticks from here and decamp to the West Country? Leaving friends and family behind? Colin doesn't seem to realise how much his mother sees of us where we are now. Then there's my parents as well. And the boys are getting on so well at their new school.'

'Would you have to move them?'

'It would either be that or spending most weekends driving back and forth.' Nicky gazed disconsolately down at her glass.

'But Colin thinks it can work.' Mark didn't make a question. 'What's the firm like he's gone to see?'

'Oh, I don't know. Old-established firm of family solicitors, sort of outfit he's with at the moment except a hundred and fifty miles away,' Nicky said bitterly. She and Colin had argued most of last weekend about this trip.

'It won't commit me to anything,' he'd protested. 'It's just reconnaissance. You know what they say: time spent in reconnaissance is seldom wasted.'

'You're determined to make this move,' she'd snapped. 'You're just hoping to wear me down.'

'Look,' he'd said gently, 'I've shown you the figures. You've seen what this house could fetch now that the property market is moving again. It's an extraordinarily good prospect and this whole idea could make a real difference to our finances.'

'You haven't any idea of the sort of house we could get down there,' Nicky burst out. 'Anything decent would probably cost much more than you expect.'

'That's why we should go down and check things out together. Come with me,' he urged. 'You can explore the house market while I talk with the legal eagles. And they're bound to want to meet you as well.' He waited, his face eager and expectant.

'I can't,' Nicky said baldly. 'I have to work on Friday.'

'Ask for time off, I'm sure you could get it.'

'No, we're too busy.' She was at her most stubborn. He knew better than to press her but gave an exasperated sigh. 'OK, then, I'll go on my own. But I shall stay for the weekend, check out houses, schools, the lot. I'll bring back lots of information and we can go through it together.'

Neither of them had said anything more about the trip and the week had passed in a state of non-communication.

'What's really getting to you?' Mark asked gently. 'I can see something is.'

It wasn't often he displayed that sort of insight and it touched Nicky. All at once she could feel tears dangerously near the surface. 'Oh, it's nothing,' she said, giving her head a little toss, making her copper curls swing, then gazed down at her shoes like a gauche schoolgirl.

'Come on, I can see there's something,' he urged, leaning forward slightly, trying to see her face.

Nicky could contain herself no longer. 'It's just that Colin never even considers me! He seems to think I can just walk away from my job and find something else in Exeter. That what I do doesn't matter.'

'Ah,' said Mark softly.

'I mean, how would you like it if Louise suddenly suggested you should move to the other end of the country because it suited her and the twins, and that meant you would have to give up your job and find another?'

Mark looked startled. 'I hardly think that's likely!'

'No, because you're like Colin. You don't think a woman has any right to a life of her own!' Nicky gave vent to her resentment.

'That's not fair! Louise has always led her own life. I don't interfere with her, she does exactly as she likes.'

Nicky gave up. She was never going to get him to admit he didn't want a working wife, anymore than Colin would. They liked to

234

think they were modern men. In fact, they were every bit as chauvinistic as their fathers had been. 'The thing is,' she said reflectively, 'Colin and I have always had a very open marriage.'

'You mean, affairs with other people?' Mark looked astounded.

Nicky giggled. 'Good heavens, no! I meant that we've always discussed everything together.'

'You don't approve of extra-marital affairs, then?' There was a note of something that sounded very like uncertainty in his voice.

Nicky gazed at him in surprise. ' "For richer, for poorer; for better, for worse; in sickness and in health, till death us do part!" ' Then she looked at him more closely, an edge of excitement forcing its way into her chest. Could this possibly be a come on? Of course, she wouldn't be interested – but Mark and she had always had a bit of a thing going. Nothing to worry anyone, of course, just a little mild flirtation, a sort of mutual admiration society. It didn't mean anything, she knew that. At least, she thought she did.

'Not that I've ever really been tempted.' She looked up at him through her eyelashes. Enough to encourage him if he was hoping to take things further but nothing that said she was on offer. Because she wasn't. Not even for Mark. Still, it would be something to have him test the waters, as you might say. She could do with a bit of morale-boosting after the way Colin had shot off yesterday morning with no more than a quick goodbye. He hadn't even kissed her.

But Mark was gazing moodily into his glass. 'What if you ever suspected Colin of . . . well, of going off the rails?' He raised his eyes. 'Has he ever?'

'Mark, what is this? Of course he hasn't. Well, perhaps I shouldn't say "of course". But I think I'd know if he did. I mean, there are all sorts of ways, aren't there?'

Mark seemed to pull himself together. 'I'm sure you're right. After all, look at Polly and Willoughby. I suppose that's what I'm thinking of. He suspected she was having an affair and it turned out she was.'

The news hadn't surprised Nicky at all.

'Willoughby can't imagine what he's done,' Mark said sadly. 'He says he's always been a good husband.'

'Oh, yeah! In between his little peccadilloes! Bet he didn't tell you about those?'

Mark looked uncomfortable. 'Well, he did mention there'd been one or two little flings. But they didn't mean anything,' he added hastily. 'Anyway, how did you know? He didn't confide in Colin as well, did he?' Disbelief coloured his voice.

Nicky gave a cynical smile. 'Only tried it on with me – at that supper we had at your place!'

'No? He didn't?' Mark looked first shocked and then amused. 'Bet you gave him what for!'

'Bet I did,' agreed Nicky. 'So how he can say he's been such a good husband, I can't imagine.'

'Well, he's always provided for her: nice houses, designer clothes, exotic holidays.'

'And that's your definition of a good husband?' Nicky stared at him dumbfounded. 'Come on, Mark. You know better than that!'

Again, he shifted uneasily in his chair. 'I didn't mean that quite as it came out. But, according to his lights, Willoughby has always been loyal. I wonder if Polly could say the same?'

'Loyalty,' Nicky mused. 'That's really important, isn't it?' A sudden vision of Colin trudging round schools and houses came to her.

'I'd say it was the most important thing of all. Husband and wife should be a team, each considering the other.'

Dream on, Mark, thought Nicky. You haven't the first idea what loyalty is about – or what teamwork really is.

Then her hostess's instinct asserted itself. 'Poor Mark, all I've done is bend your ear. I haven't offered you anything to eat yet. I've got some crisps in the kitchen. Not Kettles, I'm afraid, but they're not bad. I'll fetch them and you can nibble away while I do the vegetables.'

'I'll come with you, then I can nibble and watch you at the same time. Much more fun than gazing at the fire.' He eased himself out of the chair in one supple movement.

'That'll be great.' Nicky rose with what she hoped was equal grace and led the way into the kitchen.

She gave him chicken quarters done in condensed mushroom soup, easy-peasy and flung together before she'd sunk into a reviving bath after spending the day cleaning the house. It was accompanied by the remains of the white wine and all the bottle of claret Mark had brought. As they ate, she got him to talk about his job.

She had thought it would be difficult, Louise had said once that he never liked talking about the office and she'd given up trying to be involved in what he was doing, but Mark seemed happy to describe some recent deals he'd worked on.

'People think figures are dull,' he said, helping himself to another slice of the ice-cream gâteau she had got for the boys' next exeat. 'I say, Nicky, this is good. I must tell Louise she should get some.' Nicky couldn't see Louise feeding her husband on a ready-made pudding but said nothing.

Later she got out a large piece of Brie. Colin was very fond of Brie and liked it for supper sometimes. She'd bought it as a bit of a peace offering for his return. Before Mark had arrived, she'd wondered whether to cut it in half but thought the result would look too mean. She placed the cheese on the table.

Mark's eyes lit up. 'Any more wine?' he asked, cutting off a large slice and putting it on his plate.

Nicky went to the cupboard under the stairs. All that was in there was Colin's best, gift of a grateful client at Christmas. Without hesitation she picked out a bottle and brought it back to the table with the Screwpull.

'Would you like some coffee?' she asked.

Mark nodded, helping himself to yet another piece of cheese; there wasn't too much left of the Brie now. He looked across the table at Nicky filling the filter machine. 'You think I'm pretty much of a shit, don't you?'

She turned, genuinely startled. 'Mark! Of course I don't!'

He leaned back in his chair, one arm on the table, eyes focused on the hand toying with a half empty glass of wine. 'You're thinking to yourself, What a hotshot he thinks he is. What right has he to be so confident? Isn't that it?' he shot at her, suddenly looking up.

She was taken aback at the expression in his eyes which bore no resemblance at all to Robert Redford's now. These were the eyes of a man who was suffering.

'Mark,' she started, then stopped. She had no idea where to go from here. 'I think you're – well, one of the greatest guys I know.' She swallowed hard. 'I've always . . . well, I've always thought Louise was the luckiest girl alive.'

His expression hardened. 'You did, did you? I don't suppose she'd agree with you. Nor would anyone else.'

Nicky thought she understood. She was amazed but it made a sort of sense. She came and sat down again at the table and took his hand. 'She's crazy about you, Mark, always has been.'

He gently freed his hand and drew it over his face, pulling at the skin under his eyes. Nicky could see their whites were bloodshot. 'Nobody's crazy about me, Nicky, nobody. All they see is a man who understands figures but can't understand women.'

'I'm crazy about you,' she whispered, beyond conscious thought now.

Mark's hand wavered towards her face. He gave her cheek a clumsy caress. 'Are you, little Nicky? That's sweet of you.'

She held her breath as she looked deep into his lonely eyes. Then, very slowly, she closed hers.

Colin returned mid-afternoon on Sunday.

Nicky heard the front door close as she finished clearing out the boys' bedrooms. Dressed in jeans and two sweaters against the cold, she'd managed to work up a good sweat as, refusing to think, she'd conducted her *blitzkreig*. She'd stripped beds, stuffed away discarded clothes, computer equipment, books, records and other impedimenta that seemed to silt up their rooms like tidal detritus on a beach, and vacuumed dustballs from under the beds as though a regimental inspection was due. Only when each room looked so impersonal and neat that neither boy would have recognised it as his did she slow down.

It was as she lugged the vacuum cleaner to the top of the stairs and stopped, wondering whether she should now attack the master bedroom, that she heard the front door close. She looked over the landing banister, straight on to Colin's bald patch as he hung up his coat and hat.

He glanced up and saw her. His own expression was wary. 'I'm back,' he said.

'So I see.' Nicky was equally wary. 'How did it go?'

'Come down and I'll tell you.' His shoulders were hunched but she couldn't tell whether it was against the cold or because he was disappointed with his trip.

'Have you had anything to eat?' she asked as she deposited the vacuum cleaner in the cupboard under the stairs.

'Only breakfast.'

'Come into the kitchen and I'll see what I can find. I haven't had lunch yet.'

'You look as though you've been having a spring clean.' Colin smoothed down the remains of his hair and followed her. He leaned against one of the cupboards as she lit the oven and left the door open, then went and investigated the contents of the fridge. 'Haven't you had the heating on today? The place is freezing!' He hugged his arms across his chest then pulled up the collar of his suit jacket, worn over sweat shirt and jeans.

'Every time I flick that switch, I see ten-pound notes going up in flames.' Nicky took out a packet of sausages and some eggs. 'As long as you keep on the go it isn't too bad. And I've laid the fire in the drawing room.'

Colin strode into the utility room and switched on the central heating, waiting until the ancient boiler lit with a threatening roar. 'We aren't that poor,' he said through clenched teeth as he returned and took up his previous station.

Nicky started to grill the sausages. 'Fried or scrambled eggs?' she asked in a colourless voice.

'Scrambled, please.'

'So, how did it go?' she asked again, her back to him as she melted butter in a saucepan and beat eggs in a small bowl.

For a moment Colin didn't say anything. Then: 'Why's Mark's car outside?'

Nicky stopped beating the eggs. 'Oh, he came round for supper last night and had rather too much to drink. So he took a taxi home.'

Colin did not seem to find this strange. 'Sorry I missed him. I'll give him a ring later and say I'll drive it round for him, then he can run me back.'

Nicky turned the sausages and said nothing.

238

'Well,' Colin continued, 'the firm looks to be everything I want.'

'Are you everything they want?' Nicky asked, her voice coming out more sharply than she'd intended.

'They seem to think so,' he said quietly. He levered himself away from the cupboard and started to lay the table, his movements careful and deliberate. He gave her details of the firm, its size, the partnership, the spread of their business. It sounded as though he'd gone into everything very thoroughly. And it was obvious that he liked both the partners and the whole shape of the firm.

'I looked at houses. There's not a lot on the market but I saw one I think you'd like. It's in a little village, not far from the M5. It'd only take twenty minutes or so for me to get in. And I asked about schools. There are a couple that might work.'

Nicky finished scrambling, removed the plates she'd put to warm in the oven and portioned out the eggs.

Colin put the bread on the table, found the low-fat spread in the fridge and added that. Then saw the last of the Brie and his face lit up as he placed that on the cheese board. 'A feast,' he said happily as he sat down and Nicky placed the plate of sausages and eggs in front of him.

'So, as far as you're concerned, everything would work?' she asked as she sat down opposite him, her expression unreadable.

Colin looked at her anxiously. 'Yes, as far as I'm concerned, it all looks great. But I'm not the only one concerned here. There's you as well. I don't want to force you to do anything you're not one hundred percent sure about.'

Nicky looked at his kind, worried face and something turned over inside her. 'We have to talk,' she said.

Chapter Twenty-Eight

The sun in Sarasota on the Gulf of Mexico was as hot as on the Atlantic coast of Florida but in the shade of the luxuriant trees there was a chill. A fierce breeze came off the water and Louise pulled her light jacket around her, feeling cold for the first time since she'd left England. Ahead of her, Jake was assisting Gladys to negotiate a path through the park dedicated to Hernando de Soto, an early explorer. She was using both her sticks although the path was level and easy.

It had been Sam's idea that Jake should drive them over to Sarasota. 'The west coast is so different from the east, you really ought to see it. It's resort land, full of lush holiday retreats and smart shopping. Apart from the coastline, which includes the Keys, those finger-thin islands off it, there's very little development. And you should drive across the Florida peninsula, it will give you quite a different feel for the place. You shouldn't leave knowing only the east coast.'

Over the other side of the park was a small compound where demonstrations were given of how the early explorers lived. It was now preparing for the last show of the day. Louise watched Gladys stump determinedly towards the compound, getting slower and slower. 'I think we should suggest we find somewhere to stay tonight,' she muttered as she caught up with Jake. He nodded.

But Gladys would have none of their suggestion. 'Nonsense! We're here to see everything. I want to watch this.' She sat herself down on one of the wooden benches provided for the audience and proceeded to give a good impression of someone enraptured by actors in sixteenth-century garb cooking a stew over a fire, then demonstrating how blunderbusses were fired.

Louise slipped off her jacket and laid it round Gladys's thin shoulders as she saw her hunching them under the light T shirt she wore; she'd scorned the suggestion she might need anything warmer. More trees shaded them from the sun and the air was cool.

'We'll all huddle up together,' Gladys said, pressing a grateful hand on Louise's. 'Come on, move up.' She shifted on the bench towards Louise, pressing her against Jake.

Without her jacket, the chill had feathered Louise's arms, turning them to gooseflesh. Jake's warmth was welcome. She felt his arm come round her shoulders and hold her lightly, could feel his ribs, bony and hard beneath his sweat shirt. Could feel, too, the thud of his heart against her ribcage.

'That's better,' said Gladys, her bony frame pushed hard against Louise's softer body.

Louise hardly heard her. All she was conscious of was that rapid heartbeat pounding in time with hers. Jake had his eyes fixed firmly on the little clearing and the actors reloading their primitive weapons. But the hand clasping her shoulder was warm – so warm it seemed to burn her flesh.

She sat fighting panic. This wasn't what she wanted. She prayed the show would end so they could move, so she could escape from the sensations that were flooding through her.

Never before had Louise been attracted to any man but Mark. During the nearly twenty years of their marriage, she had been totally content with him. Oh, she'd occasionally flirted lightly with someone she sat next to at dinner or met at some function, but nothing more. Certainly they had never stirred her. Not like this. She felt breathless and wondered if she'd be able to stand when, at last, the actors took their bows and the small audience began to rise and depart.

'Quite amusing,' cackled Gladys, levering herself up on her sticks. 'I enjoyed that. Makes me realise how lucky I am with electricity and a microwave.'

Jake removed his arm and stood up as well. He didn't look at Louise. 'We'd better find somewhere to stay,' he said.

His voice seemed to come from a long way off.

'Well, Louise, you sitting there all night?' Gladys demanded.

She struggled to her feet and picked up the haversack, glad she had something to do so she could hide her face. She knew it was burning.

'What a close-knit little trio we've become,' Gladys observed smugly. She appeared to have revived. 'Well, we'd better find Jake's car.' She didn't seem to find it odd that neither of her companions appeared able to say anything, but started making her way painfully towards the main path to the car park.

'You all right?' Jake asked Louise.

She nodded, unable to speak, all too conscious of his proximity now. And was that shyness in his eyes?

'So where do we find somewhere to lay our heads down tonight?' asked Gladys as Jake helped her into the car.

He drove them through Sarasota and found a luxurious motel on the other side, not far from a circle of smart-looking shops and a causeway leading on to one of the Keys.

'I shall have a rest, it's far too early to eat yet,' Gladys said at the door to her room as Jake placed her small case on the luggage carrier and Louise added the haversack. 'Why don't you two go for a walk?' She gave them a regal smile.

Outside, Jake looked at Louise. 'What about it? Would you like a walk or are you pooped too? There's always the TV.'

'No,' she said, not looking at him. 'I'd love a walk.'

'Let's drive on to the Key and find a nice beach.'

Louise had no fault to find with this idea but it proved easier to suggest than carry out. Each side of the long, thin island seemed to be covered with hotels or condominiums, all with secure entrances. Casual visitors, it seemed, were not encouraged. Eventually, though, they found somewhere they could park the car that offered access to a sandy beach alongside the Gulf of Mexico.

Louise took off her shoes. She was wearing shorts and her legs were bare. The fine, silvery sand oozed between her toes. The wind had died and the last of the sun was warm on her back. 'According to Mark, it's below freezing at home,' she said as they set off. 'I can't really believe it but apparently there is snow everywhere, only the motorways are clear.' She looked out at the sinking sun that was turning the sea to molten gold. 'And here we are, pretending it's summer.'

'Yeah. Up where I come from it's darn' chilly too. I spoke to my next-door neighbour yesterday and in Massachusetts it's definitely winter. Snow ploughs out and roads regularly gritted.'

Jake, too, had taken off his docksider shoes, knotted together the laces and was walking with them hanging round his neck. He was between Louise and the last of the sun, casting a shadow. She should have been chilly but her skin had never felt so warm. 'When are you going back?' The question was so banal. She wanted to ask something personal, something that would drag their conversation on to a meaningful level, suddenly there was so much she wanted to know about Jake, but she was terrified of their talk leading some-where beyond her control.

'Next week, I daresay. I don't think Sam ever expected to accommodate a house guest for so long,' Jake said with a ghost of a laugh.

'It's been wonderful for Gladys and me to have your company all this time,' Louise said impulsively.

Jake stopped and put his hands on her shoulders. 'You must know it's meant everything to me,' he said and stooped to kiss her.

Louise froze under his touch, then found her arms reaching up around his neck as her mouth opened beneath his and she rose on her bare toes to reach up to him.

A multi-petalled flower opened in her breast, pressed against her ribcage, swelled with bloom and filled her with a suffocating sensation. She wanted to melt into his skin, have her bones dissolve into his bones.

Jake gave a long sigh and released her.

Louise buried her face in his chest. Then pulled away and looked

243

at him her eyes filled with distress. 'Oh, Jake, this is terrible.'

'No, it isn't,' he asserted, putting his arm around her shoulders and starting to walk along the beach again. 'I've been wanting to do that since the first time I saw you at the airport. There I was, amongst all that crowd, looking for Mary's mother. She'd said Gladys would probably be using two sticks. Simple enough to spot, you'd think. Instead, all I could think about was the most beautiful-looking girl I'd seen in my life. It took forever for me to realise that beside her was a woman wielding a couple of canes.' He pulled her closer and Louise couldn't stop herself from leaning her head against his arm. 'When I realised it was you I'd come to meet, I felt as though I'd won the jackpot.'

For a moment she allowed her feet to move in rhythm with his, his arm to curve round her shoulders. Then she stopped and tore herself away from him.

Jake stopped too. 'What is it?'

'I'm sorry,' she half gasped, half sobbed. 'I can't do this.'

He screwed up his eyes incredulously. 'What are you saying? You must feel what I feel? I can't be that wrong.'

'No . . . I mean, yes . . . I mean – oh, Jake, it's so difficult.' She turned and started to walk back towards the car, dragging her feet through the sand.

The fiery disc of the sun slipped beneath the horizon, the magic path of golden sea disappeared and the light rapidly began to fade.

Louise quickened her steps so that Jake had to hurry to catch her up.

He caught her by the shoulder as she started up the beach towards the car. 'Louise, you can't do this to me!'

She felt bitter tears begin to scald her eyes.

'Look at me,' he insisted, pulling her round to face him. 'You can't tell me you still love that bastard you're married to?'

'He's not a bastard!' she shouted at him. 'Mark's . . .' She couldn't think how to describe him. 'He's my husband, and I love him. I *do* love him.' Then she burst into tears.

Jake gently took her in his arms and rocked her, holding her head against his chest so that once again she could feel the beating of his heart.

She stood fighting the new sensations all around her, trying to control her tears. She forced herself to be aware of the sand between her toes, its heat against the soles of her feet, the resinous smell of pines drifting past her, someone shouting at a dog a long way off, the gentle murmur of the sea.

Eventually she had herself under control again. She dug in the pocket of her shorts for a tissue and scrubbed at her eyes. 'I'm sorry,' she muttered, not looking at him.

'We have to talk, Louise, Jake said firmly. 'There are things that have to be said.'

She made a jerky gesture, dismissing the suggestion.

'We have to,' he repeated firmly. 'But not now. Later, when you're calmer. I shouldn't have grabbed you like that but – well, you were irresistible.'

Louise got into the car and sat in silence as he started the engine. All the way down the long Key and on to the causeway neither of them spoke.

Back in the motel parking lot, Jake switched off the engine and sat with his arms over the steering wheel, looking straight ahead. 'After dinner, we'll see Gladys back here and then we'll go for a drink,' he said, brooking no argument. 'You owe me that.'

Louise thought she probably owed him a great deal more than that. Part of her wanted to turn to Jake and fling herself into his arms. She wanted to let the world go hang. This was what she needed, what she must have. But part of her wanted to flee from the car and from him, pack her bag, tell Gladys she couldn't stay another moment longer, and then take the first plane back to England.

Was this what Polly had felt when she fell for Jean-Paul? Had she been torn in half, not knowing whether to go to him or stay with Willoughby and Caroline?

'All right,' Louise said slowly, reluctantly, and got out of the car.

Jake leaned across before she could shut the door. 'I'll go and find somewhere nice for us to eat,' he said. 'Seven-thirty do you?'

Louise nodded. 'Gladys should be rested by then.' She wondered if she could plead a headache and let them eat by themselves.

But she was employed by Gladys to look after her. Somehow she was going to have to control her feelings and get through the remaining few days until they went home.

When Gladys knocked on Louise's door later, she looked revived, spry and excited. 'This looks really interesting,' she told Jake as they went into the restaurant he'd found at St Armand's Circle. She hardly seemed to realise that neither he nor Louise had much to say for themselves. Her bright eyes took in everything: the low-key decor, the fact that the other diners seemed to be middle-class professionals who didn't look like tourists, the Californian-style cuisine that was mainly fish-based.

And gradually, under the influence of her continuous chatter, the other two relaxed. By the time dessert arrived Louise felt they had almost re-established their previous easy relationship. But she had a sense of marking time, of a peaceful interlude before she was plunged into rougher waters.

'I'm really glad Sam suggested this trip,' Gladys said as they sat over coffee. 'He's quite right, this coast is very different from Palm Beach and Miami.'

'I think it's more like this a bit further north on the Atlantic coast,' Jake said. 'I remember going up there with Sam when I came down a few years ago.'

That must have been while he was still married. Had his wife come too? Had they also visited here too, was that why he knew it so well? Louise suddenly felt incredibly jealous of the beautiful Bonny.

'There's a place called Jupiter Island where the really, really rich live that's preserved some of the simplicity of old Florida. Just very luxurious houses hidden behind shrubs and sand dunes, bordering the Atlantic. It's all very civilised, nothing like the overdeveloped tourist resorts.' It was the longest speech he'd made so far that evening and Gladys's eyes seemed to gleam approval.

'Sounds interesting. I suppose we haven't got time to go there as well?' she suggested.

'No,' said Louise sharply.

Gladys looked at her, head on one side, like a bird considering possibilities. 'How about if we put our return off another week? I'm having so much fun with you two.'

'Gladys, I'm sorry, but if you want to stay longer, you'll have to get Shirley out here. I have to go back this weekend,' Louise forced herself to say firmly.

Once again she felt torn. Part of her badly wanted to remain here where she was having so much fun. Yet another part of her cried that she must get back to England. She had to return to her husband. And there was her mother, and Victor. He'd sounded so tired the last time she'd spoken to him on the phone. Why hadn't Mark been to see him? She'd rung and asked him that and he'd reacted badly. Mark hated being made to feel guilty. He'd been very busy, he'd said, he'd go at the weekend. Why hadn't he been the previous one? Louise asked, which had been a mistake. He'd finished the conversation abruptly. But what had he been doing? No, she knew it was more than time she went home.

Gladys shot her one of the keen, challenging looks that were her speciality. 'Hmm, well, perhaps you're right. We'll talk about it tomorrow. Now, dears, I think it's time I went to bed. Old woman, one foot in the grave and all that.'

She listened gleefully to their automatic disclaimers but was quite firm about being taken back.

Louise saw her to her room. 'Can I help you undress?' she asked. Down in the car park, Jake waited for her and she was afraid of what being alone with him could bring.

'No, my dear. I'm fine, thank you,' Gladys said firmly and closed the door on her.

Louise took a deep breath. Should she go to bed and just leave him waiting for her?

No, she couldn't do that. Not only could she not do it, she found she didn't want to. She realised that all through dinner an under-current of expectation had been building in her. She wanted this time with Jake. More than that, she needed it.

246

She returned to where he waited by his car, leaning against the side, his long body tense as though he'd feared she wasn't going to come back. He straightened up with a smile of relief. 'Now,' he said, opening the passenger door,' 'we'll go for that drink.'

The air was soft and warm, the cicadas singing their song, and the sky was a tapestry of stars. Louise was very aware of Jake beside her. Every few minutes he would look across at her, a smile on his face, as though he couldn't quite believe she was here with him.

He found somewhere to park the car near the Circle where they had dined then slipped his hand underneath her elbow and gently guided her towards a pleasant bistro-type bar that catered for both drinkers and diners.

'What will you have?' he asked.

'Wine, please,' said Louise. 'A glass of white.'

As Jake ordered, she found herself studying his profile. It was so familiar to her now she'd forgotten just how sharply beaked his nose was. Then he turned and his wide mouth split into a smile that brought all his features together into the endearing expression that was – just Jake. A sharp jolt of panic went through her as she realised how involved she had become with this man. It was as if the focus of her entire world had shifted.

'There,' he said, putting two glasses of wine on the table. 'Best Napa Valley Chardonnay. Sometimes I wonder if there's another white grape being grown in the world.'

'Semillon? Reisling?' offered Louise, smiling up at him as she lifted her glass. Some uninvolved part of her mind noted how endearingly bushy his eyebrows were.

'Oh, well, if you're going to get technical,' he teased her, lifting his own glass in a silent toast.

Louise said nothing more. This drink was Jake's idea and he was going to have to set the agenda.

He gave a brief sigh and raised one of those bushy eyebrows. 'I want to hit you with logically ordered reasons why you should stay here with me but all I can do is look at you. Oh, God, that sounds like some stupid, sentimental song.'

Louise gave him a wobbly smile.

Jake leaned forward and grabbed her hand. 'Darling, when you look at me like that, I know you feel the same way I do. Why are you fighting it? Just because you happen to be married to some cold bastard who doesn't appreciate you?'

Once again he'd made a serious mistake. Louise drew back her hand and sat up stiffly in her chair. 'Jake, Mark is not a bastard.'

'Sure he is. Gladys told me all about the way he wouldn't take you to the airport and why you took the job with her in the first place.'

A little flame of anger lit in Louise's heart. 'Gladys knows nothing about me or my marriage,' she insisted, wondering just what she

247

must have revealed on the way over. She knew she hadn't discussed it since. Every time Gladys had gently probed, Louise had deftly changed the subject. Had this told its own story?

'She's one hell of a smart lady. And don't think I haven't noticed how the only times you've mentioned your husband have been when you've either failed to get him on your damned phone or you've had a two-seconds chat with him. That's not a successful marriage, Louise! A successful marriage is when you spend hours on the phone talking about nothing in particular, just keeping in touch with what each of you is doing, filling in the gaps so you don't drift apart.'

Oh, dear, he had something there, Louise told herself, keeping her eyes firmly fixed on the glass of wine she held on the table.

'A successful marriage,' he continued remorselessly, 'is when you pepper your conversation with comments about your mate – how smart he is, what he's doing, things he's said – because he's so much a part of you, you can't stop yourself.'

Was that how Jake had been with his wife?

'I've heard a lot about your children but very little about Mark,' he told her.

He paused. Louise said nothing and wouldn't look at him.

'Another thing. When I meet this lovely lady at Miami airport, the first thing that strikes me is how unhappy she looks. It's as if she's carrying some terrible grief within her.'

At that Louise did glance up. 'I can't have looked like that!'

'But you did. Then, as we settled down together – and I'm talking here about our little group, not just you and me. I'm talking about Gladys and Mary and Sam as well – I see Mary and her mom getting along where Sam told me they constantly bitched together, and Mary and Sam closer than before. And I see it's all because of this lovely lady with the sad eyes. She defuses the tension before it arrives.'

'Jake, this is all nonsense! I've done nothing special.'

'Sure you have! You calm everybody down, get us involved with cards or interesting discussions. It's something you're good at, like you've had a lot of practice.'

'James finds it difficult to get on with his father,' she said involuntarily.

'There you are!' Jake was triumphant. 'I said you'd had practice. It's your special talent, smoothing out the atmosphere. I just love to watch you at it. But then, I just love to watch you anyway. And to talk with you.'

'But you're a university professor!' she protested involuntarily. 'I'm the girl with no brains. I don't see what you can find interesting about talking to me.'

In fact, it was one of the things that most attracted her to Jake: how easily conversation flowed between them.

248

He stared at her. 'You're no dummy. You're smart, you must know that?'

Louise shook her head, feeling confused. Nothing about this conversation was going the way she'd expected.

What *had* she expected? Protestations of undying love? A paean of praise for her looks? Would that have made her feel more comfortable?

She had a sudden sharp memory of Mark holding her in his arms shortly after they'd met, when the world had seemed reborn in fresh colours. 'You're so beautiful,' he'd murmured into her ear, his hand doing wonderful arousing things to her left breast. 'So beautiful and such fun. Everything is more fun with you.' He'd never told her she was bright, though. But then her mother had always drummed into her that you should never make a man feel threatened by your intelligence.

'They like to feel they have the brains and you need to be looked after,' Betty had said to Louise in a dozen different ways as she grew up.

'Look.' Jake leaned towards her again. 'It's you who've given me the first real idea I've had for my next book.'

'Me?' She was astounded. 'What idea?'

'The industrialisation of Florida. How technology first tamed and made attractive, then destroyed its wild beauty.'

'But I never said all that.'

'Who was it who said it was air conditioning that meant people could enjoy living in Florida?'

'Good heavens, how can that have given you an idea for a book?'

He leaned forward. 'It suddenly encapsulated the battle that has been going on in Florida this century; materialism versus the simple life, greedy developers exploiting retirement dreams, oh, so many factors.'

'My.' Louise said faintly, unable to look away from the intensity in his eyes.

'And that's just one of a number of perceptive remarks you've made. Louise, you don't realise how smart you are. You've an instinctive intelligence that makes sense of whatever it's presented with.'

'But I don't have a degree or anything like that.'

'You could have, if you wanted. Even now. There are mature students in England, just as there are in the States. Remember I told you about Bonny getting a law degree in her late-thirties?'

Tom had told her she should have gone to university. For the first time in her life, she began to believe it could have been possible.

Jake sat back and smiled at her. 'Listen to me, trying to talk the girl I've fallen in love with into going back to college! Talk about sweet nothings!'

'Look, Jake,' she started, feeling cornered. 'It's no good talking about falling in love and all that.'

'No good!' he interrupted her passionately. 'My God, you Brits can be cold! How can you deny what we feel? Your response to me this afternoon was real, don't try and tell me otherwise.'

'I know,' she said hopelessly. 'If things were different, if I weren't married, yes, we could be at the start of something.' She refused to dwell on how wonderful that something could be. 'But I am married, and happily. All right,' she continued as Jake looked to contradict her, 'maybe Mark and I have been going through a difficult patch. Every marriage has them.' She suddenly thought of Polly and Willoughby. That was more than a patch, it had driven a ruddy great motorway through their relationship. 'All right, we've got our problems. The children leaving home was disruptive and, well, Mark is having a tough time at work.' She suddenly stopped, remembering what Val had told her about Mark feeling his position was challenged by Robin. She'd dismissed that at the time. Should she have probed a bit further? Had she failed to understand his difficulties, just as he'd failed to understand hers? 'It's a time of change,' she hurried on. 'I'm trying to find a new role, build some sort of career.'

'Because there's something lacking in your life,' he interposed. 'Don't you see, Louise, that that's because your relationship with your husband is flawed?'

'It's something we can work our way through,' she insisted, knowing she didn't feel nearly as confident as she tried to sound. Again panic shot through her. What if Mark, far from being professionally challenged by Robin, wanted to make a new start with her? What if there was nothing for her to go back to? The need to return home was paramount now, overriding everything she felt for the man studying her so intently.

He sighed and sat back. 'OK, here's how I see things. We're two people in love only one of us feels loyalty to her present partner.'

'I bet you wish your wife had felt loyalty,' Louise burst out. 'If she'd made more of an effort, perhaps you'd still be married.'

She could see that she'd shaken him from the way he passed a hand over his face for a moment. 'Lord, Louise, how you get to the heart of things!' He sat thinking for a moment.

She drank the last of her wine and watched him, her heart aching, knowing she was right, that she had to get back home. There all this would seem like a dream, a mad moment she could perhaps remember with nostalgia but no regret many years hence. Until then, she was going to put the lid on Florida and not think about any part of it.

'Look,' he repeated, 'I hear what you're saying. Believe me, I do. But I still can't accept that what we have should be cast away.'

Louise stirred uneasily.

'I want to lock you up, prevent you from going back. I know it wouldn't do any good, though. Your integrity is part of what I love about you. You have to do what you have to do. So what I hope is this: that you'll go back and open your eyes to just how empty life is for you back there. That you'll recognise your marriage is over. Then you'll pick up the phone and tell me to meet you once again at the airport. Except it won't be Miami this time but my home town.'

Louise gazed at his dark eyes and felt their intensity burn into her very soul. She felt his love enfold her, warm her with its depth of feeling. Mark and home no longer seemed like magnets drawing her back.

Louise took a grip on herself. No, this wasn't what she wanted. She couldn't turn her back on her family. Maybe Mark didn't want her any longer, maybe she had to face that, but it could only be done in England. And it was to England that Emma and James would be returning within the next few months. She had to be there for them.

'Promise me you won't forget?' Jake insisted, his gaze boring into hers. 'You won't forget that I'm going to be waiting for your call?'

'At your home?' asked Louise, and immediately wished she hadn't. The hope that leaped into his face gave additional weight to the idea she might ring and say she was catching that plane.

'Yes, I'll give you the address and the telephone and fax numbers. I'll be going back there as soon as you leave. I'll let you know if I return here for research.'

'No!' Louise said, so sharply he winced. 'We're not going to write to each other.'

'But . . .' he started.

'No,' she insisted. 'I'm going home, Jake! I don't intend to contact you again.'

Hope refused to die in him. 'That's what you say now,' he told her gently. 'I know you're not going to be able to keep to it. We've got too much going for us.'

How confident he sounded! Louise was both appalled and comforted. She stood up. 'I want to go back to the motel,' she said.

He looked at her, seemed to recognise there was nothing more he could do. Without another word, he rose, escorted her to his car and drove them back.

He accompanied her to the door of her room, took her key and opened it for her. As she went in, he caught her shoulder. 'This is our last chance,' he pleaded and his voice cracked as he touched her cheek. 'Let me . . .'

'No,' she said tersely. 'Please, Jake, just let me go.'

But he didn't. He caught her in his arms and pulled her against him, his mouth pressed against hers, insistent yet tender at the same time.

251

It was like pressing a switch – electricity flooded through her.

Louise managed to raise her hands and push against his chest, forcing him to let her go.

'I'm sorry!' His shoulders slumped dejectedly. 'I just can't bear the thought that you could walk out of my life.'

Louise stood quite still. Every instinct in her shouted that she should take this moment and make the most of it. Wasn't feeling this way what life was about? 'I'm sorry, too,' she said quietly, clenching her fists until her nails cut into the palms of her hands. 'Please, Jake, go?'

For a long moment he held her gaze with his while she struggled to remain implacable, then he gently laid a hand against her cheek.

She closed her eyes, knowing that if he made another move now, she was powerless to resist him.

'I'll do anything you want, you know that. Sweet dreams, my darling.' It came out as softly as a sigh, then he was gone.

Louise closed her door and leaned against it. Emotions churned within her till she felt physically sick. The back of her hand pressed against her mouth, she rushed to the bathroom.

She went to the basin, ran water and rinsed her dry mouth. In the mirror the clear, harsh light showed shadows under eyes that looked as though she had a fever.

That was what it was. A fever. Once she was home, everything would be all right again.

She had to believe that.

Chapter Twenty-Nine

Mark's phone rang. He reached for the receiver but his eyes remained firmly fixed on his computer screen.

'It's Mrs Russell,' June's voice informed him.

'My mother-in-law?' Mark was surprised, Betty never phoned him at work. 'OK, June, put her through.'

'Mark?' She sounded upset.

'What is it, Betty?' Suddenly he thought of one reason why she could be ringing. 'Louise hasn't called to say she's not coming back tomorrow, has she?'

'Good heavens, no! Whatever made you think that?' Betty's voice became more robust. 'She'd ring you if that was the case, not me.'

'Of course she would,' he agreed heartily. 'So what gives me the pleasure of hearing your voice?' He strove to sound confident and carefree, the devoted husband looking forward to his wife's return.

'It's your father, Mark.'

'Dad?' He swung his chair away from the computer screen and frowned at the opposite wall. 'What's the matter?'

'Well, dear, I popped in on him this morning, for a cup of coffee. I do from time to time, you know?'

Unease started to seep into Mark's bones.

'Well, he seemed all right at first, except that, well, he wasn't quite as smart as usual, then I noticed that he was very short of breath and didn't really look himself.' Betty's voice had regained its initial anxiety. 'I asked him if something was wrong but he said he was fine, he'd just had a nasty cold. I mean, there're some terrible bugs around, which is what I told him when I asked if he'd had the doctor.'

'And has he?' Mark cut in sharply.

'Well, he said not. That there wasn't anything a doctor could do that a bit of rest and a couple of Aspirin wouldn't. Then, just before I left, he had a bit of a turn.'

'What do you mean?' Mark was thoroughly anxious himself now. 'A bit of a turn?'

'Well, I don't know how to describe it. He just seemed to lose it.'

'Lose it?' Mark started to grow irritated.

'He was sitting in his chair and I was saying it was about time I was going and perhaps he'd like to pop over for lunch one day soon – he does like his food, your father, and he's absolutely no good at cooking himself – when I realised he wasn't hearing a word I was saying.'

Mark felt like saying that was sometimes a natural reaction to Betty's conversation, then realised she was seriously worried. 'You mean, he had some sort of attack?'

'Not attack precisely but something happened, I know it!' Betty's voice rose as though he mightn't believe her. 'I was just about to ring for the warden when Victor came round again and said something about the weather, as though nothing had happened.'

'So he was all right after all?' Mark felt enormous relief.

'I don't know. We chatted for a little while longer and he did seem more himself. I said goodbye and told him I'd pop in again soon. But the more I thought about it later, the more I thought someone ought to do something. Your father should see a doctor, that's what I think.' She ended emphatically and Mark realised that this was what she had been working up to.

'You want me to have a word with him,' he said, making it a statement. 'I'll give him a ring now.'

'No, I think you should go and see him,' she said firmly.

He looked at the piles of paper on his desk. 'I don't think . . .' he started.

'Mark, he's your father! At the very least you should ring one of your sisters and tell her to go and see him.'

'Have they been over recently, do you know?' he asked cautiously.

'Your father said he hadn't seen anyone since Louise went to Florida. I do think you might have popped in,' Betty said tremulously.

Mark shifted position in his chair and picked up a pencil, flicking it between his fingers. 'You're right, of course. OK, I'll manage to organise something here and run down and check him out. He'll probably be fine. Old people do drift off every now and then, you know.'

'I suppose,' she said doubtfully.

'You didn't have a word with the warden?' He flicked the pencil faster between his fingers as possibilities tumbled over themselves in his mind.

'Do you think I should have?' his mother-in-law asked anxiously. 'I did wonder, but it didn't seem my place.'

'No,' he soothed. No point in Betty getting herself all upset when she'd obviously had to gear herself up to call him. 'You did absolutely right. I'll give the warden a ring now, and ask him to check on Dad then I'll arrange to go and see him as soon as I can get away from here. You all right?' he added courteously.

'Oh, I'm fine. Looking forward to seeing Louise again, of course. It seems ages since she went. You are meeting her, aren't you?' Betty seemed to have forgotten how against the trip she'd been.

'If I can,' he prevaricated. He'd by no means made up his mind on this point. 'I told her if I wasn't able to, I'd lay on a car. She'll be taken care of, don't you worry.'

'I'd meet her myself if it was Heathrow but Gatwick's so much further and there's been all this snow and more threatened . . .' Betty's voice tailed away.

'I wouldn't hear of it and nor would Louise,' Mark asserted. 'Thank you for ringing. I'll let you know how Dad is after I've seen him.'

He put the phone down and sat for a moment, still flicking the pencil, considering what she'd told him. He felt guilty. He should have gone to see the old man. Or at least rung him more often. If only Louise hadn't gone away, she'd have noticed anything wrong with his father.

Mark flipped up the number of the warden at the sheltered housing complex on his Rolodex and picked up the telephone again.

He felt no better after their conversation. The warden didn't think Mr Henderson had been looking too well for several days or so but he'd been assured that it was just a touch of 'flu. 'There're so many bugs around and he's always been such a sensible chap, not like some of our residents! I didn't think it was anything serious but I'll pop round now and see how he is. Do you want me to tell him you're coming down?'

Mark hesitated, tapping the pencil against his teeth. 'No, thanks. I think I'll surprise him. Otherwise he'll get worried.'

'Oh, okay! I'm sure you're right.'

'You've got my mobile phone number, haven't you? Just in case you want to report back to me? I'll be leaving the office any minute.'

'Yes, I've got that right here. I won't ring unless I'm particularly concerned. I hope he's all right. We don't have nursing facilities here, you know,' the warden added with a note of caution in his voice.

That was what Fiona had said at Christmas, one of the reasons why she had wanted Mark and Louise to have Victor living with them.

Mark glanced down at his diary then picked up the phone again and spoke to June. Within minutes he'd arranged for her to cancel the two appointments scheduled for that afternoon and field all calls. He stuffed several computer discs and some files into his briefcase, took a last look at his desk, then gathered up his coat and left the office.

He hesitated for a moment outside Robin's door then lifted his hand to knock.

It opened before he could do so. 'She's not here today,' Robin's assistant said. 'Anything I can help with?'

'No, nothing that can't wait until Monday.' Mark glanced with dislike at the young man, one of the pushy sort, always at Robin's elbow whispering suggestions to her. No doubt bright, Robin wouldn't have him around otherwise, but not likeable.

'I'll let her know you wanted her,' the assistant said and went off to his own office.

As Mark drove down to his father's, his mood grew blacker. Guilt at neglecting Victor vied with unease about Louise. Even now he wouldn't be surprised to hear that she and that employer of hers had decided to stay on longer in Florida. Certainly there seemed little to bring them back to England. The car's tyres splashed through melting snow as he turned off the main road towards the sheltered housing complex. There'd been snow again last night with more forecast for the weekend. Not a cheerful prospect for anyone and especially not when viewed from sunny Florida.

And how welcoming had he been to his wife whenever she'd managed to get him on the phone? Their short conversations had said nothing. Was it any wonder that her initial enthusiasm for telling him all she was involved in over there had gradually given way to a brief recounting of the bare facts? How much of what had been going on there had he actually been told? Deep unease gripped Mark as he swung his BMW through the entrance gate of the purpose-built sheltered housing in which his father had bought a share.

A short but unpleasant walk from the car park brought him to Victor's front door. Mark mentally chalked up several points to Betty. It said a lot for her that she had braved the weather to visit his father. His own neglect lay even more heavily on his conscience.

Mark rang the door bell, knocking snow off his shoes by tapping them against the doorframe. Nobody answered. He rang again. Just when he was deciding he would have to go and find the warden, there was a shuffling sound, the door was slowly opened and Victor stood there.

Mark stared at his father. He'd never seen him anything but well turned out before. Today Victor was wearing slippers, an old pair of trousers, and a tieless shirt under a plain sweater topped by a threadbare cardigan. He hadn't shaved. Was this how he'd been when Betty called? She'd said only that he wasn't as smart as usual. What diplomacy – or did her eyes need testing?

'Hello, Dad,' Mark said gently, coming in and closing the door behind him, protecting the little hothouse from the raw cold outside. He kissed his father's cheek.

Victor blinked. 'Mark! Good to see you. Come in, dear boy.' Mark realised immediately what Betty meant about the shortness of breath – Victor positively wheezed. Mark followed his father as he shuffled in the direction of the living room.

Each unit in the sheltered housing had a reception room, a bedroom, a small kitchen and bathroom. Should anyone want a guest to stay the night, the complex had three communal bedrooms available for hire. When Victor had initially moved in, Mark had been horrified by the size of the rooms after the spaciousness of the

256

family home. How, he'd asked, could his father contemplate living anywhere so poky?

'My needs are few, dear boy, thank you. I'll be very comfortable here,' Victor had replied.

Over the years, Mark had grown used to Victor's home and had never had any reason to suspect his father regretted moving into his little nest. After all, it was very cosy and did offer all the conveniences.

The television was on, perhaps that was why Victor had taken such a long time to hear the door bell, and a paper lay on the table beside his chair. It looked unopened.

Victor carefully lowered himself into place opposite the television set. Time was when the only programmes he watched were the news and current affairs. Now there was some soap opera showing.

He picked up the remote control and flicked the set off. 'Sit down and we'll have a nice talk. Or would you like some coffee?'

'It's almost lunchtime, Dad, I thought you might like to come out for a meal with me.' Mark hovered beside a chair, uncertain whether to sit or not. The suggestion about lunch had just slipped out but he felt it was a good one.

'What's up, you not working today?'

Louise would tell him the truth, that she'd come because she was worried about him. Mark couldn't bring himself to do that. The old man's dignity was precious to him. 'Thought I'd take some time off and see the house is all right, ready for Louise. She's coming back tomorrow, you know?' His voice was indulgent, a parent reminding a child about some treat.

Victor's face lit up. 'Is she? That's good. It seems a long time since I've seen her. She's been ringing me, you know? All the way from Florida. On that phone I gave her.'

'It was a good idea, Dad. One of your best. Well, how about lunch?' He sneaked a look at the way Victor was dressed. Did the old man realise what he looked like? 'We could go to the house, I'm sure I can rustle us up something.' Louise kept the deep freeze pretty well stocked, there was sure to be something there. If not, he could slip down to the supermarket.

Victor gazed at him silently for a few moments. 'That would be nice,' he said finally. 'Good to have a bit of a chat. Haven't seen you in some time, have I?'

Mark's heart grew heavy. He couldn't believe how much his father had deteriorated in the few weeks since Christmas. All right, he hadn't looked on top form then but he'd been in full control. After all, he'd gone out afterwards and bought Louise that phone, hadn't he? Mark wouldn't have placed any odds on his being able to do anything like that today.

Victor eased himself out of his chair. 'Just get my coat.'

The housing complex had a communal dining room which provided a midday meal for any of the inhabitants who wanted it.

Late last year, Victor had started to eat there. Mark thought now that he should have recognised that as a sign of deterioration.

While Victor went to the bedroom, Mark checked the fridge and the cupboard his father used as a larder. 'Dad, what are you eating for supper these days?' he called as he found nothing but a bottle of milk in the fridge and a tin of sardines in the larder. There was no bread, no eggs, no butter or spread, nothing as far as Mark could see that would make a meal beyond that sole tin of sardines.

Had Victor been eating his way through his reserves? Waiting for the weather to improve? But the warden offered a shopping service for frailer inhabitants.

Victor appeared in the doorway doing up his Crombie overcoat. 'Don't find I want supper these days. The old don't need to eat much, you know. Always get a good lunch.'

Mark went over and wrapped his scarf carefully round his neck. 'Can't have you getting cold, Dad,' he said. For the first time in his life he felt protective of his father.

'Car's parked outside, is it?' Victor asked, moving towards the front door.

'Hey, Dad, you've still got your slippers on.'

Victor looked down with surprise at his feet. 'Slippers? So I have!' He started to shuffle back to the bedroom.

Mark followed him. The bed was unmade and dirty clothes were piled on one of the chairs. He came to a decision. 'Tell you what, Dad, why don't we take your things with us and have you to stay for a few days? Louise would love to find you there when she gets back tomorrow.'

Would she, though? Mark remembered with a sinking heart how upset she'd been at the suggestion Victor should come and live with them.

Still, she had said her distress was nothing to do with Victor himself and assured him that she wouldn't mind if he came and lived with them.

Mark prayed that she'd meant it as his father sat on the dishevelled bed and felt blindly beneath it for his shoes.

Mark got down on all fours and fished them out, wondering when his father had last worn them. Then he found a case and rapidly flung a suit and several shirts and ties inside. He couldn't find any clean underwear or socks. He added all the dirty clothes, then had to find another case to hold the overflow, plus Victor's toiletries, pyjamas and dressing gown. Just before he closed the second case, he remembered to add the slippers. 'There, all ready now.' He went and helped his father up from the bed. 'OK, Dad? Manage, can you? Or shall I come back for the cases?'

'I'm fine, Mark, just fine.' Victor placed his feet carefully one in front of the other and made for the front door.

Cold air gusted towards them as the door was opened and Mark

258

saw his father flinch. He put one of the cases down. 'Come on, I'll take your arm. Can't have you slipping and that path's treacherous.' He took Victor's arm and guided him towards the car, restraining himself from hurrying his father against the wind. Once Victor was safely inside, fiddling with the seat belt, trying to get it anchored, Mark went back for the other case and shut the front door. Then he went round to the warden's door and rang the bell. The man came to the door with a napkin in his hand, obviously in the middle of his midday meal.

Mark explained that he was taking his father home for a few days. 'Has he been coming in for lunch?' he asked.

'He missed yesterday but I thought he was probably visiting friends,' the warden said. He saw the expression on Mark's face and hurriedly added, 'If he hadn't been there today, I would have checked his condition as I did when you called. I rang him and he said he was fine.'

'I think you would do well to check whenever one of your inhabitants fails to turn up, if you'd seen him, you wouldn't be quite so complacent,' he said curtly. 'I know my father is meticulous about letting you know if he isn't going to eat on any day.'

He walked back to the car seething. But his anger was directed against himself as much as the warden.

At home he left the car outside the front door and helped Victor into the house.

His father stood in the hall with his face lifted, as though drinking in the house's atmosphere. Mark had been afraid it would be desperately cold, but the place was warm, if not as hot as Victor's little home.

'Come into the kitchen, Dad,' he said gently as he put the cases down. 'It should be warmer in there. I'll get us something to drink then see what the freezer can offer.' Somewhere in the depths of the house he could hear the roar of the vacuum cleaner.

'Mrs Parks!' he called. 'Can you come down?'

She entered the kitchen as he was placing a whisky in front of Victor.

'Why, Mr Henderson, I didn't expect you!'

She was dressed in fur boots, a long grey tweed skirt and a pink woolie Mark would have been willing to swear was cashmere worn over a yellow polo neck. A navy blue knitted hat was pulled down over her head.

'I've brought my father back for lunch. Do you know if there's anything available?'

Mrs Parks pulled off the hat, revealing blonde curls that looked newly bleached and permed. She pulled down one side of her mouth dubiously. 'I doesn't have much to do with the freezer. But I'll have a look, bound to be something. You very hungry?'

'Hungry, Dad?'

Victor's face was pinched and pale, as though the effort of getting here had been too much for him. He took a sip of the whisky. 'Don't eat much these days, Mark, anything'll do for me.'

Mrs Parks looked at him sharply. 'Good bit of soup, that's what you need, Mr Henderson. Mrs Henderson usually has a jar of that nice ready-made French fish soup in the larder. And there are plenty of eggs – brought some with me in case you needed some supper. Bread, too.' She opened the fridge to display its wares. In addition to the items she'd mentioned, there was cheese, butter, bacon and a slab of country pâté. 'Didn't want Mrs Henderson to come back to an empty fridge.'

'Mrs Parks, you're a marvel! You didn't manage all this on your bicycle, did you?' Mark congratulated himself on remembering her mode of transport.

She nodded, her small, dark brown eyes gleaming with satisfaction. 'Got a nice carrier bag on the back and a basket on the front. Can take ever such a lot.'

'But the weather!' He shivered as he glanced out of the window at the dreary day outside.

'Not nice,' she agreed. 'But I've tackled worse. Now, suppose you take your father into the snug and light the fire there? I put the heating on when I came in so the house isn't too cold but it won't be really warm for several hours yet.'

'Do you always work this late on Friday?' asked Mark, feeling humble. He hadn't thought at all about getting stuff in or making sure the house was thoroughly warm for Louise. Indeed, if it hadn't been for Victor, he'd probably have gone to the airport straight from town. He'd planned to stay late at the office that night, working.

Mrs Parks shook her head. 'Nah, mornings I do. But Mrs Henderson told me I could come when I liked while she was away. So I arranged to spend the day here, making sure everything was right for her when she gets back tomorrow.' She paused and looked at him. 'She is coming back tomorrow, in't she?'

'Yes, Mrs Parks, I'm happy to say that she is.'

'I'm glad to hear you say that, Mr Henderson. Not only that she's coming back but that you're happy about it.'

Startled, he looked at her. 'Has she said anything to you?' Really, it was too bad of Louise to gossip.

'Now don't get your toe in a rag, Mrs Henderson only told me she was off on a job to America. For a fortnight.' She let the phrase sink in. 'It was Mrs Russell as rang me and said Mrs Henderson would be away for another week.' The implication that Mark should have left her a note was clear.

Another little burden was added to his load of guilt.

'I'm very pleased to see you, Mrs Parks,' Victor suddenly said. 'Will you have a drink with us?' He raised his whisky glass in a graceful salute to her.

260

'Thanks, Mr Henderson, that's very kind of you but I don't think so. I'll have a coffee later. Now, Mark's going to take you into the snug and I'm going to bring you in some lunch.' She spoke slowly and clearly to him and that, almost more than anything else, brought Mark to the conclusion he should have reached when Victor first opened the door to him.

'Mrs Parks, could *you* perhaps help my father into the snug and light the fire?' he suggested, turning to the telephone on the kitchen wall.

In no time she'd taken charge of Victor's whisky, had him on his feet and was propelling him carefully but efficiently out of the room.

By the time she returned, Mark was replacing the receiver. 'I've made an appointment for the doctor to come and examine my father this afternoon,' he told her as she opened the larder door and started scanning the shelves.

'Getting them to make house calls is like turning coal to gold,' she said, her hand lighting on a tall jar filled with an orangey liquid. 'You must have used a powerful lot of persuasion.'

'Paying for their time works wonders,' he told her. 'Should I warn my father, do you think?' He was amazed at himself, asking Mrs Parks's opinion of anything but particularly this. However, there was something very solid and reassuring about her obvious intelligence and common sense. For the first time Mark understood just why Louise relied upon her so much and paid her so well.

She shook her head. 'Nah, I wouldn't. Just bring him in and act as if it's all entirely normal. You go and keep him company and I'll bring this in in a jiff. Followed by scrambled eggs. That man looks half starved to me and you don't want to tax his stomach too much. I'll see if I can find some chicken in the freezer for your supper and something for lunch tomorrow. Mrs Henderson won't want to start in cooking the moment she gets back.'

'You're a treasure, Mrs Parks, that's what you are.'

'That's what all my ladies say,' she agreed imperturbably.

'And I'm going to ask if you can be even more of a treasure.' Mark went and collected Victor's suitcases. 'There's a whole lot of stuff here needs washing . . .'

'You leave it all to me. I'll sort it out and put the clean stuff in the big spare room.'

Mark had been going to suggest Victor should use the small guest room but realised at once that Mrs Parks was right. Small was all very well for sheltered accommodation but when Victor was back here, he'd expect space. Mark thought with sudden amusement that he hadn't been proved wrong so many times in one day since he'd left school!

Mark waited at Gatwick the following morning, walking up and down the arrivals hall, his mind churning. Outside it was still dark and more snow had fallen overnight.

The arrivals board clicked away and relayed the message that the flight from Florida had been delayed. The new landing time was half an hour away.

Mark sighed and took himself off for a warming cup of coffee. He hoped his father was all right. Victor had gone to bed early the night before, expressing a charming regret at having to leave his son's company. 'But if I don't go up now, I shall just fall asleep in front of you. So rude when you're such a good conversationalist.'

'Don't worry, Dad, I'll bring you some hot milk, shall I?'

For a moment there'd been a flash of the old Victor. 'Hot milk? Stuff for babes and geriatrics!' Then his face had become rueful. 'Well, I suppose I belong to the latter group now and perhaps it would be nice.'

Mark had taken it up with a couple of shortbread biscuits he'd found in a tin, the last of the baking Louise had done for the Christmas festivities.

Lying back on several pillows in the large double bed, a wrap around his shoulders that Mark had found in the cupboard Louise kept supplied with guest items, Victor had looked more his old self. He was reading a book from the bedside table. 'Good this,' he said, waving John Murray's *A Gentleman Publisher's Commonplace Book* at Mark. 'How about this from Horace Walpole: "The world is a comedy to those who think, a tragedy to those who feel." Spot on, eh?'

Mark had nodded. He'd taken the book and leafed through it, amused and interested by turn at the pithy sayings, until his eye lit on one from Seneca: 'Nobody is despised by other people unless he has first lost his respect for himself.' He closed the book and handed it back to his father. 'I'll be off to the airport very early tomorrow morning to collect Louise,' he'd warned. 'You'll be all right until we get back?'

'Of course, dear boy, of course.' Victor's nose was already back in the book.

'Don't forget your hot milk.' Mark had waved a hand at the mug he'd put on the bedside table.

Victor shook his head, then, as Mark reached the door, he'd looked up and said, 'Thank you, dear boy. Very kind of you to bring me back like this and to get the doctor and all. Not been feeling quite the thing for a while, really. Silly not to do something about it. You sure Louise won't mind my being here when she gets back?'

Mark had shaken his head. 'Of course she won't, Dad. You know how fond of you she is.'

Now, sitting over his cup of cappuccino, eating the grated chocolate off the top like a small boy, he fervently hoped this was true.

As he scraped off a bit more froth, he found himself considering

262

the distance he and Louise seemed to have travelled apart. He had an uneasy feeling that much of the fault was his. He didn't understand just why she had insisted on taking this job, or all the other little jobs she'd taken on since the twins had left, but he was beginning to see that he had reacted in entirely the wrong way.

He remembered Nicky's scorn that evening she'd given him supper. The memory made him squirm. They'd both had too much to drink, of course. That was why he'd thought she was making a pass at him. He'd always had a soft spot for Nicky, never really understood what she'd seen in solid old Colin. And that evening, his ego badly bruised by Robin's brush off, Nicky's admiring face raised to his, her eyes closed, was like a crystal clear spring to a thirsty man.

Her lips had been soft, had tasted of the wine they'd been drinking. They'd opened under his and he'd slid down on to the floor beside her so he could take her into his arms . . .

And that's when it had fallen apart. For both of them, it seemed. Nicky just wasn't Louise and he wasn't Colin. Mark couldn't remember who had disengaged first but it hardly mattered. He'd sat on the carpet, breathing raggedly, his head down, brain awash with alcohol, trying to grapple with the situation.

Nicky had dragged herself back upright. 'No, Mark, no!' she'd said, over and over again. Then she'd burst into tears.

Typical woman!

After a bit he'd gathered that she was blaming herself, that things hadn't been good between her and Colin but that she really, really loved him.

It seemed to be confession time and he badly needed to tell someone how mixed up he felt about the way things were with Louise.

Nicky had made more coffee and he'd talked. He didn't suppose now that it had made much sense. He remembered rambling on and on about how different everything was with Louise not being there and how awkward it was not having her around. None of the right things came out, that he was sure of now. Like how he hated not having Louise around, not because she made his life comfortable but because of the way she'd tell him little things that had happened, make a joke out of them, chuckle in that lovely way she had, then ask his opinion about something as though she really needed to hear what he thought.

And how he missed the way she'd hum when she was getting up in the morning or going to bed at night. And how empty his bed seemed now. He'd wake at two or three in the morning and find himself listening for her quiet breath, that elusive fragrance that wasn't quite a perfume, just a sweetness that was the essence of Louise. Not there, anymore than the curves of her body were. Only acres of empty sheets.

But none of that seemed to come out as he followed Nicky into the kitchen while she boiled the kettle and he wittered on about clean shirts and having to make his own supper and Louise not even asking if it was all right if she stayed another week in Florida – she had just told him she wouldn't be back that Saturday. That had jolted him more than anything else.

Nicky had waited until they were back in the living room and she'd stoked up the fire again.

'The thing is, Louise doesn't seem to trust me anymore,' he'd ended on a note that made him flinch as the memory came back to him. Talk about self-pitying!

'Trust!' Nicky had spat, standing holding the poker as though she'd half a mind to take a swipe at him. 'Trust? Why should she trust you? When have you ever made the slightest effort to understand what it's been like for her with the twins growing up and leaving home?'

He'd collapsed into a chair and stared at her. He couldn't remember now all the things she'd said: something about his being totally selfish, how Louise really needed to find herself again, how he was too immersed in his own world to be able to help her.

And he'd been so taken aback by her attack, he'd sat there and said nothing until she'd drifted on to more general accusations: how men just didn't understand. They seemed to think, even in this day and age, that a woman's real métier was running a home, that they should give up their own careers to follow their husbands anywhere, that's what men thought.

Which was when he'd told himself that the crux of the trouble wasn't him and Louise at all, it was Nicky and Colin.

The evening had ended with her in tears again and him patting her shoulder and telling her it would be all right. Colin wasn't like him, Mark assured her, his voice slightly slurred. Colin would understand, Mark was certain he would.

Upon which her eyes had blazed at him even more fiercely than they had before and she'd told him he was a fucking idiot and she didn't know why she'd wasted her time talking to him. Then she'd phoned for a taxi without asking him if that was what he wanted and had gone about with tight lips, clearing up after their meal until the taxi had arrived.

At the time he'd left with a deep sense of injury, feeling he'd once again been made to look a fool. What he'd thought would be a relaxing evening with an attractive woman stroking his ego had turned into an experience akin to a Gestapo interrogation.

The next afternoon, still nursing the remnants of a nasty hangover, he'd taken another taxi over to collect his car, driving away without letting them know he'd been there. Only when he got home did he ring up, thank Nicky briefly for the evening and explain he'd reclaimed his car.

She had listened, said, 'Thanks for telling me, Mark,' and rung off. Since then he'd heard nothing from either her or Colin.

All in all it had been a thoroughly disturbing experience. One that he had attempted to push to the back of his mind in the same way he'd tried to bury Robin's brush off.

Robin had been as good as her word that night. She never betrayed the slightest hint that she remembered the way he'd pounced on her. Not that it had been much of a pounce. He couldn't even get that right! Still, though they no longer chatted as they had before that evening, she had made it possible for them to work as colleagues without difficulty.

Which he supposed he should be grateful for.

Still stirring his cappuccino, Mark seethed with discomfort as memories of the two disastrous evenings returned with remorseless clarity.

At last, in the clear light of early morning, he forced himself to survey them dispassionately. And saw that no help had been needed for him to make a fool of himself.

He faced what both Robin and Nicky, in their very different ways, had told him. His difficulties had come about because he felt Louise no longer needed him. He was no longer the centre of her universe, she needed other interests now. He'd seen it as a rejection of himself as her husband, and at a time when he'd been trying to cope with the way Douglas had brought Robin into the department. He'd felt he'd had to prove himself not only at work but also at home as a husband. No, not as a husband, as a man.

Mark almost groaned out loud as he realised that what had really been hurt was his amour-propre.

Because of that he'd neglected his father – worse than that, failed him – and alienated the person he loved best in the whole world.

He drank the rest of his coffee and sat staring at the froth left in the cup. What was going to happen when he met Louise? Was she going to be glad to see him? Could they somehow get things together again?

He looked at his watch and rose.

Back in the arrivals hall the board indicated that the Florida flight had landed. A short while later it said that the baggage was in the hall.

Mark took a grip on himself. He found his hands were shaking and perspiration was beading his forehead.

Passengers were coming out in straggling groups to be met by friends, relatives or professional greeters. Or they walked straight ahead with no expectation of being met.

He saw a slight girl in a short-sleeved blouse and mini skirt swept up by a hairy young man in a shell suit and passionately embraced. She flung her arms around his neck and gave herself up to a kiss which looked as though it could go on forever. Even when they

265

came up for air, his arms remained around her, gently swaying her from side to side while his eyes scanned her face as though he needed to remind himself of every tiny feature.

Mark felt like a voyeur and looked away. He went back to scanning every person coming through from customs, increasingly disappointed not to find Louise among them. He wished he smoked, he needed the nicotine to give him courage and the cigarette for something to do with his hands.

Then, suddenly, there she was. A slight figure, beautifully brown, her curly hair longer than he remembered, wheeling a cart holding a couple of small bags.

Joy rushed through him on a huge, uplifting wave. He raised a hand and waved frantically, almost jumping up and down to make sure she saw him.

And she did. For a moment she stopped and looked surprised. Surprised and then cautious before the faintest of smiles lit her face.

Some of the joy seeped out of Mark, as he hurried towards her he told himself it had been stupid to hope that she'd rush to him, that everything could be forgotten in a rapturous reunion at the airport.

'Hello, darling,' he said as they met. He bent and kissed her. He'd intended just to make it a quick and light one but as he felt her mouth under his, he couldn't help prolonging and deepening it. Louise stood passively, waiting for him to finish. He dropped his hands from her shoulders as though she'd burned him.

'Where's your charge?' he asked, trying to mask his dismay, looking around for an aged woman.

'She decided to stay another couple of weeks,' Louise said expressionlessly.

She had, had she? And Louise had decided to come home. Which must be a good sign. 'Is this all you took?' asked Mark, taking charge of the trolley.

She nodded.

'Not much for three weeks,' he said, for the sake of something to say.

'I thought it was only going to be two, remember. Anyway, the weather was like summer, I didn't need much.'

'And you didn't fall for the temptations of factory shops,' he said flippantly, trying to remind her of their trip to Disney World, when she and Emma had run riot amongst a complex of cheap clothing outlets.

Louise shook her head but said nothing.

The press of people made it difficult to talk if the other person seemed disinclined and for the moment he was content just to have Louise walking beside him.

'Anyway,' she said determinedly as the car came into sight, as though continuing an uninterrupted conversation, 'how are you? Still working hard?'

'I'm fine. Work has gone on as usual, I suppose.'

'How's the office? Appreciating all the effort you put in, I hope.'

He thought what a curious thing it was for her to say. Louise normally never commented on his standing with the company, she took it for granted.

'You know me, Mr Indispensable,' he joked as they reached the car. He opened the doors, put her bags in the boot and helped her into the passenger seat. She looked remote, sitting there, staring out of the windscreen.

He put the key in the ignition then, instead of starting the car, he turned and drew her to him. 'I can't tell you how much I've missed you, Lulu,' he said, and had another go at kissing her properly.

This attempt was no more successful than his first. 'I'm sorry, Mark,' she said, drawing away. 'It was impossible to sleep on the plane and I'm very, very tired. The last few days have been extremely hectic.'

He swallowed his chagrin and started the car. 'You've got quite a lot of post waiting for you, mainly thank you letters for Christmas presents, I think. But there's a letter from Emma and James, posted in Hong Kong, with a photograph taken of them in China. They looked terrific.'

'Did you bring it with you?' Louise asked with the first sign of animation she had given.

Mark cursed himself. 'Sorry, I didn't think.' Typical of him, he thought. Why couldn't he have realised that of course she would want to see it at once. He thought of something else. 'Oh, and Val Lewin called. Wants you to phone her as soon as you get back. Did I tell you they had me to supper a couple of times?'

'Val? How nice! I sent her a postcard but I don't suppose she's got it yet. Have you had yours?'

He shook his head. 'Usual story, postcards always arrive days after the sender has returned.'

'What did Val want, did she say?'

'No, I took it she just rang for a chat.'

'Yes, that'll be it.'

'She'll be wanting every detail of your trip: Gladys, her daughter, the weather, everything.' If he'd thought that would produce some details for himself, he was doomed to disappointment. Louise said nothing.

He waited until he'd found the way out of the airport and was on the main road before he said, 'Dad's at home.'

It seemed that managed to get through whatever it was she'd armoured herself with because she turned to him in concern. 'Why? Has something happened?'

He held the car at seventy miles an hour on the slushy road as he told her about his visit to his father. 'The doctor's arranging for a series of tests on Monday. He thinks Dad's got bronchitis and is

267

suffering from angina. There's also a possibility of the early stages of Parkinson's Disease. Apparently every now and then Dad goes a sort of mental walk about. And his hands shake.'

'Oh, Mark! I am sorry!'

'The doctor's put him on antibiotics for the bronchitis and says that both the angina and the Parkinson's, if that is the problem, can be controlled by medication.'

Louise drew a deep breath. 'It sounds as though he was in a dreadful way!'

'The doctor thinks that's partly because Dad hasn't been eating properly.' Mark felt renewed anger at the warden. 'I think I should sue that sheltered housing place. They should have been keeping an eye on him.'

'It's not really their fault,' Louise said gently. 'The warden's a sort of safety net, not a social worker.'

'I still think he should have kept more of an eye out.'

'Yes, I agree, I think he probably should have.'

Mark waited for her to say that he should have done so too and felt deep gratitude when she didn't.

'I think we'd better have him to live with us, don't you agree?' Louise said matter-of-factly, just as though they hadn't had a fierce argument about it before she'd left.

'Oh, darling, I hoped you'd say that! I know it will be a lot of work for you and an invasion of our privacy and everything, but I think he'd really like it.'

'With Mrs Parks to help, it shouldn't be too much trouble. And we can arrange things so that he has his own flat. He'd like that, having some independence. He'd hate to think he was imposing on us.'

'His own flat?'

'Yes, the billiard room would convert nicely into a bedroom and living room and we could easily build on a separate bathroom and kitchenette for him. The plumbing from our bathroom comes straight down that wall, it'd be no trouble at all.'

'The billiard room!' Mark said in dismay.

Louise turned to him, her tired face earnest. 'I know we've had lots of fun out of it but your father's more important, isn't he? Or have you some other idea how it can be arranged?' She didn't sound anything but helpful.

Mark had sort of taken it for granted that Victor would take over the big guest room, perhaps as a bedsitter, and share the house with them.

'I don't think he finds stairs easy these days,' Louise continued. 'We could put a stair lift in, I suppose, but it would be much better if we could arrange things so he lives on the ground floor. And have you thought about sharing every meal with him?'

Mark hadn't. He was fond of his father but they'd never had a

268

great deal in common. He sighed. 'You're right, of course.'

They drove in silence for a little then Louise said with a note of determined cheerfulness, 'Tell me what you've been up to, darling? I hope you haven't been working all the time?'

Mark took a deep breath. How much should he tell her? 'Mostly work. We're incredibly busy at the moment. We've got two new accounts, one of which is Willoughby's company.'

'Oh, darling, that's terrific! That means you're credited with bringing in the business, doesn't it?'

He was pleased but surprised, he hadn't realised Louise understood that sort of thing. 'Yes, and it's a sizeable account so it was champagne all round.'

'Who brought in the other account?'

'Robin,' he admitted gloomily.

'Ah!' There was a pause. Then, 'Are you getting on any better with her?' Louise asked carefully.

'Well,' Mark prevaricated, 'I think we've got a better understanding of each other.'

'You mean, you've both admitted you want the top job but team spirit is what brings in the company bacon?' Louise asked with a ghost of a smile.

Mark shot her a quick glance. When had she started to talk in these terms? 'Something like that,' he said briefly.

Louise said nothing else and when he stole another look at her, he saw she was asleep.

Victor was up when they got back. Not only had he managed to dress himself with his old smartness but he'd laid the table in the kitchen for breakfast.

'Louise, my dear,' he said, a catch in his voice as Mark brought her to the house. She dropped her bag and went towards him immediately, flinging her arms around him. Mark reflected ruefully that his father was receiving a far warmer welcome than he had.

'I'll make breakfast,' he said heartily. 'Wonderwoman Mrs Parks has supplied us with eggs and bacon, so that's what's coming up.' He brushed aside Louise's offer to do it. 'Just take off your coat, sit down with Dad and watch me at work. It doesn't happen often so it should be a real treat.'

Perhaps it wasn't the best eggs and bacon in the world but it didn't seem to matter.

When they'd finished and Mark had put some toast on, he turned to his father. 'Dad, Lulu and I would really like it if you came and lived here with us.'

Victor looked at Mark and then at Louise, visibly moved. 'My dears, it's very sweet of you but I'm fine where I am.' He hesitated for a moment then looked Mark straight in the eye. 'I know I wasn't in too good shape when you came yesterday but once I'm on whatever medication the doc prescribes, I should be A1 able to take care of myself.'

'Wouldn't you like to be back here, Dad?' Louise asked gently. She put a hand on his. 'We would so enjoy it. Mark and I were discussing it in the car. We can arrange for you to have your own quarters, your own front door even. So you'd be independent but also part of us. We could have chats every day.'

Mark looked at Victor's large hand underneath Louise's smaller one; saw the liver spots of age, the arthritic swelling of the knuckles, the slight shaking as he gently removed it and raised his napkin to wipe the crumbs from round his mouth. The old man's really old, Mark realised. Somehow, perhaps because Victor was so much more himself this morning, this hit Mark far harder than the state he'd found him in yesterday.

'Don't say anything now, just think about it, Dad.' Louise spoke in a tone that was particularly loving. It was the tone she used when anyone was unwell or needed comforting. Mark couldn't remember when she'd last used it to him. Of course, he didn't get ill and he made a point of hiding his troubles. For the first time in his life, he wondered if showing a little vulnerability now and then mightn't be a good idea. 'After breakfast,' Louise continued, 'we'll show you how we thought it could work, where you would live.'

'A granddad flat, you mean,' Victor said with a shaky smile. He spread some butter on a piece of toast then added a dollop of marmalade. As he raised it to his mouth, the marmalade fell off.

'Louise,' Mark said briskly, 'I think you should have a rest. I'll clear up breakfast.' She looked at him in surprise. 'Is there any shopping you'd like done or have you enough in the freezer for the weekend? We can go to the golf club for lunch tomorrow.'

She yawned. 'Thanks, Mark, but I think it'll be better if I keep going, otherwise I won't sleep tonight and I'll never get over the jet lag.'

Later he realised he'd made a mistake in not insisting she should have a rest.

After they'd settled Victor down and had retired to their own room, Louise turned to him, her face incredibly weary, and said, 'Mark, I'm sorry, I don't want to share a bed with you tonight. I'd go to the small spare room but your father's certain to hear me moving in there and it'll upset him. Would you mind sleeping in your dressing room?'

Chapter Thirty

Val Lewin opened the door of her Hampstead house with a broad smile. 'At last! I can't tell you how I've been looking forward to seeing you, it seems ages!'

'I'm sorry,' Louise said, stepping inside out of the miserable raw weather. 'There's been so much going on.'

'I know, you've been to Florida!'

'Not just that. It's a bit complicated.'

'Then let me take your coat and you can come and tell me all about it. Do you mind the kitchen?'

'Sometimes I think it's my spiritual home,' Louise laughed, rubbing her cold hands together and beginning to feel a little warmer. 'Why aren't you at work?'

Val made a face. 'I've got a builder coming this afternoon so I had to take time off. It's a wretched nuisance but I thought I could do some work while I waited. Then, when you rang, I thought, let's make the most of it and have lunch here. I hope it hasn't been too fearful a trek for you? Did you come by car?'

Louise shook her head as she followed her friend into the bright and warm kitchen. 'I thought public transport would be easier. After one train, two tubes and a fifteen-minute walk, I'm not sure it was!'

'Sit down and catch your breath, I'll open some wine.'

Louise sat on a small sofa fitted into a wall recess and watched Val wield a corkscrew. 'You look marvellous,' she said.

Val was wearing a bright red dress. Straight and waistless, it was trimmed with black buttons cut like jet and looked vaguely military. It suited her strong features and dark hair. Louise thought she looked happy and confident and her laugh at the compliment was a sunny sound, as warming as the kitchen or the wine.

Louise needed all the warmth she could get. It had not been easy since she'd got back from the States.

'Bet you miss the Florida weather?' Val said, putting a casserole dish in the microwave and switching the gas on underneath saucepans of water.

Sudden tears pricked at the back of Louise's eyes. Yes, she missed Florida and all she'd found there. She told herself she wouldn't even think of Jake.

271

'You got back, what, ten days ago?'

Louise nodded. 'Sorry I couldn't come up before but we've got my father-in-law living with us now.'

Val came and sat opposite her. 'You mentioned something on the phone. What happened?'

Louise grimaced. 'The tests confirmed angina and early stages of Parkinson's.'

'Oh, Parkinson's is awful, I am sorry.'

'Apparently it's quite a mild case and now he's on medication it shouldn't cause any great problems. But Mark and his sisters don't think he should live on his own any more, so we're making a proper self-contained flatlet for him so he can retain his independence. It should work very well. Except,' she giggled briefly, 'Mark's losing his billiard room!'

'Oh, my! How's he taking that?'

'On the chin. It's his father, after all. I'm just very glad it isn't my mother.'

Betty had heard of the plan with approval. 'Quite right,' she'd said. 'Victor needs looking after. Who knows? When my time comes, perhaps you can find room for me as well!' She looked archly at Louise.

It was as though iron bands were being clamped around Louise. Everything was conspiring to force her to remain at her post whether she wanted to or not. But she did want to, she told herself. That's what she'd told Jake and that's what she'd meant.

She just hadn't realised how hard it was going to be.

'You wouldn't believe how co-operative Mark is being, not only over his father but life in general. He's stopped staying up in London when he works late. In fact he's only had to work late once, and hasn't been away at all since I've got back.' She smiled a little bleakly. 'I don't know how long it will last!'

'Perhaps you should arrange to go away regularly, keep him on his toes,' suggested Val, who sat nursing her glass of mineral water, wearing a Cheshire cat smile.

Gradually Louise began to realise there was something behind Val's invitation other than a desire to hear about Florida. 'You've got something to tell me,' she said, leaning forward. 'Tell me all! Have you got a new job or been made financial director?'

Val shook her head. 'Neither, though I think the directorship will be coming along later this year. Whether I'll want to take it up is another matter.'

'Why on earth wouldn't you?' Louise started to say, then she gasped, 'Val, you don't mean – yes, you do. You are, aren't you?'

Val laughed, 'I am what?'

'Pregnant!'

She nodded triumphantly, a beaming smile splitting her face.

'Oh, that's wonderful!' Louise got up and hugged her friend. 'When's it due?'

'End of July.'

Louise did some finger counting. 'So you're what, four months?'

Val nodded again. 'I went to the doctor just before Christmas. I couldn't believe it at first, I've never been very regular and I just thought it was one of those blips, you know? Then I started feeling dreadful in the mornings so I went for tests and, what do you know? Bingo!'

'Oh, that's just so wonderful!'

'Heavens, Louise, you sounded really American then. "That's just so wonderful!" ' Val repeated in an exaggerated accent. 'Don't tell me you've gone native?'

It was an ideal opening to tell her everything but Louise found she didn't want to tell her about Jake. If she actually put into words what had happened in Florida, somehow the abstract would become concrete reality. If she didn't tell anyone about Jake and what had passed between them, then just maybe it would fade away and she could forget it.

She looked at Val, glowing with happiness, and said, 'Me, gone native? How can you even suggest it? Now, come on, tell me what Neil said when you broke the fabulous news. Is he over the moon?'

Val laughed as she got up to put beans in the boiling water. 'He was so shocked when I first told him he sat there saying nothing with steam coming out of his ears.'

'And then?'

'Then he gave the most enormous Red Indian whoop, picked me up and whirled me around – no mean feat given the difference between my height and his – then almost dropped me and went into overdrive on the fragile piece of porcelain bit. Insisted I should be sitting down with my feet up.' Val leaned against the stove, her mouth curving into a soft smile. 'Seriously, yes, he's over the moon.'

'No reservations at all?'

'Absolutely none. He's already bought up every baby book there is, been to pre-natal class with me and had a session with the doctor on everything from sex during pregnancy to potty training.'

'And you, Val, how do you feel?' What a stupid question. It was quite obvious that she, too, was over the moon. If was as if an electric light had been switched on inside her; not one bulb but a whole street's worth. Even as she thought of the analogy, Louise remembered the electricity that had zinged through her that night in Sarasota when Jake had kissed her. 'I'm so pleased for you. And are you really thinking about giving up work?'

Val shrugged her shoulders. 'I'm not sure. At the moment I can't imagine I'll want to go back to the office, at any rate until whatever it is is ready for school. Yet something tells me I may well miss my work.' She turned back to the stove, tested the beans and took them

273

to the sink to drain off the water. 'What do you think?'

'Don't come to me for advice, I never worked after I had the children.'

'That's exactly why I'm asking.' Val put the vegetable dish on the table at the precise moment the microwave pinged. The casserole joined the beans. 'Help yourself,' she said and fetched a dish of rice from the oven.

Louise took a seat at the table.

'I mean, I know you enjoyed bringing up your two and never wanted a job but aren't you at something of a loose end?'

'I'll say. Spinning around like a useless top with nothing to do. Not even tennis to play in this dreadful weather.' Louise helped herself to the chicken and vegetables. 'Would I be any better off if I'd had a career and kept in touch with it as the children were growing up?' She gave an exaggerated shrug of her shoulders. 'Who can say?'

'But you must have some idea?' Val persisted.

'No one can make that sort of decision for someone else,' Louise suddenly burst out. 'I've just been in America with a career woman who worked all through her children's childhood. She has difficulty communicating with her daughter but I think that would have happened anyway, Gladys is a difficult woman.' Louise smiled reminiscently. 'But her daughter, Mary, has always worked and she and her child get on very well. Mary says she learned from her experiences with her mother and what she reckoned counted the most in bringing up Beth was allowing her to make her own decisions and giving her, in that lovely phrase, quality time.'

'Quality time?' mused Val.

'This casserole is delicious, by the way.' Louise ate some more of the chicken and considered Val's question more seriously. 'As for me, yes, I think I do now regret not having had a career to go back to but I don't think I'd have wanted to carry on working while bringing up the children even if I'd been a doctor or an accountant.' She thought some more. Val waited, studying her face. 'At least, I don't think so. Maybe I'd have done a little part-time work, if I could have found it,' she said finally.

Val looked amused. 'You're backtracking!'

'All I'm saying is, see how things go, don't make decisions before you know the circumstances. You could find small children so unutterably boring you'll fly back to work.'

Val gave a soft smile. 'I'm sure I won't.'

'Don't depend upon it. There were many times I could have screamed with our two and felt my brain was addling. I longed for conversation that used words of more than two syllables and had a logical train of thought. Other times, well, I wouldn't have swapped my life with anyone.'

'How are the twins? Where have they reached?'

274

'Australia.'

'How much longer are they going to be away?'

'A couple of months but a lot depends on whether they can do any topping up of their funds. It's illegal for them to work but I don't suppose that will stop them if they can find anyone to fork out the cash.'

'I bet you're desperate to see them again?'

Louise nodded, suddenly unable to speak. She longed to have Emma and James home, then maybe she'd feel her life could be put together again.

The front door bell rang.

'Damn,' said Val. 'I bet that's the builder. He promised me he wouldn't come before two thirty.' She glanced at the clock, which said 1.35, then went to the door and let in a young man in designer jeans with an expensive-looking leather jacket worn over a jazzy sweat shirt. He apologised for interrupting them. 'The thing is, previous job got finished early, we always likes to finish early if we can, and it was only just round the corner so I thought I'd pop round. If you weren't here, well, no harm done!' He smiled at them with easy charm. 'Now, what was it as you wanted done?'

'Do you mind, Louise?' Val asked. 'It's the nursery, you see!'

'Can I come up too?' she asked. She placed their plates in the still warm oven. 'We can finish this later.'

Val led the way up the steep, narrow staircase, past the first floor and on to the second. This contained two reasonable-sized front rooms and a much smaller one at the back of the house. 'We thought we could convert this into a bathroom,' Val told the young man. 'And we'll want the two front rooms redecorated.' Downstairs the house was smartly finished in a very contemporary style: clear colours, modern furniture, uncluttered rooms. On this floor the rooms were wallpapered in what looked like early Laura Ashley and furnished in stripped pine from the same era. 'I always said I'd wait to do anything up here until we had a child!' Val spun round excitedly.

'Pregnant, are you? That's nice,' the builder said. 'What did you have in mind for the bathroom, then? The full suite?' Val looked blank. 'Bath, toilet and bidet?' he elaborated. 'Most people go for the bidet these days.' The final 't' of bidet was just pronounced. 'Though if it's for the nursery, per'aps you wouldn't want to go that far. Quite useful with kiddies, though.'

Twenty minutes later Val and Louise descended to the kitchen, leaving the builder measuring up.

They'd finished the casserole by the time he came down. 'Think I've got everything now. But I'll 'ave to send a plumber round. Need to know exactly what the piping will involve, you see. Early next week do you?'

Val looked dismayed. 'I didn't think anyone else would need to visit.'

275

'Sorry, lady, plumber's got to see it. Work, do you? Always difficult that. Electrician should really call too but, well, the job looks straightforward enough as far as he's concerned. If I build in a contingency in case of any trouble, that should take care of it.'

Val looked bemused. 'Would you like a cup of coffee?' she offered.

'Nah, thanks very much. Be on me way. Got a coupla other jobs to see to.'

Val saw him out.

'How many other quotes are you getting?' asked Louise, helping to clear the plates away.

Val got out a cheeseboard and biscuits. 'Only him. He was recommended by someone down the road. It seems quite a small job. More quotes means more appointments and I don't want to have to take extra time off.'

'Can't you bring work home again? That chap looked to me as though he could be expensive. "Build in a contingency" probably means he'll come back to you halfway through and say they've struck a problem and everything's going to cost more than he originally said. In my experience you have to get every detail worked out before they even start, so you can get a firm quotation that they have to stick to. Change even one electric outlet and the bill soars.'

Val poured her some more wine and seemed to lose some of her sparkle. 'This is all beginning to sound rather heavy going.'

'What happened when you did all this?' Louise waved a hand round the kitchen.

'Oh, that was just after we were married. I was looking for a job then and could oversee it all. Even so we made terrible mistakes and ended up paying nearly double what had originally been quoted. I don't want to spend more than we have to now, not if I may not be going back to work!'

'It's quite simple,' Louise said. 'I'll look after the job for you. I'll get some more quotes, be here when the builders call round, check their estimates, discuss everything with you, then oversee them on the job. Like Marsha did for me. Only I won't charge.'

'You will!' Val said firmly.

'Don't be silly, you're my friend and I'd enjoy doing it. I learned a lot from Marsha. We're about to get the builders back to do the conversion for Dad and I'm really quite looking forward to getting down to working things out with them. Looking after your job as well should fit in perfectly. After all, Orphan Annie's doesn't seem to have anything to offer me at the moment.' She cut herself a piece of Stilton.

Val's face cleared. 'Oh, Louise, it would be such a help! That man got me more than slightly worried. It's not just the time. I'm out of touch with decorative techniques and I have no idea what sort of

276

bathroom tiles we should be choosing or whether we need a shower unit, let alone a bidet!

'Leave it all to me,' Louise said with conviction. She felt excited at the prospect.

'Only if we fix a proper fee?' Val insisted.

Louise made up her mind. 'All right, if it will make you happier.'

'Neil wouldn't have it any other way, I'm certain of that. I mean, look at the distance you'll have to come across London! Now, tell me more about Florida and this extraordinary woman you had to look after.'

Carefully avoiding any mention of Jake, Louise did so.

On her return home, Louise told Victor all about her lunch and the idea of looking after Val's building job. 'Dad, don't you think there could be other people out there who go out to work and want building work of some sort done? You know, alterations to the kitchen, bathroom repairs, that sort of thing. I bet lots of them would gladly pay someone to look after it all for them.'

'I'm sure there are, my dear.' He smiled at her enthusiasm. 'I'm glad to see you making plans.' They were in the kitchen, Louise getting supper ready, Victor sitting on the banquette, drinking a cup of tea and trimming sprouts. He liked to help. He was wearing Fiona's Christmas present, a sweater in a complicated pattern in browns and golds, with a smart pair of brown cords, plus toning shirt and tie. He seemed quite his old self. 'Forgive me for saying this, but you've appeared rather down since you got back.

Louise continued to stir the sauce she was making.

'Is there anything you want to talk about?' he asked gently. He put the last sprout in the colander and sat back, leaving the little pile of outer leaves sitting on the piece of newspaper on the table.

Louise felt her equilibrium sway dangerously. It would be so easy to tell Victor everything. He was so understanding, so sympathetic. But so fragile now. She had no right to burden him with her problems. And he was Mark's father. 'It's just this awful jet lag,' she said, her back to him. 'I don't seem able to get back into a proper sleeping pattern.'

She was using the jet lag as her reason for keeping Mark sleeping in his dressing room. Louise was uneasily aware that these days her insistence on always telling the truth was being steadily undermined. She wasn't actually lying yet but she was no longer transparently honest. This made her even more uncomfortable. Where was it all going to end?

Chapter Thirty-One

'Good heavens, Louise, this looks like a builder's yard!' Willoughby picked his way clumsily over a couple of planks then tripped over the legs of a stepladder.

'Whoops!' Louise caught him, dropping her clipboard in the process.

It was Friday evening, some four weeks after she'd returned from Florida.

Willoughby brushed awkwardly at dust stains on his business suit. 'Your father-in-law said you were in the billiard room, what on earth is all this?' He waved a hand at the screen of two-by-fours that was dividing the room into two, one part rather larger than the other, at the piles of dust sheets, plaster board and builders' impedimenta.

'We're converting this into a granddad annexe,' Louise explained as she helped to get rid of the dust. 'Mark's not going to be back until late, I'm afraid.'

'It wasn't him I wanted to see, it was you.' Willoughby straightened and adjusted his tie, which seemed after his tumble to have ended up underneath his left ear.

'Me?' Louise retrieved her clipboard and looked at him in surprise.

'Yes, well, it's got something to do with all this.' He glanced around the room again as though he wanted to commit the scene to memory. 'I saw Mark on Wednesday and he said you'd started a little business looking after people's building jobs. Must say, though, I didn't realise you were handling something here as well. What's he going to do for a billiard room now?'

'Manage without,' she said sweetly. 'Do you want to have a look at what's happening?'

'Might as well,' he said with the air of a man who felt it could be the right thing to say.

'This will be Dad's living room.' Louise indicated the larger of the two areas with her hand. Then she walked through a gap in the two-by-four screen. 'And here's his bedroom. We're adding another window over there.' She pointed to the short wall where a rectangle had been drawn. 'Now back in the living room,' she returned to the larger area, 'we're going to knock through here,' she indicated another, larger rectangle drawn on an outside wall, 'and add a small extension. There'll be a hallway with its own front door, a bathroom off one side and a kitchenette on the other. Then Dad will be completely independent but, of course, still part of the household.' She made a note on her clipboard to have the rectangle moved another foot down the wall. 'Have you a job you want me to look after?' She couldn't think of any other reason why he should be here, not if he didn't want to see Mark.

He continued looking about as though trying to take it all in. 'Mark's going to miss his billiards,' he said finally.

'Yes, well, life moves on, doesn't it?' Louise said crisply. She had, though, been relieved that Mark had taken the loss of his toy so well.

'Do you have a job you want to discuss, Willoughby?' she asked again as he showed no sign of coming to any sort of point. She rubbed her upper arm and tried to restore the circulation. 'Sorry about the chill in here, the radiators have all been turned off. Let's go and have a drink in the television room and you can tell me why you came.'

She led the way to the small room they used most often, discarding her clipboard on the hall table as they went. As they entered, Victor switched off the early-evening news.

'Don't let us interfere, Dad,' Louise said, going over to the drinks tray. 'Anything for you?'

He shook his head. 'No thanks, Louise. And you're not disturbing me, headlines are over and there's nothing to get excited about. The government's not resigning, war hasn't broken out and the FT index is up ten points. All's well with the world.' He turned to Willoughby. 'I see you found her.' Then he looked at him more closely. 'Didn't we meet at the Boxing Day party here?'

That dreadful party, thought Louise. When the whole Polly/Jean-Paul affair boiled over.

Willoughby instinctively squared his shoulders and his eyes narrowed dangerously.

Victor seemed to realise something wasn't quite right. 'Seems a long time ago,' he said smoothly. 'I've come to live here since then. Made all the difference to me, Louise and Mark are so kind.' He smiled fondly at her.

'We love having you, Dad,' she told him. 'Willoughby, what can I get you?'

He asked for a whisky and soda and sat in the chair farthest from Victor.

Louise poured him a stiff one and handed it over. Then she went and found some cheese straws.

Victor was doing his best to make conversation when she returned, asking intelligent questions about Willoughby's business while he was giving as little by way of answer as he could.

As Louise handed round the straws, Victor stood up. 'Got some

280

things I want to see to,' he murmured. 'I've enjoyed our little chat,' he said to Willoughby. 'Good to keep in contact with the real world,' he added as he left the room.

'Now,' Louise sat down opposite their visitor with a glass of white wine, 'what can I do for you?'

He crunched noisily on a cheese straw, scattering crumbs down his front, then slurped a goodly proportion of his drink. 'Want to do something at Whiteways,' he said finally.

'Yes?' She looked at him expectantly.

'Polly's talking about coming over for Caroline's next exeat. She doesn't want to share a room with me, of course,' he said bitterly, shifting awkwardly and taking another straw. More crumbs scattered down his front. 'Thought I might organise her a proper apartment. Not as elaborate as your effort,' he waved his hand, still clutching a cheese straw, in the direction of Victor's flat, 'but somewhere she could sort of call her own. Might help, don't you know?' He looked at her in appeal and Louise was shocked at the naked unhappiness in his face.

'When's Polly coming over?'

'Oh, it's the weekend after next, I think.' Willoughby fiddled in his inside breast pocket, brought out a diary and checked. 'Yes, weekend after next.'

'I'm afraid it couldn't possibly be done by then,' Louise said gently.

'No, I don't suppose it could.' Willoughby sat gazing at his drink. 'But if I showed her the plans, you know? Showed her what I had in mind? Might help with Easter, you see?'

'Has she mentioned coming over then as well?' Louise asked carefully. She found it difficult to accept that Polly, happily ensconced in Paris with Jean-Paul, could be thinking of visiting Willoughby.

He shrugged his shoulders in a hopeless gesture. 'We haven't got as far as that. Thought if she knew she had her own sort of bolt hole, it might mean she'd think about it.'

'I see,' Louise said, wondering just how far Willoughby was deluding himself. 'She's definitely staying in Paris, then?'

Once again he shrugged his big shoulders. 'Who knows with Polly? Don't think this chap can be any great shakes. Wasn't there to meet her when she went to him, you know?'

Louise looked at him, shocked. 'He wasn't?'

'Some mix up with messages.' Willoughby looked slightly shifty. 'Claims he tried to get her to delay her arrival.'

'Oh, poor Polly!' Louise thought of flying across the Atlantic to be with Jake and then arriving at the airport without his being there. She couldn't imagine what she would do. 'But it all worked out in the end?' It must have done, surely, otherwise Polly would have come back, wouldn't she?

'If you can call it working out,' Willoughby said bitterly. 'What do you think? This the sort of job you handle?'

Louise nodded. 'Exactly the sort of thing.' She got up and went to the desk she used in the corner of the room. 'Let me show you one of my brochures.'

These had been Mark's idea.

Louise had been surprised by how helpful he'd been over the project. Victor had got her to tell Mark about her idea the same evening she'd mentioned it to him. 'I think she could have something there,' he'd said to his son after she'd finished.

Louise had braced herself for some cutting remark.

Instead, Mark had looked at her with what seemed like real interest. 'Yes, I can see what you mean,' he'd said. 'Could be a market niche.'

'Do you really think so?' she had asked eagerly.

'Well, I think you'll need to go into it carefully and not commit much capital before you see how things are going,' he said cautiously.

'But that's the beauty of it,' Victor said quietly. 'She won't need any capital.'

'If you're really thinking of it as a business rather than something to dabble about with, then you'll need to spend a bit of money,' Mark said thoughtfully.

'What will I need?' Louise asked promptly, getting a piece of paper and a pencil, prepared to make the most of his unexpected helpfulness.

'Headed notepaper and business cards to start with,' he said when she'd sat down again, pencil at the ready. 'You've got to appear businesslike. You can probably design the letterhead on my computer, though.'

'Really? You'd let me use your computer?' she breathed.

He'd smiled at her and for a moment she saw a much younger Mark, one amused by her enthusiasm and willing to co-operate in putting it into practice. Like the time she'd decided they ought to learn bridge. For a time, they'd been quite good. But it was years since Mark had decided bridge took up too much time. 'Computer? Why not?' he said lightly. 'As long as you don't tamper with my files and don't want to use it when I do.'

'Of course not!'

'I can set you up with a simple accounting programme as well, so you can keep track of your expenses, and show you how to invoice.'

She'd gazed at him breathlessly. Everything he said seemed to bring her idea into clearer focus.

'You'll need to think of a good name for your business.' Victor smiled at her. 'Something people will remember. *Your House, My Service* . . . that's not catchy enough, but you'll think of something.'

'Your major expense to start with,' Mark went on, 'will be advertising.'

282

'Advertising?' Louise looked dismayed. 'I thought I'd start in a very small way, do I really need to advertise?'

'How were you thinking of letting people know you're in business?' Mark enquired, but he said it in a helpful way.

'Publicity, that's what she needs,' Victor interjected before Louise could say anything. 'Editorial is always worth much more than advertising.'

'How on earth would I get publicity?' Louise felt alarmed. Between them, the two men had taken things much further than she'd envisaged when she first mentioned her idea to Victor.

'Tell you what,' Mark suggested, getting up and starting to clear away the supper plates, 'take that Marsha woman out to lunch and get some ideas from her. She must have made a nice profit out of this job. She owes us one.'

Louise thought that an excellent idea. She'd got on very well with Marsha while the house was being done. So she'd rung and taken her out to an extremely nice lunch in London.

Now she fished one of her slim brochures out of the desk. They were her major expense so far. She'd gone to a graphic designer, who'd recommended a copy writer and a good printer. The finished result looked attractive and read authoritatively. She handed it to Willoughby.

'Very impressive,' he said, skimming through it. 'You charge by the hour, I see. How do I know how long you'll have to spend on looking after my job?'

'I give you a rough estimate,' said Louise in a businesslike way. 'Sometimes it works out a bit more, sometimes less. I guarantee it'll be within ten percent, unless you change what we originally decided on.'

Willoughby tossed back his whisky and sat looking at the brochure.

'Another one?' Louise suggested.

He held out his glass. 'What's the next stage?'

'I make an appointment to come round and see what you want done. This can be any time to suit you. Then I get a proposal together, with builder's estimates, colour schemes, all that sort of thing, and you go through it. Then we have another meeting and decide on everything. After that it's all down to me to see the job's carried out the way you want.'

Willoughby looked a little more cheerful. 'Sounds reasonably trouble-free,' he said generously. 'Could you come round tomorrow morning? The sooner it gets under way, the sooner it will be finished.'

'Sure,' said Louise. 'Any time you like.'

In the old days she'd have felt she had to make sure what Mark was doing at the weekend before she made any arrangements for herself. Now, unless he'd said he wanted to do something in particular, she told him what she would be up to. It seemed to work. Mark hadn't so far objected to her disappearing for odd evenings or at the weekend.

'How busy are you?' Willoughby asked curiously as he tucked the brochure into his inside pocket.

'I've got three jobs on the go so far,' Louise said proudly. One was Val's, one was for a friend of Val's and one had come through the flyer she'd had delivered with the local newspapers. 'With yours as well, I think that's about enough for me to be coping with at the moment. It's all a very new venture and I'm learning as I go along.'

'You're quite a girl,' he said slowly. 'Pity Polly couldn't have done something like this rather than running off with that Frenchman. I know, I'll suggest she has a talk with you when she comes over for Caroline's exeat. Perhaps she'll offer to help you.'

'You really do miss her, don't you, Willoughby?'

'Nah.' He rose and walked to the window, staring at the drawn curtains and jingling the change in his pocket. 'Hell, no. If she doesn't want to live with me anymore, it doesn't worry me.' He came back, sat down again and mutely held out the whisky glass.

Louise got him another drink and thought about him returning to his big, empty house. 'Would you like to stay for supper?' she asked. 'It won't be much, Victor and I usually have a main meal at midday if Mark isn't going to be home, but you'd be very welcome.'

'That's kind, Lulu, I'd love to,' he said simply, suddenly looking much more cheerful.

Louise left him sitting in front of the television, went through to the kitchen, took a steak out of the deep freeze and put it into the microwave to defrost.

The telephone rang as she was in the middle of laying the table. These days there was always a little thrill, a glimmer of hope that it might be a new client. She'd developed what she hoped was a professional way of giving the telephone number.

'Louise?' said a voice she would have known anywhere.

She put out a hand and grasped the edge of the table as her knees felt likely to give way.

'Louise,' said the voice again, breathing her name as though it was something he said often to himself.

She sat down abruptly on one of the kitchen chairs. 'Jake,' she said simply. Then, angrily, 'You said you wouldn't ring.'

'I expected you to call me,' he said gently. Then, again, 'Louise.'

'Oh, Jake,' she sighed, and found herself unable to say anything more. She wanted to remind him she'd said she was going home to her husband and family, that she'd never promised to come back or even to contact him again. Only if she found life impossible without him.

She hadn't considered whether life was impossible or not, she'd taken herself through each day as it came. And each day had offered tiny new threads that gradually built into a web that held her more and more firmly. There was Victor, who needed her to help him put his life together again; her mother, who would be so desperately hurt if Louise suddenly abandoned her; Val and her other clients who seemed to rely on her; there were the twins who, one of these days, would be returning home and for whom it wouldn't be home if she wasn't there; and there was Mark – above all, there was Mark. Gently, lovingly, he had also managed to show her how much he needed her. So she had begun to think that maybe, if she kept on going, life would show her that not only was this where her place was but this was where she wanted to stay. Now her faith in that tenuous belief lay in ruins about her, brought down by the sound of Jake's voice.

'You told me you'd ring when you'd sorted things out over there. When you knew when you were coming back,' he said softly, persuasively. 'I've been waiting. Every time the telephone rings, I pick it up hoping it's you.'

'Oh, Jake,' she said, leaning back against the wall and closing her eyes. The timbre of his voice was doing crazy things to her. She could almost imagine he was in the room with her.

'I couldn't go any longer without hearing your voice,' he murmured in her ear.

'Oh, Jake,' she repeated. Then tried to gather together her scattered defences. 'I can't talk to you. Not now.'

'When can you?' he asked, his voice still gentle.

'I – I don't know,' she stammered, holding the telephone tightly against her ear, unable to bring herself to say, Never. 'But, please, don't ring me again.'

The door opened and Victor came in. 'Supper ready?' he asked. 'Oh, I'm sorry, I didn't realise you were on the phone.' He made to leave.

'It's all right, Dad, I've finished,' Louise told him. 'I've got to go,' she said steadily to Jake. 'Goodbye.' She replaced the receiver and summoned up a smile for her father-in-law. 'Willoughby's staying for supper, I think he's very lonely.' She picked up the cutlery and went on with laying the table, putting the knives and the forks on the wrong side of each place.

Victor looked at her closely. 'Everything all right, Louise?'

'Yes, of course, Dad. I – well, the Polly and Willoughby situation is a little upsetting.'

'I see,' he said, quietly reversing the knives and forks on the table.

Louise continued getting out china and cutlery in a daze. Not once had it occurred to her that Jake might ring. Every nerve in her body reverberated with the echo of his voice. Never again would she be able to answer the telephone without a thrill of anticipation – and of dread. She didn't want this, she told herself.

As Louise got the meal ready and found ways in which Victor could help, she worked at pushing the memory of Jake back into her

285

subconscious. She listened with every appearance of fascination to Willoughby telling Victor about his company's latest takeover, taking in details of offers, counter offers and letters to shareholders as though they would be needed for an exam, and attending to her duties as a hostess as if she would be marked out of ten at the end of the meal.

She watched Victor's eyes become slightly glazed under the onslaught of Willoughby's verbosity. As they rose for coffee, he apologised and said he had to be going to bed. 'I'm not a night bird these days, Willoughby, but it's been great having you this evening. Quite like old times, hearing about dealings in the City. Reminds me of my relief when I sold my company.' He kissed Louise on the forehead. 'I expect Mark will be back soon, my dear. Say goodnight to him for me.'

She had found a good bottle of Burgundy for the meal. Victor was off alcohol and she hadn't had more than a modest glass but the bottle had been finished. Now Willoughby accepted the offer of a brandy with alacrity.

He settled himself comfortably in the television room. 'This has been a most pleasant evening, Lulu,' he said, drawing out each word, not quite slurring them. 'I'd forgotten what a quiet evening at home with a lovely woman was like.'

Louise wasn't sure what she could say to that. She poured him a cup of coffee.

He leaned forward to take it, holding the delicate china in his large hands, making the cup look like a child's toy for a make-believe teatime. 'Can't you tell me, Lulu, can't you tell me why?'

She looked up at him, slightly bewildered.

'I mean, why she had to go?' he demanded, small eyes alight as they searched her face. 'All of a sudden, just like that?'

'I don't think it was all that sudden,' Louise said slowly. 'I think she thought about it for a long time.'

'Long time? What does that mean? Weeks, months, years? Don't tell me it was years, I know it wasn't. I've known about all her little flings.' Willoughby drained his coffee and placed the cup on the table beside him with sufficient force to rattle it in its saucer. 'Not that it took much detective work. It was almost as though she wanted me to know. But none of them meant anything, I knew that. So I let her have her head. I thought that was what she wanted.'

He sat twisting his hands as he talked, lacing his fingers together.

'So what was so different about this Frenchman? Eh, Lulu? Tell me that?' he ground out angrily.

Louise decided he wasn't expecting an answer. She sat quietly and listened, noting how restless his gaze was, how he looked from her face to the coffee pot, to the cup he'd discarded, back to her face, then to the fire and the blank television screen, his hands unable to keep still.

'All right, I left her on her own a lot. But, Lulu, that's what happens in my business. Look at Mark. He spends as much time away from home as I do, maybe more, but you don't run off to other men, do you?'

Again she said nothing.

'I'm her husband, for fuck's sake! Caroline is her daughter.' He paused for a moment, his gaze on his hands. 'Caroline rings me practically every evening. She never asks if her mother has come back but I know that's why she's calling. She's told Polly she'll only see her at Whiteways, that it's no use Polly thinking she'll go and visit her in Paris. That's why Polly's coming back for the exeat.'

'She loves Caroline,' Louise said at last. To her ears, her voice seemed to come from a long way away.

'So why's she done this? Tell me, Lulu, tell me!'

Louise took a deep breath. 'I'm sure she loves Caroline, and in a way I think she loves you too. But sometimes there's another kind of love, something all-consuming, that you can't do anything about.'

Willoughby stared at her. He grabbed the brandy glass she had placed beside his chair and drank half of it down without pause. 'What the fuck's that supposed to mean, Lulu? You sound like those ridiculous romantic paperbacks, what's their name, Mills and Doon?'

'Mills and Boon,' Louise said automatically.

'Well, thank you for that,' he said sarcastically, finishing the remainder of the brandy. 'Thank you for correcting me on that point.' He put down the glass and suddenly pointed a finger at her. 'But don't try to liken my wife and that fucking Frenchman to Romeo and Juliet or any other star-crossed lovers of history.' His face was tight and angry.

Louise closed her eyes. Inside her a small voice cried out: 'But it is like that, it is! You get swept away on a tide of passion and nothing else matters. She knew that had she made love with Jake, that's what it would have been like for her. She had run away rather than accept what would have been an overwhelming experience. Polly hadn't. But now, after Jake's telephone call, even running away mightn't be enough for Louise. She tried to hold on to the thought of Emma and James. She held tight the memory of their last telephone call from Australia and their cheerful voices saying they were postponing moving on to the States. But that only brought her thoughts back to Jake. She felt very, very tired. There was nothing she could tell Willoughby that would be any help.

She heard him give a small moan and opened her eyes to see him once again interlacing his fingers, his face a mask of pain. 'What did she find with him that she didn't have with me?' He gave a great sniff and passed the back of his hand across his nose. 'I'm a tiger in bed, I can tell you. A tiger!' he repeated, but to Louise his voice sounded hollow.

'Willoughby, I'm so sorry,' she said softly and laid a hand on his knee, moved by his unhappiness but unable to find words that could assuage his distress. 'Let me get you some more coffee.' She picked up the cup and refilled it, then poured more brandy into the glass. That was probably a mistake but what else could she do? He needed to find oblivion in something.

Willoughby pinched his nose and screwed up his eyes. His hand trembled slightly as he picked up the cognac. 'I just don't understand,' he said, sounding bemused and exhausted.

The door to the television room opened and Mark came in. Louise had never been so pleased to see him, she was near collapse herself. 'Hullo!' he said in surprise, coming forward. 'Willoughby! Didn't expect to find you here.'

Louise looked up at him, her eyes wide in warning. 'Willoughby came to see if he could use my new services and I asked him to stay for a meal.'

He gave her a keen look.

'Mark, old chap, good to see you.' Willoughby made a half-hearted attempt to rise.

Mark placed a hand on his shoulder and pressed him back into the chair. 'No need to jump up just because I come back.'

'Nothing going on,' Willoughby assured him with deep solemnity. 'Would never pinch another man's wife. Know what it's like!'

'Willoughby, for heaven's sake,' Mark said, half laughing.

'I think Willoughby's a little sensitive this evening,' Louise said. 'Would you like coffee, or can I get you something stronger?'

'Coffee, please, darling. I think maybe I'm going to end up driving Willoughby home.'

Louise went and made more coffee then said she was sorry but she was about to fall asleep and would have to go to bed.

She felt a momentary guilt as she went upstairs leaving Mark with Willoughby, but knew she was incapable of dealing with anything else that evening.

She lay in bed, too tired to sleep, and tried to make her mind a blank. It was hopeless. Jake's voice whispered in her ear, his body lay beside her where Mark's should be, his very essence seemed to fill the room. Eventually she felt as though she was drowning in him.

Much, much later, she heard Mark come in from driving Willoughby home. She hunched herself under the duvet and pretended to be asleep.

Chapter Thirty-Two

Mark dropped the report he'd been reading on to his desk and called one of his juniors into his office.

Bill Nye came in with an expectant look on his face.

Mark waved him to a chair and gave him a smile. Bill had come on a lot in the last few months. Mark picked up the report. 'Good work, Bill, I like your ideas.'

The young man flushed with pleasure.

'Now, have you thought . . .' Mark started, and began to analyse the report, building on it in a way that involved his junior.

Half an hour later an ebullient Bill left the office with the report clutched firmly in his hand, saying he'd work some more on it over the weekend and bring the revised version back to Mark on Monday.

He grinned to himself as he remembered his own enthusiasm at that age. It felt good to be able to help someone else develop. It was time-consuming but rewarding.

Robin popped her head round the door. 'Got a moment, have you?'

'Any number,' he said and waved her in.

She was wearing shocking pink today, a departure from her normal grey, and her eyes looked bright.

The rivalry between them had been openly acknowledged by Douglas who had divided the department into two and given each of them responsibility for half with himself in overall command. He had justified the step by citing the amount of new business they had attracted recently. It wasn't by any means an ideal system but at least everyone knew exactly what the situation was. Soon Douglas was going to have to decide between them. At least Mark had managed to restore reasonably comfortable relations between him and Robin. He still winced when he thought of that disastrous evening but she never so much as hinted that she remembered what had happened.

She took the seat that Bill Nye had just vacated. 'Thought you'd like to know that I've managed to sort out those details we were discussing. There'll be a draft ready by Monday.' Another one going to be burning the midnight oil.

Then the faintest of blushes crept over Robin's face as she added,

'I've given it to Peter to work on.'

Given it to her assistant, had she? Mark took another look at the shocking pink suit. 'Going away?' he asked casually.

The blush deepened. 'Off to the country. I've been asked to spend the weekend in Gloucestershire. A hunt ball.'

'Sounds fun,' Mark commented, amused by her patent delight in the prospect. 'Who's the lucky man?'

Robin's eyes sparkled even more brightly. 'Someone I met over Christmas. He's a lawyer.'

'Sounds very suitable. I hope you have a good time.'

Robin hesitated a moment then asked, 'Heard from your children yet?'

Mark flipped through the pages of his diary. 'No, but I'm sure we will. It's just a matter of time, you know what the young are.' Then he thought that she probably didn't.

As so often she surprised him.' Yes,' she said. 'I've got a much younger brother. He's always putting the fear of God into our parents but somehow manages to turn up more or less intact.' She looked across at him. 'I'm sure Emma and James will surface soon.'

'And I'll have their guts for garters when they do,' Mark promised. 'They have no business not contacting us for so long.'

Going home a little later, he worked out that it was exactly fifteen days since Emma and James had rung home. Before that, the longest period they hadn't heard from them had been nine days. It wasn't enough to get really worried about, he told himself.

But the moment he got into the house, he went to find Louise. 'Have you heard from the kids?' he asked.

'No,' she said briefly. She was working at his computer in the study. She pressed the 'Save' button and rose, dragging a hand through her dark curls, her eyes tired. 'I'm sure they're fine, Mark. We've never heard from them that regularly.'

She sounded as though she was trying to convince herself as well as him. He put an arm round her shoulders and gave her a brief squeeze. 'Of course you're right, darling, we shouldn't be worrying.' To his intense regret, she moved gently out of his reach.

'I've got some telephoning. Do you want to be in here or the television room?'

He swallowed his disappointment. 'I'll shower and change, then go and have a word with Dad. What time is Nicky expecting us?'

For a moment she stared at him, her eyes wide. Then: 'Oh, my goodness, do you know, I'd forgotten! Of course, it's Friday, isn't it? I think Nicky said eight, just let me look in my book.' She picked up a fat diary from beside the computer. As she flicked through the pages, he could see each was filled with appointments. 'Yes, eight o'clock. I'll have to get ready as well.' She stretched her arms in a tired gesture. 'I've been on the go all day, I could do with a good soak in the bath. I'll make the calls as short as I can.'

How times had changed, Mark reflected as he stood under a hot shower, soaping himself. It used to be him who forgot their social engagements.

As so often these days, he found himself worrying about Louise. When she had finally got over her jet lag from Florida, he'd thought they could manage to put behind them the rift that had developed over Christmas. But though on the surface things seemed to have got back to normal, it was as though he'd lost contact with some essential part of her. By now he had begun to wonder if things between them would ever really be right again.

And now there was this worry about the children.

Mark shampooed his hair and ran through what was known of their current movements. Last time they'd rung, they'd been in Sydney. Emma had said they were thinking of leaving Australia for the last leg of their journey, America. They planned to fly to San Francisco where they had the address of a youth hostel. From there they thought they might make their way via Greyhound bus to Texas, where Mark had given them the name of a business contact who'd said he'd be delighted to offer them hospitality. Mark had rung Al that afternoon. Al's voice had boomed down the phone that he hadn't heard from them then he promised to give Mark a ring immediately he did.

All they could do was wait.

Mark towelled himself dry, trying not to feel too anxious.

He dressed in beige slacks, a blue knitted shirt and toning wool jacket. 'Casual,' Colin had said when he'd rung. 'It'll just be us. Ages since we've seen you and we've lots to bring you up to date on.'

There'd been an undercurrent of excitement in his voice. 'Move to the country going through, is it?' Mark had asked.

'Tell you all on Friday,' Colin promised.

That was another change, the men making the dates instead of the girls. But Louise was so busy these days and Nicky had a full-time job, so why not?

Since his evening with Nicky, Mark hadn't seen anything of the Webbers. He supposed he should have rung Colin to see what was happening with them. After all, that supper had been all of two months ago. No, two and a half, it was the middle of March now. But what with being so busy in the office, he seemed to be much more involved with the staff these days. It was proving productive but time-consuming, and having Victor living with them, Mark didn't seem to have had a spare minute.

He knew also, though he didn't like to admit it to himself, that he hadn't wanted to get involved in Colin's difficulties with Nicky. Stay clear of other couple's problems had always been his motto. It had been bad enough having to deal with Willoughby and his troubles. He still seemed devastated by Polly's departure. Mind you, Mark could understand that. He didn't know what he'd do if Louise suddenly left. Then he stood quite still, his hand arrested in the act of slipping money into his pockets as a new thought, devastating in its effect, sprang fully formed to his mind.

He pushed it away, combed his drying hair into place, went downstairs and knocked on the door of the old billiard room.

Victor opened it immediately. 'Hi, good to see you,' he said, standing back to allow Mark inside.

Victor had moved into his flat the previous week. The builders had done a marvellous job, mainly due to the way Louise had kept after them. There was no doubt she was managing her little business very efficiently.

'How're you doing, Dad?' Mark asked, looking around him, still not quite able to accept the transformation of his precious billiard room.

'Fine, Mark, fine.'

He was pleased to hear the contented note in his father's voice. It must be good for the old man to have a home of his own again.

They'd brought Victor's furniture over from the sheltered housing and added a few more pieces from the house. It was a good, masculine room, with dark green walls hung with the watercolours Victor had collected over many years, comfortable chairs upholstered in leather, and a few nice antiques. Heavy silk curtains in a lozenge pattern that toned with the walls hung at the window.

The bedroom had been decorated in warm apricot shades and Louise had insisted on buying Victor a double bed, not a large one but a double all the same. You'll like the extra space, she'd told him. And Mark had thought the old man would appreciate the possibilities it offered, even if he knew he wouldn't take advantage of them.

Victor's television set flickered silently in the corner, its sound killed before he'd opened the door. 'Going out?' he asked Mark.

'Yup, to the Webbers.' An unpleasant thought struck Mark. 'You weren't expecting to eat with us, were you?'

Victor shook his head. 'I've had supper. I quite like pottering about in my little kitchen these days. You and Louise have been very kind but we all have our own lives to lead, haven't we?'

Mark felt proud of his father. Since he'd been put on the right medication and Louise had made sure he ate properly, he was almost back to his old self.

But not quite. Mark could see that he'd aged in the last six months. It brought home to him once again how old Victor was. He felt a moment of quiet panic. He didn't want to lose his father. Especially now they were getting on so well.

Everything seemed unsettled these days and Mark was finding it increasingly difficult to cope with all the changes. He went over and looked at a watercolour of the Thames painted at a point not far from where they were. He looked at but didn't see the willows, the grassy banks, the curved line of the bridge. 'How does Louise seem to you?' he asked his father abruptly.

'Ah,' Victor said on a note of understanding.

Mark turned back to his father and jammed his hands into his pockets. 'She doesn't seem herself. Ever since she came back from America—' He stopped abruptly, afraid to say anything more in case his father agreed with him.

'She's had a lot to adjust to,' Victor said gently. 'You need to give her time.'

It wasn't a comment that brought Mark much comfort.

'I suppose you haven't heard from the kids yet?'

Mark sighed and sat down. 'No, but I'm sure we will.' There didn't seem much else to say about that so he started to tell his father about the rather interesting new account that it looked as though he might have found.

Colin opened the door to Mark and Louise. Mark saw immediately that the hunted look had gone from his eyes.

'Come in, come in,' he said expansively. 'Nicky will be with us in a minute.' He helped Louise out of her coat. 'My, that's a knock-out outfit.'

'This? I've had it for ages. But thanks, Colin,' she added hastily.

Mark looked at the wide cream silk pants with a matching long-line cardigan worn over a silk shirt in a deeper shade and recognised it from the previous year. He realised that Louise hadn't bought anything new for a long time, not since well before Christmas.

Colin supplied them with drinks, then Nicky came in with a dish of chicken livers wrapped in bacon and a plate of smoked salmon on brown bread. 'Starters,' she said with a beaming smile.

Mark went and kissed her. 'Great to see you again, Nicky.'

She twinkled back at him and he lost the slight feeling of awkwardness he'd had ever since the night she'd given him supper.

Louise helped herself to one of the chicken liver titbits. 'Wonderful,' she said with a smile at Nicky. 'I never seem to have time to do things like this these days. How on earth did you manage it?'

'Got up early this morning.' Nicky grinned at her. 'I was determined that tonight wasn't going to be supermarket special.'

'So, what have you to tell us?' asked Mark, looking from one to the other. It was obvious they were bursting to come out with their news.

'You say,' Nicky told Colin. 'It was your idea after all.'

He gave a small smile.

Mark looked at his tweed suit, worn with a country checked shirt, and the way he was lounging back in his chair. There was something very solid about him and Mark reckoned he knew exactly what he was going to say. Somehow everything had slotted into place for his old pal.

Colin took off his glasses, polished the lenses with a handkerchief and replaced them. He cleared his throat. 'We've just accepted an offer for the house. I've arranged to join the practice in Exeter I told you about and we'll be moving down there at Easter.'

'You've done it!' Mark said and realised he felt as happy for Colin as he obviously felt for himself. Then he felt a sharp sense of loss as he realised that his friend would no longer be living round the corner.

Colin nodded. 'It all made a great deal of sense.'

'And what about your job?' Louise asked Nicky.

She surprised Mark then. He expected her to be resigned, even play the martyr slightly. Instead she fizzed with excitement. 'I'm going to work with Colin and study to become a solicitor!'

'No!' exclaimed Louise.

'It was all Colin's idea,' said Nicky.

He said modestly, 'It came out of something one of the partners told me. They're losing one of their office managers so I thought, why not suggest Nicky? She could be exactly what they need?'

'And then he thought,' she interjected, 'why didn't I become a solicitor!'

'I've always known she was bright,' Colin said, beaming quietly. 'And the way she took charge of this job she's been doing, well, it seemed obvious to me that she needed a challenge. She'd mentioned starting Open University, so I thought, if it's study she's interested in, why not something really useful? And I can't think of anything more satisfying than working with my wife.'

'We talked the whole thing through, not once but lots of times. Really went into everything,' Nicky added happily. 'Now it's all arranged and I leave the school at the end of term.'

Mark remembered the summer evening when she'd been so excited about getting her job. She'd obviously come a long way since then. Fancy little Nicky studying to become a solicitor! Then he surprised himself by saying, 'Good for you, Nicky. You'll make a good lawyer.'

She went pink with pleasure. 'Do you think so, Mark?'

He nodded. 'You're like Louise. You can attend to detail and sort out priorities. And you're very good at assessing what's important. With Colin to help guide you, you should be qualified in no time.'

'Not no time,' protested Nicky, but she looked even more pleased.

'What about Riff and Raff?' Louise asked. 'What about the holidays?'

'Office manager isn't a full-time job, it's organised on a shared basis. That's why I can take on studying as well. The other manager's children are all grown up and she thinks we can arrange

294

things so I can spend more time at home during the holidays. And there are so many things for the boys to do down there. Sailing, riding, lots of sports. They're going to have their time pretty well taken up.'

'And what about school?' Mark asked. 'Will you keep them where they are?'

'Not sure,' Colin said. 'We'll see how the exeats and driving go during the summer term. Riff will be leaving next year anyway and I hope we can get him into somewhere down there. We've seen one place that looks very promising.'

'You seem to have it all worked out,' Louise said, 'I'm delighted for you. At Christmas we were really worried. Well,' she glanced at Mark, 'I was anyway. I couldn't see how you were going to resolve what seemed quite opposing needs. Now, here you are with everything sorted.'

'I'll drink to that.' Mark raised his glass.

'And we've seen a house we like,' Nicky said excitedly.

Mark watched Louise as she sat listening to Nicky's account of the country cottage they'd fallen for. Although she seemed to be absorbed in all the details of inglenook fireplaces and squint holes, Mark could tell that part of her mind was somewhere else. Where! With the children, wondering what they were doing and why they hadn't rung? Or somewhere else? Looking into the depths of her grey eyes, he wondered if she would ever be completely his again.

'Mark?' He heard Colin say – and realised he'd completely missed the previous question.

'Sorry, Colin, too taken up with gazing at our beautiful wives,' he said, and they all laughed.

As Nicky got up, saying she'd get the meal on the table, Colin repeated his question, which was where were Emma and James now?

Which meant they had to say they hadn't heard for a little while and Colin said, as he was bound to, that they shouldn't worry, the twins were certain to be all right.

During supper Mark got Louise to tell Nicky and Colin all about her venture, *Home Concerns*. Both Nicky and Colin thought the idea was brilliant and seemed genuinely interested in hearing about the jobs she was doing but they had to work quite hard to get the details out of her.

'Tell them how well Val's nursery suite has turned out, darling,' Mark urged. 'And about that magazine you've got interested in doing a feature on it.'

Louise coloured slightly but began to talk more easily. 'And, guess what? Willoughby's commissioned me to turn part of his house into a mini-apartment for Polly!'

'No!' Nicky sounded astounded. 'You don't mean she's actually staying with him? Has the gorgeous Frenchman disappeared, then?'

'I don't think so,' Louise said. 'It's just for when Caroline's back from school. At least, that's the impression I got from Willoughby.'

'I always thought it sounded too much like a fairy tale.' Nicky handed round dessert plates and brought out a chocolate mousse. 'Like something out of a Hollywood romance. I don't blame her for leaving Willoughby, though.'

'Oh, he's not so bad,' Mark said, feeling he had to stick up for his friend. 'After all, he's supported her for, what is it, sixteen years?'

'And you think that's justification for staying with someone?' Nicky shot at him.

Louise said nothing.

'Well, I suppose if you put it like that, probably not,' Mark admitted and felt Louise's eyes fixed on him.

'I think marriage is something you both have to work at all the time,' Colin asserted, passing round the chocolate mousse. 'And I have to tell you that this pudding is to die for. Nicky makes it better than anyone I know.'

She flushed with pleasure.

After supper, Colin took Louise through to the drawing room and Mark said he'd help Nicky get the coffee.

'I never really thanked you for looking after me when Louise was away,' he said, putting a pile of plates on the dishwasher and opening the door. 'I seem to remember I was anything but the perfect guest.'

'Oh, that!' She looked at him with a conspiratorial smile. 'I think we both needed a little home comfort.'

'And I'm truly delighted things are working out so well for you and Colin.' Mark started stacking the plates in the rack.

Nicky paused in measuring out the coffee grains. 'Things not so good with you and Louise, then?' she asked.

As so often, Mark was amazed by the way women could read between the lines of what you said.

'What do you think of her this evening?' he asked.

'Louise?' Nicky finished adding coffee to the filter and switched on the machine.

'Yes, do you think she's her old self?'

'Well, she's obviously worried about Emma and James,' she said slowly, and put a tray on the kitchen table.

'It's more than that.' Mark abandoned the dishwasher and leaned against it. 'She doesn't seem to have been herself ever since she got back from Florida. I know I was a pain in the butt before she went but I've really tried since she's got back, Nicky. I really have tried.' It had been like learning a whole set of new habits. So many times he'd swallowed his instinctive reaction and substituted one that recognised Louise's point of view, or the point someone else was trying to make to him. He'd been amazed to find that the harder he tried, the easier it got.

296

Nicky shot him a straight look then went to get out the coffee cups from a cupboard the other side of the kitchen. 'Having your father to live with you can't have made her life any easier,' she said quietly.

'I know, and I thought at first that that might be the trouble but now I really don't think it is. She seems to enjoy having him. It's almost –' He broke off and looked at his suede shoes. 'It's almost as if it's easier for her not to be on her own with me.' It hadn't been easy to say but at last he'd got it out, the worry that had been gnawing away at him, biting deeper and deeper.

'Ah!' said Nicky.

Mark waited for her to say that she was sure he was imagining things but instead she went on laying the coffee tray and seemed to be thinking.

'She hasn't said anything to you, has she?' he asked at last.

'About what?'

'Well, about meeting someone in Florida.' This, too, hadn't been easy to get out but ever since the thought had struck him like a lightning bolt earlier this evening, he'd been desperate to have someone tell him the very idea was ridiculous.

'We've both been so busy, we haven't had time for chats,' Nicky said.

Which meant, Mark was certain, that the idea didn't seem ridiculous to her at all.

He couldn't think why it hadn't occurred to him before. The way Louise had asked if he could sleep in the dressing room because of her jet lag; the way she'd distanced herself from him, even after they'd got together again; the way it was always he who took the initiative when it came to lovemaking. It was all so obvious, it hurt.

'Is there anything in particular that gives you that idea?' Nicky asked carefully.

Mark remembered Willoughby describing how he knew Polly was involved with another man. 'No, nothing concrete. No telephones that go dead when I pick them up, no letters found hidden in odd places, nothing to suggest she's hiding anything.'

'But you still think there might be someone?'

Mark nodded miserably.

'Have you asked her?'

He thrust his hands deep into his pockets. 'No, because I know she'd tell me the truth.' That was the hell of it. Louise was so damned honest, she wouldn't lie to save his feelings. And Mark didn't want to know there was anyone else in her life but himself.

'She's been back sometime now,' Nicky said slowly. 'What is it, two months?'

He nodded. 'Just over.'

'If she did meet someone, and I'm only saying *if*, she'd surely have done something by now if she was going to.' Mark got more

297

worried. It seemed Nicky was taking the suggestion really seriously.

He gave a crooked smile. 'You think so? It took Polly six months to make up her mind to leave Willoughby.'

'I'd have left him years ago,' Nicky said in a disgusted voice. 'I think it shows great character on Polly's part that she stayed with him as long as she did.'

'What do you think I should do?' Mark said after a moment.

'Go on as you have been,' Nicky said without hesitation. 'Try and show her how much she means to you but without putting any pressure on her. Nothing's worse than someone begging to be loved.' She added cream and sugar to the tray. 'There, that's ready.' She looked up at him. 'Poor Mark, I can see how hard this is for you.' He waited for her to say something to the effect that he'd had it coming to him, or he deserved it. Instead she gave him a warm smile. 'Cheer up. The sky's darkest before the dawn, or whatever it is they say when things look really tough.'

' "And westward, look, the sky is bright!" Isn't that what they say also?'

She laughed. 'I'm sure you don't really have to worry, Mark, Louise knows what she has in you.'

In his present state of mind, he didn't find this reassuring.

Chapter Thirty-Three

'And this is the plan for the bedsitting room.' Louise placed a large sheet of card in front of Polly marked up with a floor plan, shade cards and swatches of material. 'I've done a couple of alternative colour schemes and I can produce lots more swatches if you'd rather put it together yourself.'

Polly glanced disinterestedly at the plan. 'I have complete confidence in your taste, Lulu.'

'I couldn't get a reliable promise of the work being done by Easter so I suggested to Willoughby we start after the holidays. I didn't think you'd want to be worried by builders while Caroline was home?'

'Too right!' Polly got up from the sofa and walked over to the french windows. She looked immensely chic and thinner than ever.

She had rung Louise the day before, saying she'd just arrived and asking if Louise could come round for coffee. It was a weekday and Willoughby was at work.

Louise collected together her plans. She didn't know if she'd expected Polly to be interested in the project or not but she found her dismissal of any discussion very revealing. It seemed to demonstrate that Polly had severed all ties with her marriage.

All except one.

'When does Caroline break up?' Louise asked, picking up her cup of coffee.

'Tomorrow.' Polly turned back into the room. With the light behind her, Louise couldn't see her face clearly but she had an impression of tension. 'Willoughby is letting me go and get her – and her trunk!'

'That's nice of him.' Louise hesitated for a moment then said, 'He had supper with Dad and me a few weeks ago. He seems very upset about the break-up. I think he'd do anything to get you back.'

'Anything except meet me at the airport,' Polly said, and grimaced as she came and sat down opposite Louise.

'Airport? You didn't use Eurostar?'

'From New York?'

'New York? What on earth were you doing there?'

'Jean-Paul's bank has transferred him,' she said ruefully.

'Good heavens. You mean you just got settled back in Paris and then had to up sticks again?'

'Just like the old days,' she agreed ironically.

Louise could see her properly now. Underneath the immaculate make up, there were new lines on her face that had nothing to do with jet lag. Was the perfect romance falling apart? Had it been Jean-Paul or Paris Polly had really fallen in love with?

'It's not actually like the old days at all though. Jean-Paul is a world away from Willoughby!' she added.

'So you're happy?' Louise asked softly.

A glow lit Polly's face. 'Oh, Lulu, sometimes I have to pinch myself, it's all so wonderful. You can't imagine how marvellous Jean-Paul is.'

'I've met him, remember?'

'So you have! But that doesn't mean anything. It's the little things: the way he's so considerate of me, really worries about what I'm thinking, whether I'm happy, what he can do to make life better for me.'

'Sounds rather different from Willoughby,' Louise commented dryly.

Polly giggled as she poured out more coffee for them both. 'Willoughby comes from a different planet. He hasn't the first idea how to treat a woman. I can't think how I stood him all those years. When I think of the way I made sure his life was comfortable, created marvellous homes for him, entertained for him, fetched and carried for him. And what did I get in return? Designer clothes!'

'And Caroline,' Louise pointed out. 'How is she?'

'My little Pooh?' Some of Polly's glow vanished. 'Still very upset and angry at me. Won't come out to New York, still insists she'll only see me here. Come home, is what she says.'

'How do you manage, being in the same house as Willoughby?' Louise tried to imagine how she'd feel if she'd gone off with Jake, then had come back to stay with Mark in her old home to be with Emma and James. She couldn't, it was too big a leap. But at the thought of Emma and James, her heart contracted.

Polly shrugged. 'It's not too bad. Willoughby thinks if he's patient, I'll get bored with Jean-Paul and come back. If it wasn't so sad, it'd be funny. He leaps to his feet when I come into a room, opens doors for me, buys me presents, brings me breakfast in bed, looks at me with those pleading eyes like a spaniel asking for a titbit. Brrr, I can't stand it! He never bothered when he had me, and if I came back this behaviour wouldn't last a twelvemonth. It's not in him. I mean, even now he won't really put himself out. Won't give up a morning at the office to come and meet me at the airport. I had to take a taxi yesterday.'

Polly stopped and shrugged her shoulders. 'But it doesn't worry me now. I just wonder how I can persuade Caroline to come out to

300

America and stay with us instead of me having to be here.' She looked at the plan Louise had put to one side, 'Sweet of you to organise all this for Willoughby, though. How are things going with your little venture? You hardly told me anything on the telephone.'

Louise filled her in on *Home Concerns*. 'It's certainly keeping me busy, I'm getting lots of enquiries!'

'And how is Mark reacting to having a business wife?' Polly asked with a raised eyebrow.

'He's being really helpful. No need to look so surprised, Polly. He's set up a simple accounting system for me, given me lots of names to send my brochure to and is always mentioning me to his business contacts. And he never seems to mind if I have to go out to clients in the evenings or at weekends.'

'Wow!' Polly sounded impressed. 'Good for Mark! That reminds me, Caroline seems to have a boyfriend – Mark's nephew! Apparently they got together at that Boxing Day party we nearly ruined for you. Willoughby says they send each other e-mail.' She suddenly looked thoughtful. 'Reliable, is he?'

'What, Jeremy? Good heavens, yes. At least, I think so. I haven't seen him since Christmas and you can't be sure how any of them develop, can you?' Louise looked at Polly more closely. 'What plot are you hatching now?'

'Oh, nothing. I just thought, if I suggest she can bring Jeremy, perhaps Pooh would think about coming out to New York in the summer holidays? We're going to take a place on Long Island so we can get away from the humidity. Jean-Paul will commute. There'll be sailing and swimming and I can try and find somewhere with lots of young people.'

'Sounds good,' Louise said gently, watching Polly getting carried away with her plans. This was what it was like when you broke up a family.

'Jean-Paul thinks she's a great character and he wants her there as much as I do. We could have such fun together,' Polly said with unaccustomed wistfulness. Then she changed the subject. 'Anyway, that's enough about me and mine. How are yours, the terrible twins?'

Louise couldn't help it, she burst into tears.

Polly was beside her in an instant. 'Darling, what's happened? Here I am wittering on about things and all the time . . . tell me, please, what has happened?'

Louise sniffed hard and used the heel of her hand to wipe her eyes, leaving smudges of mascara. 'Nothing, I hope. It's just that we haven't heard from them for nearly three weeks. We're going out of our minds with worry.'

'Three weeks doesn't sound awfully long,' Polly said slowly.

'But it's never been more than ten days before. And they said they were going to the States and they don't seem to have arrived there. Mark found out the number of the youth hostel they told us they were going to stay at in San Francisco and they've never heard of them!' Louise gulped unhappily, found her bag and fished out a tissue. 'I just can't stop thinking about them and wondering where they are and what's happening to them. Mark keeps on telling me not to worry, that we'd have heard if they've had an accident or are in trouble of any kind, but I know he's just as anxious as I am.'

Polly slid her arm around Louise's shoulders. 'Of course you're worried, I'd be out of my mind. I know it's hard to be sensible but I'm sure Mark's right, you'd know immediately if anything awful had happened.'

'But think of the people who're murdered in deserted places and aren't found for weeks and weeks! Suppose Emma and James hitchhiked, or fell for some smooth-talking chap, and have been killed by a psychopath or a serial killer?' All Louise's worries spilled out. The things she couldn't say to Victor, that she tried to hide from Mark and knew he was trying to hide from her. These days she felt she could read his mind without his having to say a word.

'Shhh,' Polly soothed, holding her tight. 'Nothing like that has happened to them, I'm quite, quite certain. You know what the young are, they've probably lost their telephone card.'

'But they could reverse the charges!'

'Or got whisked off somewhere exciting and lost track of time.'

Gradually her quiet certainty became infectious.

'There.' Polly gently released Louise and sat back. 'You probably feel much better now you've let everything out. It was like that with me in Paris, when Jean-Paul wasn't there and I imagined all sorts of dreadful things, like he didn't really want me after all. Then when Mitzi made me spill everything out, it was like turning the light on in a darkened room, all sorts of shadows just disappeared.'

'Willoughby told me there'd been some mix-up.' Louise gave a last sniff and looked in her bag for a mirror.

'He did, did he? Did he also tell you he wiped Jean-Paul's message off my answering machine?'

'No! Did he?' Louise gazed at her in disbelief. 'Did he tell you that?'

'He didn't need to. He thought that when Jean-Paul wasn't there to meet me, I'd come back.'

'Poor Polly!'

'Yes, well, if anything could have shown me any more clearly that I couldn't live with Willoughby, that was it. Just be glad you're married to a man like Mark. Funny, I used to think he and Willoughby were a bit alike.'

'Mark like *Willoughby*!' Louise almost shouted. 'You can't mean that!' She thought about how understanding Mark had been ever since she'd returned from America. It was more than recapturing the way he'd been when they first met, she couldn't ever remember Mark being so thoughtful before. If they weren't madly in love

302

anymore, the way they once had been, the way she'd felt with Jake in Florida, Louise thought they were closer than they'd been for many years. Particularly now, with their worry over the twins.

She found the mirror. 'Heavens, I've turned into a panda. You should have told me!'

'Plenty of time to repair your face,' Polly said calmly. 'You never look anything but beautiful, Lulu. Now, I'm going to get us a drink, I think you can do with a pick-me-up.'

Polly tried to take her out to lunch but Louise said Victor was expecting her. 'I try and give him a proper midday meal at least three times a week. He's beginning to pick up his old friends a bit now, goes out quite a lot, but he enjoys our chats. So do I,' she added. 'Having him with us is working out really well.'

'We'll get together before I go back,' Polly promised, seeing her off. 'I want to tell you more about Jean-Paul.' It was obvious she had difficulty not talking about him.

Louise wasn't at all certain she wanted to hear more details of Polly's romance. Her radiant happiness when she mentioned her lover's name showed Louise all too plainly what was missing from her own life.

That evening Louise was trying to bring her accounts up-to-date before Mark came home. She was entering details of her expenses on to the computer when the telephone rang.

She answered in the crisp, businesslike way she had developed, hoping against hope, as she did every time it rang, that it would be Emma or James.

'Louise,' breathed a quiet voice. Its timbre cut through to her very soul.

'Oh, Jake,' she said despairingly.

'I'm still waiting for you to call me,' he said. He sounded as though he'd been drinking. Louise did a quick calculation and reckoned it was lunchtime where he was.

'I miss you so much,' he went on as she said nothing.

'Jake, I can't,' she said gently. 'I can't call you and I can't come over there. My place is here.' As soon as she'd spoken, she clamped her hand over her mouth to stop herself from gasping for breath. She felt as though something inside her was rising up from the depths of her being, filling her completely. She could see him sitting in a chair, holding the telephone to his ear; could see his large hand with its long fingers, could see his head held back, his eyes fixed on the ceiling, his tall, rangy body stretched out, lean shoulders pressing against his T shirt. No, where he lived it must be much colder than Florida, he'd have a sweater on. Just that small adjustment, and the whole vision fell apart.

'No, Louise, no!' he said in a pain-filled voice. 'You can't say that.'

303

'I've got to,' she said, the words almost choking her. 'Jake, I can't talk to you again, you must understand. Please, please don't ring me anymore. Get on with your life, get on with your book.' She hesitated then added, 'Send me a copy.'

There was a long silence. Feeling as though she was suffocating, she very gently lowered the receiver and waited another moment before putting it down.

'I'll dedicate it to you,' he said, his voice once again so quiet she could hardly hear. Then: 'Goodbye, Louise,' drifted out of the ether. 'I'll always love you, but you know that.'

The voice faded away, the line went dead.

She replaced the receiver and burst into tears.

She cried for the loss of a dream. She cried because she no longer had what she and Mark had started out with. She cried because she couldn't feel anything anymore. She cried because she was terrified she'd never see her children again.

The study door opened and Mark was there.

'Darling, what is it?' He came across to her instantly and held her, soothing her as Polly had done that morning. He held her tight in his arms, her head cradled against his neck, his chin resting on her hair. 'Have you heard something about the twins?'

She could feel the thudding of his heart, knew he was holding his breath, waiting for her to tell him whatever it was that had caused this breakdown.

She thumped gently at his chest with a clenched hand, unable to speak coherently, trying to shake her head.

He pulled away from her, still holding her shoulders so he could look into her face. 'Darling, tell me, please. Tell me!'

The two men she'd loved in her life, both begging her for words she couldn't give. She shook her head again. 'Nothing to do with Emma or James,' she finally got out. 'Nothing at all!' Except it was. And it was to do with him and she couldn't tell him that either. And it was to do with Jake, whom she must never, ever think of again.

She stood up, supported by Mark, taking deep, hiccoughing breaths, trying to regain control.

The phone rang. Automatically Louise reached out a hand.

'Let it ring,' said Mark savagely. 'Let the answering machine take it.'

Louise let her hand drop, knowing she'd be unable to get out anything coherent, dreading to hear Jake's voice trying to make her change her mind. But what if he left a message on the machine? If he did, she knew she was powerless to prevent the consequences.

'Darling,' said Mark, 'you must tell me what the matter is. If it isn't the children, what is it? Not Dad?' he asked on a sudden intake of breath. She could see anxiety creasing his face.

'No, no,' she got out as the telephone continued to give its statutory number of rings before the machine clicked in. The

304

repeated sound resonated in her head and made it impossible to think. 'Dad's all right,' she managed. His eyes searched her face; he looked at her with such intensity, it was as if he wanted to reach her very soul and reveal all its secrets.

She closed her eyes, the sobs still racking her body. Any moment now the machine would take the call and she'd hear Jake's voice again – and so would Mark. She waited hopelessly.

'Hello? Mum, Dad? Bugger, don't say you're not there!'

Mark grabbed for the phone. 'Emma, where the hell are you? Why haven't you been in touch, we're out of our minds with worry!' His voice was hard and full of anguish as he pressed the conference button so they could both hear what she was saying. 'Hey, Dad, no grief, huh! Jimmy and I are fine!' Emma sounded injured. 'We're here, on-line, OK?'

'But where have you been? You told us you were going to San Francisco and would call from there. I rang the youth hostel and they said they'd never heard of you.'

Louise clung to Mark, listening to the anger in his voice. 'Darling,' she said, her voice warm, 'we're so relieved you're all right. We've been so worried.'

'Hi, Mum. Yeah, we're fine. Here's Jimmy, he'll tell you what we've been doing.'

'Hi, folks.' It was James's voice, deep but soft. 'See, what it was, Ems and me met this guy in Sydney whose folks have this place in Brazil . . .'

'Brazil!' Louise said faintly.

'Yeah, it's like a sort of plantation, they grow rubber here. Used to be millionaires – still pretty rich though he says the market these days isn't strong for rubber. Anyway, he said why didn't we come with him, visit Brazil? He was going so it seemed like a good idea.'

'Heavens,' said Louise as she tried to absorb the fact that the twins had left Australia but not for the States.

'We didn't tell you,' it was Emma back on the line again, 'because we thought you'd only worry. You said it would be better not to go to South America.'

'I specifically said you weren't to go to South America,' Mark said grimly, still upset.

'Yeah, well, we reckoned that meant without contacts or any-where to go. Having met Ramirez, it seemed OK. His family are respectable, I mean really respectable. We were going to ring when we got here but Ramirez had rung and said we were coming with him, so they organised a cruise for us on the Amazon and we had to fly off as soon as we arrived. I did ring but the phone was engaged so I thought better wait until after. The trip was absolutely brilliant!' Emma's voice was high with excitement.

Louise's eye was caught by a photograph of the twins Mark had put on the desk. It had been taken two years ago, on a summer

305

holiday in Brittany. The two of them were hauling a boat down into the sea, dressed in shorts and T shirts, bare legs tanned by wind and sun. Louise remembered their enthusiasm for learning to handle the little yacht and she could see exactly how they would have met the exotic challenges of the Amazon.

'I bet it was.' Mark's voice softened.

'They took us to meet the natives who live there. Can't wait to tell you about it, Dad.'

'And were you up the Amazon for the whole three weeks?' Mark asked sceptically.

'Well, no, but there were other things that had been arranged. They've just been so kind. They wanted us to ring you but by then we thought it was better to wait until we knew when we were leaving.'

'You mean, you didn't want to be told to get out of South America,' Mark said with grim humour.

'Oh, Dad, it's been the most splendiferous end to our trip we could possibly have had,' Emma said pleadingly. 'I'm sorry if you've been worried but you should have known we can take care of ourselves.'

'You said "end",' Louise interjected. 'Does that mean you're not going to America, that you're coming back here?'

'Here's Jimmy again.'

'Hi, yes, Ems is spot on. It's been spectacular, really cool. But we seem to have run out of money. I mean, flying here wasn't cheap and then we went with Ramirez to Peru . . .'

'Peru?' murmured Louise, now quite beyond being able to take it all in.

'So we thought we'd save the US of A for another time and come home.'

'Home?' Louise repeated softly. 'You're really coming home?'

'Yup, in two days' time. Want our flight details?'

Mark grabbed a piece of paper and a pencil and told him to go ahead.

'That's wonderful, darling.' Louise felt like crying all over again, but such different tears. 'I'll meet you, of course.'

'I'm sorry,' Mark said. 'I've got a meeting scheduled then that I don't think I can do anything about.'

'What's new, Dad?' James's voice was resigned.

'But I'll be back early that evening, promise. Can't wait to see you, son. Can't wait to see both of you.'

After the call had finished, Louise and Mark stood and looked at each other.

'They're coming home,' she said in wonder. 'The day after tomorrow they'll be here!' She couldn't believe it. Not only were Emma and James both safe but she was going to see them in two days' time.

Mark was still looking at the receiver that he'd replaced. Slowly he turned to her. 'Why were you crying when I came in?'

She stared at him and could find nothing to say.

He gently touched the skin beneath her eyes. 'Your mascara has run,' he said softly.

'It was nothing,' Louise said. 'Not now we know Emma and James are safe. We must tell Dad!' She rubbed at the smudges for the second time that day then gave up, took Mark's hand and pulled him out of the room towards Victor's door.

Mark insisted on taking Louise and his father out to dinner. 'We must celebrate,' he urged. 'And I'm going to book a taxi so none of us has to worry about driving. Why don't you see if your mother can come as well?' he suggested to Louise.

They went to the Italian restaurant they always used when they wanted to celebrate, where the food was superb and ambience extremely pleasant. The head waiter welcomed them with every appearance of delight. 'And how is the beautiful *signorina*?' he asked as he led them to a table.

'Coming home the day after tomorrow,' Louise said happily as she followed him.

It was a delightful evening, all of them drunk on the relief of knowing the twins were safe and on their way home.

As their desserts arrived, Louise looked round the table and thought, This is my family, and soon it will be complete again. This is where my life is, where my heart is. In the inner recesses of her mind she heard a whisper that breathed, 'Louise,' and gently shut a door she knew would now stay closed.

'Eight months Emma and James have been away,' said Betty, attacking her *gelato* with gusto.

'They'll have grown up,' said Victor wisely. 'Changed.'

'We've all changed,' said Mark quietly.

A little of Victor's euphoria left him. 'Yes,' he said in a rather more subdued manner. 'That is so.'

'Betty put a hand on his. 'We're all getting older but you do it so gracefully,' she said gently.

He smiled at her and said, 'If I were any younger, you'd be in severe danger.'

Her smile became playful. 'Careful, Victor, you'll have me chasing you.'

The waiter came up and poured the last of the champagne into their glasses.

Mark raised his. 'A toast. To Emma and James.'

'To Emma and James,' they all repeated.

'And when I've got them home, they're going to be told what keeping in touch really means,' he added lightly.

'Oh, don't be too hard on them,' begged Betty. 'They're really very responsible.'

'That's not what you said when I told you they'd at last been in touch,' Louise reminded her.

Betty swallowed the last of her *gelato*. 'Well, I'd been worried,' she said in justification.

Victor snorted with laughter and Mark gave her a delighted smile. Louise felt very content.

Later, as they climbed the stairs to their bedroom, she asked Mark, 'Can't you dump whatever that meeting is and come to the airport with me to meet them?'

'Darling, I wish I could. But it's Douglas. He fixed it before going away for a couple of days. It's the only time he can do and he made it sound important. I have to be there.'

'You mean, he's finally going to decide between you and Robin?' Louise turned to him in excitement.

'He didn't say so but I'm pretty sure that's what it's about. He's going to have to announce his retirement soon and choose one of us to take over.'

'Oh, darling, I'm sure he'll choose you.' Louise put as much conviction as she could into her voice. But since she'd returned from the States, she'd come to realise what an effective force Robin was. It was strange, she thought now. As her knowledge of Robin as Mark's rival increased, her jealousy of her had disappeared. Was it because of her own feelings for Jake or had she realised Mark wasn't interested in his colleague as a woman? 'I wish I could be as confident as you,' he said, entering their bedroom behind her. Then he reached out and drew her gently into his arms. 'Why were you crying so desperately when I came home today?'

Louise stood very still. What could she say? The truth would hurt him far too much. But anything else would be a lie.

So much of her life these last few months had been spent evading the truth, was it never going to end?

She slipped around in Mark's arms so that her back was to him. 'Will you undo me?' she asked in a low voice.

She was wearing a silk dress that buttoned down the back.

Mark slowly undid the little hook and eye at the top then released the first of the buttons. 'You were crying as though your heart would break,' he said, but his voice sounded remote as he started on the second button.

Louise let out a long sigh and stood with her head slightly bowed.

Mark undid the third and then the fourth of the little silk-covered buttons. He appeared so concentrated on this task that he had forgotten the question for he said no more. Then as the fourth button slipped through the material, Louise felt his lips gently kiss the skin just above the fastening of her bra. His touch sent little shock waves along her spine, made her catch her breath.

Mark undid the bra then his fingers moved on to the fifth button.

His breath was coming more quickly now.

He dealt with the last button then undid the zip on the skirt.

Louise gently pulled down first one sleeve, then the other, taking the bra and her slip with the dress. The materials rustled gently to the floor, leaving her standing in panties and gartered stockings. She turned to face her husband.

She hadn't seen a look like that on Mark's face for many years. Inside, she could feel the bubbles of the champagne they'd drunk that evening working like yeast, raising her spirits in a long-forgotten way. She felt an incredible lightness. It was as though her feet hovered above the floor. She reached out, closing the short gap between them, placing her arms around his neck. 'Darling Mark,' she said dreamily. 'I feel seventeen again, it's as if we've only just met. Hold me as you did then.'

Gently, oh, so gently, he pulled her tight against him, bent his head and found her mouth with his.

Then all of Louise's body came alive and she gave herself up to him with an astonished joy.

Chapter Thirty-Four

Louise stood in the airport waiting nervously for the twins to arrive. Their plane had landed twenty minutes ago. Soon now they would be coming through from the customs hall.

It seemed impossible that eight months after she'd seen them off they were coming back to her.

Watch it, Louise told herself. Remember, they will have changed. Don't expect everything to be as it was.

She wished so much that Mark could be with her. He'd gone off this morning swearing he'd be home as soon as he could. She'd known, the way he'd said it, that he would have done anything to have gone to the airport with her. Anything but tell Douglas he couldn't be at their meeting. Well, Louise supposed, it was his future. No, their future.

'Mum!' a voice shrieked – and there was Emma. And behind her was James, pushing a trolley with their bags.

Louise waved frantically and moved towards the end of the barricade that kept those emerging from the customs area from their meeters and greeters. She felt elated and also slightly numb. Emma and James looked so wonderful, so healthy and so *familiar*. Her children, home again.

Then someone grabbed her shoulder and shouted, 'Hello, kids!'

She looked round, disbelieving. It couldn't be, but it was. Mark. He'd made it! Together they moved towards the twins. Emma dashed up, kissed Louise then was engulfed in a crushing hug by Mark. 'Oh, it's wonderful to be back.'

Behind her came James. 'Sure is,' he said with a wide smile.

Louise pulled his head down and kissed him. 'Oh, I can't believe it. You're actually here!' She stood back and looked at him. 'You've grown!'

He had filled out. The coltish quality had gone. He was still only eighteen but he wasn't a boy any longer. There was a new confidence in the way he held himself. He looked reserved rather than shy. Emma, too, was different. Was it just the hair, no longer short but waving Hollywood starlet style around her shoulders? The sun had added platinum highlights, her skin was a golden tan and she looked sensational.

Then both Louise and Mark saw the diamond in her left nostril.

It wasn't very large but it scintillated with every move of her head and drew attention to the pertness of her nose and the satiny smoothness of her skin. Emma finally realised what they were looking at and her hand automatically went to the little jewel. Then she stood waiting for their reaction, her eyes more than a little nervous.

'Quite something, isn't it?' James said mischievously.

Louise waited, resigned, for Mark to explode.

Intense but unidentifiable emotion crossed his face.

'Quite something,' he agreed. 'Come on, let's go home.'

'You haven't got to go back to the office?' Louise asked in amazement.

He shook his head and grinned at her. 'Not today.'

With Emma chattering excitedly and James interposing the odd remark, they made their way to the car park. 'I thought you'd come back with much more luggage than you started with,' Louise said as Mark and James hefted the haversacks into the boot of the car.

'Emma would have done if I hadn't imposed a bit of control,' James said, grinning.

'He was impossible, Mum! Every time I found something really good, he refused to let me have any money!'

'You kept control of the funds, then, did you?' asked Mark, looking amused.

'You bet, Dad. If it hadn't been for me they wouldn't have taken us any further than China!'

'He looked for bargains everywhere. I called him a skinflint.' Emma tossed her hair and looked challengingly at her twin. 'But who was the one who engineered all the hospitality, eh? Who was the one who knew exactly who would be good for a night or so's lodging along the way?'

James dipped his head in acknowledgement. 'True, sis, your judgement in that regard was unerring.'

'God, you're pompous!' Emma gave him a small jab in the arm.

'I can see you had lots of fun.' Louise got into the car. 'We can't wait to hear all about everything. Have you taken lots of photographs? We've loved the odd snap you sent us from time to time.'

'Not enough of them, though,' complained Mark, starting the engine.

'You'll be bored long before we get to the end of them,' promised James. 'How's Grandfather? It was a bit of a shock to hear he had Parkinson's and couldn't live on his own any longer. Is he really that bad?'

Louise swivelled round so she could see the twins in the back seat. 'Don't worry, he's managing very well.'

'I think it's great he's living with us,' said Emma. 'It means we can tell him everything and not have to rush it, like if we went to see him or he came to us.'

312

'Have you really converted the billiard room?' asked James. 'I couldn't believe it when you told us. I mean, what are we going to do without it?'

'I can think of a hundred things,' their father said cheerfully. 'By the time you've monopolised the telephone for the rest of the day, I should think you'll have fixed enough engagements with your chums to occupy every moment between now and when you go off to college.'

'Dad!' they both protested.

'But you don't have to worry. I'm going to build another billiard room on top of the garage.'

Louise turned to him, deeply surprised. Then she realised she hadn't asked him what had happened at his meeting with Douglas. She noted the excitement that hung like an aura around him. This was more than delight at his children's homecoming. She caught her breath as she realised what it had to be. 'Douglas has made you Head of Department!'

He nodded and gave her a quick grin as he drove out of the car park.

'Golly, Dad!' James sounded greatly impressed. It was a change from his attitude before he'd left; then he would have been dismissive of bloated capitalists seeking further advancement.

Mark accelerated smoothly into the main stream of traffic round the airport. 'Yes,' he said. 'And Robin's leaving,' he added.

'No! Because you've been chosen as Head?' breathed Louise.

'She's going to be Financial Director of an emerging conglomerate. 'She's very excited about it.'

'So the field's all yours.' Louise felt enormous relief.

'But I'm not the only successful business person in the family,' Mark said over his shoulder to his offspring. 'Your mother has started her own company and it's going great guns.'

'Really? Mum has?' Emma's astonishment was patent.

'Your mother has surprised us all,' Mark continued imperturbably. 'I always knew she was efficient but her business acumen is considerable.'

'Wow!' said Emma.

'That's great, Mum,' said James. 'Now you're really flying!'

Louise smiled at them. They were sweet. They were her family. The summer loomed pleasurably ahead. The noise and bustle the twins would make, the steadying presence of Victor, the sweetness she'd found once again with Mark.

Emma and James would not be back for long, soon they'd be off to university. But this time she'd have something else in her life. She felt as though she also had come home after a long journey.

313